Daniel's Daughter

Daniel's Daughter

anna kelly

POOLBEG
Crimson

Published 2008
by Poolbeg Press Ltd
123 Grange Hill, Baldoyle
Dublin 13, Ireland
E-mail: poolbeg@poolbeg.com
www.poolbeg.com

13 5 7 9 10 8 6 4 2

A catalogue record for this book is available from the British Library.

ISBN 978-1-84223 -336-8

Typeset by Type Design in Sabon 10.5/14

Printed by
Litographia Roses, Spain

Note on the author

Anna Kelly is a Dubliner, born in the city centre, and now lives in Sutton. She has two sons and two granddaughters. She began writing fiction in childhood and returned to it throughout her life time and again. In recent years she went back to education as a mature student and studied Art & Design & Culture & Heritage. In past lives she was a supervisor, a sales person, a secretary, but always a writer. After a life-changing episode she began writing in earnest. *Daniel's Daughter* is her first novel. She is currently working on her second book.

Acknowledgements

Words fell from the tip of my pen
and formed in lines on the page,
but the book you hold in your hands now
is a tribute to Poolbeg's gauge.

Paula, Gaye, Niamh and the team
were there at every call,
with patience, tolerance and encouragement
– but for them it wouldn't have happened at all.

Words from the mouths of family and friends
encouraged, supported, true.
You know who you are who was there for me,
and I am indebted to you.

To Karl and Ivan
with Love

Prologue

Angela Brennan looked in horror at the man lying on his back on her kitchen floor.

A minute earlier he had been on his feet, grappling with her. In unbridled anger he had closed his hands around her throat. Only her terror-induced struggles had at first prevented his mallet-like hands from getting a solid grip.

Then, as her struggles grew weaker, his grip tightened and became vice-like. Her world grew dark and a myriad of thoughts flashed through her mind, not least being the fact that there was no one to come to her aid. There was only Thomas, nine years old, and he was out somewhere in the fields as usual.

From the small loft window in one of the outhouses Thomas had spotted the man prowling around. Then he saw him go into the house by way of the back door. In alarm he jumped down via some stacked bales of hay and ran across the yard. He heard the scuffling inside as he reached the back porch. He burst into the kitchen

1

and, seeing his mother's plight, picked up the first thing that came to hand – the coal shovel from the stone hearth. He began to hit the attacker on the back.

In fury Christopher Cleary rounded on Thomas, who dropped the shovel and ran like a shot to the other side of the table, where fright made his legs unsteady. Cleary made to follow, but instinctively Angela thrust out her foot and suddenly her attacker was going down. The side of his head and the corner of the table met with an awful smack, and the force twisted his body so that he landed face up. The fall knocked his cap from his head, and long greasy strands of hair lay like black snakes beside his ear.

He stared up at her. Sick with fear and unable to divert her eyes she stared back. In an instant he would be back on his feet again, and God help her then.

He didn't move. Just stared.

Thomas edged his way back around the table cautiously, silently, and looked down.

"He's dead," he said flatly.

"He's not!" Angela's eyes involuntarily transferred to Thomas in disbelief.

"He is!" Thomas insisted.

"Fuck it!" his mother swore. Then she thought again. "How the fuck would *you* know?" She eyed the prostrate form warily as she spoke, watching for the smallest sign of movement.

"I've seen dead birds in the field. And a dead dog too. They had the same kind of stillness as that."

Revulsion took hold of Angela. Her uncle's eyes still stared up at her from the floor. Just as she couldn't get her eyes away before, now she couldn't bear to look down. And neither could she move away without having to step over the body. He had landed quite close to her feet, and the prospect of coming in contact with him again, however slight, immobilised her.

Thomas held out his hand. "Gimme your hand, Ma."

She did. She closed her eyes and jumped across the body. The two of them stood back then, unconsciously holding onto each other.

"Jesus, Tomo, what are we going to do? Oh God! Oh fuck it, fuck it!"

Thomas looked up anxiously at his mother. He could feel her shaking. She was becoming increasingly agitated, her head moving continuously in an irregular manner, her fingers beginning to dig into his shoulder. Then she began to babble and what she said made no sense to him – he even heard her mention the name of Redser Reilly. He feared his ma was losing it. Suddenly his young mind knew with certainty that if anyone was going to deal with this situation it was going to have to be him.

"Come on, Ma," he urged as he encouraged her towards the door. "We'd be better off out of here."

He wanted to get out of the kitchen himself. He guided her up the three steps that led into the front hall and then into the drawing-room where he sat her down in an armchair. He tried to think what his nan would do if she were here. And suddenly he wished she was. Nancy Brennan could cope with anything. Well, almost. Thomas then thought of some brandy. He remembered hearing his nan call for brandy once when a neighbour's child was knocked down on D'Arcy Avenue. He looked for brandy now in the long sideboard opposite the marble fireplace, while keeping a watchful eye on his mother. She was mumbling a load of stuff that seemed to have no bearing on what had just happened. She was nodding to herself as if something had just fallen into place, and only now made sense.

"I knew it all along, I knew it, I knew it wasn't my fault," she was saying.

"Drink this, Ma!" He held a glass to her lips.

She kept pushing the glass away. "I know now," she was whispering, "I know now."

Thomas was getting terribly worried about her, and he didn't *really* know what to do, try as he might to make it look like he did. He needed to con himself as much as his mother. He tried with the brandy again.

"This will help, Ma. Just have a little sip," he pleaded.

She took the glass and drank, then looked at him with more awareness in her eyes.

"Are you all right, Ma?"

She nodded determinedly.

"Did he hurt you badly?"

She would have answered him but for the fact that a noise startled them both. In their fright they could not decide where it had come from, or exactly what sort of noise it was.

Both of their heads swivelled towards the door together, then in alarm they looked at each other, wide-eyed. A terrible silence prevailed while they waited for something awful to happen, their hearts almost stopped in suspense.

4

Angela got to her feet and felt Thomas's restraining hand on her arm.

"Don't go, Ma," he whispered, even as he moved with her.

As stealthily as a cat stalking a bird they moved into the hall and towards the kitchen. Thomas had left the door open, and from the doorway they stooped low and looked across the room under the table.

Christopher Cleary was gone!

"Oh Christ!" Angela moaned.

"He can't be gone!" Thomas couldn't believe his eyes.

"I thought you said he was dead!" Angela hissed.

"Well, I thought he was! But where *is* he?"

She feared he might still be in the house. She was too afraid to turn around. It occurred to her that she should phone someone. They needed help. What if Christy was lurking around? What if he had collapsed and died outside in the yard?

"Ma, he's the oul fella we always see on his bike," Thomas was whispering.

"Thomas," she said, trembling, "that oul fella is not just any oul fella. He's Daniel's older brother, and he's pissed off that we got this place, instead of him."

The boy's mouth fell open. He stared at her in disbelief.

"Swear to God!" she insisted, her throat sore and her voice rasping. "Patrick told me. Now, come with me, I'm going to phone him."

She immediately felt a little better. Patrick Cullen would know what to do.

Chapter 1

In D'Arcy Avenue the Brennan family was at dinner. Paddy Brennan was making full use of his audience to expound his usual theory: Angela Brennan was useless. Totally fuckin' useless. He'd been saying it for years. Any time he got half a chance. An uneasy but familiar embarrassed silence befell those around the table.

"Part-time," he was saying derisively, "what bloody use is that? Why can't you get a proper full-time job like anyone else, for Christ's sake? There's two of yis there to feed, y'know!"

As he spoke he wagged his knife in Thomas's direction. Thomas had long since learned when to keep his head down. He cast a quick glance sideways at his mother. Angela's eyes were fixed on her plate. With her fork she stabbed at her food, and it was clear she had lost her appetite.

Nancy came to her daughter's defence. "It's better than the last job," she pointed out. "There's more hours and the money is better –"

"It's no better than the countless bits of jobs she's had since she left school!" Paddy cut in. "And as for the money? It'll probably go on hair dye or more bloody muck for her face! And what fuckin' improvement will *that* make? Tell me that! None!"

Twenty-one-year-old Finbar had heard it all before. He got to his feet.

"Where do you think *you* are going?" his father snapped.

"I have exams tomorrow," Finbar answered shortly. "I have to study."

Fergus got to his feet also. "Me too. Excuse us, Mam." He followed his twin out of the room.

Paddy fumed but said nothing. He was losing his audience, but he knew he was on thin ice when it came to the exams. Nancy wouldn't hear of anything getting in the way of them. Thomas took his chance and slid quietly from his chair. No one said a word as he followed his uncles up to the bedroom. He climbed onto his bed and picked up a comic.

"I'll be quiet," he pleaded, "you won't even know I'm here."

Finbar and Fergus gave each other an understanding look and said nothing.

In the kitchen Paddy sat facing his wife and daughter.

"It's a pity *you* hadn't the brains to pass *your* exams!" he flung at Angela. "It would've answered you better than to go whoring around –" With a cry Angela leapt to her feet and ran from the room, but her father followed her into the hall, his voice roaring after her up the stairs,

"At fifteen!"

Upstairs a door slammed loudly. The whole house felt the vibration. Paddy returned to the kitchen, slamming *that* door equally loudly.

Nancy was scraping the unfinished dinners into the bin, including her own. Her nerves were at breaking point, and she was heartsore and weary of the same argument.

"If you didn't keep on at her she might have the confidence to get something better," she said quietly.

"Oh, so now it's *my* fault, is it?"

"I didn't *say* that."

"That's what you meant. You're the one who wanted her to have that bloody young fella in the first place. He should never have been born. If I had had my way –"

"Keep it down!" she hissed. "We know what you would've done if you'd had your way!"

The voices rose as one word borrowed another.

In her room Angela clamped her hands over her ears. Then she turned on her stereo and turned the volume up. But that only further fuelled tempers downstairs, and the arguing got worse.

Suddenly she grabbed her jacket and clattered down the stairs in her high-heeled shoes and left the house, slamming the door behind her. She half-walked, half-ran down D'Arcy Avenue, desperately trying to hold back the tears, and was grateful for the fact that it was already dark. Seeing a bus approach the stop ahead, she ran forward, put her hand out and stopped it. It took her into town, where she wandered for hours, cold and miserable. On Batchelor's Walk she paused in her aimless rambling to rest by the Liffey wall. The Liffey looked like a long, black, oily streak stretching endlessly into the night. There was no wind to ripple its surface, and the reflection of the streetlights on the narrow quays seemed unable to penetrate its depths. A late frost glistened on the thick granite walls of the silently ebbing river and on the roofs and windscreens of the cars parked alongside the uneven flagstone footpath. It was a bitterly cold night. She moved on. The balustrade of O'Connell Bridge provided little protection from the freezing cold air arising from the water. The cold of the ancient granite easily penetrated her short, lightweight skirt, and she regretted having dashed from the house with only a flimsy jacket against the night air. She wished for the warmth and comfort of her own bedroom.

She was the problem. She and Tomo.

There had been peace in their house. Then Thomas arrived. The arguing began as soon as her pregnancy was confirmed. Her father went spare altogether. Not wanting her in the house. Not wanting the baby. But her mother had put her foot down. Nancy Brennan stood firm for the first time in her life. They'd manage. Somehow they'd manage. No one asked what Angela wanted. The arguments became constant. They were always about her, or Thomas, but never included her.

In his own inadequate way Paddy Brennan was still trying to come to terms with the disaster which had foisted itself on their lives. When she became pregnant he was devastated. Though not the youngest in the family, Angela was his baby, his little girl. His angel. She adored him. Never ever did he dream that anything would or could spoil their relationship. But this unwanted bastard she carried demolished all that. He couldn't bear to think of his darling girl being mauled by some spotty, sweaty wimp, and her enjoying it. The thought repulsed him. When did she start this carry-on? She was only fifteen, for Christ's sake! How many had she been with? Oh God, he couldn't bear the sight of her swelling belly! How could she continue to pretend to be his little innocent? The hypocrisy of it! Anger surged through him like some raging torrent. Well, he was finished with her for sure. He had no daughter now, and she had done it herself.

Neither could he understand Nancy's new-found determination. That surprised him and made him angry at how she could defend her whore of a daughter the way she did. Did she not think of his position as head of the house? To him, it was ganging up on him. Usurping him. Women! You couldn't trust them. How dare they do this to him? How was he going to face his workmates when "it" couldn't be hidden any more? He could just imagine it now, the snide remarks behind his back in the job. He'd be talked about for the duration. He was determined that he wasn't going to cough up to pay for its rearing. Money was tight enough as it was. They could go out and get jobs. The pair of them. He worked all the hours he could and he wasn't going to be taken for some kind of soft touch of an eejit. In fact, it would answer her better to leave his house and get herself somewhere else out of his sight. Get rid of it. Before it became too noticeable. While they still could. But there again Nancy surprised him, railing against him, appalled at the very mention of getting rid of it and insisting their daughter be given the support she needed. Support which would cost *him*. The arguments raged on never-endingly.

Nine years now and if anything, things were worse. Thomas was more of a handful the older he got.

Angela was freezing cold now. And it was late. She was on early in the shop in the morning. She made her way to the stop and took the bus home.

Calmer now, she walked back up the avenue, noticing as she went that the light was on in the Reillys' porch. So the job was finished. It looked well. A bit over the top perhaps, a conservatory-cum-porch on the front of a terraced council house, but it was well done. Of all the neighbours on the avenue the Reillys were always the first to get something new. Nancy always declared she never knew how they did it. No one in the house ever seemed to have a proper job, but clearly there was no shortage of money. Thomas was constantly telling them the Reillys had this and the Reillys had that, despite the fact that Angela was forever telling him not to hang around with them.

She had slowed down passing the house, taking as good a look as she could in the dark.

A car came to a sudden stop beside her and a man jumped out of the back seat, pushing the door shut behind him.

She stopped in her tracks in fear. The car sped off up the road, and she found herself standing facing "Redser" Reilly.

Word had been that he was "out" again but no one had seen him. Till now.

For a split second she hesitated, then she tried to side-step. He moved so as to block her way. She tried the opposite way. He blocked her again. He was enjoying this. The grin on his face chilled her. It had to be nearly ten years since she was last so close to him, but time had not diminished his ability to strike instant fear in her. Most of that time he was back "in" again.

Aggravated assault was his favourite thing, but there were also rumours about drugs.

Everyone believed the rumours – after all, there was no smoke without fire. Redser's viciousness was legendary around the estate. No one could remember a time when he was not a problem. From a young age he was in trouble, regularly getting into fights just to prove he was the toughest. When he first pulled a knife it was in the church where he carved his initials into the wooden pew. To do this in the church had the desired effect. Only a "hard man" would dare do such a thing. But a knife slicing wood was no kick. It wasn't long before the feel of the blade in real flesh gave Reilly the high he wanted. Either he was lucky or his expertise developed quickly because he managed to cut without causing a life to be lost – because that was never his goal. He preferred to see the terror in his victims' eyes before the lightning flash of the blade followed by a thin red line forming on the skin. At first he cited any imaginary insult as a reason why he attacked someone, but he soon gave that up as a waste of energy. He was Redser Reilly. He needed no reason. He did it because he could. The gang that gathered around him thought themselves favoured to be associated with him but soon found that once Reilly selected them there was no way out. He ruled over them with absolute power and was known to be involved in one way or another with most of the local crime and gangland feuds. Spending time inside was seen as yet another feather in his cap and Reilly used these experiences to his advantage, often having planned his next "job" even before his release after the last one.

It was often Tomo who brought the stories home, relating what he had heard from the youngest member of the Reilly household. Now, the eldest of the brood stood before Angela, and the knowledge of what he was capable of greatly intimidated her. He was barely the same height as she, but he was built like a bull. Solid and broad, the result of much pumping iron.

"Well! If it isn't little Angela! Long time no see."

It sounded more like a jeer than a greeting. He manoeuvred himself so that he had her back to the garden wall. She could smell the alcohol on his breath.

He could smell her fear. She flattened herself against the wall to stay back from him.

"Yeah," he almost slobbered, "it's been a long time . . ." His eyes swept over her, taking in the improvements the years had made to her.

He made her feel dirty.

"Let me pass." Her voice sounded small and weak.

He feigned surprise. He held his arms out to the sides. "I'm not stopping you."

She was almost afraid to move in case he grabbed her.

"Go, if you want," he said. "Or maybe you like it where you are, right?"

His face came sickeningly close. The blade-one red stubble on his shiny scalp earned him his nickname. She slid sideways. His hand was instantly on the garden wall, stopping her.

"Remember – you haven't seen me! Got that?"

She nodded wordlessly, her eyes wide with fear.

"If you talk," he growled into her face, "I'll know it was you!" He traced a stubby finger down the side of her face.

She recoiled as the touch of his hand made her skin crawl.

"It'd be a pity to spoil that lovely complexion . . ." He removed his hand with a snigger of a laugh. He loved the smell of fear. He stepped back only enough for her to move without brushing against him and she started to run up the road. There was no one else around, and the sound of her running feet echoed in the quiet of the night.

Her family had lived on D'Arcy Avenue as long as she could remember. The avenue, with its thirty houses and their small front gardens, some still fenced off with black painted railings, had not changed much over the years. Her house was the last one at the top of the road, on the corner. There was a large open space facing it. An eyesore, where gangs congregated at night and where bonfires were lit. This was where Redser Reilly and his gang graduated. Used syringes and condoms were often found, but it was the horses which caused the most annoyance to local people. Tethered to stakes in the ground by long ropes they sometimes broke loose and wandered into gardens. Local youths owned them and rode them bareback around the fields. Thomas had his mother pestered. He wanted a horse. It was all he seemed to think about. He spent all the time he could over in the field. Sometimes Angela would look out her bedroom window and see him riding up and down, despite her having told him umpteen times to stay away. She had often opened her window and roared across at him to come in this minute. That in turn would bring a shout from her mother downstairs to give over shouting out the window like a common rossie.

Now, as she approached the garden gate she was relieved to see that the light was on in the big front bedroom window. She would not feel safe till she had closed the door behind her.

The house was quiet. For now.

Her mother would be in bed reading, as she often did, till the small hours of the morning. Most likely her father was sound asleep, snoring. Tomo was in the back bedroom he shared with Finbar and Fergus.

Quietly Angela let herself into the house and listened.

The only sound was her father's snoring. She slipped the bolt on the hall door, and went up to the small boxroom that had always been her bedroom.

As she passed her parents' door she heard, "That you, Angela?"

"Yeah."

"Night, love!"

"Night, Mam."

Exhausted, she was asleep almost as soon as her head hit the pillow.

Chapter 2

In the age-old cemetery on the western slope of Baltinglass Hill, outside Baltinglass town, a small group of women gathered by an open grave. Standing back a bit to allow room for relatives and friends by the graveside, they waited for the hearse to arrive. From their elevated vantage point they watched as it approached on the sharply curving road which climbed steeply from the main street to the gates of the graveyard and beyond.

The hearse and the mourning car turned into the cemetery and slowly made its way up the narrow path as far as the old tower. It stopped, and the coffin was hoisted carefully onto the shoulders of six men, none of whom were related to the deceased, but all of whom considered it an honour and a privilege to be allowed to take him to his final place of rest. The women waiting by the graveside watched as the oak casket was carried up the narrow path between the headstones.

They stood gathered together, as they did at every funeral in the parish, summoning their most sorrowful expressions, with their rosary beads wrapped around their fingers.

"I knew his wife's mother well," said one, claiming her absolute right to be there.

"Heart attack at fifty-two!" said another with a disbelieving shake of her head. "What on earth's to become of us at all?"

"God only knows," someone answered, sighing heavily, "God only knows."

They stood in silence a moment, watching the deliberately slow progress of the funeral procession.

"It's not going to be the same in the shop now," said Maisie Mac, who owned the small newsagent's shop, dabbing at her eyes, claiming monopoly on the grief. "Every evening he came in for his milk and the paper." She sniffed a second time to emphasise just how much she was going to miss him. "Oh, it's just not going to be the same!"

Someone at the back of the group coughed pointedly. "So you said. But he was nice to everyone. He was just that sort of person."

Maisie Mac ignored the remark. It *wasn't* quite the same. It was different when he winked at her. She *knew*. She had been engaged once. Long time ago but she *knew*.

"*You* always think –" The antagonist began another digging remark but an elbow in the ribs on her left side cut short her comment.

"He wasn't at all like his brother, thank God," Maisie

commented. "How the same parents produced such chalk and cheese I'll never know."

After elbowing her neighbour, Betty O'Gorman got in her own say before another unkind remark could raise the horrible possibility of an argument at the graveside.

"Speaking of Christy – I suppose he'll get the house and land. I mean, there's no one else, is there? I wonder what will become of the workshop and the paintings?"

"Firewood!" Maisie Mac said sarcastically. "That's what Christy Cleary will make of them. That man has no appreciation of nothing!"

The pallbearers were approaching and the women turned their heads to look in sympathy at the brother of the deceased. Christopher Cleary was walking behind the coffin, alone and unsupported. Everyone knew there was no love lost between the Cleary brothers. Christy's resentment of his sibling's good fortune had put the kibosh on their rather distant relationship many moons ago. Now as he followed the coffin he held his cap with both hands tightly pressed against his body, his balding head bowed. A few oily strands of hair were brushed across his scalp – the wind, sweeping up the hillside and across the exposed graveyard, played havoc with his occasional efforts to keep them in place.

His face was set in a frown. This funeral business was a total nuisance. He saw no reason why he should be there. They could have had the burial just as well without him. Besides, he wasn't comfortable being the centre of so much attention. Adding to his discomfort was the fact that he was confused and ill at ease, not knowing how he should react at the sudden and untimely death of his younger brother.

"Wouldn't you think he would at least have put on something decent for the funeral?" Maisie Mac whispered in disgust. "That auld jacket has so many beer stains on it I'm surprised he doesn't get drunk just wearing it!"

Someone smothered a titter.

"Heard he picked on one of Mulhearn's customers the other day," another mourner offered. "Bloodied his nose because he was looking at him, I believe."

Maisie Mac's lips tightened. "That'd be Christy all right, he's unhinged he is, and he's getting worse. No one is safe from that man any more."

Not one of the onlookers contradicted her, but the thought uppermost in their collective minds was the shameful waste of such a fine inheritance.

As he walked Christy's mind would not stay still, and he found himself amused at the irony of the situation. Mary would turn in her grave at the very idea of *him* ending up with *her* inheritance. They had never got along, Christy and his sister-in-law. His "rough manners and filthy personal habits" offended her greatly, as she had been known to say behind his back. If he called to the house, he would clear his throat and spit on the grass before greeting her. He knew she hated it. In some perverse corner of his mind he felt it toppled her from the pedestal his brother put her on. Just a little. But enough to give Christy a peculiar satisfaction. But look at him now. Who could have foreseen this?

He smiled inwardly at the thought. He remembered when he had last approached this spot, stood at this graveside. How he had envied his brother his good fortune then! Even as his sister-in-law was buried Christy had begrudged his brother his inheritance. For he, Christy, still lived in the labourer's cottage where they had both been born. It had only two small rooms and an outside toilet.

Love for the quiet, sickly Mary Shields had transported his brother out of the one-bedroom dwelling and into the "Big House". Not into a fortune, as Christy had thought, but a fortune by Christy's standards.

Christy had spent all his life in Baltinglass, but his brother had spent a good number of years travelling and working abroad. It had knocked the rough corners off him. Made him more articulate and interesting. That would have helped draw the refined and well-bred Mary to him. There were only a few acres of the once vast Shields' lands remaining now. Five, maybe seven at most, Christy wasn't sure. But it didn't matter. Compared to the tiny yard at the back of his cottage, it was colossal.

And the house itself, double-fronted and two-storied, was built solidly of stone, with outhouses better than what he was living in. He had no idea of what it was worth, but he imagined it to be a fair bit. He had always begrudged his brother every penny of it.

And now it would be his! What a bloody great turn of events!

The procession approached the open grave of Mary Cleary, buried this past eight years. The priest waited while all the mourners gathered round. Christy wished they would just get on with it. His mind was still swirling as the coffin was being lowered into the ground. The priest, standing solemnly beside the impassive Christy, raised his hand, and made the sign of the cross upon himself. The people did likewise. Christy also raised his hand, and used his palm to plaster his windswept hair back across his head.

"In the name of the Father, and of the Son, and of the Holy Spirit," the priest began. "My dear friends, let us pray for the repose of the soul of our dear brother, Daniel . . ."

Chapter 3

Nancy Brennan was getting the dinner ready. In silence. One quick glance at her husband's stony face told her a multitude. Paddy Brennan was sitting across the room in the armchair by the kitchen fire, reading the evening paper, and waiting for his dinner. It was a source of annoyance to him that there had not been a pot of fresh tea ready when he came in. Nancy said nothing. He hadn't even bothered to greet her, but there was nothing unusual in that. She just made the tea, poured it when it was ready, and placed it beside him, secretly hoping it would burn the mouth off him.

Thomas sat at the table, which took up most of the centre of the small room, and was already set for the meal. A pile of freshly cut bread was on a plate in front him. A large glass jug was filled with milk. One of the things Nancy would not tolerate in her kitchen was a milk carton on the table. Paddy said she gave herself airs.

Thomas's elbows were on the table. Both his index fingers were up his nostrils.

"What are we having, Nan?" he asked.

"Mince and onions," Nancy answered. Thomas sounded like he was getting a cold. She turned to look at him. "Thomas!"

Only his eyes moved in her direction. Caught! Again.

"Cut that out!" Nancy said.

The fingers were whipped out and wiped on his trousers, but not before his granda had seen what he was being checked for and scowled threateningly.

Thomas put his hands in his lap and his nan went back to the dinner and his granda turned his attention again to the evening paper.

"Why can't I have a horse?" Thomas asked, trying to sound very deprived.

Neither of his grandparents answered or looked at him. They had been through this before. Thomas stirred the sugar in the bowl with his forefinger, brooding over how badly he needed a horse. A small one would do. Even a pony. Thomas knew his horses.

"You'd want to give over about that before your mother comes down," Nancy warned him without turning.

Thomas rearranged the slices of bread on the plate while he contemplated how cool it would be to have his very own animal, and not have to be hanging around in the hope of getting a go from one of the other lads.

"You've been told – you're too young and there's nowhere to keep it," Nancy went on. "Anyway, they cost too much, and that's that."

Thomas sighed. This was going the same way as all the other times. "Slappo Reilly has one, and he's only thirteen," he argued. Slappo was the best at giving go's.

"And he is far too old for you to be hanging around with! You've been told that before too, so stay away from him!"

"But if I had my own horse –"

He broke off as the door opened.

Angela came in, her wet hair wrapped in a towel.

"Is he on about that again?" Without waiting for an answer, she shouted at her son: "I told you, Tomo Brennan, I don't want to hear about this again! And stop mauling the bloody bread!"

Suddenly there was a fierce rustling noise as Paddy Brennan slammed the newspaper onto his lap.

"For Christ's sake!" he exploded, glaring at Thomas. "Can you not keep your filthy little hands to yourself? People have to eat that. Get the hell away from that table!"

For a split second there was a stunned silence, then Thomas jumped from his chair as if he had been scalded. But his elbow caught the jug of milk and it toppled over, splashing his clothes, saturating the bread as it spilled, spreading all over the neatly set table and flowing over the side to form a large pool on the floor.

Paddy jumped to his feet, throwing the crumpled paper away from him.

"Jesus Christ! That's it. The knackers wouldn't see fit to eat in this house!" he roared, grabbing his car keys from beside the clock on the mantelpiece. He pushed

Thomas out of his way and stormed out of the house, slamming the door.

The milk continued to spill into a pool and, for the hundredth time, Nancy mentally thanked God that she had never put carpet on the kitchen floor.

Thomas looked at her. She knew he was sorry.

"Sorry, Nan. I didn't mean it, really I didn't."

"I know, love, I know."

He knew by the sound of her that she was very upset, but his attention was suddenly drawn to his mother when she hissed, "You're nine fucking years old, and you're still messing like you were a baby!"

"That'll do, Angela!" Nancy said firmly. She reached for the roll of kitchen paper, tore off a number of sheets and handed them to Angela to start mopping the table, while she started on the floor. "Go upstairs, Thomas, and change those wet trousers and jumper and then tell the twins their dinner will be ready in a minute. And make sure you wash your hands. Go on now!"

He closed the door behind him, glad to be out of his mother's sight.

Angela turned to her mother in exasperation. "Ma!"

Nancy wiped the lino slowly so as not to spread the milk further, but the floor beyond the pool of milk was already sticky. "I keep *telling* you, Angela, if you don't want him cursing then don't curse *at* him," she insisted.

Angela wiped furiously in frustration. She was no better at coping with her son than when he was born. "But he's forever causing disasters or having accidents! When is he going to give over? It's like he's permanently messing!" She pulled more paper from the roll and wiped her hands. The milk was everywhere. "The only time he seems to have it all together is when he's on one of those bloody horses!" she added bitterly.

Nancy decided it would be better if the mopping up was left to her. Angela wasn't being much help anyway.

"Look, love," she coaxed gently, "why don't you go up and finish drying your hair? This is nearly done – I'll wipe up the rest of it."

Angela didn't need much coaxing. She rearranged the towel on her head as she made her way up the stairs to her room.

Nancy cleaned up the mess. She found herself agreeing with her daughter about Thomas, but wisely she kept her feelings to herself, and made excuses for him whenever she could. But it was a terrible strain, trying to keep the peace between them all. It was a situation that erupted at any given moment. Paddy Brennan had never got over his disappointment about Angela.

Pregnant at fifteen. Only a child still. She had been his pride and joy. There was no one like her. She was bubbly and happy, and she adored him. They often went places together and always down to the ten thirty at St Mary's, in the convent. People could set their clocks by them on a Sunday morning.

Nancy and the twins always went to the "big chapel" at half past eleven, and when they got home Angela and her dad would have the table set for dinner. That was how it was. Until the night they had allowed Angela to go to that birthday party. They were not mad about the idea of the party being left unattended by the parents, even for a short while, but they knew most of the partygoers, and anyway, Angela could twist her father around her little finger. He was disgusted when she was brought home, apparently fluthered drunk, by two friends who took her to her door and made themselves scarce as soon as it was opened.

In the weeks after the fateful party Angela was not herself, and Nancy was very worried.

Then her pregnant state became obvious.

The one thing Angela was sure of was that she had not been drinking, but her father would not believe her. That devastated her as much as the pregnancy. The last thing she could clearly remember was the party being disrupted by gatecrashers. After that things were very unclear and disjointed. Her adored father kept calling her a liar. A liar and a whore! Nancy tried to intervene in these savage arguments. She was appalled at Paddy's attitude. But he turned on her too, and accused her of shielding a whore.

Nancy was sure her daughter had been drugged, but weeks later who could prove it? None of Angela's friends seemed able to shed any light on what happened, none could remember anything helpful. Even though Angela was under age the police could find nothing to go on, and in the end nothing was really done about it. The Brennan family went home to stumble through the consequences. And they were still doing that.

As she reset the table Nancy wondered what was to become of it all. Paddy would not be back now for dinner. If he ate at all it would be in the pub, and he would certainly drink more than he ate. She tried to put the thought of him arriving home later out of her mind, but in her heart was dread at the very idea. There were definitely times when she was afraid of him, but for the sake of her family she put a brave face on it and carried on. When she had all ready again she swallowed hard and forced herself to lift her heavy heart. Then she went and called the others for their dinners.

The first to come to the table was Fergus.

"What's all the going-on about?" he asked as he sat down.

"Oh, nothing more than usual," his mother answered as she busied herself taking up the dinners. "Just Thomas being Thomas, I suppose."

The others came in then. Finbar sat beside his brother, and Angela and Thomas sat facing them as always. Nancy was in her place at the end of the table nearest the cooker and the fridge. The chair opposite her at the far end of the table was empty.

Nancy glanced around as her family ate.

The twins were grown men, replicas of their father in appearance, with their curly hair and sallow complexions. Except for their height. At almost six feet tall they both towered over him. Finbar was the more easygoing of the two, the practical one who had the knack of being good with his hands. He could fix anything, and he and his father had often spent hours out in the driveway with their heads under the bonnet of the car, fixing this or adjusting that. If they were not at the car then they were in the garden shed, hammering and banging to their hearts' content. Half the time Nancy didn't even know what they were doing. But that was then . . .

Fergus was the serious one. He knew exactly what he wanted to do in life and could often be found dug into his books, even on a Saturday, if he didn't have a match to play. He was football mad, the one who got togged out in all weathers.

Nancy was very proud of the fact that her boys were in college, doing their finals. Fergus was doing Business Studies, and Finbar, who had yet to decide what he wanted to do, was doing a BA. Not many from D'Arcy Avenue were educated to third level. It was nearly over, the struggle to find the money to keep going. It was difficult to make ends meet, and it was a serious bone of contention with Paddy that their education soaked up money like a sponge. At their age they should already have a few years' work behind them, he said.

They planned to be off to the States for the summer. They had been planning for ages, along with a group from college. Straight after the exams. All the arrangements were made, tickets, accommodation, jobs.

She thrust the thought aside. Time enough to think of them going then. Her gaze fell on her daughter. Her unfortunate, problematic daughter. Angela's education finished with her Junior Cert exam. Thomas was one then. Angela went back to school after his birth, and Nancy took care of the baby, but it soon became clear that Angela's schooldays were over, and after a disastrous exam result she dropped out of school. A series of "bits of jobs", as her father belittlingly called them, followed, and money was always tight. Angela's eye caught her mother's gaze.

"Coloured your hair?" Nancy asked, covering her thoughts nicely.

"Yeah. What d'you think? Is it too strong or what?"

Nancy considered the effect for a moment. "No. It's different, mind you. What colour did you put in?"

"A sort of plum. I'm letting it grow. The colour will fade as I wash it."

Thomas looked up at his mother's hair. He didn't think plums were that colour.

Nancy noted how Angela was always trying to change her appearance, even though she didn't go out much. A pity really. Her daughter was pretty. It was Nancy's opinion that she ought to be out enjoying herself, at least more often than she did. Angela's lack of interest in going out was a worry. Boyfriends were rare, and didn't last long.

When she was younger she was full of laughter and confidence. She had hair like Nancy's had been before the grey took over, thick and lustrous, but it was her gorgeous big expressive eyes, rimmed with thick lashes that were her best feature. Paddy was forever admiring his adored daughter. As a toddler he would bounce her on his knee, as proud a father as ever there was.

"How did I happen to get such a little beaut?" he used to say. "Where you got those lovely eyes I'll never know!"

But Nancy knew.

She used to say her grandmother had eyes like that. She lied.

Paddy rolled onto his side of the bed and was almost instantly out cold, aided both by his exertions and the Guinness. Nancy waited till she heard the snoring, then quietly got out of the bed and reached for her dressing-gown.

In the dark she made her way to the bathroom, where she gave herself a quick wash. Then, wrapping her towelling wrap tightly around her, against the cold of the night or as psychological protection, she knew not which, she made her way downstairs, and put on the kettle.

She dropped a single tea bag into the mug and sat to wait for the kettle to boil. A great sadness filled her mind and it seemed to weigh down her whole being. It was at times like this that she felt so entirely alone in the world. There was no one at all who put her needs first. Even occasionally. There was no one who even knew what her needs were. The fact pointed out so very forcibly that she had no soul mate.

She sighed heavily as she poured the boiling water into the mug. She sat again and, with both hands clasped around the warmed mug, she stared at a small solitary bubble going round and round on top of her tea till it burst.

Why didn't she stop him when he was being so brutish? Say no? At least when he was drunk. Did her conscience bother her that much? Was it guilt that made her feel she deserved to be brutalised like that? Or was she *that* much afraid of him? Maybe she should have left him, then. But she had still been in love with him. And anyway there had been more than herself to consider. Daniel already had a wife.

But she couldn't sit and dwell on herself like this. It made it all much harder to bear.

Her thoughts went back to Angela. She wasn't the only single mother around the place but it didn't seem to isolate other girls. Maybe they were sexually active already and accepted the consequences. But it hadn't been that way with Angela and her friends. Nancy was sure of it. At the time of the ill-fated party her class in the Community School were still at the stage where they all used to hang around together. They went everywhere together. The party included.

They'd all shunned her when they learned she was pregnant. Nancy thought that strange. Her gut feeling was that they knew more than they said.

A creaking stair told her that someone else was coming down.

Finbar had woken, disturbed by the sounds from his parents' room. Covering his head with the covers, he'd tried to get back to sleep, but he was aware of the fact that his mother had gone downstairs. And he had not heard her go back to bed.

She looked up as he came into the kitchen.

"God, Ma! What are you doing sitting here in the cold? You'll die of exposure!" he exclaimed, pretending to be surprised. Then, looking closer, he asked, "You okay?"

She nodded, with a little smile. The concern was nice.

"Sure?" he said.

"Of course I'm sure. I only came down for a cup of tea! What has *you* up?"

"Thirst," he lied. "Just wanted a drink of water."

Chapter 4

Nancy got the shock of her life when she opened the hall door to call Thomas in. There were two horses in her front garden and Thomas was just tethering the second one to the railings. Two other lads with him cleared the garden hedge in one leap when they saw her and ran off.

Thomas turned and knew he was in trouble again the instant he laid eyes on his nan's face. Nancy's first impulse was to let a roar at him, but he was standing between the two animals, so she dared not risk it. With a jerk of her head she ordered him inside. He made sure the knots were tight and then he slinked towards her.

"What in God's name do you think you're doing?" she demanded as she closed the door behind him and propelled him towards the kitchen with a push. Even Nancy ran out of patience with him now and then. She shouted up the stairs. "Angela Brennan! Will you get off your arse up there and come down and see what your son has done now! Look outside!"

Angela flung aside the magazine, and jumped from her bed in annoyance. "Jesus! Now what?" she swore and took a quick glance out the window. The minute she saw the horses she shouted out, "Tomo Brennan! I'll fuckin' kill ya!" and she wrenched the bedroom door open and came thundering down the stairs.

Thomas and her mother were in the kitchen and the child was trying to explain that the big fellas were going to light a fire in the field that night. You couldn't leave the horses there, he argued, they wouldn't be safe. He only wanted to leave them in the garden till tomorrow.

Angela stood glaring at him as though she could gladly strangle him. He knew well that she would have walloped him good if she was nearer to him, so he inched closer to his nan, angry and all as she was too.

"Who owns them horses?" his mother demanded.

He had no reply.

But she guessed. "Slappo Reilly!"

Thomas cringed visibly as she moved threateningly towards him.

"Why didn't he put them in his *own* garden?"

"Ours is nearer."

"Yeah!" she jeered him. "That's what that cute bastard said, isn't it? He runs rings round you! And you don't cop on, do ya?"

Thomas was by Nancy's side now, right up against her. She placed a protective arm around his shoulders. Angela was fit to murder him – she had long since run out of patience with the things he got up to and she had trouble enough coping with herself.

But the horses had to be got out of the garden before Paddy came home. The garden was his department, and Nancy knew he would have a fit if he saw the horses in it. Everyone would pay dearly for it. The grass was already pockmarked with holes from the animals' hooves.

Nancy took control of the situation before Angela totally lost it.

"Thomas," she said, "you have to put the horses back in the field –"

"But, Nan!"

"No buts! They can't stay there. Put them back in the field. Down the far end – it's big enough. I'll get Finbar and Fergus to give you a hand. Do it now, before your granda gets home, or there will only be killing!"

Thomas knew that tone. He had forgotten about his granda for the moment. Putting the horses in the garden had seemed like such a good idea. He was disappointed. It would have been great to have them there overnight. He would only have to look out the front window to see them.

His nan left to get the twins to help and Thomas went too, knowing his mother would go for him if he stayed.

Finbar was in front of his telly and Fergus was studying, but they got up willingly enough. In the garden Fergus untied one of the horses and led it out the gate. Finbar took the other one. They were unkempt and smelly animals and the twins tried to manage them without actually having to come in to contact with them. The horses took their time manoeuvring themselves back through the narrow gateway, but they were well used to being in strange situations, and were docile enough. Thomas ran alongside them.

"Give us a go! Lift me up!" he pleaded once they were across the roadway.

Out of sight of the house Fergus grabbed hold of the lad and swung him up onto the horse's back.

"Let me go on me own!" Thomas tried to take the rope into his own hands.

"No way!" Fergus said. "Your mother would kill me if she thought I let you."

"She won't see. I won't tell."

Fergus let the rein go.

"Great!" Thomas whooped as he dug his heels into the horse's sides. The animal leapt forward and Thomas headed him towards the far end of the field, and galloped the length of it.

Seeing him go, Fergus remarked to his brother, "Would you look at that! Like he was born in the saddle!"

"And *no* saddle," Finbar pointed out. "It's a pity he can't have a horse of his own."

"Angela wouldn't want the bother."

"Angela doesn't want the bother of Thomas," Finbar remarked ruefully. "I feel sorry for the little git at times."

"I know what you mean," was the reply "but he can be the craftiest little git too, when he likes. Just wait till you see the innocence when Da sees the hoof-marks and wants to know who left the gate open!"

They gave each other a sudden, knowing glance, and

burst out laughing. After tethering the animals they went back to the house.

Thomas arrived in a bit later, rather subdued for a lad who had been on a high such a short time ago. He sat at the table, a deep frown creasing his brow. There was only the two of them in the kitchen, and Nancy sensed something was coming.

"Nan, is Redser Reilly my da?"

Nan might have been prepared for almost anything else, but this totally stumped her.

Reilly! Of all people! Good Lord!

Thomas sat quietly, waiting for the answer. Both his elbows were on the table, his head resting on one hand, and with his free hand he traced the pattern on the tablecloth, his lips pushed tightly together. He cast an eye in her direction a couple of times while Nancy searched desperately for an answer.

"Is he, Nan?"

The child looked over at her. He had seen his nan's eyebrows going high up to her hairline, and then coming down together very quickly, almost meeting over her nose, while she concentrated hard on the dinner. Now she beat the boiled potatoes to a pulp and tried to sound matter of fact.

"Where did you ever get an idea like that?"

"Anto Dunne said his big brother said it." Thomas was troubled. But he wasn't done. "Anto's brother said him, Redser and his pals gatecrashed a party, and Redser laid one on me ma. Everyone was afraid to talk about it, because it was *him*, and then I was born."

Nancy smelled burning. She whipped the pot from the gas ring, her mind working overtime. The things Thomas was saying! "Laid one" on his ma! Did the child even know what he was talking about?

"Is it true, Nan?"

She sat on the chair beside him, trying desperately to find the right things to say. "Listen love, people tell stories all the time. Besides, you know how your mother can't stand the Reillys! She would never have anything to do with any of them! You know that, don't you?"

"But Anto's big brother was *there*," the child insisted.

Nancy was desperate. "You wouldn't want a da with a jail record now, would you?" She watched his reaction closely. She put her arms around him and gave him a firm hug. He would never have allowed that if anyone else had been there.

His reply was very slow in coming. "Well, at least I would have a *da*, wouldn't I?"

Her heart ached for him. They heard the hall door open. Nancy put a finger to her lips.

"Let's keep this to ourselves, just for now, eh?"

Thomas slid from his chair without another word and trudged out into the hall.

He passed his grandfather without a word of greeting from either of them. She heard his slow footsteps as he dragged his feet up the stairs. The poor little mite.

Paddy came into the kitchen, took off his jacket and threw it onto a chair.

"What's *he* done now?" was the greeting Nancy got.

"Nothing," she said.

Paddy sat by the fire and opened the paper he had brought in. "He's *always* up to something. Where's me mug of tea? And me dinner? I'm starving."

She prayed to God that he would never hear what Thomas had just said. If it was being talked about, God only knew who else had heard it.

A sick feeling persisted in Nancy's stomach. She knew what Thomas said could well be the truth. It would explain why no one would speak out at the time. She always felt that Angela was drugged, else she would have known who attacked her. No wonder her friends had deserted her. No one dared stand up to Redser Reilly.

"What's keeping the bloody grub?"

Paddy's narky tone got to Nancy. "It's coming, I said!" she snapped.

He sat himself to the table. "Don't give me that attitude," he said darkly. "I've been working hard all day. You've only had to get a dinner! It's not rocket science!"

She ignored that. She called up the stairs that it was ready. The twins appeared and thundered down. No sign of Thomas.

Nancy went up.

"Thomas?" She sat on the edge of the bed, quietly waiting for him to respond.

"Granda will kill me if he hears," he said. "So will Ma."

Reilly's son, living in Paddy's house. The child was probably right.

"They don't even want me now. What'll they do if they hear *this*?" he worried.

"Don't think like that, love. They won't do anything at all. I wouldn't let them, now would I?" said Nancy and she placed her arms around him reassuringly.

He was in sore need of the reassurance. "Promise?"

"Of course I promise. Now, come on down and don't worry, there's a good lad."

Chapter 5

Christopher Cleary lifted the tarpaulin cover from his bicycle and threw it to one side. Rainwater had gathered in the dips and it splashed down his trousers and over his shoes. He cursed about it to himself as he swung the bike around towards the door of his small backyard. He wore his cap and his belted wool overcoat and had his bicycle clips around the bottoms of his trousers. He had been waiting for ages for the rain to ease up, impatience building as he watched the blackened sky. Any other day he wouldn't have chanced it, but he couldn't wait. He'd been waiting for too long already.

He slipped the latch on the yard door and pushed the bike out through the narrow passage at the side of the cottage, and out through the front gate. He threw his leg over the crossbar and headed the bike towards Baltinglass. It was only a ten-minute cycle from his house, but his destination lay out beyond the town, on the banks of the River Slaney.

He refused to admit to himself that it was a bad idea to set out today. Doggedly he steered around potholes and roadside puddles which grew bigger and bigger as rainwater flowed and found nowhere to drain to. He had been cycling this road all his life and he knew every twist and turn, every dip and hollow, so he put his head down against the wind and pedalled as if on automatic pilot. Lost in his thoughts as he was, he failed to see the sky darken threateningly again, and even before the town had come into sight the heavens opened once more. The rain lashed down in a continuous torrential downpour. It hopped high off the roadway and fell back again, doubling the circles on the surface water.

The keys in Christy's pocket drove him relentlessly onwards. Ever since the Sergeant had handed the keys to him, his one thought had been to fit them into the lock they were made for.

Rain dripped from the peak of his cap and his nose, and his feet and legs were saturated right through to his skin. Cold began to seep through the heavy overcoat as he approached the town. The main street was almost deserted. He passed the Heritage Centre and rode into the main street, where he would turn out of the town again. But luck was not with him. He cycled through a puddle that covered a deep pothole by the side of the road and the bicycle suddenly stopped moving and lurched sideways. He was thrown against a litterbin which stood at the edge of the footpath. It toppled over and helped to soften his landing on the ground.

Maisie Mac dashed out of the nearby newsagent's, much to Christy's consternation.

"Good God, man!" she exclaimed. "Are you hurt?"

Christy gruffly waved off her attempt to help him up. He picked up his fallen bicycle and cursed the Council for the state of the roads.

"Are you sure you're all right?" Maisie enquired a little more tentatively.

Christy was examining his bike. The front wheel was buckled, and the tyre was burst.

"Fuck it! Fuck the *fuckin'* potholes!" he exploded. "Fuck the *fuckin'* Council!"

Maisie tutted loudly and Christy suddenly turned his venom on her.

"What are you fuckin' looking at?" he growled. "Piss off!"

As if he had physically pushed her Maisie suddenly backed into the safety of the shop. She had never before had an offer of help refused with such rudeness, and she was soaked to the skin as well. How Christopher and Daniel Cleary managed to have the same parents she'd never know.

Outside the shop Christy lifted the damaged bicycle off the roadway. He carried it a few doors up the street, where he parked it against the front wall of the pub, and made his way inside, still cursing rings around him about the Council and the weather.

A couple of customers were seated at a table having a drink. Another two men sat at the bar near the door end. They turned and acknowledged his presence with a nod.

"Turned out bad," one of them understated.

Christy gave them an almost imperceptible nod in return and made his way to the far end of the bar and occupied a stool there. He removed his cap and ran his hand over his head, making sure his strands of hair were in place. He placed the saturated cap on the bar counter. He removed his heavy wet coat and put it on the stool beside him and then placed the wet cap on top of it. There was no way that he was going to get to put the key in its lock today. Not now. Not with the rain and not with the bike the way it was. He cursed his luck.

Turning that key was all he had wanted to do since he got it. Weeks after the funeral, the local garda sergeant had contacted him and asked him to call into the station to pick up his brother's keys and wallet. They were all the personal items found on him when he collapsed in the street. Why it had taken the fuckin' garda so long to contact him Christy didn't know. He was almost as bad as the fuckin' solicitor. He hadn't heard anything from Patrick Cullen yet and he didn't want to contact the snot himself – didn't want to appear too grasping. He wouldn't wait much longer though – after all, it was his rightful inheritance.

At least he had the keys. But now opening that door was delayed further until the bike was fixed. He wanted to be alone when he turned that key in its lock. He didn't want anyone else snooping around with him just because they might have given him a lift out. Having to wait and get the bike sorted was a blasted nuisance. Even getting back to his cottage would be a bother now. The rain was still coming down in buckets. He needed a stiff whiskey to fortify himself and he knew there was money in Daniel's wallet – he had it with him in his trousers' pocket.

Seán Mulhearn made his way down the bar and stood before Christy.

"That's a bad one!" He eyed the saturated Christy. "What can I get you?"

Christy took out the wallet and looked inside. "Whiskey. Double."

He smiled a crooked smile to himself and mentally thanked his brother as he selected a note to pay for his drink.

"Things looking up, Christy?" one of the men at the other end asked.

It put Christy on the spot.

The barman sat his drink on a beer mat.

"Give them whatever they're having," Christy muttered with a large degree of begrudgery, "and them too." He jerked his head back indicating the two other people seated behind him. Suddenly he was glad of the rain. It might keep others indoors at least till he left the pub.

But he wasn't getting away that lightly. The door opened. A huge figure of a man came in, stamping his feet and slapping his cap against his thigh.

"Christ Almighty. That's some weather. As if we didn't have enough rain already!" Mick Furlong made his way to the centre of the bar and looked left and right. "That your bike, Christy?" Without waiting for an answer he turned to the barman. "The usual, Seán, please." Then turning to Christy he enquired, "What happened to the bike?"

Christy supped his drink with a frown. He knew the answer would make him feel stupid but he was on the spot again. "Pothole," he muttered.

"Damn roads," said Furlong. "Always the same. I'll put the bike in the trailer and drop it around to Mooney's to be fixed, if you like."

"That's very kind of you."

"No problem," the newcomer said. Turning to the barman he enquired, "How's your father doing, Seán? Any better?"

Seán topped up the pint as he answered. "He says he'll be back behind the bar in a couple of days. Bad enough dose, mind you, but it will be grand to have the extra pair of hands back again."

"Time you two had a good woman about this place. Or maybe *two* good women would be better. Sure I'm always saying it."

"That's true," said Seán with a rueful smile and pushed the man's drink towards him, leaving Mick to decide for himself which sentence he was referring to.

Christy said that he would take care of it also. His foul mood was lifting with the help of the whiskey. The men lifted their glasses together in salute and commiseration.

"A fine man your brother, Christy, a fine man."

"Aye, he'll be sorely missed about the place."

"God rest him!"

Christy raised his glass in return, and surprised himself by ordering another round.

"That's mighty kind of you, Christy. Lord of the Manor, eh?" someone remarked.

Yeah. That was it. Lord of the Manor. Sort of. Well, almost. He was beginning to enjoy the camaraderie around him. He found it easier to order the next round, and the ones after that were no problem at all.

Christy's increasing inebriation was obvious to everyone. Even so, they sat and followed his lead and lifted their glass to Daniel each time a round was placed in front of them.

Mick Furlong retained his position at the centre of the bar, not too close to either end to be overheard if he didn't wish it. He lifted his pint with a sideward glance, then inclined his heavily featured face towards Seán. Always keen for a juicy comment, Seán cocked his ear towards Mick.

"What a waste, him getting the Cleary place!" said Mick, the thought of it leaving a bad taste in his mouth. "He wouldn't know what to do with it."

Seán couldn't help admitting to himself that the big farmer was right but only offered a shrewd, "And you would?"

Mick was nodding most definitely. "I'll tell you something – I've had my eye on that place a long time now. Did you know that I made an offer to Daniel?"

Seán didn't. "Get away!" He was all ears. "And?"

Mick licked the froth of his pint from his upper lip while he remembered the meeting. Seán always served an excellent pint. "Nah! Not a budge! Don't know why he was so dead bent on holding it. It wasn't as if he actually used it himself. Wouldn't let it go at any price." Then he winked at the barman. "But Christy might!"

Anticipation whetted Mick's appetite. A gleam of determination shone in his eyes. He ordered the next round and made it a double and made sure that Christy knew it. Mick Furlong had already begun his assault on the Cleary lands.

Chapter 6

The postman was late this morning. Crossing the landing from the bathroom Angela heard him push some mail through the letterbox. Thomas was in his bedroom playing games on the computer by the sound of it. He had the room all to himself now that the twins were gone to America. A couple of times, when he knew his granda was on the night shift, he had asked his nan if he could go into her bed, just till she came up.

"He's too big for that!" Angela was annoyed but Nancy made excuses for him.

"He's not used to being in a room on his own," she said. "What harm is in it?"

"You're babying him, Ma! How is he ever going to grow up if you baby him!"

Nancy had noticed a change in Thomas since he had been told that Reilly was his father. He was quieter these days. He got into just as much trouble, but something about his demeanour was different. The fact he had the big bedroom all to himself now normally would have delighted him, but it seemed to Nancy that he didn't want to be alone. She worried about him. She said nothing, but kept a close eye on him. She couldn't help but notice that if someone said something that began with "D'you know what . . ." or "So and so said . . ." he immediately tensed up and seemed alarmed. She realised that he was only waiting for the word to spread. The poor little mite was living in fear of the day it would become common knowledge.

She believed it was true. It would explain such a lot. But her own heart sank at the very thought of her husband finding out. It was a real source of worry, which she kept quiet about and simply added to those she had already lived with for so long. She prayed fervently that her worries would never see the light of day. But in spite of her devotion to her particular saint, her prayers were not to be answered. And the relative security she thought she had was about to be shattered.

Angela took her time getting dressed and then came down to the kitchen. She didn't have to be in the shop till the afternoon. Her mother was sitting at the table, reading a letter. An unopened envelope lay on the table beside her hand. Her other hand covered her mouth, and the look on her face alarmed Angela.

"Ma? What's up? Is it the lads?"

Nancy shook her head slowly but said nothing. Angela glanced over her mother's shoulder and saw the large print of the letter heading.

Solicitors! She was immediately alarmed.

54

"Thomas. Is it Thomas? What's he gone and done? I'll kill him!"

"It's not Thomas," Nancy said quietly, almost to herself. Her mind was desperately searching for a way to grasp the implications of what she had just read.

Angela looked again at her mother's face and saw the colour had drained out of it, and her annoyance quickly vanished. She sat down opposite Nancy, wanting to ask but suddenly not wanting to know.

Still she said, "Ma? What is it? *Ma.*"

Nancy put the letter down on the table, and took a slow deep breath.

"There's a letter here for you too, love," she said heavily, "but before you read it I have to tell you something . . ."

She stopped, unable to make herself say the words. Then she simply pushed the unopened mail across the table, and with a nod indicated to Angela to open it.

Angela looked at it as if frightened of it, then slowly she picked it up and opened it, all the while anxiously watching Nancy's face. She read it through, then read it again, and finally looked at her mother for explanation.

"Ma? What's this all about?"

Feeling the ice was broken, Nancy took a deep breath. "It's simple really, love," she said quietly. "You see, that man Daniel Cleary . . . he's, well, he's your father. I mean, *was* your father. He died last week."

There, it was out. Said.

And God alone knew what would happen next.

"What that says is that you inherit his estate."

Angela remained silent, staring at her mother.

Nancy waited for a reaction.

"You mean me da is *not me da?*" That was all that Angela had taken in.

Nancy confirmed it with a simple "That's right."

Not her da? Angela would never have believed it, only the proof was in her hand.

"He doesn't know, love," said Nancy.

Thoughts were tumbling over each other in an effort to sort themselves into some sort of coherent order in Angela's mind. All she could think was that he wouldn't speak to her in a civil manner, and he wasn't even her *da*. If he *had* been, surely he would never have turned on her the way he did. But he didn't *know*. It didn't take long to realise the situation her mother and herself were in now. A bomb exploded in her brain and the colour drained from her face. With a sinking heart she met her mother's eyes. The same thing was in both their minds.

"Da! Oh God, Ma! What'll happen if he finds out?"

Fear was tangible in Nancy's eyes. Suddenly an awful spectre hung over them both.

"I don't want him to find out," Angela said emphatically, her mother's fear draping them both in a blanket of conspiracy.

Nancy picked up her letter. "God, love! Neither do I. But I *do* want you to have whatever has been left you. You need to go see this solicitor and –" She stopped abruptly at the sound of the hall door slamming. Both their heads turned towards the hall in a strangled silence.

Paddy should be in work but he pushed the kitchen

door open now, already in a rage. His eyes fell on Angela who was nearest and staring at him in disbelief.

"You filthy little whore!" he spat at her as two strides put him right in front of her. "It's all over the job!" He lashed out and hit her across the face. Her head swung from the blow as if on a pivot. "*Reilly's* bastard! That's whose bastard you have! Reilly's! No wonder you wouldn't say! That scum! *In my house!*"

No! It couldn't be. He was wrong. Terribly wrong!

Nancy leapt to her feet, shouting at him to stop, and came around the table, pushing her letter into her apron pocket. He flung out an arm to block her and his elbow caught her full on the nose. Straight away it bled profusely, and Angela screamed in shock when she saw blood pour down her mother's face. Nancy was dazed and struggled to keep herself upright.

Angela's letter was open on the table. She had to prevent Paddy from seeing it. But he had sensed something when he rushed into the room and now his eyes focused on the open letter. Angela tried desperately to snap it up, but he was quicker.

"What's this? What's going on here?" he growled, pushing her away hard, taking in the name on the letter heading.

"That's *my* mail!" Angela cried in panic.

His eyes narrowed as they skimmed quickly over it. Veins pulsed at his temples and his mouth worked soundlessly as the printed words sank in.

Angela's heart seemed to stop.

Nancy felt a cold sweat run down her back as her

husband turned on her, the whites of his eyes bulging. Fury and rage gagged his words.

He swung out, knocking her sideways with his fist.

"Ma!" Angela screamed as she saw her mother go down. Then her attention was drawn to a sound on the stairs as Thomas turned and scrambled to go back up to safety.

Like lightning Paddy rushed out and grabbed him, then hauled him kicking and screaming into the kitchen, hitting him about the head as he did so.

"Scum!" he kept roaring. "Reilly's scum!"

Angela screamed at him to let Thomas go as she was helping her mother up.

"No, Granda! No! No!" Thomas's fearful cries tore at Nancy's heart.

Paddy flung the child aside.

Nancy was on her feet, trying to steady herself. "For God's sake, Paddy, stop!" she cried.

He ignored her pleas and lunged at Angela. His arm reached her and grabbed her hair, pulling it viciously. "And whose scum are you?" He thrust his purple face at her. "*Whose*! Answer me!" He wrenched her head back and forth till hair came away in his hand.

Nancy and Thomas clung to each other crying, screaming.

"You and your fucking bastard are finished in my house!" he spat at Angela. "Do you hear me? Do you fucking hear me, I said!"

She was incapable of answering.

Reilly! Oh, Jesus, she felt sick.

"Answer me, you slut! Just like your fucking slut of a

mother! No wonder you turned out to be the slut you are, with a whore for a mother!"

She did her best to nod her head. Thomas was holding on to his nan, seeking the protection she had promised, but he knew well that none of them could protect each other now.

Paddy dragged Angela into the hall. He looked back at Thomas.

"Get yourself out here!" he shouted at the child.

Nancy anticipated his intention. "No, Paddy! You can't do that. You can't!" She held Thomas close to her.

"I'm getting around to you, whore, you lying bitch!" he snarled, grabbing Thomas roughly and dragging him away.

The child roared in fright for his nan, but Paddy opened the hall door and pushed him and his mother out, and shut the door hard.

Nancy was hysterical and tried to get to them, but he was too strong, too enraged. He turned on her. The very look of him stopped her dead. Chilled her.

"That's the end of them. Get used to it! And as for you, you bitch, you'll stay here. You won't be going after them, if you know what's good for you!"

He grabbed the front of her blouse but she managed to wrench herself away from him. She turned and ran up the stairs, grabbing Angela's shoulder bag and jacket from the end of the banisters as she ran past. Thinking as quickly as she could, she stuffed the letter from her pocket and some money into the bag. Then she grabbed Thomas's jacket from his room. They were standing sobbing in the garden. She opened the front bedroom window and threw the bag and jackets down to them.

"Go to the solicitor!" she urged them. "Go see him today! The address is in the bag!"

She closed the window quickly, unable to watch the state they were in, then sank, weak with fear, as she heard Paddy's deliberate, slow, heavy footsteps reach the landing. For her there was no way out.

The noise in Brennans' had attracted the neighbours' attention. Across the road Nancy's friend Annie Ryan came out when she saw the state of Angela and Thomas in the garden. She took them into her house and did her best to help them calm down.

Angela told her what had happened.

"Promise. Promise you won't tell anyone me ma's secret, Mrs Ryan!" she pleaded.

"Don't you worry one bit. I've known something about it for years," Mrs Ryan said kindly, very worried about Nancy's fate. "Nancy had to talk to someone, you know. But what about you and Thomas?"

Go to the solicitor, her mother had urged, go today!

Wicklow! Angela didn't want to go to Wicklow; she didn't even know how far it was. She wanted to go home, but she certainly couldn't go back into the house. She looked in her bag and found the letter. She read it again, still in disbelief.

"I'll phone the solicitor for you, if you like," Mrs Ryan offered, "see if he'll be there today. Those guys spend a lot of time in court, y'know."

Angela handed her the letter.

Thomas sat so still and quiet they had almost forgotten he was there.

Mrs Ryan came back from the hall.

"You're in luck," she told Angela. "They expect you down this afternoon. And I checked with Busáras – there's a bus in about an hour."

Chapter 7

The Bus Éireann bus for Baltinglass was almost full when they climbed on board in Busáras. Only single seats were left. Angela indicated the first one to Thomas and moved further down the aisle to the next available seat. As the bus moved out into the traffic and past the Customs House she wanted to make it stop. Something akin to panic gripped her and she wanted it to go back and let her get off. But she made no sound, only watched in silent despair as the city in which she had spent every minute of her life began to slip, with frightening momentum, into her past. But there was no way back. Home didn't exist any more.

The city gave way to the suburbs, and the suburbs gave way to country fields. Now and again the bus stopped, sometimes in the middle of nowhere it seemed. People got off, people got on, and the bus continued its journey, transporting its two reluctant passengers to an alien world. Angela barely moved. Thoughts of the situation they had left her mother in made her feel physically sick. She was riddled with guilt when she tried to squash them. But her mind continually whirled around what had brought her to this. Unattached, unconnected events which had begun before she was born. Now they had come together to catapult her into another life. Even though she did not yet know what it might entail, she knew for certain it was a life she did not want, in a place she had no earthly wish to go to. The prospect of being on her own with Thomas filled her with dread. How could she be expected to cope with him alone? Half the time she couldn't stand the sight of him. He was the cause of all her problems with her father. Without him all would have been well. Suddenly she felt the shockwaves of that last thought reverberate through her body.

And there wasn't any truth in it. The fact was without Reilly and her mother's affair all would have been well. Not Thomas's fault at all. Nor hers either. But it made no difference – she still knew she wouldn't be able to cope with him alone. She had no practice at it. Her mother always took the bulk of the problems with him off her shoulders. And how was he going to be without his nan to run to all the time? Somewhere in the depths of her trauma the fact that her mother had an affair sat very uneasily on her. Her steady, dependable mother. She was shocked at the very idea of it. Reliable Nancy, who rarely dressed up or socialised, had a wild dark secret. For all those years. A secret, Angela could see now, that never had very much hope of staying buried forever. And she was the result of it.

Like mother like daughter, Paddy had raged. No wonder Angela turned out to be the slut she was, he roared. What chance had she with a whore for a mother? Angela cringed visibly when she thought of the awful things that spewed from his mouth. Vile awful things, and Tomo had heard them all. She wondered how much of it he understood. She wanted to die.

Now that it was out, would her mother want to talk about it? Oh, if only she'd had the chance to say something about this Daniel Cleary! Now it would torment her, raising endless questions in her mind, because it all had such an effect on her – but that was the *nub* of it all, wasn't it? Other people's actions had her where she was, and it fell to her to pay the price. It wasn't fair. It wasn't fucking fair at all.

But she knew now very well that what she had been saying all along was the truth: she had not been a willing participant in the making of Tomo Brennan. Reilly would not have needed anyone's permission or agreement. What had happened that night at that party was still a blur. Her mind automatically cut itself off from this line of thinking. It was much too difficult to bear, too difficult to take in.

Suddenly nothing in her life was as it had seemed. She was not even who she thought she was any more. She had lost her home, her mother, her family, even her identity. And she hadn't got the foggiest notion where they were going to spend the night. She felt sick. And the rain was coming down in buckets.

Thomas was lost in thoughts of his own. In his young mind the fault was all his. The arguments were all because of him. And now it was all over the place that Reilly was his da. The *shame* of it! Reilly, of all people. Always he had wanted a da, and always he had hated Reilly even though he was pals with his younger brother. Everyone did. That was the way it was. Reilly earned everyone's hate, and fear. Even so, some of the lads were in awe of him.

Did Reilly know he was his da, he wondered? Maybe no one had dared tell him. Or maybe he didn't *want* to know, just like Granda.

But Granda *wasn't* his granda. That was hard to get a grip on. If this other man was his *ma's* da, then it was *he* who was his granda. *Wasn't* it?

It was getting very complicated but that thought gave Thomas a serious fright. What about his nan, then? She was still his nan. Wasn't she? *Wasn't* she?

He had to know for sure. He turned in his seat and looked back at his mother. But she wasn't even looking in his direction. Her face was deathly pale as she stared into nowhere, and Thomas knew better than to present himself in front of her just now. But he was worried. If he was anxious before it was nothing to what he felt now. He turned back in his seat and concentrated hard on looking out the window, mostly to distract himself from the surge of water welling up behind his eyes.

He watched for sheep and cattle in the fields and tried to count each lot before the bus passed them by. Then he saw two horses grazing. That perked him up. They were gorgeous big brown full-sized horses, with black manes and long black tails. Like the ones you see on the sports news, racing past the winning post. Much better than the ones over in the field. And *he* and his ma were going to the country! The very place for horses! There might even be some where they were going! Suddenly he saw all sorts of possibilities! But he knew in his heart that his ma wouldn't see any. They didn't even know where they would be spending the night, and if he mentioned horses to her now or asked about his nan she would only throttle him.

It began to rain heavily, and it was no longer possible to see out to watch for horses, so he sank back in his seat, despondent again, and went back to worrying about his nan.

It was still raining heavily when the bus arrived at its final stop. Thomas, being near the front, was already standing on the pavement with his coat over his head when Angela alighted. She had forgotten all about him, and he looked so out of place. Everyone else seemed to know exactly what they were about. Most of them hurried to the luggage compartment at the side of the bus to collect their belongings. Others rushed out of the rain to waiting cars. Angela looked around. The main street of Baltinglass was quite deserted. And it took absolutely no notice of her and Thomas's arrival.

She felt quite lost. Thomas looked at her questioningly. With a shrug of annoyance she dug the letter out of her bag and checked the address. She checked the numbers on the buildings.

"It's this way," she said gruffly and, pulling her own jacket over her head, she started walking up the street.

Thomas followed her till she stopped in front of a doorway with a brass plaque on the wall. The solicitor's office was on the first floor. They went up and into the reception area.

It was so neat and warm. So organised, and so quiet. A dark-haired lady in a trouser suit looked up from the desk.

"May I help you?" She looked quizzically from Angela to Thomas, her eyebrows high over her spectacles as she took in the rain-soaked state of them.

"Yes, em . . ." Angela found she was whispering. She coughed and started again. "I'm Angela Brennan." She produced the letter, "I . . . em, I have an appointment this afternoon . . ."

The lady quickly scanned the page, then looked again at Angela, this time with great interest. Angela felt like she was being examined.

"You're Daniel's daughter?" the lady said, getting to her feet, and Angela felt it so peculiar to be addressed as such.

The lady held out her hand and shook Angela's warmly.

"How do you do? I'm sorry about your father. I'm Rose." She looked at Thomas.

"And who have we here?"

Angela coughed again. "That's Tomo –" she corrected herself, "Thomas. He's my son." Thomas shot a quick glance at his mother. He had never heard her say that before. He looked at Rose. Her eyebrows were above her glasses again.

"Daniel's grandson? Well. Mr Cullen is looking forward to meeting you both, I'm sure, but he is at a meeting. He will be back in an hour."

"Oh," said Angela flatly, "I see. Well, we'll come back then. Thanks."

She took Thomas by the arm and propelled him out of the office, down the stairs and into the street, wishing she didn't have to go back again, wishing the rain would stop.

"Ma, I'm dyin' to go to the toilet. And I'm starving."

"Oh, for God's sake! There's always something up with you! Where am I going to find a loo around here?"

Thomas wrenched his arm free. "There's a pub. There's another one."

Angela needed a loo herself, but she wouldn't let on. They ran for the nearest pub.

"And I'm not buying packets of crisps, d'you hear?" she said.

Seán Mulhearn was clearing empty glasses from the bar. He was curious about the two people sitting across from him. They sat rather quietly for a girl with a child, but that was not what struck him as interesting. Apart from the fact that they looked rather out of place, there was something vaguely familiar about the young woman. They had arrived in well after lunch was finished but he had managed to serve them the lamb. The boy made short work of his food.

Seán got a chance to enquire about them when the boy came to the bar to order a glass of Coke.

"Lunch okay?" he smiled.

"Yeah. Can I have a Coke, please?"

"Coming right up, young man!" Seán put a scoop of ice into the glass. "Visiting in the town, are you?"

Thomas had perched himself on a high stool. He shrugged his shoulders while he decided. "Sort of."

Seán wasn't prepared for what came next.

"D'you fancy me ma, mister? You kept looking over when we were having our grub."

Seán grinned at the forthright observation and poured the Coke. "I was just thinking I hadn't seen you in before," he answered carefully, then proceeding with caution said, "How can you be 'sort of' visiting?"

Thomas took a gulp from the glass. He liked the way the barman spoke to him as if he was grown up. "We have to see the solicitor, cause me ma's da died."

Seán handed the lad a straw. "I'm sorry to hear that. Would I have known him, your mother's dad?"

Thomas was stirring his ice with the straw. He took a sip, swallowed, and innocently dropped his bombshell.

"Don't know," he said with another shrug of his shoulders. "Daniel Cleary was his name."

Seán's jaw dropped. Thomas didn't notice. He was busy making slurping noises through the straw. Seán took a quick glance over at Angela who was edging her way around the small table. Daniel Cleary's daughter? Good Lord! No wonder she looked familiar!

Seán looked directly at Angela as she came up to the

bar. "I'm sorry about your father, Miss Cleary. He was a fine man. Well liked." He held out his hand and thought she seemed troubled as she placed her own in his firm grip. Looking into her face he could see the clear resemblance between father and daughter. Daniel's eyes were alive there, but they were not laughing now. He could also see the blue of a large bruise on her jaw, partially concealed by make-up. That made him wonder.

Angela was about to say that her name was Brennan, but she wasn't so sure who she was any more.

"I didn't know Dan had a daughter," Seán commented, filling the gap.

"Nobody did!" Thomas piped up, but a dig in the ribs from his mother shut him up.

"I'll fix up the bill now," she said.

Seán raised his open hands and shook his head. "No no no! It's on the house. I insist. It's a pleasure to meet you – and you too, lad." He saw Angela's eye take in the time on the clock above the bar.

"We have to go," she said politely. "Thanks again. Thanks very much."

"See ya, mister!" Thomas jumped down from the stool.

Seán wiped the bar top, unaware of the little smile around his mouth. Daniel had a daughter! Well, fancy that! Christy was certainly in for one hell of a drop. The way he had been spending money the day before in the bar showed he had no notion of the complication which had just arrived in on the bus from Dublin.

Patrick Cullen was not at all what Angela had expected.

He came into the office and introduced himself, and offered them his condolences. Then he proceeded to take off his jacket and tie, putting them on a coat-stand behind the door. He took a woolly jumper from the bottom drawer in the filing cabinet, and pulled it over his head.

"Ah, now, that's much better!" he told himself aloud, then perched on the corner of his desk.

Angela and Thomas watched in silence.

"Well," he began with a big smile, "I must say I've been looking forward to meeting both of you. Your father always told me I would, one day."

Mother and son exchanged an astonished look.

"You knew about me, us . . . before?" Angela was incredulous.

"Since you were born – both of you. Daniel followed both of your lives from day one."

It was Thomas's turn to be gobsmacked. Why hadn't he known this man who was so interested in him? In them? Angela was trying to absorb this news.

"How did he know? I mean – how *can* he have . . .?" words failed her. Questions she needed to ask wouldn't form in her mouth.

Patrick lifted himself off the corner of the desk. His bottom was almost sixty years old, and it preferred a softer cushion. He moved to his deep padded swivel-chair and sat down. Stretching his arms above his head he swung himself slightly from side to side while he scratched the very top of his head with his middle finger, drawing Thomas's attention to the bald spot.

"How did he know? Simple. Your mother kept him

informed. She wrote to him every year, after your birthday, with an update. She posted her letters to this office, and he collected them. Sometimes she included photos." He clasped his hands together and rested them on the desk.

"She never said a word!" Angela couldn't believe her mother had bottled all this up inside for so long.

"Both of them were already married, and not for long, when your mother became pregnant," Patrick continued, "and although Daniel wanted to know his child, at the very least, neither wanted the risk to their marriages. So he agreed, as long as Nancy would keep him informed, he would settle for that. He also expected to have children with his wife. That wasn't to be. And his wife died the year after Thomas's birth. So he was very pleased to have a grandson as well."

He smiled at the boy as he spoke, and this acknowledgement of his presence made Thomas feel important. He smiled back broadly.

"That was when Daniel changed his will in your favour," the solicitor said to Angela.

"Your mother, of course, knew none of this. There was no contact between them. Nancy never got any feedback. She just continued to forward the letters."

Angela was beginning to understand the burden her mother had carried for years, and the very real fear of Paddy finding out. But there was a question in her mind.

"Was there only Daniel . . . my father . . . in his family?" She wasn't really sure she wanted to know the answer to that, even as she asked it. And the answer made her heart lurch.

"No."

Patrick Cullen considered his words carefully before he elaborated. He decided to stick to the bare facts. Mother and son held their breaths.

"Your father has a brother. Christopher. He's the older one." Without allowing them time to assimilate that latest information he went on. "But apart from a small bequest to his brother, Daniel has left you his entire estate. That was his wish."

"How do you mean?" Angela asked.

Thomas was listening intently, his mouth open.

"Your father has left you his house and some land and anything else he had."

This was getting a bit heavy for Angela. All the way down here in the bus, shocked as she was, she never gave a thought to what she was actually coming to. Nancy had told her to come here and said she wanted her to have "whatever has been left you", but Angela had only come because there was nowhere else to go. She had only thought of the trouble the letter had caused. Now here was a whole different dimension she hadn't considered.

Her silent reaction puzzled the solicitor. Hers was not the usual reaction of an inheritor to such good news. He was becoming increasingly curious about her as he spoke. He had noticed the bruising on her cheek and jaw which she had obviously tried to conceal with make-up, and the lad had what appeared to be the mark of fingers on the side of his face just in front of his ear.

"When did you receive my letter?" he asked in a very matter-of-fact manner.

"Today," she said. "This morning."

He thought so. They had arrived so quickly after receiving it he figured there had been trouble. They seemed to bear the marks of it.

"Thomas, my good man, would you do something for me?" he asked brightly. "Would you go and tell Rose we would like some tea and biscuits, please?"

Thomas was only too willing.

"Be sure you say we'd like the chocolate ones, won't you? Good man."

Rose got the message. She asked Thomas to give her a hand. She was by now adept at dragging out the tea-making process, and Thomas was soon thinking she was so slow she would annoy his nan something awful in the kitchen. He had forgotten his question about his nan till now. He frowned, worried.

"What's the matter, Thomas?"

Rose seemed nice. She might know.

"If Daniel is me ma's da . . ." he began hesitatingly as he put the cups on the tray when they were handed to him one by one, "me nan is still me nan, isn't she?"

Rose's cool exterior hid a sudden pang in her heart. "Oh yes! Of course she is," she gushed, delighted to be able to wipe the awful frown from his little face.

Thomas looked hopeful. "You sure? Really?"

"I'm certain. I know she is. Nothing can change that, Thomas. Ever!"

He beamed. They laughed together, and Rose took out the chocolate biscuits.

"I think the letter caused problems this morning, Angela – am I right?" Patrick had asked gently after Thomas left.

She made no response, just continued to watch her hands in her lap. What could she say? How could she tell him the awful things that had happened?

"Are you thinking of heading back to Dublin today?" he tried again.

She shrugged. "We can't go back there." She fought not to lose control. "Me da would kill us." She struggled to keep the thoughts of what might have happened to her ma from becoming pictures in her head. All day long she had battled with that. "It wouldn't be safe."

It was just the situation Patrick had expected. Paddy Brennan was not the first man to have a violent reaction to the news that someone else had fathered "his" child. In his experience she was wise to stay away. It was small wonder then that she wasn't over the moon about her inheritance. It must seem more like a gift of thorns. It was costing all her family the life they had known. And it left her with the problem of where she and Thomas would find to stay. But Daniel had entrusted him with the job of seeing to it that she received her inheritance, and see to it he would.

"We had better see what's keeping the tea," he said now and left the room, arriving back immediately with

Rose and a very happy-looking Thomas who was carrying the tray. Angela fully expected to see something hit the floor, and felt vaguely surprised when nothing did.

"When we have had our tea," Patrick said, "I'm going to take you out to see Daniel's house."

Chapter 8

At the same time as Patrick Cullen was opening the car door for Angela, Nancy Brennan was cautiously opening her door to Mrs Ryan. She was sure she was in no fit state to be seen by anyone, and had she not recognised the shape through the opaque glass she would have pretended she was out. Annie Ryan squeezed in and closed the door behind her.

"I saw him go out," she said. "I just wanted to know you're okay."

Pain crumpled her own face when she saw the swellings and the bruises. Nancy's tears started afresh when she felt the compassion of her friend.

Annie put her arms around her, and held her and just let her sob. The brute! The stumpy, baldy, bullish brute!

Nancy took a paper tissue from her pocket. It was already in flitters. She must have used packets of them already. Her face was sore, and her nose swollen. Even dabbing her eyes hurt. At the slightest sound she jumped.

She continually watched the door, fearful of his return.

Annie Ryan saw it all in silence and anger.

"Have you eaten anything today, Nancy?" she asked when Nancy seemed calmer.

"I'm not hungry. I couldn't eat."

"Even so," said Annie, "I have gorgeous thick home-made soup and I'm going to bring it over. And some lovely fresh brown bread too. I'll be back in a minute."

With the hot soup before her Nancy acknowledged the emptiness in her stomach. But she couldn't manage the bread, fresh and all as it was – her mouth was too sore.

"What are you going to do, Nancy? Did you make a complaint to the Gardaí?"

The hopelessness that hung over Nancy was dreadful to see.

"I couldn't press charges. I brought it all on myself." She shook her head, a terrible sigh of resignation escaping her. "I always feared being found out, you know. It was always at the back of my mind. Guilty conscience, what? But it never crossed my mind that Angela would inherit. Ever. He must never have had kids of his own. The letter said she was sole inheritor."

She dabbed with the tissue again, searching for a dry spot among all the holes.

Annie Ryan frowned at the self-recrimination in her friend's voice.

"But that's not what brought *him* home in such a fury, was it?" she reminded her.

No, it wasn't. But Nancy could only blame herself.

Annie was at pains to point out that it was unfortunate that the letter arrived on the same day as Paddy found out about Reilly.

"If the two hadn't happened together, Nancy, you would've worked it out somehow so he wouldn't know. And he might never have found out then, see?"

She did see. That was exactly what she had been thinking just before he had burst into the house. Even as Angela had been reading the letter Nancy's mind was frantically trying to find a way to allay the questions and suspicions that she knew would be uppermost in Paddy's mind. The likes of Angela Brennan just didn't get a house and land handed to them by a total stranger, it just didn't happen. She knew whatever she said would have to be entirely plausible. Whatever else she might think of her husband she knew well he was no eejit. She needed some time to think out how she was going to handle the problem. Perhaps they could keep it secret between the two of them till she found a way to deal with it. Talking her way around this and keeping her own dark secret was going to be extremely tricky. She didn't want it to lead to lies. More lies. Lies she had to remember forever. Like the ones she told when she became pregnant first. Lies that of their very nature never allowed her to forget them. She could never risk forgetting them. What if she didn't remember what she'd said? She could then trip herself up at some time in the future. These webs had a way of growing, a way of becoming more entangled. She wanted no more of that. But she didn't get the chance to find a way around this predicament, and it was no use going on about ifs or buts now. She had been found out, and by God everyone would pay. And would go on paying, and that was the awful part that she couldn't bear. Everyone would go on paying for her sin. That was Paddy.

"Can you phone Angela?" Annie asked. "See how she is? How things are?"

Nancy's eyes filled again, and pitifully she shook her head. "Her mobile is on her locker upstairs. And she can't phone me either." Tears spilled over her bruises. She nodded at the phone on the kitchen wall. The handset and cable had been ripped off. "He did that," her voice was barely a whisper, "so I couldn't talk to her."

Annie stared in disbelief at the amputated gadget. "The bastard," she uttered, "the cruel heartless bastard!"

Despite Annie's best efforts at persuasion Nancy refused to make a complaint. It might only make things worse, she feared. She was not seeing things rationally, to Annie's way of thinking. Annie believed a complaint would make Paddy afraid of throwing his weight around any more. Bringing him to the attention of the Gardaí should put a damper on his rage. Nancy just didn't see it like that.

They didn't know where Paddy was, or when he would be back. Whether he was gone to the pub or back to work. Or indeed, what frame of mind he would be in when he did arrive home. Annie wouldn't have put her money on it being good. She was afraid the very sight of Nancy would trigger him again.

Nancy said no, he wouldn't do it again. But she wanted to think that. She *had* to think that. She could not allow herself to dwell on anything else.

But Annie was not convinced. Far from it. She sensed fear. She sensed guilt. And worst of all, she sensed resignation.

Chapter 9

Christy woke up on his bed in his cottage. His head pounded. It felt like a sledgehammer was inside trying to break out. His wet coat and cap hung on the knobs of the iron bed-end and his keys were on the chair beside the bed, the wallet beside them. Empty. In disgust he threw it on the floor.

Then he thought again. When he came into his own he would have need of a wallet like that. He bent down and picked it up. It was a bad move. His head pounded worse when he stooped. He put the wallet into a drawer, where he would keep it until he could fill it again. Next time he wouldn't empty it so quickly, or so carelessly. He sat on the bed and looked around him. He had spent his life in this cottage, living alone since Dan left. But he had no sense of being lonely. People tended to make Christy Cleary feel crowded. In a peculiar way the smallness of the place afforded him a feeling of security. Still, he had no qualms about leaving it. In his mind living in the larger house could only lift him in people's estimation. What was it they had said in the bar?

Lord of the Manor. Yeah, that was it. Lord of the Manor he would be. They would look up to him for a change. A lot of things were going to change. What he would do with the cottage he hadn't yet decided. Things had happened suddenly and, though weeks had passed, he hadn't had time to take in the significance of it all. If only that blasted Cullen would get in touch! He had no idea of how long legal matters might take, but it couldn't be that complicated. After all, there was only him left. Daniel's darling wife had been too sickly to produce any offspring and so Daniel had inherited everything when she died.

Luckily for Christy, Daniel had never remarried. Looking back now he found himself to be a bit surprised at that. There was no shortage of available females around the place. And Daniel was very presentable, very amiable, and not short of a few bob. But Daniel had made it clear he had no interest in replacing Mary.

So, Christy assured himself, it was only a matter of time before he was on the pig's back. He just had to sit tight and wait till the solicitor got in touch with him. In the meantime, as soon as he could, he would go over to the house and have a good look around. He had the keys and he was entitled to do that at least. Ramble through the rooms upstairs and downstairs, get the feel of it. He could walk about the land. Look in the outhouses and the stable. He could walk through the fields and down to the river. He could spend the day there plodding about, going into each field, opening and closing gates, crossing every ditch, without coming across another soul.

But patience was never his strong suit, and curiosity was getting the better of him. Between that and his hangover not even his impending inheritance could keep him in good form this morning.

All this thinking was making his head worse. He looked out the window, not knowing whether to expect to see night or day. It was a rainy day but even so the light through the small window hurt his bleary eyes. He had slept well into another day in his drunken stupor. The fact that he had slept fully dressed didn't bother him in the slightest. But then a pleasant sight met his sore eyes. There propped against the garden wall, just inside the gate, was his repaired bicycle.

Well, the blessings of God on Mooney, he thought, for that was a mighty fast job all right.

Thomas was in the back seat of Patrick Cullen's shiny silver Mercedes. He positioned himself in the gap between the front seats, leaning an elbow on each one, as he watched excitedly for his first glimpse of his *real* grandfather's house. Would it be as big as his nan's, or would it have one of those strawy kinds of roof like the one on the calendar on the back of her kitchen door? Would it be painted white? He was annoying his mother with his chatter. But Patrick was enjoying his excitement enormously and said nothing, just let him ramble on. It was pity his mother wasn't having the same reaction.

Angela certainly didn't want to hear Tomo's rattling

on. The pictures he was painting were making her more depressed with every word. Her heart sank further with each turn of the wheels. They were already in the middle of nowhere. They had left the town, such as it was, behind them ages ago. How could they even call it a *town*? Not much more than one long street with a fork at the top and that was it! No wonder Dublin was so full of country people. Who in their right minds would want to live here? And by now they must surely be way out in the middle of the bog. There was nothing here. Trees, grass, no end of it. And still the car was going on! She had it in her mind to ask how far more it was when Patrick Cullen slowed down and stopped.

"Here we are!" he announced as if they had just arrived at Áras an Úachtaráin.

Thomas started to scramble from the car.

"Hold on there, Thomas – just a minute while I open the gate."

Angela couldn't see anything. The truth of it was she didn't want to look. I want to go home, she thought glumly, visibly shrinking in her seat. Patrick got back in and moved the car through the gate, then stopped once more.

"Hold it again," he said smiling, and got back out to close the gate behind them.

"What *is* it with this *gate* thing?" she muttered to herself.

Thomas was taking it all in. "There it is!" he squealed excitedly, pointing his finger. "Is that it, mister, is it?"

"It is," he was told, "that's your grandfather's house.

And it is going to belong to your mother, as soon as the will goes through probate."

The boy was not sure about that last bit, but the man had just said his ma was going to own it, and he should know.

The rain had stopped, leaving a very grey evening. There was no sunshine to illuminate the granite façade of the house. Looking through the windscreen what Angela saw was a dull old house with windows like rectangular black holes. She saw nothing to recommend it. A tall window each side of the hall door and three windows upstairs reflected the dark rainy evening. Even the porch with its pair of elegant pillars and steps up to the solid double doors failed miserably to impress her.

Thomas saw something completely different.

"Wow! Look at that, Ma!" He couldn't contain himself he was so bowled over by it. He jumped from the car and ran up the four granite steps. Angela followed, with Patrick Cullen behind. He turned the key in the lock and pushed open the left side of the door, and ushered them in. They stood in a large square hall, its floor covered in a black and white tile laid in a diamond design, and to the left a wide carved staircase leading to the upper floor.

Thomas's head tilted backwards as he gaped in awe at the height of the ceiling.

"Look at all them squiggly bits!" He pointed up to the ornate plasterwork cornice and the large ornate ceiling rose above a chandelier. "This is huge!"

"It's cold," Angela countered.

There was a door on each side of the hall, both closed, and she eyed them warily, half-expecting someone to emerge from them. But there was no sound. The house was silent. Silent like a trap, she thought, waiting for us to go a little deeper, then it will snap shut keeping us prisoners. She had no wish to like it one bit. She was unwilling to allow herself to be affected by Tomo's enthusiasm, and concluded instead that he was just being a stupid pain, as usual.

Patrick Cullen pointed to each of the doors in turn, saying, "That's the dining-room – that's the drawing-room. The bathroom is upstairs." He moved ahead of them and they followed. He led them across the hall and down three stairs at the back and into a large square kitchen. Its ceiling was average height, and two small windows on the right side let in the light. There was another door in the wall facing them, and there was a huge fireplace.

Thomas rambled around the room looking at things.

Patrick placed the keys on the table. "Why don't you stay here tonight?" he suggested to Angela very casually. "If there's no great hurry back to Dublin, I mean."

Angela looked at him with questions in her eyes. Patrick was aware of a tingle going down his back. He felt as if Daniel had given him a quick glance. Standing here in this house where there was still so much of Daniel's presence, looking at his daughter, was indeed a strange experience.

"We . . . we could? But I thought . . . I mean . . . you were saying about legal stuff . . ." she stopped, unsure of what the legal stuff was exactly.

Patrick explained. "Your father's will now goes to probate, and only when that is complete will his estate become legally yours, you see. Probate usually takes months at the least, maybe a lot more, depending on the complexity involved. But your father's will is very clear. He had me make very sure of that. His estate is to be yours; that was his wish."

So, if it wasn't hers yet, then what?

"What I'm saying is, if you would like to stay here tonight, or till you get yourself sorted, I don't see that as a problem. It might even be better than leaving the place empty, don't you think?"

He was being kind. He was familiar with her background, and probably her serious lack of any sort of financial backup as well. She could not go home, and she had no money and nowhere for herself and Thomas to stay. He was offering her a solution. She felt awkward and grateful all at once. Her back was to the wall, and much as she wished herself elsewhere, she didn't have an option.

She should thank him. She should say something. But her throat closed up on her and threatened to choke her, and no words would come out.

But he understood. He nodded and smiled and gave her a merry wink, and that was the matter sorted. He turned to Thomas.

"I have to get back to the office now," he said. "Tomorrow, when you're in the town, you'll drop in and say hello, won't you?"

"Is the town far? How many miles?" Thomas was quick to ask.

"It's barely a couple of miles straight in."

He turned back towards the front hall and they went with him to the door. He got into his car and waved as he headed it back down the drive, stopped and did the thing with the gate again, and then he was gone.

Angela's speedy arrival had made it imperative that he should see Christopher Cleary as soon as possible. But his thoughts were not on what Christy's reaction might be. Christy would be as awkward and as belligerent as ever. But the will was watertight so he had no worries on that account. And he had no worries about Thomas either. That little fellow was game for any adventure, to be sure.

Angela was the one that concerned him. Patrick Cullen knew people. Too often he had sat with traumatised people who spoke quietly and passively while all the time their minds were screaming in silent agony at the unbearable blows life had dealt them, and which had brought them to his office. Yes, he knew people, and he knew the signs. And Angela Cleary had them all.

That young girl was obviously in shock, and Patrick doubted she had ever spent much time away from home. It was very evident to him that Angela's mother's secret was a secret no longer. He'd known that Angela inheriting was more than likely going to create problems. At the time he had hoped sending the letters in plain envelopes without the usual firm's logo might be some help. Apparently not. But for young Angela to be beaten and forced out of her home like that was nothing short of criminal. Daniel would surely turn in his grave if he knew. Patrick was sure it was never Daniel's intention to cause hurt or upset, but he was determined that his daughter should have her inheritance. Patrick was now more determined than ever to make good on his promise to him, to keep a watchful eye out for her.

After Angela had closed the hall door she and Thomas stood looking at each other. This was so strange. The house around them was so big and so silent it was scary.

The kitchen was so very different from D'Arcy Avenue.

There was a huge open fireplace with hooks over the fire for cooking pots. Thomas could stand in under the mantelpiece easily. Angela wondered vaguely when it was last used for cooking. There was an electric cooker, with spills burnt onto the edge of the ring, and an original white Belfast sink, chipped at the edges. An ancient dresser was laden with assorted crockery. In this kitchen the old and the new were used side by side. There was a fridge-freezer, and a microwave oven on the worktop. A small television sat on a low table at the far side of the fireplace. A huge solid oak table, with a long cutlery drawer in its side, stood in the centre of the room. An armchair added a cosy touch by the fireplace.

Angela felt as if she was encroaching on someone's privacy.

The place looked exactly as if someone had just

nipped out for a minute. A dishcloth hung over the edge of the draining board, and a few dirty dishes were in the sink. A man's jacket hung on a hook behind the door, the ashes in the fireplace needed sweeping up. This was her father's kitchen. Her father's house. A man totally unknown to her. And even though they knew there was no one else there but them there was a strong *sense* of someone else about the place.

Angela caught sight of the bunch of keys on the table. *He* was gone without them. It struck her forcibly that *he* wasn't coming back. A wave of finality swept over her. She would never meet him. For twenty-four years he had been in the background while she poured all her daughterly love on Paddy Brennan. What a waste that had been!

Thomas disrupted her train of thought by nudging her in the side. He had been very still, as if he was waiting to be told it was okay to be there, okay to be comfortable there, in his grandfather's house, and he needed to do something about it.

"Will we look around?" His voice was a whisper, as if he were afraid someone was about to walk in and consider them intruders.

Angela was reluctant, but Thomas didn't want to explore on his own.

"C'mon, Ma, let's take a look!" Thomas, as ever, could not stay still for long.

They opened one of the doors in the hall and looked in at a large dining-room with a massive shiny table. The sitting-room, or "drawing-room" as Patrick Cullen had called it, was huge. Thomas thought both rooms very grand. Angela thought they were old-fashioned and shabby.

In the hall the staircase was very wide, a well-worn carpet covering its centre. They climbed the two flights to the upper floor. They looked in the first bedroom. The bed was unmade and the feeling of just having missed someone increased. There were two other bedrooms, equally as big, which Angela immediately decided they would use. The bathroom was across the big square landing and Thomas decided he absolutely *had* to go. The cistern was high up on top of a long pipe and you flushed by pulling the chain, which had a wooden handle. It really took his fancy. The bath stood on ball and claw legs and was not against the wall like at home and it was really deep, *and* you could see right under it. But what was best of all was the size of the room. He measured ten steps between the bath and the loo, and the sink was another eight.

"Oh, for God's sake! Are you ever coming out?" Angela never thought she'd actually seek his presence, but this was different.

"I'm hungry, Ma," he said on finally leaving the bathroom.

She was hungry herself, and she hoped there was something downstairs they could eat.

They went back down to the kitchen. It was getting slightly dark there as the only light came from the two small windows. They actually felt it was time they should head for home and it struck them forcibly that that was the one thing they could not do. Angela reached behind her for the switch and turned the light on. The whole atmosphere in the kitchen changed.

Finding where everything was kept wasn't difficult. Most cooking utensils hung on the wall and cutlery was kept in the kitchen drawer. Angela took meat from the freezer and defrosted it in the microwave and grilled it. Potatoes were in a large bag under the sink and she boiled enough for two. The smell of cooking soon filled the room but somehow it didn't taste the same as at home. The meat was overdone and dry and the potatoes were soggy. Angela swallowed hers glaring across at the faces Thomas was making trying to chew his chop.

"One moan outa you and you can fuckin' starve!" she growled across at him.

Miserably she thought that if she had to depend on her own cooking for long she would probably starve with him!

After dinner Thomas sat in the armchair and turned the television on, but obviously he was only half watching it. Every so often he got up to examine or fiddle with something, and for once his mother paid no attention to his restlessness. She was lost in thoughts of her own. She sat at the table staring unseeingly at the wall.

It was all everybody's fault. *They* had done this to her. Her mother, Paddy, even Daniel, had all brought this situation about. Things they had done were what she was now paying for. It wasn't fair. How the hell was she supposed to manage? What the fuck was she going to do with herself down here in the fucking *bog*? She wasn't going to stay. That was definite. As soon as possible she was going to get herself out of this god-forsaken place!

How long she sat there she didn't know before she noticed that Thomas had begun to fall asleep in the armchair and she was stiff and getting cold. She shook Thomas awake.

"Get up, you can't sleep there."

Up on the landing once again Angela pointed to one of the doors.

"Take that room. I'll take this"

She pushed open her door and went in. Thomas was left there on the landing looking after her. Taking his courage in his hands he went into the darkened room alone, and got himself ready for bed in record time. He was in the bed like a shot. He pulled the covers right up to his nose and closed his eyes tightly, so that he would not see the shadows around the room.

He listened to the sounds of his mother moving about in the next room. When there was silence he called out with his eyes still closed, "Night, Ma!" and listened for the reply.

"Go to sleep, Tomo Brennan," she answered into the darkness.

He called out "Night, Ma!" a few more times before eventually there was silence.

Angela did not get to sleep as easily.

Without street lighting outside the window like there was at home, the blackness of the country night was dense. She left her curtains open so that the moonlight could brighten things a little. The furniture was big, made for the large rooms, and it created strange, unfamiliar outlines in the dark. The dressing table had an oval mirror, and it reflected the shapes in the room. It kept catching her watchful eye, and finally she got up and threw her jacket over it.

She slipped into an uneasy sleep, and sometime during the night she woke with the distinct feeling that there was someone there, quietly watching her. With a start she was wide awake and saw a shape over by the doorway.

"Can I get in with you, Ma?" Thomas was standing there in his vest and underpants.

"For fuck sake, Tomo Brennan!" she exploded at him in terrified relief. "Get back to bed! You're nearly after frightening the fuckin' shite outa me!"

Chapter 10

Next morning was bright and sunny, and in the town people were out and about, glad the rain was gone. High, widely dispersed white clouds held the promise of long sunny spells. There was a particular buzz about the place. On the steps of the church after Mass, Betty O'Gorman was given the most interesting piece of information she had heard in ages. She made her way down towards the main street, past the 1798 monument with its statue of Michael Dwyer, and headed for the newsagent's. She just *knew* what she had to say would stop Maisie Mac dead.

"I know, I heard," was the smug reply when she imparted her earth-shattering news. Maisie could draw news like a magnet. It niggled Betty sorely every time.

"Have you seen her? The daughter?" she asked, peeved that she had to capitulate to Maisie's superior capacity for always being the first to know.

"Not yet," Maisie hated to admit as she glanced out

the doorway, "but there's Christy now going down the street on his bike, and hell bent for leather he is too."

She pulled her beige cardigan tightly around her, as if the mere sight of Christopher Cleary had sent a sudden chill through her. Betty noticed that Maisie was bristling with anticipation. The broken red veins in her cheeks seemed to be just a little more noticeable, and her habit of scrunching the fuzz in the front of her tightly permed hair was a dead giveaway.

"Do you think he knows yet?" Betty wondered aloud.

Maisie shrugged. She hated to be asked a question to which she didn't know the answer so she avoided it completely. "I'd rather not be in that girl's shoes, y'know, inheritance or no inheritance. Not with *him* for a relation," she said.

"Me neither. There's a grandson too, you know."

"Haven't heard any mention of a husband . . ." Maisie slowly drew her breath through her teeth, making a slight hissing noise, and nodded her head knowingly at Betty.

That was Maisie for you, Betty thought as she left the shop, always assumed she knew more than she heard. Still, she was the one to go to as she could always be depended on for the latest bit of gossip.

Patrick Cullen left his office and crossed to his parked car. He was on his way out to see Christopher Cleary. He had not seen him last evening after all, and the fact that Angela was now in Daniel's house meant he could not delay it any longer. In his pocket was the official notification of Daniel's wishes, but he had to do

Daniel's Daughter

Christopher the courtesy of presenting it personally. He did not relish the task. He was so deep in thought that he didn't see Christy go down the street on his bicycle.

A tractor and trailer was causing a blockage on the road, a normal occurrence in the town since it was surrounded by farmland, but when Patrick pulled out to go around it he almost ran over Betty O'Gorman who also was hell bent on where she was going. He jammed on the brakes. A surprised Betty stopped in her tracks, then smiled apologetically, gave him a weak little wave and hurried on.

The task he was about this morning centred his thoughts on Daniel and his recent demise. It was hard to believe they would never share a drink and a confidential friendly chat anymore. Often these "chats" took place in Daniel's house. There they could chat, eat, drink, and then sleep it off without the whole town getting wind of it. Patrick was Daniel's confidant, but Daniel also provided a very valued and valuable friendship for Patrick, something which the solicitor had to be very careful about in such a small town.

Patrick missed his friend. Down the years he and Daniel grew close. He was the only one Daniel could talk to about his daughter, and Daniel liked to talk about her, particularly after he received a letter from Dublin giving him an update. They arrived once a year and Nancy, safe in the knowledge that she could talk freely, did just that. She wrote about everything from how Paddy was mad about *his* little girl, to how things changed when Thomas arrived. In spite of the difficulties *they* were having over

Thomas, Daniel was pleased to have a grandson. He would have liked to communicate that to them, but he had sworn an agreement with Nancy, and he would not break it. In time he did what he could. After he inherited from Mary, he went to Patrick and together they made out a will, as watertight as possible, in Angela's favour. Patrick well remembered the night they celebrated the making of that will.

It began with a couple of drinks in the town early in the evening, then dinner, then more drinks in various pubs, and after closing time they continued in Daniel's house until the small hours.

There Daniel raised a glass, the last of many.

"To my beautiful daughter! To Angela, that some day she may know the love of her real father!"

He sank heavily into a chair then, muttering incoherently to himself, while Patrick in his inebriate state decided what was needed was another drink. But Daniel was asleep before the next one was poured so Patrick, feeling quite obliged to keep the party going, did his level best before sinking into oblivion himself, in the opposite chair.

The following day found they were the talk of the town as curiosity as to the reason for the celebration ran rife.

But Daniel had given his promise to Nancy, so his lips were sealed. Their drinking nights were held in private thereafter.

They often talked afterwards about that night. Daniel derived a great deal of satisfaction from having made the will, and he gave Patrick strict and explicit instructions as to what he should do if he, Daniel, should be the first of them to go. They both felt that was unlikely since Daniel was the younger by almost a decade. But one never knew.

In the event of Patrick being the first to go his nephew and partner in the firm was the one who would then see to Daniel's wishes. Daniel was happy. All eventualities were covered.

Patrick had followed those instructions implicitly. And after meeting Angela and Thomas and hearing their story he was more determined than ever to see his promise through to the letter.

Now he pulled up outside Christopher's cottage, took a deep breath, and got out of the car. But he knew even before he knocked that the house was empty. The front gate was open and the side gate also, and that meant that Christopher was out somewhere on his bike. Damn it, he cursed quietly. He did not want Christopher to hear the news about the town before he got to him.

Chapter 11

Angela woke, and for a split second she thought all was well. When the memory of yesterday flooded back her heart plummeted. She was reluctant to open her eyes and have the nightmare confirmed. A wide shaft of brilliant yellow sunlight slanted sideways through the long sash window.

She got up and dressed, wishing she had a change of clothes. Looking in the oval mirror she twisted her hair into a knot and held it with a gold-coloured hairgrip she took from her handbag. She went to the window and looked out. As she stood she was vaguely aware of the heat of the sun through the glass. Outside there were trees, grass, hedges, hills not too far distant – the countryside was looking its best, but there was nothing of interest to her. The road beyond the front hedge was the one they had arrived by last night she figured, and even that was deserted, except for the occasional car or tractor.

Thomas came to her door. He was up and dressed before her.

"Isn't it great?" he enthused. "If you look out the back windows you can see a river!"

"What are you doing in that manky track-suit?" she snapped at him.

The boy was taken aback. "It's all I have," he said defensively.

She was sorry she'd mentioned it. She turned away from him and went down the stairs. Halfway down Thomas passed her, sliding on the mahogany handrail. He reached the end of the stairs and slid off the handrail onto the floor, landing on his backside, and looking quite amused with himself.

"That was great," he laughed up at her. "You couldn't do that on the stairs at home!"

His mother showed her annoyance by refusing to be amused.

He ran ahead of her to the kitchen, jumping down the three stairs from the front hall. They looked in presses for whatever could suffice for breakfast.

Thomas put his nose to the milk carton. "Yikes! It stinks. It smells like it's been there for a week!"

It was. At least a week. Angela found the bread bin. What was there was covered in green mould. She threw it out. The milk was washed down the sink so they set out some dry cornflakes and apple juice for breakfast. Angela went to the phone and dialled her mother's number, anxious and needing to hear her voice. All she got was the engaged tone. She tried a few times more without success. It worried her. Thomas crunching loudly on his dry cornflakes irritated her. Her own sat in the bowl, untouched.

"Where on God's earth do you get milk around here?" she muttered.

"There are loads of shops in the town," Thomas offered, trying to sound helpful.

Angela glared at him. "Don't get smart with me," she warned him. "The town is two bloody miles away!"

Thomas's mouth was full of flakes and he looked across at her, willing her to be less unhappy. "Ma," he said when he had swallowed the flakes, hoping he was choosing the best words, "it's lovely out and it wouldn't take that long – and –"

She silenced him with a gesture of her hand. He was being totally practical but she hated the way he was giving in to their situation so easily.

He went back to crunching his cornflakes.

"We'll go when you're ready," she surprised him by saying suddenly. Anything would be better than sitting around here in this god-forsaken silence all day.

"I'm ready!" He downed the last of the juice and went straight out the front door.

Angela grabbed her bag and jacket, locked up and joined him outside. They set off down the drive.

Thomas closed the gate after them, remembering how Mr Cullen had made a point of doing that. Angela was glad she was wearing her trainers for the walk, but that in turn reminded her that she was in yesterday's clothes and, just as bad, she had hardly a screed of make-up on

– there had only been a stick of concealer and a well-used lipstick in her bag. In all of the horror of yesterday, make-up was the last thing on her mind – apart from her efforts to conceal the bruising on her jaw – but today she was going into the town, and she felt naked without her face properly on.

They walked along the road, Thomas absorbing anything and everything around him. A tractor passed, and the driver saluted them. Thomas waved back with a big grin. He jumped up and down trying to see over the hedges. They passed some cottages, and further along some fairly new bungalows.

As they rounded a curve a man came cycling towards them. He wore a belted overcoat and a cap despite the fine weather, and he had to swerve and pull up to avoid hitting Thomas. They heard some foul words about "bloody tourists" as he pushed off again, keeping his eyes fixed on the road ahead.

"Did you see the steam rising from that oul fella's coat!" Thomas was incredulous. Angela made no reply. The last thing she needed was to bother about some oul fella going around on a bike in a damp overcoat. Fool.

When they came into the town Angela was struck by how different it looked in the sunshine. It was quite busy. Cars were parked bumpers to the kerb all along both sides of the main street, and also on both sides of the paved pedestrian island where the Michael Dwyer 1798 monument stood on the point of the fork dividing the street. At this point the road rose in a V, one side rising up to the right past the Credit Union, to the church of St

Joseph with its magnificent spire overlooking the town. The other side of the fork curved upwards and left, towards the graveyard set on the side of Baltinglass Hill, and beyond. At the other end of the street the road bridged the River Slaney which they had crossed yesterday when they arrived.

"Can we go in to see Rose and Mr Cullen?" Thomas wanted to know.

"We'll see," he was told.

His attention was drawn to a man crossing the road. He was wearing a felt hat. His trousers were tucked into his wellie boots and he carried a plastic bucket.

Angela gave Thomas a nudge on the shoulder. "Stop staring," she said.

"But *he* is looking at us!" Thomas protested.

"Let him."

They continued along the street. At the supermarket they passed an elderly man with a walking stick. Smiling, he stood while they passed, his head turning to look after them. In the supermarket two elderly ladies took to smiling at them as well.

"What the hell are they all gawking at?" Angela muttered, while Thomas simply smiled back.

He wanted a large bottle of Coke but he was told it was too heavy to carry two miles back to the house. Angela only bought what they could carry with ease, and could have strangled Thomas when he kicked up about the Coke. Anyway she only had money for necessities now that they were on their own, but she hardly wanted to say that all over the shop. She was becoming quite uncomfortable. The whole supermarket seemed interested in them.

"Well, can I have a small Coke, then?" Thomas wasn't giving up. "I'm thirsty!"

Angela was mortified when one of the ladies handed him a can of Coke. That silenced him. He knew he was now "in for it". But he still took the Coke.

I'll swing for him! she swore to herself. I'll fuckin' swing for him!

Back in the street she was about to let him have it when a friendly voice halted the tirade before it got started.

"Ah, there you are, Angela! I was trying to get you by phone at the house. But you must have already left. Good morning, Thomas."

Patrick Cullen was getting out of his car which he had parked in its usual spot by the kerbside. He was just back from his fruitless drive to Christopher's cottage. He put some papers into his briefcase, and slung his jacket over his arm.

"Have you time to come up to the office?" he asked.

Angela liked the way he made it seem as if it was she who made the decision.

Rose was pleased to see them.

"How was your first night in Baltinglass?" she enquired.

Angela answered, "Fine, thank you, Rose" and followed Patrick into his office. Immediately Thomas was over to Rose's desk. She lowered her glasses to the tip of her nose, indicating she was ready to listen.

Thomas watched them for second, amazed at how they didn't slip completely, so precariously were they perched.

"D'you know something?" he whispered as if he was imparting some deep secret he would not admit to anyone else. "It was real scary last night." His eyes were wide with the memory of it. The tilt of Rose's head encouraged him to go on. "It was pitch black. Ma didn't leave a light on, and the house is so big and scary in the dark. There was only me in this big room. I didn't like that."

Daytime is better, he decided.

In Patrick's office Angela waited on the phone while Mrs Ryan went across the road to get Nancy. Mrs Ryan had left her number with Rose earlier on. She explained that Nancy's phone was out of order. Patrick left the room so that Angela could make her call in private.

She heard her mother's concerned voice.

"Angela? That you, love? How are you? You all right?"

Angela swallowed hard. "Mam, oh Mam! I was so worried about you! I feel so *guilty* for leaving you there!"

Nancy only wanted to hear that they were okay. She wouldn't go into what happened after. She couldn't have voiced it aloud, not even to Annie Ryan, who could only guess at the humiliation she had been made to suffer.

"Tell me, love, are youse all right? How's Thomas? Where did you stay last night?"

She listened to her daughter's misgivings about the situation. About how they were in the arsehole of nowhere. There were no buses, no shops, and a two-mile walk to the town!

It was terrible! The house was old and Angela didn't like old. She could never stay there. When the legal stuff was sorted out she would sell it and move back to Dublin. She couldn't wait.

Nancy was more concerned about their safety.

"Don't be worrying about all that, Angela. You and Thomas are safe there. I couldn't bear to think what would happen if Paddy laid eyes on either of you. Be glad you have there, at least at the moment."

Angela couldn't be glad. She didn't fit in down here. But her mother was being practical, and if Angela could admit it for a minute she would have to admit also that her mother was right.

"I'm sending some clothes down, love," Nancy went on. "You'll need them now, so I've made a parcel for the two of you and Mrs Ryan put it in the post this morning. Rose gave me the address. I put your mobile in as well. You should have it tomorrow."

"Why isn't the phone working?" Angela asked. "It was okay yesterday morning. I was trying to get you last night, and before we came into the town this morning."

Nancy was caught off guard. Her hesitation told Angela the answer.

"*He* did it, didn't he? *He* broke it. That's why you couldn't get me! The bastard! You can't stay there, Ma. What if he takes it out on you again?"

Nancy felt leaving wasn't quite as simple as that. He would never let her go. His ego had taken a severe battering. He would have to maintain some degree of authority as the head of the household, to salvage his male pride. No, he wasn't going to let her go anywhere. He wasn't going to let her forget it either. She couldn't think about that now. She mustered up as much conviction as she could.

"He won't. Don't worry, love. I'll be all right."

She never mentioned the fact that Paddy had not been home since yesterday morning. Nor that she was terrified of him coming home. Nor that he said if she was out when he got back "she would know all about it".

"When you get your mobile we can keep in touch through Mrs Ryan's for the moment. Is Thomas there with you? Will you put him on? Just for a minute. We can't hold up that nice Mr Cullen's phone all day."

Thomas was a tonic for Nancy right then. It was good to talk to him. He gushed on about the house, and the countryside, and about how nice everyone was. And he missed her. And he was glad she was still his nan.

Chapter 12

After he had almost mown Thomas down, Christopher Cleary had pushed off on his bicycle and headed up the road again. Bloody tourists all over the place! It was hardly safe on the roads any more! Tractors and cars were one thing. Even cows or sheep had a right to be there, but bloody tourists never seemed to know where to put themselves. They were a positive danger to themselves and everyone else! And kids? They were the last straw.

He had not stopped in the town on his way through. He was in a hurry and having to look out for and avoid tourists on the road was a waste of his precious time. He muttered away to himself as he pedalled, until the vexation left him, and he got his thoughts back on track. The sun beat down on him but the cap stayed in place and the heavy overcoat remained closed.

Mooney had done a grand job on the bike, he noted. It even seemed to be a bit easier to push. But although he was pleased to compliment Mooney's work, it never crossed his mind to ask if the man had been paid for his trouble, or about the cost of the repair.

It was a long time since he had been down this road. He had never felt the need to travel it. He and Dan got along just fine without the need to keep in touch. Now that it occurred to him, he couldn't think of the last time he had spoken to his brother. No matter – when he moved into the house there would probably be plenty of reminders around. He could sort that out too.

Ahead he saw the upper story of the house above the hedging. The hipped roof with its two chimneys was a smashing sight. He liked the way the house could be seen from a distance. His cottage was barely visible above its front hedge. As he drew nearer, the whole structure could be seen from the road. He liked the way it was not hidden or surrounded by trees. Country houses were often protected from the elements by tall trees which were planted too close to the house to allow much natural light through. But Christopher's reason for not wanting trees was he wanted everyone to see clearly what he had inherited. It was a fine house. Strong and well maintained. His heart made its presence felt by fluttering in unaccustomed excitement and anticipation. Christy wasn't used to feeling much of anything except annoyance or irritation and he felt quite heady now as he approached the front door.

The granite steps were indeed quite impressive, he thought as he stood on the top one and drew out the bunch of keys from his coat pocket. With a tremble in his hand he selected the correct one and reached it towards the lock. In his mind's eye he was already standing in the hall. The hall was large enough to fit his present sitting-room into, and more. The hall with the diamond-shaped black and white tiles. Vaguely he wondered if they were still there. The key sat into the lock and automatically his hand turned.

But the key did not.

He turned his hand again. He assumed he had not done it properly the first time in his excitement. He still had no luck. So he withdrew the key and inserted it again, telling himself to get a grip on himself and do the thing properly. This time he noticed that the key was not sitting all the way home. He used a bit of force and tried again. But the lock continued to defy him. He looked at the other keys. There were two others and neither looked remotely like it would fit a Yale lock. Getting annoyed now he tried the key again and again, even after it became very clear to him this key was not going to open that door. His annoyance grew rapidly. He shouldered the door. And kicked it. He cursed and swore loudly at it. But he was still on the outside. He decided to try around the back of the house. Leaving his bicycle lying on the steps he walked around to the back, and into the yard.

There was an older type of lock on the back door and he selected the longer key with the round shaft for it. It didn't fit either. It would not turn. He looked along the back of the house. The kitchen windows were small and too high for him to see in. The ground was lower at the back of the house. Going back to the door he looked long and hard at the lock, trying to figure out why the key would not work. Then he noticed it. The lock looked old but the barrel was shiny, and he realised it had been changed! He hurried around to the front door and found the same thing. The lock itself was dull and old but there again the barrel was shiny.

They had been changed!

A passionate frenzy consumed him.

Thwarted again, he lost control and beat at the door with his fists till they hurt. He kicked at it. Spat at it, cursing the worst he could think of. Breathless and sweating he stopped, and tried to reason it out. The garda had said the keys were from Dan's pocket, along with his wallet. Were they an old set? If so, where were the new ones? Why did Dan have the locks changed in the first place?

Christy seriously considered breaking a window. Or else, he should be able to put in the back porch door with a couple of good kicks. It was only timber slats, reinforced on the inside. But his miserable nature would not allow him because he knew it would cost him to have to replace any of them. He turned back down the granite steps and picked up his bicycle. Then he remembered the workshop.

Daniel always called the small low stone building at the side of the yard "the workshop". It was the original cottage that was built on the site. Built of stone with a slate roof, it would have been a fine house at the time. Over the years it was used for various purposes: housing animals, storage, even for hiding rebels. Dan converted it into his workshop and put a couple of Velux windows in the roof for light. He never referred to it as his "studio". That would be a bit presumptuous. Even so, it was in here that he indulged his passion for painting. He often spent hours on end totally absorbed in it, especially after Mary died. It helped him maintain his sanity. His life was sadly empty then.

But, unknown to his brother, unknown to his neighbours, he had a daughter who became more and more important to him. Although he could not be a real father to her, and God knows she needed one, her existence was the thread that kept him going. So he painted. Working from photos Nancy had sent him over the years he produced paintings deep in substance and emotion, always disguising his subject's identity. Often he painted other subjects, sometimes he exhibited, and sometimes he sold. A few special works very dear to his heart never saw the light of day.

Christy approached the workshop and found a padlock on the door. The last key opened it without any problem at all. He stepped inside, a strange feeling of familiarity sweeping over him. He could almost feel Daniel's presence. He didn't like it. His eye swept around the single narrow room. Paintings were stacked against the walls. Frames, both old and empty, leaned untidily against each other under the window. An easel stood in the centre, under the roof windows, its canvas wrapped in an old sheet.

Brushes of all shapes and sizes were clean and neatly

lined up on a table nearby, and tubes of paints sat alongside them. There was an order to the apparent chaos of the cramped room. Daniel's life was here. Daniel's cosy, cushy, life! He had his job, his fine house, his nice wife, and his painting. How sickening. How fuckin' sickening!

Christy lashed out with his foot, to left and right, sending frames, brushes and paints across the floor. He kicked the easel and it crashed to the wooden floor with a loud clatter, the cover remaining on the canvas. He kicked at it again so that it slid away from him quite easily across the floor.

Satisfied with himself, he left without bothering to lock or even close the door.

He went back to his bicycle, picked it up and pushed it down the gravel driveway, kicking at the small stones as he went. Out on the road again as he cycled back towards the town, he considered whether he should go to the Garda Station or the solicitor's first.

He settled on the Garda Station simply because it was nearer, and he wouldn't be adding too much mileage onto his journey. But after his trouble of going there the garda Christy wanted was off duty, and the young one at the reception desk wasn't sure exactly when he would be in. This time Christy kept his cursing well under his breath. Youth! What did they know? He left the station and headed the bicycle determinedly for the solicitor's office. Something was wrong. He knew it in his gut, and it was high time someone told him what it was.

Chapter 13

Thomas and Angela got back to the house, and Thomas noticed straight away that someone had been there, because the gate was open. He said so as they trudged up the gravel driveway, but his mother was only concerned with complaining about the length of the walk, the weight of the few groceries, and bemoaning the fact that there was no local bus service in the country.

"No bloody buses! How are you supposed to get about down here, for God's sake?" She placed the shopping on the step and took out the key.

"Look, Ma!" Thomas pointed to the marks at the bottom of the door. "I told you, someone was here while we were out!"

"Don't be ridiculous. What would anyone want to do that to the door for?" Angela concluded the marks had already been there, they just hadn't noticed them.

Thomas said nothing. While his mother took the shopping into the kitchen he stayed outside to ramble around. There was so much space! He wandered around the ground in front of the house, rambling along by the hedges and finding himself a young thin branch which he promptly stripped of its leaves and whipped the grass as he went. In no time at all he was really far from the house and yet he was still in the front garden. It only had grass in it. His granda would have a ball if he had all this space to plant things. In D'Arcy Avenue theirs was the biggest front garden, because it was on a corner, but Paddy Brennan had every inch organised and complained there wasn't enough space for the ideas he had. And Thomas had never been allowed play in it.

Thomas became troubled at the thought of his granda, and he kicked at the grass and lashed the air with his home-made whip. His brow was creased in a deep frown, his head bowed in thought. He climbed a gate into the field and the house disappeared from view behind the hedge. He sat in the grass with his elbows resting on his knees, and his head fell onto his arms. While the sun beamed down on him he cried quietly where no one could see or hear him. Forlornly he swished the stick back and forth through the long grass. Then he sniffed loudly and wiped his eyes and his nose with his sleeve, and got up and plodded on.

All around was the sound of birds. The crows and the magpies were high in the trees. Smaller birds favoured the safety of the hedgerows. Thomas heard their melodic twittering and noticed how they fell silent as he passed. He wondered at that. How clever they were! He saw the sun glistening on the waters of the river, the one he could see from the back windows of the house. He made his way towards it, climbed a nearby tree and positioned himself in the lower branches to watch the swollen river gush past. He sat quietly, looking all around him at a different world. He watched sheep grazing in a field. They had black faces, and their black legs looked so skinny compared to their woolly bodies. They were like balls of wool with knitting needles through them. His nan always pushed the wool onto the needles when she left her knitting down. He felt sad at the thought of her. But his attention turned to the cattle in the next field. He watched how their ears twitched as they swatted flies away. Bigger and bulkier than the sheep they grazed just as quietly, munching away contentedly in the glorious sunshine. Across the river a tractor was at work, the sound of its engine carried on the light breeze. It was the only manifestation of people Thomas could see from his branch. Further away there was a bungalow here and there, but the countryside belonged to Mother Nature. He absorbed the peace and tranquillity around him. He listened to the birds sing. He watched the river flow, and decided to get down for a closer look.

He gripped the branch and was about to swing himself to the ground when a movement to his left caught his eye. A man had entered the field through the gate and was striding purposefully towards him. Something about the man's manner made Thomas hesitate in dropping to the ground. But it was obvious the man had seen him. He reached the foot of the tree and glared up at the lad.

"What are you doing up there?" he demanded.

He was the biggest man Thomas had ever seen, and he stood with a walking stick hooked over his arm. His trousers were tucked into knee-high green rubber boots. Surprise caused Thomas to hesitate in answering. The man pointed the stick up at him and waved it threateningly in the air.

"Get down out of that tree!" he ordered. "You have no business being on this land!" Thomas did not take kindly to that remark. Mr Cullen had told them this was going to be his ma's. And Mr Cullen should know. All of a sudden Thomas was not afraid of this huge hulk any more.

"Who are you?" he demanded, safe in his branch.

Mick Furlong was quite taken aback. The child was no more than eight or nine, and as cheeky as be damned! He glared up at him.

"None of your business! You are trespassing and you had better clear off before you land in real trouble!"

Thomas laughed out loud. He had heard those words lots of times before in his short life, so often had he and his pals in D'Arcy Avenue been chased off by various people. Sometimes for writing graffiti on walls, or for hanging around where people assumed they were up to no good. He leaned forward, still laughing down at the farmer, somehow knowing that this time the shoe was on the other foot.

"My ma will run *you* off!" he declared. "She wouldn't like trespassers on *her* land!"

He enjoyed watching the man's reaction. He thought

he was going to burst a blood vessel. Over his nose his dark eyebrows met, forming a thick continuous line.

"Don't you mock me, you blasted little gurrier! You're up to no good!"

"You don't *own* this land," Thomas called down, "so *you* clear off!"

That was true, Mick thought, he didn't own it. Yet. But he would. But how would this child know that? By the sound of him he wasn't from around here. Dublin, most likely. Probably trouble as well. But he was not budging from the tree, and Mick knew he could not force him down.

He tried another approach. The one he probably should have tried in the first place. He smiled and relaxed his manner, hoping to get the lad off the defensive.

"So, how come you are here all by yourself, then?"

Thomas wedged his bottom in the fork of the branch and let his legs dangle. He swung them back and forth, deciding to stay where he was till the man was gone.

"I'm not all by meself," he replied, quite comfortable with the situation now, "and Mr Cullen says it's okay. You can ask him if you want to know!"

Mick Furlong was getting a sense of something that made him uneasy. The lad was sitting up there in the tree as if he was in his own backyard, and he was not intimidated in the slightest.

"You from Dublin, lad?"

Thomas changed the sequence of the swinging of his legs. He could not have articulated what had changed between himself and the man, but something had, and he was quite enjoying himself.

"Yeah. Are you a farmer, mister? I never met a *real* farmer before."

Mick acknowledged that he was indeed a farmer, and Thomas then wanted to know where his farm was. Mick pointed with his walking stick in a rather vague manner.

"Are they your sheep and cows?" Thomas indicated the grazing animals with a nod of his head.

This young lad was more curious than a body would like. "Sheep and bullocks," Mick corrected him, beginning to realise he was not as in control of the situation as he would have wished.

Thomas's ears picked up. "What?"

"*Bull*ocks," Mick repeated stressing the *u* sound. "*He* cows."

"Oh, yeah, I know!" Thomas laughed out loud. "Ha ha, *he* cows? Who ever heard of *he* cows? It's the way you talk!"

Mick felt very stupid and his first reaction was to become angry. But he held back and eyed this youngster more thoroughly.

"So where do *you* live?" he asked curiously.

"Here," came the simple answer.

"Here? Where here? Do you mean in the town?"

"No, here," Thomas insisted, "over there in that house." He waved his arm back in the direction he had come from.

Mick did not need to follow the movement. He knew the house "over there" as the lad had put it. "You don't live

126

there," he disputed, "that's Cleary's house. I know that for
sure." He straightened himself up to his full height, pleased
he had caught the lad out in a downright lie. He placed the
end of his walking stick on the ground between his feet and
leaned both his hands on the crook. A nasty little smile
hung about the corners of his mouth as he waited to see
how the lad would get himself out of that one.

"Well, you don't know. Me and me ma live in it now.
I told you, ask Mr Cullen."

The sense of unease slammed back into Mick's
stomach with a wallop.

"And who would you and your 'ma' be?" he enquired
with a narrowing of his eyes and a forward movement of
his head, as if he didn't want to miss a single syllable.

"You go first," the lad said.

"What?" said Mick.

"You tell who you are first! You've lived here the
longest!" said Thomas with a childishness that irritated
the hell out of Mick.

This was getting to be *too* ridiculous for words. But
there was no leaving it now.

"Mick," he said, almost through his teeth, "Mick is
my name. Now you. Who are you? And how come you
are in that house, as you say?"

"'Cos Daniel Cleary left it to me ma, didn't he, 'cos
he's her da!" Thomas was quite pleased to say.

Shock jerked through Mick's considerable bulk, and
the walking stick slipped on the grass under his weight.
He just managed to save himself.

Thomas tittered at the sight.

Chapter 14

Angela's eyes followed Thomas for a while as he went exploring. When he climbed the gate into the field alongside the garden and disappeared out of her sight she turned away from the window with a heavy sigh. The silence and emptiness of the house seemed to scream at her. She stood with her hands clasped over her mouth, unwilling to let a sob escape. Afraid if she started that there would be no stopping her. She almost wished she had gone rambling with Thomas. She must be getting desperate – even *his* company was beginning to seem better than no company at all.

And he was Reilly's! She groaned inwardly. Of *all* people! How did she not see the resemblance before? Or did she only see it now because of what she knew? It struck her then that he could have been born with red hair, like his father. Jesus! That would have been drastic! She would never have been able to look at him again. Her mind was running away with her, and it was so turbulent with everything that had happened it was impossible to sort out what her feelings were. One thing she was absolutely certain about was how much she hated Reilly.

And with good reason. He had ruined her life.

Many other people hated him too, but for what he was. Or because they had reason to fear him. Reilly never forgot what he considered to be a disservice of any kind, and just how exactly a person could fall foul of Redser Reilly was decided only by Reilly himself.

Now she could understand just why no one had dared spill the truth about what had really happened the night of the birthday party. How could they have known what they were sentencing her to by their silence? But Paddy still didn't know the true circumstances. He was more concerned with his own standing among his workmates.

Perhaps he had unknowingly done both her and Tomo a favour by forcing them out of the house and putting them out of Reilly's reach. It occurred to Angela then that being out of his way was probably the only positive angle to this whole sorry mess. But it suddenly came to her that Reilly being Tomo's da meant that Slappo was his *uncle*, not only his pal! And that meant the whole family were his *relations*! Grandfather, grandmother, aunts and uncles! Jesus Christ! Relations from hell. Who the fuck needed that? And Thomas was already far too palsy with them. It had become impossible to keep him away from them. They were like some kind of fatal attraction to him.

She glanced out of the front-room window, but there

was no sign of him, and she wondered what he was getting up to. She hoped it wasn't trouble. She had more than enough to be going on with on her plate, thanks very much. She couldn't remember how much land Patrick Cullen had said there was with the house, but she was sure it was a whole lot more than Tomo would need to get himself up to something! He was getting on her nerves the way he was going on about everything, as if they really had arrived at Áras an Úachtaráin.

This place was crap, in the arsehole of nowhere. There were no shops nearby, no buses, no nothing. A two-mile walk to the nearest semblance of civilisation was ridiculous. Whoever decided it was only two miles must have done it in a car, she figured. At top speed! It suddenly struck her that Daniel Cleary apparently had no car. That was insane!

Everything in the house was old. Her mother probably would say "antique", but it was still old. She went out into the hall and into the room facing her. They hadn't really looked around properly last night. She had put on as brave a front as she could manage, but all the while she could feel something she had trouble identifying, and in her upset state she could not tell if it was good or not. She had simply tried to ignore it. She had come close to naming it when Tomo appeared at her room door last night and scared the living daylights out of her.

She knew he was nervous too, and she almost felt sorry for him. She wondered vaguely if he had any thoughts on Redser being his da. He hadn't said a word about it. It never crossed her mind to actually ask him.

Now that she thought of it, he hadn't said a word about anything. That wasn't like him. Too often he had too much to say about things. Many times she had run him, because he was earwigging when she and her ma were talking. Little pigs have big ears, her mother used to say, and she would send him upstairs with instructions to clear up his stuff in the bedroom. Thomas was always being sent to do that. Angela sighed again, and decided she had better change her train of thought.

How long was she going to have to stay in this place? She would go demented if she didn't get back to Dublin soon. It was like solitary confinement down here. And what had she done to deserve such a sentence? Got herself born, by the looks of it, that was all.

She looked about. This "drawing-room" was huge. It was the full depth of the house, and had a long sash window at each end. Like the dining-room on the other side of the hall it had a huge fireplace, only this one was black stone. It had a couple of occasional tables and a number of armchairs, some with high backs. If someone was sitting in one, it would be hard to tell from behind. There was a long sofa-type thing with an arm at only one end, and it had a matching roly-poly cushion.

The stuff in this house was ancient, she thought. She had to admit it was all very well kept though. She realised with surprise that there was very little dust on the furniture. She almost expected to see cobwebs draped here and there. Someone had been doing the housework. Was it Daniel? Did he have a housekeeper? If he was this well off, probably he did.

The furniture was easily twice the size of what they had at home. Then she noticed the desk by the back window and the computer on it, and the boxes of files beneath it on the floor. A leather swivel-chair stood in front of the computer. She sat on the chair, and looked at her faint reflection on the darkened screen.

He sat here. This was where *he* spent at least some of his time. Suddenly she wondered what he had worked at. Was he a farmer? She didn't think so somehow. There were no animals on the land around the house, at least as far as she knew. She hadn't actually taken a look. It hadn't crossed her mind till now. She swung very slightly back and forth on the chair, her fingers on the keypad.

There was no chance of her turning on the computer and checking out what might be on it. Her computer skills never really got a chance to develop at school. They only had three computers when she was there. Lack of funding. The reason for the school shortages was always put down to lack of funding. Of course she had to be *in* school to get a chance on the computer in the first place.

But as she played with the keys the feeling she could not identify came back. Straight away she quickly withdrew her hands, and clasped them together, pressed into her lap, and stared at the screen.

Thoughts of Daniel filled her mind, and she felt strange. Yet she told herself she was being silly. How could she be thinking of someone she never knew? Why then should she suddenly feel familiar with him?

Perhaps because she was sitting in his chair?

She pushed the swivel-chair away from the desk and

spun it around, as much to make sure she was definitely alone as anything else. She stood up and briskly left the room, hoping the feeling would then leave *her*. She turned and went up the stairs, deciding to tidy the beds, purely to keep occupied. Certainly not from any house-proud tendency.

Going up the stairs she was reminded of Tomo sliding down the banisters that morning. It seemed like ages ago. This house was doing *something* to her.

She reached the landing and stopped, looking at the door which led to Daniel's room.

She decided against going in and turned instead towards the bathroom.

It was something else. The utilities were very far apart. The free-standing enamelled iron bath stood on its ball and claw legs, with its taps to the wall, a shower rail and curtain suspended over it from the ceiling. Across the room was the hand basin, with large sturdy solid brass taps. The loo was against the third wall, its cistern high up, connected to the pan by a long down-pipe. The handle hung on a long chain. Angela had only ever seen the likes of it in magazines, before the makeover. It was so old-fashioned that some designers were even bringing that style back!

She put down the toilet seat and sat on it. She could see the fields through the small window facing her. How much of that land was hers, she wondered? Why on earth was Daniel so intent on leaving it to her? Surely there must have been *someone* in Daniel's life he would have preferred to leave his estate to? Someone he actually *knew*? Or was he a loner? Apparently not. Not according to the things Patrick Cullen said about him. She tried to remember these things. Daniel and Patrick had been very close. Good friends. Everybody liked Daniel. The whole community was in shock at his sudden death.

Practically everybody in the town had attended his funeral. The overall impression she got was of a fine man, an honest upstanding person, friendly and outgoing.

But then, she remembered, although she did not know him, he knew her, didn't he?

Okay, it was certainly from a distance, but Nancy had kept him well informed about her. Imagine it. Every year he waited for news of her. Year in and year out his interest never waned. Even when she had Tomo. What had he made of that? She would not have been surprised if he had stopped wanting to know her then. But he did not react like Paddy and refuse to hear any more of her. He did not cut her out of his will. Why didn't he condemn her like Paddy did? Why would he still give her his house and land after she had let them all down so badly? Her thoughts swung to and fro like a pendulum. Wouldn't it have been great to have had the support of your father when you needed it so very badly? When your entire world went into utter chaos and you lived in fear of waking in the morning and finding *it* was still there. Wouldn't it be great to have had your father on your side, a father who would stand between you and the world?

Daniel would have done *that* for her?

Daniel would have done that for her.

Why was he being so persistent in installing himself into her mind like this and doing his best to make her so aware of what she – *they* – had missed?

A gnawing feeling of loss crept into her mind and settled itself securely at the back, even as resentment at Paddy for not being different surfaced quickly and sat in the forefront. It prevented her from dwelling on the positive aspects of her situation. That in itself was hardly surprising. For years she had been filled with anger and bitterness over her situation, which led her quickly to believing she was inadequate and useless. Wasn't Paddy forever pointing that out, how useless she was, every single chance he got?

What would Daniel have thought?

How different would he have been if he had the chance to be her father? The thought that it would definitely have been very different presented itself, and she could only imagine what it would have been like. But it was pointless to be thinking things like that now. There were some things she might never know, really be sure of, and that must certainly be one of them.

She stood up and rambled out of the bathroom. Sunlight streamed in through the tall window, filling the landing with light. How different it looked from last night when they couldn't even find the light switch. There was another window at the turn of the stairs – it had a curved top to it. She looked out and saw the river that Tomo had been so excited about. It looked full and fast-flowing and dangerous after all the rain. For long stretches there were no hedges obscuring it, or offering protection from it. She could see in places how the land ran right to the water's edge. She would have to make sure he stayed well away from it. Neither she nor Tomo could swim. She remembered in D'Arcy Avenue some of the kids went to the canal during the summer holidays. They brought fishing nets and buckets and had their swimming trunks on under their clothes. Tomo always threw a tantrum, wanting to go with them. Nancy would not hear of it. Angela would have let him go. It would have got him out of her hair for a while.

She looked down into the back yard and saw the old stone building by the hedge. It was curious the way it had a relatively new roof with a Velux window in it. The thought came to her that she ought to go out and take a good look about the place. She should at least know what she was inheriting. Or better still, what she would have to sell when it came to it.

Her impression of the house and its land had moved up a notch or two in the bright light of day, although it was still anything but where she wanted to be. Who knows, perhaps it would even get a good price, and she could then afford a nice place in Dublin, well away from D'Arcy Avenue and the Reillys. And Paddy. And maybe, since it wasn't such a crappy place after all, the house might sell fairly easily so that she could get herself out of the arsehole of nowhere and back to Dublin that much quicker.

Chapter 15

Mick Furlong regained his balance, turned quickly on his heel and set off towards the gate without a word. Thomas looked after him, surprised by his sudden departure.

"Hey, mister! Where are you going?"

He got himself down from his branch as quickly and as safely as he could, but the farmer ignored his call, and continued to stride away up the field, his big fist clenching his walking stick halfway down its shaft. Thomas ran to catch up with him, and suddenly something soft squelched under his foot. He looked down and saw his trainer half embedded in a pile of dung. Trying to wipe it in the grass as he ran, he half-hobbled half-limped up towards the gate. Mick had gone through and was heading to the house. Thomas did not like the determined way the farmer marched up the granite steps and banged on the door with the crook of his stick.

139

"We have a bell," he informed the man as he finally caught up with him.

Straight away the farmer's manner changed. Mick Furlong was aware he had a tendency to go headlong at things, when often a softly touch would more likely work better. Silently he was thankful to the lad for checking him.

Angela jumped at the sudden banging on the hall door. She went to the front landing window, positioned over the door, and looked down but saw only the roof of the porch. Assuming it was Thomas, she hurried down the stairs and across the hall, annoyed with him even before she laid eyes on him. She wrenched the door open and a mixture of surprise and alarm registered on her face, as the great bulk of Mick Furlong, firmly gripping his walking stick like a weapon, filled the opening.

Angela could just about see Thomas standing behind. Surprise registered with Mick also – he'd disbelieved what the lad had claimed and had not really expected an answer – but he was the first to recover. This slip of a girl surely would not present that much of a problem.

"Good day to you, Ma'am," he nodded, hooking the stick over his arm.

Angela nodded in return, waiting for the complaint about what her son had just got up to which had brought this man banging on the door. But it was Thomas who spoke next, as he squeezed into the hall between Mick and the doorframe.

"I told him Mr Cullen said it was okay for us to be here, Ma."

"What's going on here?" Angela asked. "Who are you?"

Mick was suddenly at his most charming. The last thing he wanted was to get on the wrong side of her. That would do his purpose no good at all.

"Mick Furlong," he smiled widely as he introduced himself. "Please let me explain. I came across your son in the field, and I assumed he was trespassing, you see –"

"*You* are the one who was trespassing!" Thomas butted in, despite his mother glaring at him.

Mick merely smiled at the interruption and went on. "He said Dan Cleary was your father and –"

"That's right," Angela cut him short, "what of it?" Was it any of this stranger's business? That flustered the farmer quite a bit. He was somewhat stuck for words. But not for long.

"Then I must offer my condolences," he managed to say. "You'll have to forgive me, I never knew Dan had . . ." he stopped himself before he really put his foot in it. He held out his huge hand and Angela shook it without an awful lot of enthusiasm. "Your father was a very nice man, very well liked indeed."

She wasn't being very forthcoming, he thought to himself. She just nodded her acknowledgement.

Mick Furlong obviously had a lot of questions about her and Thomas, she could see it in his face, but it seemed he knew better than to ask them of her, and she was not about to fill him in.

But he could not just walk away. He had to find out more about this latest obstacle to his plans.

"Might I ask – are you from Dublin?"

141

There was no harm in answering that, she thought, he'd probably guessed anyway. "Yes, we are. Do *you* live around here?"

Thomas's arm waved in the same direction as Mick had waved his stick, but he said nothing. He was watching cautiously, not trusting the change in the farmer's manner.

"We are neighbours so," Mick said, still smiling. "My land is next door, so to speak. You must find it strange here. Not like at home, eh?"

She had to agree with that. Was there a touch of understanding in his voice?

"I imagine you probably won't stay? I mean, you being from the city? Don't be stuck with this place, now. I'm sure we could come to some agreement if you want to head back to Dublin. I would oblige you by taking it off your hands, for a good price of course."

"No! No, Ma! No!" Thomas cried, even as the meaning of the words was sinking in with Angela. Then turning to the farmer, he added vehemently, "We're not selling!"

Again Mick ignored Thomas – the lad was only a nuisance. His mother's city upbringing was the thing to concentrate on.

"A place like this takes an awful lot of managing. You could get yourself some nice house in Dublin instead of being landed with this." Mick warily looked up at the house as though it was about to fall down around their ears. He was careful to make it sound as though he was thinking aloud.

Angela's apprehensive gaze followed his, afraid she was going to see huge cracks and damage she had heretofore missed.

"Oh, sorry, it's just that I know only too well what keeping a place like this involves."

He smiled apologetically, with a large dose of sympathy thrown in for good measure. She half smiled in return, but he could see with satisfaction that the seed of the idea he wanted to plant could well take root, if it wasn't already there. A city girl like this one surely would never want to stay here? He decided to risk laying it on a bit more.

"There's always something or other needing to be done with these old buildings. If it's not the plumbing, it's the electrics or God only knows what else." He tapped the palm of one hand with his walking stick, tut-tut-tutting away to himself. "Don't rightly know if Daniel kept up the maintenance or not in recent times," he mused.

Thomas's alarm was growing. He stood right next to his mother as if to make his words her words too. "We are not selling! My granda wouldn't like that! He wanted *us* to have it" he declared stoutly.

"Be quiet!" said Angela, annoyed.

Mick allowed himself a silent congratulation. Discord among the opposition ranks was always a good way to beat the enemy. It was time now for him to make a retreat, for the time being. Besides, there were other things he could be working on.

Christopher Cleary was one of them.

He wondered just what Christy thought about all this. If his guess was right it was entirely possible that he might not even know of it yet. He certainly knew nothing the other day in the pub when he spent all his money, buying drinks all round him. Mick did not have any sympathy for Dan's brother. He was a no-gooder anyway, and in Mick's estimation he definitely did not deserve to inherit his brother's estate.

But there was a lot that Mick had to find out and so he took his leave, assuring Angela he would be glad to be of any help he could.

Thomas was quick in his unconscious attempt to undermine Mick Furlong.

"I don't like him! He threatened me in the field with his stick! I was just sitting in one of our trees. And *he* was the one who was trespassing on *our* land! Marching around like he owned it or something, and he shouldn't even have been there!"

Angela was not listening. And that worried him. She could be thinking about selling! And they were only after getting there. If Daniel knew, he wouldn't like it, Thomas was sure.

"He only wants us out to get it for himself!" he stressed.

"He has a point," was all she said.

Thomas felt sick. Feck that farmer anyway! Feck him and his bloody greedy ideas!

"He's right," said Angela. "This house must take an awful lot just to keep it as it is, never mind updating it. Look at the size of the rooms! Imagine the amount of paint you'd need just to do one room! And how do you get up that high?" She looked up at the ceiling. She didn't notice that it had been recently painted. "You'd have to pay someone to do that! And where are we going to get that kind of money?"

Thomas was *very* worried. He didn't know anything about decorating. Or the cost of it. His granda never let him help when he was decorating in D'Arcy Avenue. Thomas knew he could move a brush up and down a wall as good as anyone else, if they would only let him. But they never did. Certainly not after he had stepped on the lid of the white gloss paint without knowing it and then walked up the stairs to the loo.

"The man has a point," he heard his ma say again. "With what we might get for this, and the land, we could buy a house in Dublin, a nice one not too far from me ma – wouldn't you like that?"

Thomas didn't know what sort of an answer would be the best one to that question.

He was caught between liking the possibility of being near his nan and dismay at leaving here, and neither a yes answer nor a no answer would answer the question properly or fully. But he was afraid to say nothing. He worried that their future here could hang on what he said now.

"Yes and no," he said, very much afraid his answer might put a seal on some unfavourable plan in his mother's head, which could never be reversed.

"That's a great help," Angela sounded irritated. "I might have known better than to ask *you*. What's that

145

fucking smell? Did you *fart*? That's some stink!"

"No! It wasn't *me*!" He immediately looked towards the hall door. "It must have been that . . ." His voice trailed off, remembering the dung pile. Lifting his foot he saw that his efforts to clean his shoe off had not been thorough enough.

Angela ordered him outside until he had removed all traces of the offending manure.

"See?" she told him. "If we stay here in no time we'll be up to our necks in it! That's the country for you, nothing in it but shite!"

A very dejected Thomas took himself outside to clean up his shoe.

For the first time since they had arrived Angela had shown a spark of interest. Only it was interest in leaving. And it worried him that she would not give it a fair chance, being here. She was grasping at the first suggestion that might get her back to the city. And even worse still it was that farmer's suggestion, and Thomas had already decided not to like Mick Furlong.

Thomas had not thought of his pals in D'Arcy Avenue since he had got here. In his mind something told him they were not a part of his life now, and the realisation of that did not bother him in the slightest. He was happy enough to be so far away from Reilly, even if he was his da. He now had a granda instead. Okay, he was dead, but he was a granda who really wanted them here. And he was happy about that – it made all the difference. As far as he was concerned there were no problems down here. They had all been left behind in Dublin. That was the way it was then, and this was the way it was now, and the thought of going back did not seem remotely appealing. Here was better. He looked for something with which to clean off his shoe, and then he remembered the farmer's green wellie boots, and he realised why he wore them. If by some miracle they got to stay here in Daniel's house his mother would have to get him a pair. He could just picture himself in them, a real country young fella.

But he couldn't ever imagine his mother in anything like them.

Angela went back to the kitchen and put on the kettle. She frowned as she did so and knew well why. Mick Furlong was right. This house would take a lot of upkeep. But even if she agreed with him on that she wasn't stupid. She could see exactly what he was at. Of course he would want this place and it right next to his own. How very handy. His visit had only served to heighten her misgivings.

But what bothered her was that Thomas was also right. Daniel wanted them to have his house. He wanted his daughter and grandson to have it, live in it. He had decided that years ago, when his wife died. That's how certain he was. And Angela already wanted to leave it. Hardly a day in it and she thinking of selling. It didn't feel right either way.

Chapter 16

Rose had dealt with difficult and upset people and clients in the office before on numerous occasions, and thought she had seen it all, but Christopher Cleary was in a league all of his own. The man was without any sort of normal behavioural pattern or rational thinking. There was no talking to him, no reasoning with him. Patrick had met him coming up the office stairs as he was headed down to drive to Christy's cottage, for the third time.

"Ah! There you are, Christopher!" he said, "I was just on my way out to see you . . ."

Christy growled something about it not being before time, as he removed his cap and settled his strands of hair, and dismissed the solicitor's efforts to explain that the nature of the business necessitated seeing him personally.

"And I want to see *you* personally! If my brother knew what a lousy solicitor you are he wouldn't lie easy in his grave!" was the gruff retort.

The sudden concern for his brother's resting in peace was obviously blatantly false, and Patrick ignored the remark. No use in fuelling aggression in an already tricky situation.

Since Daniel had died he had spent sleepless nights wondering how to break the news to Christy that his dear departed brother did not trust him, and did not want him anywhere near the house he would leave to his daughter. Daniel had made precise decisions because he knew his brother well. He insisted that Patrick promise to change the locks on his house *immediately*, if he should die before his brother. To this end a spare set of house keys and locks had always been deposited in Patrick's possession, along with the will. And Patrick had followed the instructions to the letter.

He indicated a chair to Christy, but Christy was not about to sit when told, like a dog.

He rummaged for the keys in his pocket and, dragging them out, flung them with a clatter onto Patrick's desk.

"Why don't these open the door to *my* house?" he demanded. "And my brother's affairs need sorting, and I haven't seen hide nor hair of you since he died! Some solicitor you are, I must say!"

Patrick searched desperately for words that would not antagonise him any further. But found none. There was no way he could soften the blow that was about to land on the man. He decided to be straight and quick about it. He sat at his desk and assumed his most officious tone in an effort to distance himself personally from what he was about to declare.

"I'm afraid I have not got good news for you, Christy." He used the familiar version of the name in the hope it somehow might dilute the inevitable reaction. "That is why I've been trying to see you in person because, you see, your brother has not left his estate to you. With regard to the keys, on Daniel's instructions the locks on the house were changed immediately upon his death. This will come as a great shock to you, I'm sure, but the reason for all this is that Daniel has a daughter."

Patrick paused to allow the words time to sink in. He watched the slight tilt of the head, the narrowing of the eyes. The working of the mouth without sound as the jaw sagged slightly. Spittle sprayed as Christy's stunned reaction struggled to articulate itself.

"Your brother has a daughter," Patrick repeated, hoping to help the fact sink in, "not Mary's obviously but a daughter none the less and a grandson. He left his estate to her, which he was legally entitled to do." Patrick paused slightly, then continued, feeling more wary as he spoke. "He has left a sum of money to you. Not very large, but it is something. I'm sorry, Christy. I know it must come as a terrible blow to you, but that is his will. Those are Daniel's wishes."

Rage gripped the mind of Christopher Cleary, which instantly dismissed the words he had just heard. He loomed over the desk, glaring with wild eyes at Patrick. His hands gripped his cap and screwed it into a roll before his fist slammed down onto the desk.

"Liar! Don't you try and cheat *me* out of what's

rightfully mine. I know your lot! Daniel has a daughter! You'll have to come up with something better than that, you fuckin' liar! Daniel has no daughter. Everybody knows that! You bloody snots are all the same. You think I'm fuckin' stupid. You think you can swindle me just because you know the law!"

Patrick rose indignantly to his feet. This was getting too much out of hand. It was expected that Christy would be angry. Very angry, knowing him. But to insult his professional integrity was going too far. He pushed a copy of Daniel's will across the table at Christy.

"I assure you your brother left a valid will, this is a copy of that will, and as such it stands. And yes, he *has* a daughter. And yes, he *has* left his estate to her. Everything I'm telling you can be verified. You will, of course, receive a copy of the will."

The authority that exuded from Patrick Cullen halted Christy in his tracks. But only temporarily. Blind rage consumed him and with surprising agility he was beside Patrick like a shot and made a grab for him. He got a hold of Patrick's jacket and jerked him back and forth, snarling into his face, spraying him with spittle as incoherent words tumbled from his curled lips. A shocked Patrick tried to hold his balance but Christy was surprisingly strong, and the two men fell against the desk, toppling the chair backward onto the floor with a crash that brought Rose running in. She pushed open the door as the struggling men fell down onto the upturned chair. One of its legs struck Patrick in the back between the shoulder blades and winded him, leaving him at the mercy of his attacker. Christy put the boot in, and Rose began to scream at the top of her lungs, startling Christy momentarily. She raced for her phone and dialled 999, but the people in the offices above had heard her screams and instantly running feet were heard thundering towards them down the stairs. Christy heard and reluctantly ceased his attack. He let go his grip on Patrick, pushing him towards the floor in the process, and snatched his cap from the table. He left the will there in disgust.

"You haven't heard the last of this!" he hissed at the prostrate solicitor, and marched out through Rose's office.

"Who the fuck do you think you're staring at, bitch?" he flung at her. "With your fancy fuckin' suit and stuck-up hairdo!" He swung his arm out and pushed her aside, then he reached out over her desk and with his cap he sent all her paperwork sailing onto the floor in one sweep. "Fuckin' solicitors! This isn't over. Not by a long shot!"

He pushed his way through the group of people crowding in from the small landing, and cursed his way down the stairs and into the street where he grabbed his bicycle and swung it around, catching a passer-by on the leg with his wheel.

Even as he made his way out, Rose dashed to help Patrick to his feet. He was pale and badly shaken. She turned his chair upright again and he sat down. Someone from upstairs had got him a drink of water, and enquired if an ambulance was needed.

Patrick insisted there was no need. He just needed to recover for a minute. A police car arrived very promptly in answer to the 999 call, and Garda Joe White took in the disarrayed state of the office as he came in. He looked at Patrick, who had begun to gather himself together.

"Disgruntled client?" observed the garda.

Patrick rubbed his side where he had been kicked and nodded. Rose was relieved to see him make a rueful half-grin.

"Occupational hazard," he replied taking some of the water.

"Would it have anything to do with Christy Cleary? I saw him leave just as I pulled up outside. He was quite agitated, it seemed to me."

Rose thanked the people from upstairs as they left and she closed the door behind them. "Christy was not named as Daniel's heir," Patrick said. "He just found out. It did not go too well, as you can see."

He noticed as he spoke that the garda did not express any surprise.

Rose made strong tea. They needed it. The policeman joined her and Patrick in a cup.

"You want to press charges, Patrick? You have witnesses, no doubt."

Patrick pursed his lips and brought his brows together in a thoughtful frown. "I'm not sure about that," he said hesitantly. "I think maybe I'll give it some thought."

Joe White nodded understandingly. He was well

aware that there was no one in a better position to judge the situation than Patrick himself.

"If you don't mind, I'll take a statement anyway," he said, taking out his notebook, "from both of you," he smiled at Rose. He flicked over the pages as he spoke. "So, Christy is not to have the house and land, eh? I heard something about a young girl and a lad. That so, then?"

Neither Rose nor Patrick was surprised that the news had spread, nor that it had spread so quickly. It was the talking point of the town, and would be for some time to come, most likely. Patrick nodded in answer to the question. Rose coughed politely.

The garda took their statements, carefully, slowly, writing down all they said. He then placed the notebook back in his breast pocket, and gave it a habitual pat with his hand.

"The boul' Daniel! A daughter. All this time, well, I only ask you!" He gave a low silent whistle, shaking his head. "You never know, do you?" He looked from one to the other. "Mind if I ask what she's like?" He settled his cap on his knee.

"The spit of her father," Patrick replied in a tone that did not invite further questions on the matter.

The garda gave a little "Ah, yes" as he got the message.

It was time he was getting on with things, he said, getting up to leave.

He patted his breast pocket as he turned to the door. "Let me know if you want to do something about this,

Patrick." He lifted a hand to stop Rose getting up and smiled at her, "I'll see myself out, thanks. Good day to you both." He tipped his hat at them and was gone.

"How are you *really*, Patrick?" Rose turned to him with concern. "That was a very vicious attack. I'm sure you're going to be quite sore. Do you think you should let the doc see you?"

He grimaced as his side hurt when he drew a deep breath, more in relief that he was all right than anything else. He felt quite sure that he was only bruised.

"I'm fine, Rose. I am, really," he insisted. "I'm more concerned about Angela and Thomas. That Christopher Cleary is out of control by the looks of it. You wouldn't know what he might get up to, the way he is right now."

Rose had to acknowledge he was right. She was feeling the same concern herself, but was almost afraid to admit it.

"Perhaps the Gardaí will keep an eye on them, do you think?" she asked anxiously.

Patrick set his cup aside. "I think they will more likely keep an eye on Christopher, at least until he gets over the shock he got today. He's not exactly noted for holding his temper, as you know."

That was the understatement of the year. He was thinking it would be advisable for him to call out and see Angela and Thomas, and try to warn them without causing them any more anxiety, if that was at all possible. Daniel's brother was unpredictable, given to fierce bouts of temper and violence without warning. He had taken the news very badly. Christy had just assaulted the news bearer – what would he do if he came across Angela? Maybe he would not leave it to chance. He might just make it his business to come across Angela!

Patrick found a bad feeling of unease had taken hold in his gut. Christy's history was dotted with violence of one kind or another.

Patrick remembered Daniel telling him of the incident of Christy's neighbour's dog. The dog was doing what dogs do, protecting his own patch. But this little mutt had taken a definite dislike to Christy. True, it was mutual, and every time Christy cycled past the gate the dog barked its head off. Christy was known to have dismounted from his bicycle and kick the gate, antagonising the little animal even further. After it was unfortunate enough to find the gate open one day the dog chased Christy a good half mile down the road. It was the last time it did anything of the sort. It was missing for a couple of days and then it was found dead by its owner's hedge at the side of the road. Poisoned, the vet said. Everybody had their suspicions, and Christy was wordlessly acknowledged as the culprit. But it wasn't the only incident giving an insight into what Daniel's brother was capable of. There were others. And they were not only aimed at animals either. People were certainly included in Christy's range of targets. The one that landed Cleary in Court was the episode with the young lad in the town. He had jeered after Christy who had just barged against him on the footpath. Leaving his bike lying in the way of traffic Christy returned and grabbed the lad by the arm, shaking him so violently that the lad's shoulder was dislocated. Charges were pressed and eventually a suspended sentence was handed down, but from that day onwards a definite question mark hung over Christy Cleary's mental state. If it had been suspect before, and it was, people now had their own unambiguous thoughts on the matter. They were left with an uneasy feeling about the effect the outcome would have on Christy's attitude towards the judicial system. They were right. It proved to be derisive and contemptible, giving Christy a dangerous feeling of being untouchable and immune.

People had learned to give Christy a wide berth. A polite but distant greeting was the norm from most people if they came upon him about the town. It suited Christy well. He was not the one for socialising, always being ill at ease around people. He didn't trust them. Didn't even like them, didn't drink with them, and certainly did not like it if he felt the wool was being pulled over his eyes. People were always trying to do that, put one over on him, he was sure of it. He knew he had to be always on his guard, and sort out whoever he suspected of conniving against him. Patrick had only briefly mentioned Christopher Cleary to Angela and Thomas when they first arrived. He deliberately did not dwell on the fact that Angela had an uncle, one who was disinherited solely because of *her*, and therefore not at all likely to be happy to learn of her existence. She had enough on her plate as it was for now. Patrick was quite sure she was having a hard time of it with all that had transpired in her life recently. He had no wish to make it any tougher for her, or to cause her unnecessary stress.

Now he felt things had changed drastically with Christy's reaction. Now he was worried, really worried, and with good cause. Christy was in no mood to take this lying down, and Patrick knew that Angela and Thomas could well be sitting ducks. Daniel trusted Patrick would do his best for his daughter, and he was not about to let his friend down, even posthumously. But how to fulfil the civil aspect of Daniel's wishes was going to be the difficult bit. Maybe even the *dangerous* bit!

Chapter 17

"Package for Angela Brennan," the postman declared. He was holding aloft a large parcel wrapped in plenty of strong brown paper and tied with thin twine. For good measure Nancy had also used lots of sticky tape all over it. The postman looked quizzically at Thomas who answered the knock on the door.

"Ma! Postman!" Thomas called back into the house.

The postman looked into the hall beyond the lad with great curiosity. The word was out, and he was in a prime situation to be among the first to view the newcomers first hand. He held onto the parcel. He was not about to hand it over to the boy and then have to leave with the feeling that he had missed the main feature. He looked intently at Thomas.

"Your mother must be busy settling in, eh?"

Thomas wished that was so but whatever she was doing he was sure it wasn't "settling in". He called again. "Ma!"

Angela appeared on the landing above. "Stop roaring, I'm coming!" She ran down the stairs.

She looked at the postman, not surprised at the long searching look he gave her. She felt like a bit of a sideshow down here. Every one wanted a good look.

"Package for you, Miss," he said pleasantly. He handed her the parcel.

She noted he had used her correct title. It told her the locals could put two and two together just as fast as anyone else. Maybe even faster, some of them.

"Best of luck with things here, Miss. Hope you settle in okay."

She glanced up from the package to see a warm smile on his face. "Thank you," she stammered, "I don't know – I'm not sure –"

"Things will work out," he said. "It's always strange at first. I'm a blow-in myself, you know. Mind you, I'm here nearly twelve years now. But you'll be grand, you'll see. I'm sorry about your father. Lovely man, lovely man, God rest him."

She was touched by the kind thought. A warm positive feeling rose within her for the first time in ages, and she found she was smiling warmly in return.

Thomas, watching this exchange in silence, found himself smiling also. People were nice. The postman left. He was nice. Rose was nice, and Patrick Cullen was too. Thomas really wanted to stay here. And his mother was smiling a *real* smile. That was good.

"Let's see what we got, Ma. Is it from Nan?" he asked excitedly.

"Of course it's from her! Who else would be sending us stuff?"

No one else even knew they were there, she thought bitterly, the warm feeling melting fast.

They took the parcel to the kitchen table. She had to cut away the paper because there was so much sticky tape.

"Ma made sure this wouldn't get torn in the post," she muttered as she cut. She opened the parcel out, while Thomas waited impatiently. Inside were the promised changes of clothes for both of them. Nancy had placed a plastic bag in the centre of the clothes, and filled it with Angela's mobile phone and her make-up, Thomas's Game Boy, a short letter and a couple of photographs, and whatever money she had in her purse.

Angela flicked through the photos. She came to one of herself and Thomas with Nancy in St Steven's Green at the pond, feeding the ducks. She remembered the day well. It was one of the good ones, just after her twenty-first birthday. There was just the three of them out for the day, which would have accounted for it being good, so someone else had obviously taken the snap. Angela remembered her mother asking a man sitting on a nearby bench to take the photo for them. Angela was mortified. Nancy always made a thing of having photos taken. The man went back to his bench and his paper, and Thomas continued to feed the ducks. Some of the fowl had hopped from the water onto the path and Thomas threw them the bread they had brought with them. The last photo was of Nancy herself. Both Angela and Thomas fell silent at the sight of it. Suddenly Angela burst into tears. Harsh, anguished heart-rending tears, and Thomas was shocked. He could only stare at his mother, his mouth agape.

She put the photo down and became aware of him staring. "What are you gawking at?" she cried, her anguish mixed with anger, and both emotions boiled over uncontrollably. "This is all your fault! If it wasn't for you things would have been different!" She collapsed onto a chair and cried hopelessly, inconsolably. "Why don't you just get lost, you fuckin' little nuisance!"

Thomas paled and backed away as if she had just pushed him. It was never said so plainly before. He already believed all the trouble at home was because of him. But the venom in his mother's voice was a huge shock to him. He put his Game Boy back on the table and ran from the room.

Angela never heard him go. Sobs racked her body as everything tumbled out in a seemingly endless torrent of tears and pain.

After what seemed to be a very long time the sobbing subsided. Her head rested on her arms on the table, and when she lifted it, it pounded like mad. Her eyes were so puffed from crying they would not open fully. A feeling of resignation had descended upon her, and that depressed her even further. But something else troubled her, and she was ashamed and reluctant to examine it. A picture of Tomo's shocked face was stuck in her head. She knew she had gone too far this time. Much too far. She admitted to herself that he was probably in turmoil too. But she had not given that fact even one minute's acknowledgement till now. She was well aware of how attached he was to his nan. Sometimes she had even been jealous of that. So he had to be missing her very much.

He would not miss Paddy. If anything Paddy was most of the reason why Tomo didn't wish to go back, and she couldn't blame him. Before and after he was born he was unwanted, both by her and by Paddy, and he would have been a fool if he had not become aware of that. And Tomo was no fool. A messer, yes. A pest perhaps, but no fool. In her heart she knew full well that none of this was his fault. And none of it was hers either, even though she was guilty of taking her frustrations out on him. What had her in this position was all other people's doings, or other people's inability to cope. It wasn't fair that the burden for that was let fall on her shoulders. Hers and Tomo's.

Slowly she dragged herself to her feet. She felt old. She felt weighed down. And she knew that if she didn't find Tomo and tell him that she didn't mean what she had said the weighty feeling would not lift.

Her eye caught sight of her mother's short letter, and she read it through. In it Nancy thanked God that they had Daniel's place to go to. She urged Angela to stay put, at least till things settled down. She wrote that Mrs Ryan was going to get her a mobile phone for herself and show her how to use it. Mrs Ryan even knew how to programme the video recorder and she also used a computer in the house. Nancy said how she missed them, and explained that the money was all she had right then.

She did not say that Paddy was only giving her the barest amount for food. Neither did she say that often he did not come home, or that she was glad about that. She never mentioned that *she* paid for it when he did. He got no mention at all, and in her own mind Nancy willed that he would cease to exist.

The letter was brief, probably rushed off in a hurry and yet Angela knew she had gathered much more from it than her mother had written. She sighed heavily but remained dry-eyed – she was all cried out. She folded the letter and put it in a drawer and went to look for Thomas.

She expected to find him in the garden. Because her head pounded unmercifully she was not inclined to call out as she normally would have done. So she went out to look for him, fully expecting to see him from the doorway. But there was no sign of him. She rambled down the front garden towards the gate. It was a lovely morning but the breeze was strong and a bit nippy. She rubbed her arms under her sleeves and was glad a change of clothes had arrived.

Money. It was a good thing that her mother had sent some. But it made Angela realise one thing. Work was what she really needed to keep a steady inflow to the house. She was going to have to get something to do. They could not depend on what Nancy could send. Angela had the feeling it was she who should be sending some to her mother. Paddy's angry voice sounded clearly in her head: "There's two of yis there to feed, y'know! It doesn't grow on fuckin' trees! Why can't you get a proper job like everyone else, for Christ's sake!"

The last thing she wanted was to have to admit he was right about that, but it was quite obvious she needed an income. If they stayed or not, she had to get work.

Now where could Tomo have got to? He had said something the other day about sitting in a tree watching the river and the sheep and cattle. She wished she had paid more attention. She crossed over to the hedge and looked through it but could see nothing. She walked faster, beginning to feel unease at the fact that she had not seen him yet. His little face had registered such shock that she was quite concerned at his whereabouts. She listened, but all she heard was birdsong. A tractor passed by on the road, drawing her attention. A man waved. From the driving seat he could see over her hedge, but he was too far away to ask if he had seen Tomo. She stopped, wondering if Tomo might have gone into the buildings at the back of the house.

She made her way around there, for the first time taking in all that made up her inheritance. The yard behind the house was part concrete and part flagstone, huge big squares offset against each other. Angela headed for the buildings on the left. In more prosperous times they were the stables and the barn, and above them, the loft. It surprised her to see a couple of bales of hay stored against the wall as she went in. The stalls' doors were gone, only the strong hinges attached to the sturdy wall remained. A flutter of wings above her head made her look up, thinking that Tomo must have climbed up there. But all she saw was a startled bird making good its escape. Silence returned, apart from the wind blowing through the tall building, and Angela really began to worry. She hurried out into the sunlight again, and crossed to the building with the Velux window. As she approached she noticed the door partially open, and with relief she pushed it in, a sharp rebuke ready on her lips. Her eyes met with a mess of paints and brushes and frames all strewn about the long room. She could appreciate the work being done here, and therefore she was appalled at the deliberate mess someone had made. Under a cloth on the floor a canvas was just about visible. She picked it up to put it in a safe place, and took a peek at the painting beneath.

She gasped at what she saw. The painting was of a young woman and a boy by a pond feeding ducks. Their laughing faces were partially shaded by the shadow of overhanging trees, but there was no mistaking who the subjects were! In the background a man sitting on a bench was watching them and smiling. Although he was a little obscured by distance, Angela knew she was looking at a self-portrait of her father.

"Jesus!" she whispered in astonishment. "You! *You* took that snap!"

She held the painting further away in an attempt to get a clearer look at him, but it was cleverly done so as not to completely identify any of the subjects. Yet it depicted a day of sunshine and laughter and happy people. She tried to remember it more fully. Embarrassment swamped her when she thought of how she had objected to her mother bothering the man.

Nancy must have let him know they would be there. How often would she have done that? How many times were she and Tomo close to him without knowing?

She studied the smiling face, and tried to see it clearly, but it had not been painted so.

It occurred to her there might very well be actual photos of him in the house. She stood the easel back on its legs again and set the painting on it, and backed away a little to view it better. Again she had the distinct feeling of having missed something, being just a little too late. Her thoughts came back to Tomo, and she wondered if he had been in here. Horrified, she suddenly thought he might have caused this destruction because of what she had said to him!

No! He wouldn't! He wasn't that bad . . . was he?

Where was he?

She rushed from the workshop, realising it was now quite some time since she had seen him, and she was afraid in his upset state he might have an accident of some sort. She began to run towards the river. The water levels had subsided in recent days and the Slaney flowed peacefully on its way. Access to it from where she stood was not easy, and she turned towards the house hoping Tomo would have come back. If anything happened to him her mother would kill her. She couldn't even look after her own child. In a panic by now, she ran into the hall and searched the downstairs rooms, running from one to the other, a horrible feeling tightening in the bottom of her stomach. Nothing! Oh God. Oh Christ Almighty, where *is* he?

Thomas had run from the room and then upstairs, looking for somewhere to hide himself. He wanted nothing more than to find a place where his mother wouldn't have to see him, maybe wouldn't even look for him. He couldn't bear to see that look on her face again when she looked at him. He suddenly felt sick, nauseous, and he hurried into the bathroom where he threw up violently into the loo. He was so weak afterwards that he didn't have the strength to reach for the chain to flush the toilet. He felt so awful that he thought he was going to die, and he didn't want to die on the loo floor, so he dragged himself across the landing to go to his bedroom.

And then he saw the closed door of Daniel's room. Drawn like a magnet he opened the door and went in. The feeling of desperate aloneness eased a little and he climbed into the bed. His mother wouldn't look for him here. He curled himself into a ball and pulled the covers over his head. Only then did he allow the tears to fall. Silently they soaked the pillow, and he did his best to be very quiet.

Angela found him there, curled up in the big bed, fast asleep, exhausted from all the emotional upset. He was right. It was the last place she looked.

Chapter 18

It was a strange sight these days, watching Thomas clearing the table. Nothing got spilled or broken. She was able to allow him get on with it without having her heart in her mouth, waiting for the inevitable crash of cutlery or crockery. There was no comment made about it, lest the magic wouldn't last.

But Thomas was still as likely to come out with surprises as before.

"Ma, can we go and see Daniel's grave?"

For a minute Angela was quite taken aback. "What for?"

"I'd like to see it," he informed her, very matter-of-fact, as if it was something he was used to doing regularly.

"That's fuckin' morbid!" she replied strongly, hoping he would change his mind. "What would you want to do that for?"

Thomas was not sure just why he felt he would like

to do that. He was very curious about Daniel Cleary, but he didn't need to analyse why. He just was, and that was that. But his mother seemed to need a reason, so he thought about it for a minute.

"Well, I'm waiting," she said.

"I just thought since he is your da, and he gave us all this," he waved his arm indicating the house and all, "that maybe it would be nice to visit him."

He spoke as if Daniel was actually expecting a visit from them and it gave Angela a peculiar feeling.

"I'm not going into any graveyard," she declared.

Thomas thought about that too.

Angela didn't like this habit he was developing of thinking on things – you never knew what was coming next any more. Since they arrived here his brain seemed to work way ahead of hers. She didn't like it.

"If Granda Brennan had died you'd have gone to the funeral, wouldn't you?"

"Of course I would!" was her impatient reply.

"Yeah – and he's not even your *real* da, *is* he?"

He had her there, the crafty little git, and she was annoyed because she should have seen it coming. He made her feel ashamed and ungrateful. And in many ways she was. Daniel had wanted her to have "all this" as Tomo put it, but had he considered whether *she* would want it? Would she want the changes it had wrought on all concerned? It occurred to her then that because Reilly was Tomo's da, Paddy Brennan probably would have dumped them out anyway. Maybe she should be *more* than grateful for "all this".

"So can we, Ma?" Thomas's voice interrupted her thoughts.

"What?"

"Visit Daniel?"

"Oh, I suppose so. Maybe tomorrow . . . or the next day."

They did not wait till tomorrow or the next day. A walk to town for groceries was needed. Thomas was eating like a horse ever since they arrived here. There was no more picking or "I don't like that". Anything she put before him went down without objection. Where he was putting it all Angela did not know. All she was sure of was that any money they had was spent on food.

Rain was forecast for later on in the afternoon, so they set out after breakfast. They had become avid weather-forecast watchers, mainly because of the walk to and from the town.

When they reached the old wrought-iron gates of the cemetery Thomas hesitated. "How will we know which one, Ma?"

"We'll find it," she said, steeling herself to go in.

They made their way as far as the old tower and looked around. From there Angela spotted the freshly dug mound of earth, covered in withered floral wreaths. She sent Thomas to see what name was on the headstone. When he beckoned her over she took her time. But eventually she stood looking at the name of Mary Cleary etched into the polished black marble, in gold coloured lettering. Daniel's name would go below that of his wife, and the day he was born, and the day he died. Thomas was worried when he read the headstone.

"Why is Daniel's name not on it, Ma?"

"They'll put it on, don't worry."

"Who will?"

Angela wanted to be gone. This was far too much of a dose of reality for one morning. She made the sign of the cross upon herself, using it to signal the end of the visit, and stepped back. Into her head flashed a picture of the painting of the pond scene. The man on the bench in the background was not there. Troubled, a shiver ran down her back.

"Let's go!" she said suddenly.

"*Who* will put Daniel's name on, Ma?" Thomas was insistent.

She looked at the headstone for a long time, a feeling of responsibility coming over her. Thomas waited. She was deep in thought, but presently she took a deep breath.

"We will," she said finally. "In a while we'll find out how, and we'll get it done."

They walked briskly down the hill again into the main street, Thomas happy that he was going to be able to do something for his *real* granda. Angela was surprised at him. She was seeing a whole different Thomas to the one who lived in D'Arcy Avenue. The *things* he concerned himself with!

"Hey, Ma! Look! There's a fire station!" he burst out suddenly, pointing across the road. She laughed. He was still only a child.

And he wanted crisps.

"Just this once, please, Ma?"

"Here, we'll get them here," she answered.

They were passing the newsagent's. If she got them in the supermarket he would probably put five or six packets in her basket.

Maisie Mac was made up. Daniel's daughter and his grandson in her shop! She stared at the young woman who stood before her and silently she marvelled at the resemblance to Daniel, the interesting face, the same good looks. But Maisie had already decided she was not going to like this blow-in from Dublin, this brazen hussy without a father for her son, who came to fill Daniel's place, even if she was his daughter.

"What can I get you?" she asked sweetly.

"Just the crisps, thanks," Angela replied.

"You're *her*, aren't you? Yes, of course you are," Maisie answered her own question, and added, "You have to be, looking like that, don't you?"

A surprised Angela had no reply to that.

It didn't seem to matter. Maisie Mac went on talking anyway. "I knew your father very well, you know," she said with more than a touch of self-importance. "He never mentioned a word about you."

Angela bristled at the slight, and was about to tell this fuzzy-haired auld bitch to fuck off and stick her bleedin' crisps, when Rose suddenly appeared in the shop doorway.

"I *thought* that was you I saw from up the street!" she greeted them warmly. "Hello, Thomas, aren't you coming up to see us?"

"We were just up visiting my granda's grave, Rose,"

Thomas happily informed her. "Ma says we are going to have his name put on the headstone soon." He held the crisp packet towards her. "Want some?"

Angela paid for the purchase. Maisie leaned her elbows on the counter, and smiled a different smile as they left. Well, well! So they were doing right by Daniel. Perhaps *that one* was okay after all, bastard son or no. And apparently they were well in with the solicitor and his stuck-up secretary. Probably best to keep on the right side of them so, just to be sure.

Angela never saw anyone produce three cups of coffee as fast as Rose did.

"I saw you going into the shop, Angela. I thought you might need a little rescuing, if you get my meaning? Our Maisie can be a bit caustic sometimes."

Angela sipped her coffee and made no secret of the fact that she was about to let Maisie have it just as Rose showed up, while Thomas talked to Patrick who seemed extremely interested in what he had to say.

"Doing anything Friday night, Angela?" Rose enquired casually.

Yeah, she was about to say, ruefully, watching the *Late Late Show* on telly. Exciting night.

"We are having a table quiz in the Lalor Centre," Rose went on, "we need one more to make up another table. Fancy coming along?"

Angela was suddenly short of a reply, and not so sure about going. She knew nobody. She wasn't sure she had anything suitable to wear, and she certainly did not want to make a fool of herself in front of a group of strangers either! And what about Tomo? That was it. She couldn't go and leave Tomo alone!

But she hadn't actually answered Rose, who suddenly said, "That's settled then. Thomas can come to our house. My son Owen will be glad of the company, and his father will take you both home afterwards. Great! Orla will be pleased. She's looking forward to meeting you!"

Angela felt something akin to panic. Like a ball had started rolling and she never even had the slightest grip on it to begin with. "Who's Orla?"

"My eldest," Rose replied, delighted with the arrangement. "She's around the same age as you. She teaches senior infants in the school."

A teacher! Angela's heart sank. *She* would be the dunce! She would make such a fool of herself! This was terrible, but she didn't see how she could get out of it.

"I'll pick you both up, about eight, and we can go down together. That's great! It's for the Day Care Centre, a good cause. It will be good fun."

Angela was dismayed. Even Rose would be there to see her make an ass of herself! Patrick declared himself not busy at the moment, and offered them a lift home after the supermarket, if they liked. In the shop Angela would have forgotten half the things she had come to get, but for Thomas, who was quick to remind her that they did not have this or that. She told herself to pull herself together – the quiz was just a bit of craic and it wasn't as if she had never been to one before. Well, one.

Thomas loved being in Patrick's car. The leather seats were so soft and thick. It even had really wide armrests that would have done him for a seat, saddle style. He missed the horses in the field in D'Arcy Avenue. He had been telling Patrick all about them, and he had listened very attentively.

When they reached the house and Thomas had gone outside, Patrick took his opportunity to bring up the issue of Christopher Cleary. He began with the possibility of Christy lodging a claim.

"He is your father's older brother, his *only* relative actually, and I know I mentioned him before," he said, "but I do so again because it is possible that he might make a claim on Daniel's estate."

"And if he does?"

"Well, it would hold up probate while his claim is being investigated," Patrick replied. "That would delay everything. I don't believe he will be successful, but he *could* harbour bad feelings, because he expected to inherit, you see."

She did see. It certainly did not make her want to meet this new uncle. The fewer complications she had to encounter the better. At least for the moment.

"Do I have to meet him, or anything?" she asked, half-afraid the answer might be in the affirmative. "I mean, is there any reason why I should?"

He understood her concern. "Legal necessity? No. No legal requirement there at all."

She felt relieved about that. But not with what came next.

Patrick was very concerned that Christy might make trouble for her any way he could, and that he would be very bloody-minded about everything. He more or less said that he would not be surprised if Christy turned to anything to get her out of the house. The fact that it was hers to keep or sell regardless could well be lost on him.

As if she had read his mind she asked, in a very serious tone, "Do you think this uncle might be trouble, like do us harm or anything?"

He had the feeling there was a particular reason behind that question. "What is on your mind, Angela? Did something happen?"

"I'm not really sure," she said. She told him about the mess made in the workshop, the way the easel and paintings, brushes and paint tubes were all scattered about. "I almost blamed Tomo for it," she admitted, but did not elaborate on why she thought he would have done it, "but he was in bed fast asleep, and he thinks too much of Daniel to even think of doing anything like that. They say artists' studios are a mess of a place anyway, but this looked like someone had done it deliberately."

Patrick frowned, pushing his lips forward. He did not like the sound of that. It sounded very much like an outburst of Christy's temper. He asked if she had seen anyone about the place, or had she noticed anything else. She shook her head, but Patrick's frown did not disappear. Christopher had been to the house and tried the keys on the front and back door. Patrick had seen to it that both locks had been changed, but there was a padlock on the workshop, and he realised now that they had overlooked that one. He could well imagine Christy venting his anger on Daniel's cherished paintings. But

Christy did not know at the time that he was not going to inherit! If he had known he might have done worse!

"Are any of the paintings damaged?"

"No. Tomo and me went in and sorted it out. We took some of them into the house. We were thinking we could hang them in there somewhere."

Patrick interrupted his own thoughts while he answered. "That would be nice. Your father never hung them, you know, the 'personal' ones. He painted them and tucked them away. Others he sold. I used to say to him he should hang some in the house. But clearly they were very personal. Hanging them in full view in his house might have invited questions he didn't want to answer. He didn't want to risk letting the cat out of the bag, I think."

"Do you think it might have been Christy who made the mess? Would he do something like that?"

"Well . . . *someone* clearly did it. Was it *he,* or someone else knowing the house was empty? Who can say? But I would advise you and Thomas to be careful. Don't go out and leave doors unlocked, close windows, you know, that sort of thing. If your Uncle Christopher should happen to call on you, I would advise you to give me a buzz immediately. Whatever you do, do not invite him into the house. And tell Thomas the same. That is very important. We would not want him claiming you said he could stay, now, would we?"

The more Angela heard of this newly acquired family member the less she liked it. Why couldn't she have *normal* family relations, like everyone else? What with the Reillys and Paddy Brennan, did she really have to have a lunatic such as Christopher Cleary as *well*? Just the sound of him was enough to strike fear in her. She certainly didn't want him anywhere near her. Or Tomo. One vicious mad man in their life was more than enough, and Christopher Cleary was already reminding her sharply of Paddy Brennan. She kept this similarity to herself. It was too horrible to even contemplate. But unknown to her then, this new and veiled threat to their future caused a tiny undetected degree of anger to be born in the pit of her stomach.

She tried to keep any fear or apprehension from her voice when she answered, "He sounds like a total nutcase. Do *you* think he's likely to make a claim?"

Patrick attempted to assess her reaction. Was she getting the picture? "All I can safely say is that in my long experience of working with families in all sorts of circumstances, anything is possible. And I mean *anything*. Sometimes what you think will surely go one way, doesn't – and what looks like it definitely won't happen sometimes does. But you need not worry about your Uncle Christopher making any difference to the fact that you inherited. Your father charged me with looking after you from a legal standpoint, and I am not about to let Christy, or anyone else for that matter, cause you any problems on that score. He is entitled to challenge your father's will, if he wishes. As I said, all it could do is hold up probate, but he cannot change the terms of a valid will. And Daniel was very concerned that his will be watertight, and between us we ensured it is."

Angela was quiet for a while, thinking over what

Patrick had said. He must have been very close to her father, for he was being extremely diligent. She felt the better for having him in her corner.

Her next question was a surprise to Patrick, coming as it did after such a short time in the house.

"Could I sell this place, do you think – I mean, when it's mine?"

To gain some time to try to assess what she might be thinking, he countered with "Is that what you're thinking?"

She half-shrugged her shoulders. "It was suggested to me the other day, by someone who would be interested in buying it. This house and all would take a lot of upkeep and I wouldn't have that kind of money . . ."

"That sounds like what someone would say if they were trying to persuade you to clear out," Patrick interjected when her words faltered. "Can I ask who would like to get their hands on it?"

"Mick Furlong."

Patrick was nodding his head. He was not surprised. It sounded like the determined Mick was not letting the grass grow under his feet.

"Mick Furlong tried to get your father to sell also. According to Daniel he was quite persistent at the time. That was after Mary died. But Daniel would not hear tell of it. He now had something substantial he could leave to you in his will. That was his thinking."

Angela felt like a right heel, and was disgusted with herself for asking. "It would mean I could go back to Dublin," she attempted to defend herself, her voice very small. "I didn't want to come here in the first place."

He watched her discomfort at the whole situation. From the beginning it had been clear she was a fish out of water.

"Of course you could sell, Angela. You will be able to do what you wish. But first you must wait for probate. You cannot do anything until the legalities have been completed." He felt sorry for her. She looked miserable. "Thomas seems to like it," he added.

"Yeah," she had to agree, her voice laced with sarcasm, "you'd think he was born on a farm or something, the way he has taken to it."

Patrick smiled and stood up. "There *is* some money in Daniel's estate, you know, he *did* have some savings. Not a huge amount but you won't exactly be penniless, that's for sure. You'll have something to be going on with." He looked at his watch. "Now, I must be getting back, I have some appointments logged in. Mustn't keep them waiting."

"Thanks for the lift," she attempted a smile herself.

Patrick picked up his jacket. "You know, that was something your father thought of," he remarked thoughtfully, "the fact that you might not like it here."

"Really?" That surprised her quite a bit.

It actually pleased her too, that she and Daniel had the same thoughts on the matter. Somehow, it validated her feelings, told her it was all right for her to have her own thoughts about it. And to think that Daniel had foreseen the likelihood of that!

Standing at the front door she smiled to herself as

Patrick made his way down the granite steps to his car. He glanced back just before getting into it, satisfied to see what he interpreted as a positive look in her eyes. He pulled the car door shut tight behind him.

"We need a lot more intercession up there, Dan," he muttered quietly, casting his eyes upwards. "Don't give up on her yet." He turned the key in the ignition, and the sleek Mercedes moved off down the driveway.

Thomas appeared then from around the side of the house, and ran shouting and waving after the car till it reached the road. He closed the gate after Patrick and only turned back to the house after he had received a long departing beep of the horn.

His mother was sitting thoughtfully at the kitchen table when he went into the house. She was wondering how she should tell him what Patrick Cullen had been saying. But Tomo was so obviously delighted with life here in "the arsehole of nowhere" as she called it, and she did not like the idea of bursting his bubble.

This was a new feeling for her. In D'Arcy Avenue she would not have considered his feelings for one minute. She hadn't been in the habit of acknowledging he even had any, and she would have blurted out all Patrick had said, and if it worried the lad, well tough. Actually, now that she thought about it she realised she would have left it to her mother to tell him.

Nancy would have found a way.

That was what she needed to do, she realised, find the way Nancy would do it.

Chapter 19

In Seán Mulhearn's bar Christy Cleary sat on a high stool, and propped himself up by means of his elbows wedged between the brass bar that ran the length of the counter at its outer edge and the bar itself. His pint glass was less than half full yet he managed to miss his mouth and slosh some of the black liquid over his sleeve. He muttered incoherently as he made a second attempt to empty the glass. People on either side of him had begun to leave him well and truly to himself. Any pretence at conversation with him was being rapidly dropped as he became more and more inebriated. Common knowledge by now, and the talking point of the moment with everyone, was the fact that his brother had pretty much left him out of his will.

Even those who were sympathetic to him backed off because he could be so unpredictable. He had a fair sup taken, only this time his drink was Guinness. He no longer had his brother's wallet to dip into, so his splurge was over and buying whiskey was now out of the question, and no drink was bought for anyone sitting around him at the bar either. He begrudged having been so bloody stupid as to spend money like that.

There were others who had no shred of sympathy for him. They were almost relieved that the girl and her son had showed up to claim the house and land. That property would have been wasted on the likes of Christy Cleary. He would have deliberately allowed it to go to rack and ruin, some said, and taken a perverse pleasure in its deterioration. Christy's own cottage was not somewhere anyone chose to visit – he did not make any attempt to keep it presentable, nor himself either.

When Mick Furlong came into the bar he strode up to Seán and leaned across the bar to him. Seán leaned forward to hear Mick's lowered voice.

"How is our Christy? Been here a while, has he?"

Seán nodded and lowered his voice too. "Too long. If you ask me, he's going to get carted out again."

It was getting to be a bit of a nuisance, carrying Christy Cleary off the premises, and getting him home, when he would otherwise be a danger to himself and everyone else, if he was capable of cycling his bike.

Mick gave Seán a conspiratorial wink. "Leave it to me, I'll sort him out."

He went along the bar and edged his big frame in beside Christy. Customers willingly made space for the big farmer. He placed his own pint next to Christy's, and leaned towards him. No one heard what was said, but Mick clearly had the other man's attention. Then Christy raised his arm and placed a Guinness-soaked sleeve across Mick's shoulders. They were in deep conversation for a while, then Mick downed the rest of his drink and raised his hand to Seán.

"Goodnight, Seán. Thanks, man, see you again!"

He helped the very unsteady Christy to his feet and handed him his greasy cap. Dogged to the last, Christy insisted on going through the motions of emptying his already empty glass while Mick held him steady. Then he made an issue out of fixing his cap at just the correct angle before allowing himself to be guided from the pub.

Once Christy was in the car, his bicycle once again left propped against the wall of the pub, Mick opened the windows and drove out along the road towards the cottage. After a couple of minutes Christy roared he was bleedin' freezing. Mick watched him closely and when he figured he was about to throw up, he stopped the car, got out, pulled his passenger from his seat and plonked him on the grass verge.

"What the fuck do you think you're doing? You're not fucking leaving me here!" a very belligerent Christy shouted.

"And you're not going to fuckin' throw up in my car!" Mick told him in no uncertain terms. "Now get it up, because you're not getting back in my car till you do! And make sure it goes on the grass, not all over you!"

Christy sat in the dark on the grass, taking short heavy breaths. His arms rested on his knees, his head hanging between them, his strands of oily hair hanging on his shoulder. The language that came from him was so atrocious that even Mick, sitting in the warmth of his car and well used to foul tongues, was appalled. Eventually Christy parted company with the offending liquid, making as much noise about it as he could, and Mick allowed him back into the car.

"Me fuckin' arse is wet!" Christy complained.

A wary Mick threw him a disgusted look. "It had better be because the bloody grass was wet! Else you'll pay for the cleaning of this car!"

Christy gave a derisory sly laugh. "With what? My dear departed brother hardly left me a tosser! He dips his wick and then leaves everything to his bastard daughter!" He gave twisted snort. "I wish I'd known! I could have got great mileage out of the snotty Mary over it!"

Mick made no comment on that. He always had great respect for Mary Cleary. She was a real lady. But that didn't stop him having great designs on her land.

"I wanted to talk to you about that," he said.

"What? Dan cutting me out?"

Mick threw him a sharp glance. He wasn't *that* drunk!

They let themselves into the cottage and Mick coughed at the smell. He could stick it long enough to get business done, he told himself. He was reluctant to sit anywhere, but if he wanted Christy's attention he had better not risk giving offence. He sat at the table. Christy sat heavily onto the wooden chair opposite, then slid his cap from his head and placed it carefully on the table, beside his arm.

Mick came straight to the point. "I was over by Daniel's place the other day." He waited for a response but there was none. Christy was waiting for whatever was coming next.

"I met the new occupants. Came as some surprise, that did. The spit of her father, she is."

The venom that spilled from Christy Cleary's mouth was vile. "I don't give a shit what she's like! I'd rather bleedin' guzzle them both!"

"And who could blame you?" Mick fed the other man's simmering anger. "Must be some shock all right. Have you seen the solicitor yet?"

A string of expletives gushed from Christy at the very thought of Patrick Cullen. "Fat lot of use it did me. The fucker told me I could see him in the courts if I like! Where would the likes of me get the money to do that, I ask you?"

"And if you lodge a claim against the estate?"

"He said Dan made a watertight will, a valid one, and I wouldn't be successful in changing it even *if* I had the money. They can prove she is his daughter, his next of kin as he puts it, so that's me out, money or no money." He spat on the floor in loathing.

Mick turned his head away momentarily.

"It sickens the pit of my stomach to see her get it. What I wouldn't do to get her out!"

"The thing is," Mick remarked, trying to sound as if the thought had only then occurred to him, "even if she was out, that doesn't mean it would go to you."

"I fuckin' know that!"

That surprised Mick. Our Christy wasn't as thick as people assumed.

"Do you think I'm bleedin' stupid?" Christy growled nastily. "She has the boy. Even *he* would come before *me*. Or she could sell it and I still wouldn't get a penny!"

Mick decided more sympathy would not go amiss here. "I can well understand how hard done by you feel. But there is a way that you could get something out of it."

He watched as the drink-sodden brain struggled to get his meaning, and failed.

"What you getting at?" The eyes narrowed to slits, suddenly more focussed than they had been all night.

Mick figured what he was about to say could go either way for him. If Christy felt he was being used – then that would be his plan down the tubes. So he prefaced his words carefully with some that he suggested Christy already knew.

"Well, you know, don't you, that I offered more than once to buy Dan out, after Mary died?"

Christy didn't know. That was news to him, but he did not want to admit it. "So? What if you did?"

"Well," Mick went on carefully as though they were hatching a plan together, "what if *I* was to buy her out? She's a jackeen. She would be better off back in the city. My guess is with a little persuasion she would be glad to sell up and clear out." He watched Christy's face closely. It was unreadable. "I could afford it," he went on carefully. "And when it's mine I would make it worth your while. A nice tidy sum to spend as you wish would be far better than having that house hang around your neck like a noose, wouldn't it? Property like that is more bother than it's worth if you don't have the finance for the upkeep."

He could almost hear the other man's brain jerking into action. Christy slumped his arms forward on the table, his keen eyes narrowed, his jaw worked wordlessly. He scrutinised Mick for what seemed like forever.

"What would you call a nice tidy sum?"

"Five thousand."

It was enough, Mick figured, to get him on board.

"Five." Christy was muttering to himself. "And what do you suppose I'd *do* exactly for five thousand, like?"

Mick had decided he didn't want to be specific. "You're a clever man," he said emphatically. "*You* think of something."

Christy eyed him suspiciously. The farmer sat there perched on the edge of the chair, his back straight and his hands in his lap. He would leave the cottage without actually having come into contact with anything. Christy despised him for his fastidiousness.

"And if I can manage it without getting *you* involved then better again, eh?" He watched as Mick shifted uncomfortably.

Mick Furlong was no fool, and he realised to take Christy for one would be a big mistake.

Christy wiped his hand across his dirty scalp. A nervous excitement caused perspiration to form on his upper lip. He wiped that also.

"You're done here," he said suddenly, holding out the hand. "Thanks for the lift."

He had his own thoughts on the matter but he wasn't going to share them with Furlong.

Mick had no choice. He gripped the sweaty hand for the briefest moment and stepped after Christy to the door, realising as the door closed behind him that he was unsure of exactly what the handshake was for. Was it agreement? Or a mocking thanks? With Christy you wouldn't know.

Chapter 20

"I'll never get the hang of this, Annie," Nancy lamented as she sat in the Ryans' front room, her new mobile phone in her hand. "I just can't get it into my head. I think I've done it wrong again!"

"Let me have a look. It's really simple, you know." Patiently Annie took the phone and deftly pressed a couple of buttons. "I'll write it down in sequence for you, if you like, Nancy. And you can have it on vibrate only, just in case it rings when *he's* around." She never referred to Paddy by name any more. Not since he had beaten Nancy up and thrown Angela and Thomas out. He was subhuman in her estimation, not deserving of identification. "There, I've put it on vibrate for you."

Nancy really wanted to get the hang of it, as she said. She badly needed more contact with Angela and Thomas. When Paddy was at work she would be able to have nice long conversations with them. When she last spoke to them she was unsure of how they were managing on their own. She was reluctant to ask too much, wounds were too raw, and she didn't want to upset them in the solicitor's office. Neither could she constantly be in Annie's house ringing them. Paddy had refused to replace the handset on the phone. There was badness in him that disgusted her. He never asked how they were, never referred to them, and wouldn't listen to any of her concerns about them. It was as if they never existed. The silence was almost the worst. With the lads gone to the States, and now Angela and Thomas gone also, Nancy spent long hours alone. It was never like that in her house before. Now the silence told her forcibly that they were going about their lives elsewhere, and that did not include her, and it left a gaping hole in her heart.

And yet silence had its good side too. Conversation between herself and Paddy was down to zero. It was amazing how two people could live in the same house without having to resort to addressing each other. It had quickly become obvious that less talk was a good sign. She felt increasingly afraid if Paddy was talking much. She had learned the signs fast, and on some days no matter which way she moved it was wrong. Yes, she learned, it was better when he was silent.

Silent days were the good ones. At such times she tried very hard not to allow the bad days to fill her thoughts. Today was a good day. She was as sure as she could be that Paddy had gone into work. She knew he did not always. He had missed a good few shifts in recent times. Spent them in the pub, and God knows where else.

But he was gone in today. And when he was "on days", she was free for hours.

She sat on Annie Ryan's sofa, concentrating so hard on her new mobile that for a time she forgot her troubles, and began to get the hang of it.

Annie watched her, and noticed the bruises on her arms that were fading, and the new ones that were coming up.

But Nancy was busy dialling.

Fact and rumour ran rife in and around D'Arcy Avenue in the wake of Angela and Thomas's expulsion. People had witnessed and heard the rumpus in the Brennan household. And they observed the fact that Nancy had become a virtual recluse.

Paddy was as much to blame for the stories that abounded as anyone. He was apt to talk too much while sitting over a pint, in response to commiserations from whosoever was seated next to him.

And others were only too eager to listen. Nothing so interesting had ever happened before around here, and everyone had something to say about it. Some said more than they heard. Some knew nothing at all except hearsay and had something to add anyway. This was too good not to have an opinion on it. The facts were lost in among all the goings-on, and the amount of land Angela inherited increased by the day. The size of the house also grew to the point where some said she was made up for life, and that Paddy had made a big mistake in throwing her out. There were those who secretly admired Nancy for her affair, and wished they'd had the chance themselves. To have had such a memory tucked away would have got them though many a tough patch.

Talk about Nancy was sometimes defensive and sometimes unkind, depending on the marital experience, good or bad, of those who couldn't keep their own counsel. No one mentioned anything to her directly when she ventured out to the shops, which wasn't too often. It was so difficult to venture out alone. And she was ashamed in case anyone might see any bruising. She had missed Mass a couple of times and that was a major worry to her. Then Annie Ryan suddenly "found" religion again and took up going to Sunday Mass with her. Nancy knew otherwise but said nothing, and with Annie by her side no one dared bother her or be heard to make any comment unless it was favourable.

Slappo Reilly brought as much gossip home to his own house as anyone. Stories about the "huge farm" and the "big house" and the "loadsa money" sailed around the table, till his mother, begrudging anyone such good fortune told him to shut it, and bade them good riddance.

"The likes of them brought a neighbourhood a bad name," she declared.

Her youngest clammed up but he missed Tomo. The little wimp looked up to him. Slappo missed that. He was able to boss him around and the poor sop went for it every time. It was no hardship giving him a go now and then on his horse if it kept him onside and Slappo had begun to realise he had his own personal gofer in Thomas.

To be the top of your gang, you needed your own runner, at least one, and Thomas had been just proving to be the natural choice.

Now, as Annie watched, Nancy put the phone to her ear, a look of excited expectation on her face.

"Angela! Oh, God, love, it's me. How are you? And Thomas?" A sob caught in her throat – she wasn't sure whether to laugh or cry at getting through. She settled on laughing, thrilled with herself that she had succeeded. "Yeah, I'm on my mobile! What do you make of that! I'm in Annie's. She's been showing me how to use it for ages!"

Annie got up and left Nancy to have her call in private. She went into the kitchen and put on a kettle for some tea. She could hear Nancy's excited voice, the laughing and out-pouring that had been building in her this past while. It would do her good to be able to talk like this. Annie didn't know how the woman was still sane. Or still alive. The crap she was taking from that bastard was unbelievable. Annie hoped *he* didn't find out about the mobile. She wouldn't put it past him to break it, or worse. She waited till the call ended before bringing in the tray.

Nancy was sitting looking at the phone in her hand, marvelling at the miracle of technology.

"They're fine," she gushed. "Oh thank God, I was so worried about them!"

Annie set the tray down, and poured two cups of tea. "Didn't I say they would be? Angela is well able to look after both of them."

"You would never have thought it if you'd seen her over in that house before," Nancy reflected, "and Thomas too. A walking disaster that child was. But I didn't tell you the good bit! Now that I have the phone we are going to arrange to meet!" Her smile clouded a bit. "Some day when I'm sure *he* is in work. We're going to meet in the shopping centre in Tallaght. It will be easy enough for both of us to get there, and afterwards they'll be able to get the bus straight back to Baltinglass from right outside."

Annie was glad to hear it. "Well then, the sooner you arrange it the better."

"And the boys," Nancy was saying happily. "They can ring me if they ever have a few bob. They're always short! And I'll be able to phone them too!"

And the Gardaí, Annie wanted to add, you'll be able to phone the Gardaí. But she could not impinge on her friend's happy moments – they were too few and far between these days.

Nancy kept the phone in the deep pocket of her apron, and wore the apron inside out. She knew now that her children were only on the other end of the line, and that made her feel a little less lonely, not so isolated and cut off. The little smile that hung about her face, only visible if one looked for it, was in danger of becoming a broad grin, and she would have to be careful not to let it escape when Paddy was around. No one had any right to have something to smile about if he had not.

Nancy always timed the dinner so that it was ready to be taken up as he arrived home. Any delay with it was likely to result in a backlash. Much the same happened if it was too long in the oven, and dried up because he was late.

And he was late. She worried and fretted over it and finally descended into fear.

And still he did not show.

In the local pub, down from the bus terminus at the end of D'Arcy Avenue, Paddy Brennan sat staring into his drink. He came in after work with a couple of other men, who had long since gone home. He was hungry, in spite of the drink, and he was at the crossroads of a decision. He wanted his dinner, and he wanted another drink, yet he knew if he ordered another, there would be no going home till closing time. He raised his head and caught the barman's eye. A simple lift of his index finger sealed the fate of the night. Customers had begun to fill the bar for their night out. The seats on either side of him were filled, each man settling down to a quiet drink and maybe a little chat with like-minded persons.

"There y'go!" The barman placed another one beside Paddy.

He paid for it and cast a bleary eye left and right. "Life's a bitch," he remarked audibly, to no one in particular.

The man sitting on his right stared at his own reflection in the mirror behind the bar.

"You too?" he said gloomily, without turning his head, and lifted his drink to his lips. Paddy did likewise. "You work your butt off for them and what thanks do you get?" But there was no answer to his question.

The other man looked at him for the first time, then supped his drink again. "Yeah, I know what you mean."

The two men sat in silence awhile supping their drinks, a feeling of solidarity beginning to manifest itself between them. Around them the bar became noisy as people began to loosen up and relax, but the two men were oblivious to all but their own problems.

"Your girl has one of Reilly's, am I right?" asked the man, unaware of the dangerous ground he was treading.

Coming from a stranger the directness of the question gave Paddy the option of telling him to mind his own fuckin' business. But there was a clear lack of personal effrontery in the tone. And Paddy's attention was immediately arrested by the numerical implication in the question. He turned his head and looked directly at the stranger. His face was familiar. He knew him vaguely, but only from seeing him around the area.

"What do you mean 'one' of Reilly's?" he asked.

The man seemed surprised. "Just that exactly, one of Reilly's."

"You mean there are others?" Paddy was incredulous.

It was the man's turn to be amazed. He turned in his seat to face Paddy, his openly honest face too surprised to be able to give offence. "You mean you didn't know? My God, man, Reilly would be afraid to throw a stone around here in case he hit one of his own!" He imparted the information with an equally fair dollop of sarcasm and distaste.

Paddy's incredulity knew no bounds. His pint sat on the bar, his hand closed around the base of the glass. In his total shock he momentarily forgot to raise it to his mouth, which was hanging stupidly open. Then it clamped tightly shut as his mind formulated a mental picture of the situation.

And it was even worse than he had previously thought. If Reilly were *that* attractive to the women, and for the life of him he couldn't see why, then it was ten times worse that his daughter would go and throw herself at him, like all the rest! Christ, he probably had a string of them ready to jump into bed with him, at any given time! Any time he got out of the nick most likely! And clearly it was during one of his "outs" that Angela threw herself at him, and in a house crowded with people and empty bedrooms only up the stairs, and she only fifteen! God, he was disgusted to the core! Technically, that was rape, but if she threw herself at him what judge could blame him?

An unctuous ball of disgust was formulating in Paddy's stomach. Old feelings of anger and repugnance were merging with this new devastating information. *She* was her mother's daughter to the core! What else could he expect? He twitched visibly on his stool. He consoled himself with the fact that he had done what any self-respecting man would do. He had rid himself of the little whore and her bastard. The fact that he now had all the space he wanted was neither here nor there. Houses were for families, big or small, but they had to *be* your family. Not someone else's bastard. Or someone else's whore!

"At least you don't have Reilly living in your house!" the man commented innocently.

"What are you talking about?" Paddy demanded, agitated at the very idea.

The other man didn't seem to notice the change in his manner. "My young one has two kids," he went on by way of explanation. "She was living with her 'partner'. A bloody no-gooder, I say! And then he goes and loses his job, and they can't pay the rent, so what do they do? Move back in with us – kids and all. You think you're bad, having *one* extra! I have the bleedin' lot of them and me the only one working. I'm here because there's no bloody room for me to sit down in my own sitting room when I've done me day's work!"

Paddy wasn't paying attention. He lifted his glass and emptied it in one go. He ordered another, and half-emptied that as soon as he got it. Anyone else's problems were minuscule compared to his. This fella rambling on beside him was lucky to be supporting his own. To spend your life working to support someone else's was a horse of a different colour altogether. To be taken for an ass twice over was more than a man should have to take. He emptied his glass.

The other man couldn't help commenting. "You got through that fairly quick."

Paddy slid unsteadily from his stool. The fledgling feeling of solidarity that had begun to knit the two men together had suddenly dissipated and Paddy turned on him.

"Mind your own fuckin' business!" he snapped, and began to push his way through the people as he headed for the loo.

"There's no call for that!" the offended man replied, but he was talking to himself. He shook his head, and then looked in hope at the man on the other side of him, wondering what the chances were there. Some minutes later he saw an obviously unsteady Paddy make his way to the main door. His face was dark and threatening, and the man gave a sympathetic thought to whatever unfortunate person might be at home waiting for him.

Chapter 21

At the oval mirror of her dressing table Angela sat putting the finishing touches to her make-up. She was very glad that her mother had thought to include it in the package she sent. It was good to be putting make-up on at all. It was like a means of preparation, and the longer she spent on it the more ready she felt for the table quiz. It would have been nice if her mam had included her perfume as well, but she was grateful to have clean clothes to go in, and she was glad her mam had put in her new silvery top and her heels. That surprised her. Her mam was such a practical person. Angela had expected only to find a change of track suit or the like in the package.

She had been surprised too to find Rose's husband was coming to collect her and Thomas, and even though she took her time at the mirror she did not want to keep him waiting. Thomas was ready. He had been ready for ages. She had been worried about him staying in Rose's, because it was somewhere unfamiliar, and she was afraid he might get all hyper and not behave himself. He'd said he was looking forward to being with Owen for a change, but he had reservations just the same. He was thinking that he never had a "culchie" for a friend before. There were none around D'Arcy Avenue and there were none that he knew of in his school. It sort of worried him a bit that Owen might not like him. His mother had said a million times how he was to behave himself, and he was to remember his manners, and he was not to be noisy, and not to stuff himself if they had any food, and no cursing, farting or anything like that. He had his Game Boy ready to take with him, and he watched with a mixture of eagerness and anxiousness for the car to arrive in the driveway.

Angela stepped into her heels. They felt strange after being so long in her trainers, but she drew herself up to her full height and eyed her reflection in the mirror.

In trousers, top and heels, and with her make-up on, she felt a thousand times better than she did in a track suit and trainers.

Thomas came into the room.

"Wow! Look at you, Ma! You look real cool."

She looked in the mirror again and hoped that she was not overdressed for a country table quiz. She had reservations too. She hadn't gone out all that much even at home, and she had no idea at all as to what the night would be like. On top of that she felt she would be the talking point of the evening. It made her even more nervous, so what had possessed her to agree to go?

"Really?" she replied. "Any sign of the car?" She tried not to sound *too* pleased with his reaction.

He looked out of the window.

"It's coming!"

"Jesus!" she exclaimed in a suddenly panicky voice, as she checked the mirror again.

"Listen to me, Tomo Brennan, you behave yourself in Rose's house, d'you hear?"

But he was already running down the stairs.

She grabbed her jacket and bag and ran after him, holding onto the handrail because of her high heels.

"Don't let me hear there was any problem, Tomo Brennan, I'm warning you!"

Thomas had grabbed his Game Boy from the kitchen table, and was crossing the hall to open the door. "There won't be!"

"There'd better not be!" she hissed through clenched teeth as he opened the door.

Just beyond the granite steps a beautiful deep-blue coloured BMW had slid to a halt, and a pleasant-looking middle-aged man got out. Leaving the car door open, he came towards them smiling. He held out his hand and shook Angela's vigorously.

"Angela, isn't it? Rose didn't tell me you were such a stunner! I'm Brian."

"Hello," she replied. "This is –"

"Thomas, no doubt," Brian turned to the boy, shook his hand equally vigorously and tousled his hair. "You're a fine chap, you are. Owen is looking forward to you coming over. His mother was telling him all about you."

"Yeah?" Thomas was chuffed. He was grinning all over his face.

"Are we ready?" Brian asked.

"Can I sit in the front?" Thomas wanted to know.

"Wanna drive?"

That stopped Thomas in his tracks for a second, and Angela thought she would like this funny man, and she relaxed immediately and sat in the back seat.

In no time at all they were at Rose's house, and once again Brian made the introductions. Orla looked like her father, and Angela was glad to note that she had the same relaxed manner, and was just as chatty.

Thomas vanished with Owen to his bedroom, and Angela got no opportunity to warn him again to behave himself.

When they arrived at the quiz venue she could not help feeling a little apprehensive. Quite a number of tables were already occupied, but a lot of people were still standing about talking, drinks in hand. A noticeable hush befell them as they saw who had come in with Rose and her daughter. Angela almost died. Orla, bless her, noticed the sudden tension in her, and linked her arm.

"You're socking it to them, Angela!" she muttered with glee in her voice. "I'm glad I'm with you – might get me noticed!"

A genuine amused laugh escaped Angela's lips, and the tension was broken, but before she could reply a familiar face came bearing down on them.

"Well, this is a pleasant surprise!" Seán Mulhearn stood before them. "Nice to see you again, Miss Cleary,

I'm Seán. Don't you have a first name?"

"Angela." She didn't correct him on the Cleary bit, and couldn't help thinking that he was not "backward about coming forward", as her mother would say.

"This town needs a bit of shaking up, Angela, and I reckon you're the very one to do it." He greeted Rose and Orla but he didn't take his eyes from Angela for long. "You *are* going to join *our* table, aren't you?"

"She is *not*, Seán Mulhearn," Orla protested, laughing. "She's on our team. We're going to beat your lot tonight! That will mean free drinks in your place for a fortnight!"

"If you score ahead of us," he grinned, "then you can *both* treat me to dinner by way of compensation at least, surely?"

His eyes held Angela's and she laughed outright. He seemed to be a likeable rogue. She was quite surprised that he would flirt like that in front of Rose but no one paid it the slightest bit of heed, other than to be amused. They turned to find their table, and saw that a woman was standing up across the room and waving at them.

"There's Maura, my sister – she has our table," Rose said and they made their way over.

Angela was introduced yet again. Maura had a small bakery near the bridge in town.

"Rose was telling me you were going to be the fourth person," Maura said. "We badly need an injection of fresh talent in this team."

Rose and Orla gave each other a look, pretending to be offended.

"I hope I don't let you down too badly," Angela managed a laugh.

"It's only a bit of craic," Orla said. "The last quiz we did was a disaster altogether! We came third last."

"We nearly got the booby prize!" Rose remembered.

Angela managed to feel a little better and decided she might as well relax and enjoy herself. It felt strange that there were no upsets attached to the evening out. If she were at home her father would be giving out about the money she spent, when she had so little to hand up. He would be on at her about the time she got home, and even what she wore. She could do nothing at home without incurring a litany of derisory remarks.

The population of Baltinglass in the hall had transferred their collective interest to the questions at hand, and the team at table number fifteen did the same. Rose had bemoaned the fact that they had no one who could tackle the sports questions, which, she said, put them at a decided disadvantage. They joked about who would be elected to go up to collect the booby prize!

But there was a surprise in store. Years of listening to her father and Finbar and Fergus discussing the sports on the telly and in the papers had its advantage, and Angela surprised herself at the information she had absorbed, and the amount of it she was able to recall.

At the halfway stage Seán Mulhearn appeared at their table with a round of drinks, and to discuss their respective scores, pointing out that his team was still ahead of theirs.

Maisie Mac arrived at their table next, selling raffle

tickets. Her hair was newly permed, temporarily taming the fuzz, and she wore her favourite blue blouse, with a cameo brooch at the neck. Maura complimented her on her appearance. Maisie seemed a little flushed, which surprised Rose, until she realised that Maisie had imbibed a little more than her customary glass of sherry.

Angela took two strips of tickets. "One for Thomas as well," she said. "Maybe we'll be lucky for a change."

"I would have thought your luck was very much *in*," Maisie remarked with a very sweet smile, as she handed Angela her change, and her tickets.

"Depends on how you look at it," Angela replied, without the slightest hint of a smile. Maisie sniffed and gathered up her books of tickets and her tin box of money, and moved herself on to the next table.

Orla smothered a laugh. "It's not often anyone silences Maisie Mac," she remarked.

The second half of the night got under way, and table fifteen was having great fun. They managed to secure themselves a much better position on the scoreboard than before, and they attributed it to the answers to the sports questions Angela had supplied. To cap it all, Angela had a ticket drawn in the raffle, and begged Orla to go up to collect it for her.

"What if there's a choice, what will I pick?" Orla wanted to know.

But there wasn't a choice. She was handed a voucher for Quinn's Supermarket.

"Fifty Euro! Wow! That will do nicely!" Angela exclaimed, thinking she could not have done better, since what she had spent on the evening's entertainment was money she could ill afford.

With the raffle over the night came to an end, and Angela headed for the loo. The others waited for her, wondering what could be keeping her so long. Then they noticed her talking to someone near the door.

"Who's that she is talking to, Orla?" Rose asked. "I can't see."

Orla strained her neck. "It's Francie Furlong."

Mother and daughter gave each other a knowing wink, but it was Maura who put their thoughts into words. "She has caught the eye of every available man here tonight, and why am I not surprised?"

She had *indeed* caught the eye of every man, available or otherwise, Rose had noticed, but there was no need to point that out.

On their way back to Rose's house Orla asked Angela if she had a date.

"No, I haven't!" Angela laughed. "What makes you say that?"

"Francie Furlong seemed mighty interested," Orla remarked, "and so did Seán Mulhearn. Are you saying neither of them asked?"

Angela's brow furrowed. That surname rang a bell. "He's a *Furlong*? Francie Furlong?" He had only introduced himself as Francie. "Is he Mick Furlong's son?"

"Yes," Orla was surprised. "You met his father already? But of course you would have – you're neighbours, after all."

Angela mentioned that Thomas had met him in the fields, and that he had called to the house. She said nothing about his suggestion to buy her out. Patrick might have mentioned it to Rose, but she was pretty sure that Rose would not mention it outside the office. Was it a coincidence that his son had introduced himself to her tonight? He was a very attractive young man, but why did he just introduce himself as Francie? Perhaps there was nothing in it. She decided to put it out of her head.

Thomas and Owen were wide awake when they reached Rose's house, and the story of the improvement on the last quiz performance had to be told and credit was laid firmly at Angela's feet, in spite of her protestations.

By the time Brian had driven them home Angela was ready for her bed. The few drinks she'd had were taking their effect, it being quite a while since she had any at all. Thomas objected to having to go to bed. Even though it was hours past his bedtime, he declared he was not even a little bit tired. But he went to his room and got into his pyjamas. His mother bid him goodnight, and switched off his light, and pretty soon her light was out also, and Thomas knew she was sound asleep.

But *he* could not sleep. His head was full of the great night he and Owen had. He got out of bed and went over to the window, and sat on the chair there with his elbows resting on the sill, and his face cupped in his hands. He had become used to the darkness of the country at night, and the sounds of the house that had scared him in the beginning. He gazed out the window, and his eyes adjusted to the dark. He watched as clouds scurried across the moon, and saw how the surface of the river shone silvery with the moonlight on it. When the clouds permitted it he could make out the shapes of the cattle over in the field, and he thought how well it was for them, because they could stay out all night and didn't have to try to sleep when they were not tired. He'd had such a great night in Owen's house. Owen had a PlayStation and they played games as long as they liked. His father didn't seem to mind, as long as they didn't get *too* noisy. There was no shouting at them, no telling them to shut up, or telling them to go back up to the bedroom. Owen was even allowed to make popcorn, and his father wanted some as well. It was brilliant. Thomas couldn't remember ever having had such a good time before. In his mind he hoped his mother would go out more often and then he could go to Owen's. Then he felt bad. She was much better to him here than she had been in D'Arcy Avenue. She talked to him more. She even asked him to do some things that before she would have told him he would only mess up. It was seldom he thought about D'Arcy Avenue now. It seemed like ages ago that he'd lived there. If he thought of it, it was usually to do with his nan.

But they would be going to see her soon, his mother said. He was happy about that.

He wished she could come here and see the house, and spend some time with them. He decided he would ask her that when he saw her. He hoped that she wouldn't mind that he liked it better here. He thought his mother did too. But she wouldn't let on. *She* had no one always giving out to her either, and at times he actually saw a smile on her face. That never happened before. She had always been worried then. She didn't say, but he thought she liked being with him sometimes. It seemed like it.

He yawned and pulled the sleeves of his pyjamas as far as he could over his hands. He was getting cold. His bed was looking very inviting. He yawned again and just as he was about to leave the window something caught his eye. Or did it?

He thought he had seen movement by the hedge! There were no animals this side of the hedge, so what had moved? He looked harder. He watched for the slightest movement. It was a fairly calm night, and he was sure it had not been caused by the wind. He found he was holding his breath in suspense. He breathed out heavily.

There! There it was again!

But the window had fogged up with his breath, and suddenly he couldn't see out. He had to use his pyjama sleeve to clear it. He did it very fast, but whatever he had seen was gone. It had seemed too tall to be an animal, but what reason would any person have to be rambling about in the dark, on *their* land, and anyway he had not got a good enough look. He sat and waited till it showed itself again. He watched for a long time, worried that there was *something* out there, but the night clouded over with thick unbroken cloud, and made it impossible for him to see. Eventually he just *had* to give up, and he climbed gladly into his bed, and fell asleep immediately.

But his sleep was disturbed, and he dreamed that his Granda Brennan had come looking for him. But Thomas hid and he could not find him, and so he plodded about outside in the dark, searching for the way out of the field, while Thomas watched silently from his window. Although Thomas feared that his granda might look up and see him, he found he was unable to move and so he could not protect himself by moving away from the window and out of sight.

The dream stayed with him when he woke, and he sat at the breakfast table with his head resting on one hand, while he stirred his cereal listlessly with his spoon. There was no evidence of the chatty form his mother had been in last night. She sat opposite him at the table, her face was very pale and her mascara, which she had neglected to remove, smudged down beneath her eyes. Her elbows rested on the table and she held a mug of tea to her lips. A slice of toast lay untouched on the plate before her.

"Eat it," she said flatly, indicating his bowl, "we can't afford to waste it."

He stirred it a little more purposefully, and even lifted a spoonful, but he still didn't actually put any in his mouth.

"What's up with you?" she asked. "Don't start getting picky on me – I fuckin' couldn't cope with that all over again."

He put the spoonful in his mouth and swallowed, just to keep her happy. He knew it was probably not the best time, but he absolutely had to ask his question.

"Does Granda Brennan know where we are, Ma?"

She put her mug down rather suddenly. The frown on her brow deepened. "Why?"

"I was wondering, if he got the bus down here, would he be able to find us?"

It had not occurred to her at all, but now that he had asked she suddenly felt less safe.

What was to stop him coming down? But then, what reason was there to bring him here? Surely the less he saw of them, the better he would like it? She knew straight away that she certainly did not wish to see him. She looked closely at Thomas.

"What brought this on? Did something happen in Owen's last night? Was something said?"

"No."

"Well, what then?"

Thomas told her about his dream.

But he did not connect it to the shape he thought he saw outside his window last night. He was more worried that his granda would find him, and . . . and . . . he didn't know what the "and" would be, but he was sure that he wouldn't like it.

Angela had not seen him so concerned about anything recently. The difference in him of late was great to see. She could talk to him now, and she did – sometimes anyway. He was actually company, and he was always willing to help. It occurred to her as well that there was no shouting going on these days. Well, very little by comparison.

But as she looked at him now she saw the old

Thomas, and it shocked her. He needed reassurance. So did she, and suddenly it struck her that it was up to her to reassure them both.

"I don't think he could find us," she lied. "Sure why would he bother? He wanted to be rid of us, didn't he? It wouldn't make any sense for him to come looking for us, now would it?"

He looked up hopefully. "You really think so?"

"Of course I do. Anyway," she added with an air of importance which she hoped would work, "this is *our* house, and we just wouldn't let him in!"

"Yeah!" He laughed suddenly, relief sweeping over him. He hadn't thought of it that way. Imagine saying to Granda Brennan that he couldn't come in! Cool!

With his appetite renewed he started to shovel the soggy cereal into his mouth.

"Want that toast?" he asked.

She pushed the plate towards him, and watched as the toast vanished too.

In no time at all he was finished at the table, and he jumped from his chair, eager to get outside to see what he could find to do. Everything about the place enthralled him and absorbed him for hours on end. This morning he had a plan. He was going to take a good look about the barn and also see if he could get up into the loft. It was very inviting but there was no ladder.

"I'm going to have a look in the barn, Ma," he called back, before he disappeared out of earshot.

Angela sat at the deserted table, half a cup of tea in front of her, picking bits of mascara from her eyelashes, flicking them away, and wondering vaguely what *she* was going to do. Last night had been great. It had been so good to spend time in adult company, as an equal. It was company with very mixed ages, young and old. That in itself was different. And no one minded or thought it weird. She had liked that. In Dublin people her age never went to a venue where their mothers and fathers were likely to be as well.

To have been part of the craic, part of a team, and accepted as she was, was a new experience to her. When her answers were accepted without question she found herself briefly surprised they didn't contradict her, or ask how the hell did *she* know that. It felt really good.

It didn't hurt either that she had drawn the attention of two of the most eligible men in the town.

But she felt strangely indifferent about that and, equally strangely, she did not wish to examine why. Orla had been quite excited by the fact that her new friend had attracted so much notice from the most eligible Baltinglass had to offer. She didn't understand Angela's apparent laid-back reaction to it. Angela didn't either, but it was not of such major significance to her as it seemed to be with Orla. Orla decided that her apparent lack of interest was what had drawn the attentions of these two eminently desirable men.

Yes, it had been good.

But she wasn't feeling so good now.

She was a bit disturbed at Thomas being so worried about his granda showing up. She fervently hoped she was right about him not having any interest in coming down to see them. She knew well he would not have any difficulty in finding them if he arrived in the town on the bus.

But why would he bother?

He had slung them out in no uncertain terms, shouting that they were never coming back, that they no longer had a home there. From talking to her mother she knew Paddy was still of the same mind.

The horror of that morning flooded back at the slightest thought. The desperation and screams of her mother. Her face covered in blood, picking herself up shakily from the floor. Thomas's vain attempt to scramble out of his granda's way. Paddy had hit him before, that wasn't the first, but this was different. This was savage.

Angela had been sickened. Before she would have convinced herself that he deserved it, and turned a blind eye. But watching in terror that morning she knew well that this was something else. This was years of pent-up hatred and loathing being vented on a child. The viciousness was dreadful to watch. She saw it as if it was in slow motion, every movement etched onto her brain. And then he had grabbed her. Her hand went unconsciously to her hair and she felt again the wrench as Paddy's fist entangled itself in it and dragged her about. The stinging from the wallop he had landed on her face and the snap of her head back and forth were suddenly all too real once more, and she knew with the utmost certainty that if she never laid eyes on him again it would be too soon.

But if he knocked on her door? What then?

Would she be strong enough to stand up to him? Would she do as she had told Thomas and not let him in? No. She didn't think she would. She was quite sure the sight of him would strike fear in her, and that fear would make her weak just as it had always weakened her and made her unable to stand up to him. And she would not be able to protect herself or Thomas now any more than she was able to that awful morning. Years of Paddy's rejection had done that to her. All that time wanting him to see she was still the child he had loved so much. She thought of the constant barrage of insults that poured from him at every opportunity and realised that he had undermined her confidence with every word, constantly chipping away at her till she was as useless as he was forever saying.

Paddy had done more than reject her. He had caused her to reject herself.

No. She did not want to see him at her door. And no, she did not want to have to relive that morning ever again. She wanted Paddy Brennan out of her mind once and for all. Thomas had gone out into the fields, happy that she would keep Paddy away from him. She hoped to God she never had to try.

She wondered what he was getting up to. She half thought about getting out of her pyjamas, putting on some clothes, and going out to find him.

She pulled at her mascara again and got two loose eyelashes with it.

"You're coming asunder," she told herself. "Get up and get some clothes on before you fuckin' fall apart."

Chapter 22

Thomas skipped and hopped all the way across the yard towards the outhouses, like a child who had not a care in the world. And at that moment that was exactly the way he felt. He need have no worry of being found by Granda Brennan, because they simply would not let him in. He was safe again. Even though he could not name the feelings of oppression that had returned briefly, he was very much aware that it was gone again, and his young shoulders were wonderfully free of the weight.

He headed straight for the barn, and stood looking in for a minute, his small frame outlined by the huge doorway. He stepped into the cool shade and the pleasant smell of hay filled his nostrils. Bales of it were stacked all over the place and Thomas was able to jump from one to the other, which he spent some time doing, before the stable area caught his attention.

It had fallen into disrepair through lack of use. There were two wooden stalls, both doors was missing and the hay basket was on the floor. Some of the wooden panels needed replacing. There was some tack hanging on the wall opposite and an old saddle covered in mildew sat astride a saddle-rack beneath it.

Thomas was thrilled to be standing in a real stable – to him it was a magical place. He convinced himself that he could smell the horses, and the dung. He knew well how they smelled from D'Arcy Avenue. He climbed up the timbers like a ladder, threw one leg over the top and imagined himself on a horse like he used to be at home. Then he climbed down and took the slippery mildewed reins from their hook on the wall. He got back on his imaginary horse, and fixed the reins around the end post and then he set off at a gallop, across endless fields, urging his magnificent mount to greater and greater speeds. He called on his fellow riders to follow him, to race with him across the vast open spaces. Lost in his world of play he did not stop till a loud "Whoa, boy!" caused him to rein in and halt his gallop.

He stared in surprise at the figure of Seán Mulhearn, leaning against the jamb of the barn door.

"Any spare horses, Thomas?" he asked, trying to be serious. "Had to shoot mine, went lame."

Thomas laughed and jumped down from his "horse". He recognised the barman.

"Hi'ya, mister! How did you know my name?" He scrambled onto a bale of hay as he spoke, and brushed some of the loose bits of it from the front of his clothes.

"I met your mother at the quiz last night. I asked her."

"Yeah? So what's *your* name, then?"

"Seán."

"So, did you come out to see me ma? She's in the house."

The information was offered totally without guile, and Seán admired the boy's forthrightness. He remembered his last encounter with Thomas, and he decided for the moment to avoid answering the question. He stayed with the theme of Thomas's game.

"I heard all the whoopin' and stampedin' around here and came right in. Thought you might need an extra hand with the herd."

Thomas liked the barman. He liked the way he talked and joked with him. He didn't make him feel like a "bloody nuisance".

He hopped down from the bale of hay, and it wobbled with the sudden movement, causing Seán to issue a warning.

"Take it easy there, Thomas, those bales look like they were just flung there, like they were stacked in a hurry. They could topple."

Thomas stood still while he looked upwards towards the loft. "I'd like to get up there and see what it's like."

Seán's eyes followed the boy's. There were some bales up there too, but he could see that the wooden floor of the loft had some planking missing.

"It might not be safe – look!" he said, drawing the boy's attention to the missing timbers.

Even as he spoke he knew that Thomas was going to get himself into the loft anyway, sooner or later. The place was like a magnet to him. That was boys for you,

Seán thought, but he could be putting himself in real danger.

"I'd only walk on the good ones." In his ignorance Thomas was quite confident.

But Seán was concerned. He sat on the bale beside the boy, and they both looked upwards. Thomas was assessing how best to reach the loft, and Seán was wondering when someone had last stood up there. It was not terribly high as lofts go, and the bales up there looked as though they had somehow been thrown up.

It could easily be reached with a ladder, but there wasn't one, and Thomas was thinking that he could use the nearby bales and simply climb up them.

"I'll tell you what," Seán said, and was about to continue when an owl swooped into the barn and immediately flew up to the roof to where its nest was located.

"Wow!" Thomas cried. "Did you see that? I never even heard him!"

Seán put a finger to his lips, and Thomas instantly fell silent, his mouth agape as he watched for more activity above.

"A barn owl," Seán informed him. "They make no sound when they fly. Has his nest way up there in the rafters. See it? There!" He pointed. "Keeps the place free of rats and mice – they feed on them, you know. A handy fellow to have around."

"I thought owls only fly at night?" Thomas was amazed.

"No, they fly anytime, but they can hunt at night too, because of their great eyesight."

"What were you going to say before he flew in?" Thomas asked, picking a long piece of hay from the bale and wrapping it around his finger as he looked up towards the roof for more action.

Seán swiped at the bits of hay that were stuck to his trousers. "I was going to say I want you to promise not to get up there before it's checked out for safety. I could check it out myself as soon as I have time. But not now – I have to get to work in a while..."

"Would your boss mind if you were late?" Thomas interrupted.

"I *am* the boss," he laughed, "but my customers would mind, I'd say!"

Thomas stared at him in surprise. "You *own* that pub? Cool! You must be real rich!"

Seán couldn't help smiling. "Well, as I was saying, don't go up there till that floor is checked out, okay? I'll do it for you, if your mother doesn't mind."

"If his mother doesn't mind what?"

Angela had appeared at the doorway, and she was very surprised to see her son and Seán Mulhearn sitting chatting together on a bale of hay.

Thomas was impressed with the way Seán immediately jumped to his feet.

Seán felt a little stuck for words, caught as he was in Angela's barn, without first having made his presence known to her. But he covered it nicely with a big smile at the sight of her.

Angela stayed by the door – the smell of the hay was not very appealing to her. Bales of the stuff against the walls like this was *too* much country smell altogether!

"Good morning, Angela, I was just about to knock at the house, but I got a bit side-tracked with Thomas here."

"Morning, Seán." She was inwardly thanking her lucky stars that she had not come out to the barn in her pyjamas! The barman looked so very comfortable there sitting with Thomas that a stranger would have to be forgiven for taking them for father and son, and the thought shocked Angela. She wondered what age Seán Mulhearn was. His fair hair was thinning at the front, but she knew that was no indication of any great age – he might only be six or seven years older than she. "What was it you hope I wouldn't mind?"

Seán explained that he thought the loft should be checked for safety before Thomas went climbing up there, and offered to do it if she didn't mind.

She looked up. "You're not going up there!" she told Thomas in no uncertain terms, looking up through the holes in the floor. "It's too dangerous!"

"But Seán said he could sort it out, Ma!"

She glared at Seán, annoyed that he was getting her into what she felt was a "situation".

Seán understood her annoyance. "Only if you *absolutely* don't mind," he insisted as he walked towards her. "It would be no problem, it wouldn't take much to fix, and Thomas was talking about going up there as it is."

She was silent.

"It's none of my business," he admitted, beginning to

feel he shouldn't have said anything about it at all, "but I was afraid he might hurt himself with that flooring the way it is."

"I appreciate your concern, thanks," she smiled, "but I wouldn't want you to feel obliged or anything."

"I don't. I would actually enjoy it. I enjoy a bit of DIY now and again. I don't get much time for it behind the bar."

"Well, if you *really* don't mind, then I don't mind."

"Good then. That's settled. I have some free time this afternoon. I'll bring a few tools, check it out then, okay?"

She nodded. Seán insisted that Thomas promise he wouldn't go up there till it was done. Thomas made a solemn promise by wetting his finger and making a cross upon his neck. They walked out into the sunlight, leaving Thomas playing in the barn. But he watched as they rambled back towards the house together.

Seán Mulhearn fancies me ma, he thought. And imagine him actually *owning* that place! Wow!

Chapter 23

The buses from Baltinglass to Dublin were not all that frequent, and Angela was afraid they would miss it and her mother would have gone all the way to Tallaght for nothing.

"For fuck sake, Tomo Brennan! What the fuck is bleedin' keeping you?" she roared up the stairs for the third time.

Suddenly she wondered if he was up there at all. If he was over in that bloody loft again she would swing for him. Ever since Seán Mulhearn fixed the loft floor Tomo spent a lot of his time there. If he wasn't sitting watching the fuckin' nest in the rafters, he was watching out the tiny loft window. He said he could see everywhere from that window. He *knew* they were meeting his nan today, and he was holding them up!

She was just about to go out and check the loft when she heard running feet on the landing above her head. Thomas came sliding down the banisters, and landed on his feet in the hall. He always slid down the stairs like that and he had perfected the art of landing upright. His mother tutted in annoyance at the smug smile on his face and ordered him out the front door before her.

"I had to go the toilet," he declared "I was dying to do a –"

"I don't want to hear it," she interrupted quickly, "just get going. The bus won't wait for us, you know."

She was so looking forward to seeing her mother. They had arranged to meet in The Square in Tallaght because Nancy said it was easier than either of them having to do the entire journey. The truth was that she did not dare be out when Paddy got home. She was okay today till at least five thirty, but if she went all the way to Baltinglass, as she would have preferred, she risked trouble if she was home late. Angela agreed to the arrangement without question, but thought to herself how much she would have liked Nancy to come down to the house for the visit. She had hoped she would, that would have been nice, but Nancy seemed reluctant, and Angela did not push it.

Angela followed Thomas as he walked ahead of her on the road. They had become so used to the walk into the town. Usually it was relaxed and unhurried, but today Angela was anxious that they make that bus. She went on at him any time he ran up on a ditch or stopped at a gate or to listen to the various calls of the birds. He could identify most of them now, and did, but Angela declared it was only holding them up.

A horn suddenly honked behind them, and a black Land Rover jeep pulled up alongside.

Francie Furlong was at the wheel.

"Hi, Angela! Want a lift? Going into town?"

He looked gorgeous, and smiled broadly at her, and Angela beamed a smile in return.

"Yes, thanks!" she said, almost unable to believe her luck. "We are."

Thomas came towards the car, but one look from his mother stopped him from asking to travel in the front seat.

Francie opened the rear door. "Hop in," he said, and waited while they both settled themselves in the back.

Angela was disappointed. She would have preferred the front. It was a little awkward making conversation from the back seat.

Thomas sat and scowled. Francie Furlong had not even greeted him, nor did he acknowledge his presence, and his mother was all chat to him as if he was the greatest thing since sliced pan!

"I'm going into Dublin," Francie happened to say.

"Are you?" Angela replied, thinking what a stroke of luck. "We're going as far as Tallaght ourselves, I'm meeting my mother at The Square."

She waited for the expected offer to drive them that far and, sure enough, it came. Thomas would have preferred to travel on the bus. At least he would not have to listen to his mother gush all over this creep! He had never seen her smile so much. She was being so awfully nice that he almost didn't recognise her. She ignored his presence, as did Francie, and he could do nothing but sit and watch out the window as the jeep turned the corner into the town.

People were queuing at the bus stop, and the incoming passengers were alighting from the bus. Angela was thinking that the bus would remain at the terminus for a short while before leaving again for Dublin. Even so, if they had not got a lift they would have only just about made it, with no time to spare. She noticed a passenger with long straight hair waiting near the bus. It was her expensive clothes that caught Angela's eye. The black leather trousers alone must have cost an arm and a leg. Francie pulled in to the side of the road a little behind the bus, and the girl waved cheerily at him, lifted her bag and came towards the jeep. He leaned over and opened the front passenger door. The way they greeted each other told Angela they knew each other well.

Francie introduced her. Just about. "This is Clodagh," he said, and left it at that.

The two women eyed each other critically, and neither one went overboard greeting the other.

Thomas felt invisible, and scowled all the more. Getting a go in this cool jeep was suddenly very un-cool, even though he could see over all the hedges, and he wished all the more that they were on the bus.

Angela understood then why neither she nor Thomas had been invited to sit in the front. Clearly, it was being reserved for this newest passenger.

Clodagh decided to ignore this intruder in the back seat as best she could, and she was very good at it. Francie chatted to both of them, blissfully unaware of the coolness between his passengers.

Nobody spoke to Thomas. He wondered if this

Clodagh was Francie's girlfriend or what? He didn't like the smell of her perfume, and it wafted up his nose all the time. He tried holding his breath so that he wouldn't have to get the smell, but he could only manage that for very short spells, and then he had to take in big gulps of air, and that made it worse.

Clodagh chatted to Francie about things that gave Angela no opportunity to join in. They seemed to have an intimacy that automatically excluded her, and she began to wish she was on the bus.

But they were making good time. Francie liked to drive his jeep fast, and used its four-wheel-drive facility to its best advantage, especially on the curves. Thomas held on to the edge of his seat to steady himself. He had not spoken a word since getting in, and now he didn't like the feeling that persisted in his stomach.

Francie suddenly raised his voice and called back to Thomas. "You're very quiet for a young fella, aren't you?"

Silence fell while the others adjusted their thinking to the fact that a child was being addressed.

"I feel sick," Thomas said faintly.

The mood in the car changed quickly. Francie was almost sorry he had asked, as if asking had triggered the sick feeling. Thomas was seated behind Clodagh and she involuntarily moved forward in her seat, as if she was trying to put herself out of the firing line.

Angela was dismayed. Trust Tomo Brennan to put the kibosh on it altogether. She turned and glared at him, and was about to tell him he was imagining it, but the ashen colour of his face changed her words completely.

"Don't you do it in the car!" she warned him.

"It's coming, Ma," Thomas whispered pathetically, doing his utmost to hold on to it.

They heard the screech of brakes, and the sudden stop caused the unprepared Angela to hit her head against the headrest in front. But no one noticed. They were more concerned that Thomas be got out of the car before he showered them with the contents of his stomach. Angela got out with him.

Francie and Clodagh stayed in the car, doors and windows closed, trying hard to pretend everything was fine.

"For fuck sake, Tomo, what the bloody hell is up with you?" his frustrated mother asked. "Could you not be normal for once?"

Thomas spat, and wiped his mouth with the crumpled-up tissue she gave him. "I was okay till *she* got in!" His voice was a little stronger now. "It's the smell of her perfume that's making me sick."

Angela never heard the likes of it. "That's fuckin' stupid. You're getting to be a real puker, you are!"

He wasn't, and his ma saying so wasn't fair, but he was in no state to argue.

She threw the tissue into the hedge. "Are you finished now?"

His face had a little more colour in it, and he nodded his head. They went back to the jeep and opened the door.

Clodagh was positively hostile. "Perhaps you'd be better off to wait for the bus," she suggested hopefully.

"We could drop you at the next stop."

It sounded like the best idea Thomas had heard since the jeep had pulled up in the first place, but Francie thought otherwise.

"We're nearly at The Square – another five or ten minutes should do it," he said, putting the jeep into gear. "We'll take it easy." He moved off again and kept the speed down.

Sitting with the window open, Thomas was grateful for the consideration, and Angela was delighted that Clodagh's suggestion had been squashed. The mood between the two of them was now unsalvageable.

"Children!" Clodagh sighed, supposedly to herself. "Soul-destroying!"

Angela would have loved to get a grip on that long hair, which Clodagh kept tossing to great effect, and pull the hell out of it, but she chatted instead to Francie, thereby irritating the front-seat passenger all the more. A few minutes later the jeep stopped at The Square and Thomas was already opening the door.

"Thanks for the lift," Angela said to Francie while she ignored Clodagh.

Francie turned in his seat. "Hope the lad is okay," he smiled. He had such a gorgeous smile. "You going to the dance next Friday?"

"Dance?" That was the first she had heard of a dance.

"Stratford Arms," he said, "fund-raiser for the amateur dramatics."

Angela flashed Francie her most intriguing smile, while wondering if the haughty Clodagh, who was busy trying to kill her with a look, would be going also.

"Oh, yes, that one – haven't decided yet," she replied, trying to sound like she had other interesting options.

He simply winked at her, and she had no more excuse to hold the door open. The jeep moved off, and she followed Thomas towards the main entrance, her spirits restored by that one devilish wink.

Chapter 24

They were early, but Nancy was already waiting for them. Thomas spotted her first.

"Nan!" he yelled, running towards her. "Nan!"

She saw him immediately, and quickly put down the bags she was carrying, a huge smile on her face, her eyes brimming with unshed tears of joy, as she stretched out her arms. Thomas cared not one jot about anyone seeing him run into them.

"Oh my God! Look at you! I swear you've grown!" Nancy gushed.

They hugged each other tightly as Angela came up to them. She realised she was actually nervous meeting her mother again. After all that had transpired she now became aware of a new dimension to their mother-daughter relationship. For the first time in her life she had been coping without Nancy, and she also had knowledge of her mother as an individual person, with a life prior to theirs. Now, as they embraced, she was glad to find their relationship was untouched. It was still as warm and welcoming and comforting as always. But now it was also woman to woman.

"You're different, love," Nancy observed. "I hope it's a good difference."

They laughed and the tension was broken.

Angela eyed her mother closely. "You look well, Ma, but how have you been? I've been so worried about you."

"That's definitely a change! Those used to be my lines!" Nancy laughed. "Here, love, take this bag before I forget. There are a few things in it you probably could do with."

They went into McDonald's and Thomas had a large Coke and a burger, his earlier sickness now forgotten. His nan was here, and all was well with his world.

Nancy stirred her tea, soaking in the wonderful sight of her daughter and grandson actually sitting at the same table as her. She had missed them sorely, but until now she had not known how much. She needed contact with her family – it was as precious as a lifeline to her.

Thomas was bursting with news, trying to tell it all at once. He told her about the house, how scary it was at first, and about the river nearby, and about the land and how much there was to play on, and the cattle and sheep in fields around, and *everything*.

Nancy told him he was sounding like a farmer!

"I know," he laughed, delighted with her assessment.

Angela was noting how much care her mother had taken with her appearance. She couldn't help wondering how much of it might be camouflage. She didn't know how to approach asking how things were with Paddy since the day he threw them out, so she remarked positively on her hair instead.

"You coloured your hair, Ma. It looks terrific. Younger."

"You think so?" Nancy was pleased. "Thanks. I got it done early this morning, got a bit of a colour in. You know like, hide the grey and all. Hair and Beauty – you know, that place in Glasnevin where Annie Ryan's daughter goes? She always says they're very good. I badly needed a decent job done on it. They persuaded me about the colour."

"Looks great," Angela said, "takes years off you. Has Da seen it yet?"

Nancy lifted her plastic cup of tea, but didn't sip it. She hesitated with her response. She was sure he wouldn't like it. He didn't like anything these days.

Angela read the hesitation accurately. "That bad? Hasn't he calmed down, come to terms, or anything?"

"It's difficult for him, love. It was all a very great shock . . ."

They fell into a subdued silence at the very mention of the recent events and Thomas moved away from the table now that he had consumed his burger and Coke – he didn't want to listen to talk about his granda anyway. He began sliding back and forth on the low wall of a raised planted area, ducking his head each time he came to the low-lying fronds of the palms.

Up until then Nancy and Angela had skirted the serious issues, talked of trivial things. Bringing it into the open and talking about it was very sobering and Nancy sighed heavily. This was all her fault. She had triggered this mess all those years ago.

If only she could have known! But would it have made any difference? Would it have stopped her and Daniel from being together? She knew it would not. They convinced themselves very easily that no one would be hurt – if they had given consequences the merest thought, and as she remembered it they had not. No one would know. But they could not have known what lay ahead for them, or how their futures would be. If Daniel and his wife could have had children there would have been no problem. He would have left his property to them. His interest in Angela might not have been so important to him. Indeed, he might have even preferred no contact at all, in an effort to safeguard his own family. She looked at her daughter, struggling to cope with a very difficult situation, and felt very guilty and contrite.

"I'm so sorry, love – I did this to you too – it wasn't only Paddy. If I . . . if I hadn't been . . . with Daniel . . ." There was a long pause.

"That wouldn't have stopped Reilly, Ma, and that was what Paddy was furious about," Angela reminded her softly. "That was what brought him home from work that morning."

Nancy nodded quietly. She took a deep breath and went on in a hesitant voice, "I was nervous coming down to see you. I was afraid you would blame me and not want to see me . . . I was afraid you would think little of me, be ashamed of me and . . ."

Angela couldn't watch this, her mother in such a quandary about seeing her. She was immediately at pains to reassure her. "Ma! Stop, will you? Honest to God, I don't think anything of the sort. I mean yes, it was a shock that my sensible, steady mother had such a secret, a wild side to her. I still can hardly believe any of it! But I don't *blame* you. I mean, it was Daniel too . . . but I don't see it as *blaming* anyone. Okay, I admit I was gobsmacked that Paddy wasn't my da. But he treated us all so badly, from when *I* was pregnant, and he didn't even know then. If he had been different then things wouldn't *be* like this."

Nancy smiled ruefully. How she had changed from the impulsive, full-of-life young girl she used to be! Now she was paying for her . . . transgression, and so was her beloved family.

"No, he didn't know then, but in a way I knew how he would be. That was why I put my foot down when he was insisting you have the . . ." She couldn't make herself say "abortion", but Angela knew what she meant. "When I was expecting you, I was so worried about 'what ifs'. It was a different time then, and that particular – sin – was the unforgivable one. If Paddy had found out my marriage would certainly have been over, and I would have been a separated woman expecting another man's child. The worst situation on the planet to be in! Like you, I had a pregnancy that was shrouded in worry and fear. It might seem like a contradiction but I loved him and I didn't want that. Neither of us was that long married. Daniel didn't want his marriage over

243

either. He was longer married than me, and so far there were no children – that was why he wanted to be kept informed about you. So we ended it, and I hoped and prayed it would go all right for me. It couldn't have gone better, Paddy never suspected a thing. It seemed like I got clean away with it. I felt I didn't deserve that. I was guilty. But *you* were innocent. Later, when you were pregnant, I knew he was going to make you pay big-time for your situation and I could do no less than support you as best I could. I hoped in some small way it would make up to you for my . . . for Paddy not being your father, even though I still hoped you'd never find out. I was still too afraid of the consequences. I always knew that Paddy wouldn't be able to deal with it."

It was a weight she had carried in her heart forever. Always she had to be on her guard, always afraid the tiniest slip would begin to unravel her secret. It had been difficult. At times she had wondered if it would have been different without the constraints of the guilt. To what degree had that put its own cost on her relationship with Paddy? Did he always sense something he could not articulate? Was that why he was the way he was? Yes, it was her fault. She sighed a long heavy sigh. It had been difficult, but she'd just had to get it out and make things all right with Angela. She couldn't live if things were not "fixed" with her precious daughter.

Angela could see that this confession had been terribly difficult for her mother, and yet she knew she had needed so much to say it.

"Ma, will you give over? I couldn't have better than

you. I never would have got through without you, you've been the best. I don't hold *anything* against you, and I worry so much about you now. I don't like you being there all on your own with *him* – he'll keep making you pay, I know it."

It was ridiculous, Nancy thought – such a traumatic moment in both their lives and they had to talk it through sitting in the very public setting of Tallaght Shopping Centre!

She looked lovingly at her daughter, grateful for her understanding, her acceptance. She reached across the table and squeezed her hand firmly, the grip saying it all. "Paddy feels betrayed," she said quietly, "he's having a hard time . . ."

Angela, in turn, placed her hand over her mother's and returned the grip. "Don't make excuses for him, Ma," she urged strongly, and was surprised to see her mother wince. She looked down and saw the bruising on her wrist. Nancy pulled her hand away, but too late. Angela was horrified. "Oh my God! The fuckin' bastard! He's still at *that*? Ma, you can't stay there! Come back with us, please, there's plenty of room!"

"I can't, Angela," she whispered desperately, and seeing her daughter's ready objection she insisted firmly, "I just can't. It will settle down. It will. He's a proud man. It's hard for him and –"

"Ma, that's a load of shite, and you know it. I'm sorry but it is. He's no man at all, he's a bully!"

Nancy was becoming distressed, and she badly wanted to change the subject. "Angela, please, leave it.

Let me deal with it in my own way. Please." She raised a hand to stave off further objections. "Let's talk about something else. *You*. Tell me how things are with *you*. I want to hear it. It's what I came for, after all."

"I didn't mean to upset you, Ma," Angela sighed, "and me and Tomo are all right. He loves the country. You wouldn't believe it. It's like he was born there. He never even mentions D'Arcy Avenue, or anything. Not even the lads he used to play with, thank God. Getting him away from them is the best thing about all this."

"Well, *that's* good news. And what about you? Do you like it any better?"

Angela pulled a face. "It's not so bad as it was. I thought I would go bananas down there at first. There's nothing there. Not even a bus. But the people are lovely. I think it's because of Daniel. He was very highly thought of. Apparently I really gave them something to talk about, though, when *I* showed up. You can imagine! I hated that at first."

Nancy laughed. She was happy to listen to the adjustment in Angela's voice. She was safe, Thomas and her, and that was the most important thing.

"Any word from the lads?" Angela asked. "How are they getting on in the States?"

Nancy brightened up, relieved to be discussing something other than her problems at home. It was good to be able to say that they were doing okay. Although she suspected that Finbar was not that mad about "Upstate New York" as he called it. It all sounded very Americanised. The whole group kept in close touch over there, and got together as often as they could. Those were the bits Finbar liked best. The heat was horrific. They sweated buckets and hardly peed at all. Nancy worried that they were dehydrating, but they assured her that they drank plenty.

"Yeah, plenty of what, I wonder?" Angela asked, and was glad to see her mother have a genuine hearty laugh.

"So, what doesn't Finbar like about the place, then? I would have thought he'd have been the one to take to it like a duck to water."

"Me too," Nancy replied. "He didn't actually say he doesn't like it. I just get that impression, more from what he doesn't say than from what he does say, if you know what I mean."

"Do you suppose he might be a bit homesick?" Angela wondered. She knew even without asking that Finbar would never admit to such a thing. He would die rather than admit it, especially after all the hype and planning they did beforehand about how they were going to take the States by storm when the exams were over!

"Well, he has Fergus with him. That's a help, I'm sure," Nancy mused, "but the home he'd be homesick for is not the way he left it any more." She could have bitten her tongue out over that last remark, she never meant to say it, and her heart broke when she saw the anguish on Angela's face. "I'm sorry, love!" she rushed to say. "Don't mind me babbling, that just slipped out!"

Thomas tired of his imaginary jungle game over by the plants, and came back to sit by his nan. He moved right up against her and placed his hands on the table, twiddling his fingers absentmindedly, while he leaned his head against her arm. Angela was about to tell him to get lost while she and his nan had a chat, but one look at his face told her he was not even listening to them. His brow was furrowed, and his lips were pushed tightly together in deep thought.

"Why don't you come and live with us in Daniel's house, Nan?" he surprised them by asking suddenly. "We have plenty of space, and you could even have your own room!" He looked up at Nancy expectantly. "It's real nice. You'd like it, wouldn't she, Ma?"

Both women were very taken by surprise, but Nancy gathered herself together first.

"I couldn't do that, love. My home is in D'Arcy Avenue, with your – with Paddy."

"But he hit you," the boy said pointedly, "and Ma!"

Nancy was flummoxed. "He was upset . . ." she said lamely, searching vainly for justification of her husband's behaviour, and at the same time being very uncomfortable about the fact that she was giving a child the wrong idea.

"He can't do that. If I was bigger I would have hit him for you!"

Angela instantly became choked up, and clasped her hand over her mouth, not trusting herself to speak. Nancy made a supreme effort to appear normal. But she did put her arm around the lad's shoulders, and gave him a quick sharp squeeze and plonked a kiss on the top of his head. He didn't object.

"I'll tell you what," she said, suddenly busy

rummaging in her handbag for her purse, "why don't you go up and get yourself another Coke?"

"You could come and visit, couldn't you?" he asked, looking hopeful. "And I could show you around. I could show you the loft. It's safe now since Seán fixed it. And he put a ladder up too, so it's real easy to get into it as well."

"Yes. I will visit. Now, you get yourself a Coke, there's a good lad."

Nancy pressed a coin into the child's hand and he headed towards the counter. She looked questioningly at her daughter, a look of expectancy in her eyes.

"Seán? Who is Seán? Is there something you haven't said?"

"Oh Ma!" Angela protested, slightly embarrassed. "No, there's nothing *to* say. This guy offered to fix the loft so Tomo could play safely. That's all."

Nancy raised a knowing eyebrow with a hint of a smile. "So, this guy starts playing the role of surrogate dad and you still don't get the impression he fancies you? Come on, Angela! This is your mother you're talking to and I wasn't born yesterday. Do *you* fancy *him*? Is he a farmer?"

Thomas arrived back with his drink. "Is who a farmer, Nan?"

"You mind your own business, Tomo Brennan!" Angela warned him.

If Angela had a steady fella that would be a first, and Nancy was curious, so she decided to press it a bit further.

"I was wondering who this Seán is, who fixed the loft for you, Thomas."

Thomas settled himself back on the seat beside his nan, and ignored his mother's protestations of "Ma!"

"He owns the pub. He fancies Ma, so he does."

Nancy's surprise registered clearly on her face. "Owns the pub! Well, fancy that!" So, he had means. She looked at Angela who was fit to be tied.

"Will you two give over! He does not fancy me! And he does not own the pub!" She glared at Thomas. "Where did you ever get *that*?"

Thomas sipped his drink, all signs of his earlier sickness barely a memory. "He told me. *He's* the boss. That's what he said."

Angela looked at her mother, uncertain whether to believe him or not. "It doesn't matter, anyway," she spoke through gritted teeth. "I don't fancy *him*."

"No," said Thomas flatly, "you fancy that *poncey* Francie Furlong!"

Angela almost choked. Her mouth opened, but she was so gobsmacked she could not get any words out. This was what happened when you had to have a nine-year-old child with you nearly all the time. Nothing was sacred. It was impossible to have a bit of privacy. The little fecker noticed *too* much.

Nancy was equally surprised, and concerned. Men's names were being dropped all over the place. That was a total change for Angela, and she wondered how she was coping with it.

"Is there no end to the suitors down there?" she enquired, hoping to get some indication of Angela's feelings. "Who is Francie Furlong, for God's sake?"

"Nobody!" Angela cut in sharply, hoping to end this ridiculous conversation.

Thomas knew exactly who the "poncey" Francie was, and he took delight in getting this opportunity to remind his mother. "His da is the one who wants to buy us out."

"Shut up, you!" Angela warned him through clenched teeth.

Nancy looked from one to the other. She observed that Angela was ready to strangle Thomas. And Thomas was clearly delighting in living dangerously by spilling the beans on this Francie fella. It was obvious that mother and son were divided in their opinion on the same Francie. But apart from that, someone was already making plans to buy them out. Nancy did not like the feeling that fact gave her. People were known to do strange things to get their hands on land. It was not unheard of for people to be murdered because someone else wanted to claim their land.

"What's this all about? *Who* said they want to buy you out? You're not thinking seriously about it, are you, Angela?" Nancy's anxiety was written all over her face.

"Ma! Will you not be worrying? I'm not selling. I can't do anything at the moment anyway. I have to wait till probate is all sorted out before it's even legally mine. So stop worrying, for God's sake."

Nancy studied her daughter's face. She certainly had grown up a lot since she had to leave home, but she was not entirely au fait with the ways of the world as yet, and Nancy worried that any "cute hoor" with an ulterior motive who smiled at her might easily be able to take advantage.

"You'd want to watch out, love. People who would take advantage will smile while they're stabbing you in the back, you know."

"Ma, don't worry," Angela tried to ease her mother's concern with soothing tones, "I'm not about to do anything. I wouldn't anyway, not without Patrick Cullen. I'd always ask him first. If I wanted to sell he'd see to it that nobody duped me."

Nancy visibly relaxed. She was happy to hear that. From talking to the solicitor just on the phone she had the feeling that he had her daughter's interests truly at heart. Daniel had charged him with the task, he said, and he assured Nancy that he would honour his friend's wishes to the full.

She looked at her watch.

"Christ Almighty!" she exclaimed in alarm, "look at the time! I have to be going, love. I wouldn't want to miss this bus. If I wait for the next one I'll be smack into the rush hour traffic, as sure as God!" What she really meant was that she wouldn't get home before Paddy got in, and with no dinner ready either there would surely be hell to pay.

She gave the bag she had arrived with to Angela. "There you go, love, just a few things from your rooms I thought you might need." She turned to Thomas and hugged him tightly. "I have to rush, love. Don't bother coming down to the bus stop, it'll be along any minute. You be good for your mother – and watch out for each other now, y'hear?"

Nancy turned to Angela and hugged her too, tightly

but briefly, saying that she would phone tomorrow. Angela suggested they arrange another meeting when she did.

"Of course, love, I'll see you again soon."

She lifted her handbag and hurried away, hoping in her heart that nothing prevented her from seeing them regularly. She would have to be careful.

In silence they sat and watched her go, deflation taking her place. Then Angela nudged Thomas.

"You ready? We might as well go for our bus. We're too early, but what the fuck."

Chapter 25

Thomas lay on his bed thinking about the events of the day. It was not totally dark outside, because it had been a bright sunny day, and at almost ten at night there was still some brightness in the western sky. The sun was going down fast with a magnificent display of colours that ranged from pink to deep orange, to almost blood red. Thomas did not turn the light on.

He got up and went to the window and rested his elbows on the sill, watching the glow from the dying sun as it filled his room. The country was a magical place, especially at night, when it took on a totally different personality. He loved to sit and listen to the night sounds, secure in the knowledge that he was safe in his room. It was now too dark to see out and only the fact that by now he knew every shape by heart made him think he could still see. He took a last look around, assured himself that all was well with the world, and went back to his bed.

He climbed into the middle of the old-fashioned double bed and slid down under the blankets. He had a bolster pillow which was almost as wide as the bed itself and another pillow on top. He loved this bed. He could get lost under the covers and it would look like he wasn't there. His other bed had been a single one in the corner of his uncles' room and too much manoeuvring in it could cause him to fall out on the floor. It had happened more than once, driving his mother bananas.

Angela was still downstairs, watching "shite" on the telly, as she would say herself in the morning. It was great for Thomas, seeing his nan again. But now that she was gone home it all seemed like it had been only a lovely dream.

Crash!

Instantly Thomas was alert again. His heart pounded. He had been almost asleep but still he was sure the noise had come from outside. He waited for another sound but when none came he jumped from his bed and ran to the window. In the pitch darkness he could see nothing at first. He lifted the sash window and stuck his head out. There was no sound apart from the night breeze in his ears, and the thumping of his heart. The sudden gush of cold night air tore any semblance of sleep from him, and he leaned out as far as he dared. He thought it was *too* quiet out there by far.

"Ma!" he hollered, as he turned away from the window and headed towards the stairs. "Ma! Did you hear that?"

He went down the stairs two and three at a time, calling his mother as he ran.

Angela leapt from her chair in alarm and met him at the doorway as he pushed past.

"Tomo! What the fuck is the matter? What are you doing up?"

She managed to catch the end of his pyjama top and stop him in his tracks. He was heading for the back door.

"I heard a crash. Someone is outside. I heard them!"

His eyes were wide with alarm and he tried to pull himself free.

But she just laughed. "Ha! Will you get a grip for fuck sake! That was on the telly, you eejit!"

"No, Ma!" he insisted. "I heard it outside. I did!"

Angela swung him around towards the telly. "Look!" she pointed. "There! See?" She was watching a film involving a car chase, in which everything was getting smashed up. "Go out there if you want to but I'm going to bed. This film is only a load of crap anyway." She turned off the television as she passed it. "Goodnight," she said and headed towards the door. "Make sure you put the light out."

Thomas stood for a moment, unsure and unconvinced, but if he was going to be left downstairs all on his own he certainly wasn't going to go out the back. He hurried after his mother, eager for the security of his bed once again.

Back in his room he went to the window. The weather had changed. A persistent rain was falling and the moon was no longer visible. For a moment he listened to the sounds of the rain as it fell in big drops on the large broad leaves of the sycamore trees, the smooth slate roof of the workshop, the hard concrete of the yard. Only natural sounds reached his ears, so he closed the window and got into his bed. He was still so very sure he had heard that noise outside the house, and he kept listening for any more strange sounds, but none happened and he fell asleep.

Angela's thoughts were turning over the events of the day. She could not block out of her head the sight of those black bruises on her mother's wrist. She had stayed watching that tripe on the telly, trying to tire herself out so that she would fall asleep quickly, but it hadn't worked. Her mind would not let go of those awful pictures. The horror of her last morning in D'Arcy Avenue presented itself uninvited before her closed eyes, in every minute frightening detail.

She saw the blind fury that drove Paddy Brennan to viciously destroy his family. She felt again the cold grip of fear as his wild bulging eyes moved from the letter in his hand and landed on *her*. She *heard* as well as felt the hair being torn from her scalp. She heard herself scream as she watched blood spurt from her mother's nose. And the roars of Thomas as he was gripped by a fist of steel, his light body lifted from the ground by the force, and his head swinging like a pendulum from the strength of the blows. And Nancy had gone back to that. What sort of a daughter was she? She should have been more insistent that her mother should come back with her. She was riddled with guilt that she had let her go, even though she knew that Nancy's mind was made up. But that didn't prevent her from being tormented by the knowledge that nothing had improved at home. She could not understand why Nancy stayed.

Or maybe she could. Had she not stayed herself, for the past nine years, because she could not see a way out? Perhaps her mother was the same. In need of a clear path out. But Angela knew now that it needed to be a *mental* route out, because failing that she was trapped. She had not believed in her head that she could manage alone. Home was home, and she used to persuade herself that things could have been worse. That was what she consoled herself with, then.

Her mind went over all her mother had said in the shopping centre. It left Angela with a totally different view of her. She was a woman with needs and desires like everyone else, one who had dared grasp the excitement of going against convention, who had broken all the rules, and lived with the fear and worry of being found out ever since. She had been a vivacious and spirited young woman. No surprise then that she had attracted serious male attention. The surprise was that now there was very little outward trace of that person, and since the events that drove Angela and Thomas from the house all traces of the original Nancy had vanished altogether. Paddy had seen to that, but then perhaps Paddy had spent a long number of years trying to erase that person, the same person he had fallen in love with in the first place, and Angela wondered if he even knew why.

Her own tragedy, as Angela now saw it, was that he had done the same thing with her. He badgered and harassed her till she was no longer herself. Very little that was positive about her ever crossed his lips, once she had fallen out of favour. The irony of it was that Paddy, in his raging desire to make things worse for her, had actually done her a favour. And Thomas, too. She again considered the change in her son since they arrived in Daniel's house. Paddy would not recognise him! He was happy. He laughed easily. He was capable. He feared no one. The worried look had vanished from his young face.

His one nightmare was that Paddy might find them!

And the way they got on together here in Daniel's house was something she would never have expected. Nowadays he came in and chatted to her. He told her about everything he noticed out there, so taken by it all as he was, and he made it sound interesting. She realised she liked to hear what he had to say about things, whether it was the owl in the loft or the magpies trying to raid the nests of other birds, or the flow of the river after rain. He noticed it all and loved to come in and talk about it. He was her "roving reporter" on the land. She cringed when she thought of how he used to try to avoid her, fearful that she was about to swipe at him, or how he always gravitated towards her mother for protection! God! Was she really *that* bad? He had feared her like she feared her father. That did *not* feel nice.

She lay there sleeplessly, realising just how much they both had changed since arriving here. And she realised with absolute certainty that for her and Thomas there was no going back. Ever. Without knowing it or wanting to, they had moved on.

At first she was consumed by the fact that she was missing home, and missing her mother. Now she knew for sure that what she *wanted* home to *be* was what she was missing. She could see now that she had always missed it, because it had ceased to exist ever since she became pregnant.

If only her mother could see that there was life after D'Arcy Avenue! Angela felt that she could understand her mother's guilt. But she could not accept that Nancy should have to spend the rest of her days paying for it. One fact became absolutely clear as she lay there. With no going back, she was on her own. Providing for herself and Thomas was now solely her responsibility. Not her father's. Not Nancy's. Hers. The road ahead was suddenly cleared of the uncertainty that had dogged her life in the last decade. It was time to get on with it. She pulled the covers up over her shoulders and fell asleep with her teeth clamped tightly together.

Chapter 26

In her bathroom Nancy ran cold water on the face cloth, and held it to her cheek. With any luck the swelling might be gone down by morning. It was the most noticeable marking, but the sorest part of her right now was her ribs. They hurt when she took a deep breath, or when she sighed. So she practised shallow breathing, and ran more cold water on the cloth and held it gently against her jawbone.

If only the traffic had not been so heavy. If only the road works at the Red Cow roundabout were not so disruptive, reducing traffic to one slow lane. If only Paddy had not been in that little bit early or if only she had got an earlier bus from the shopping centre.

If if if.

She sat on the toilet bowl and tried hard to stifle the sobs. It hurt her ribs so much. It was not as bad this time, only because it had not lasted as long. And *that* was because in his viciousness Paddy had swung wildly, and he actually missed her with the last downward swipe and smashed his fist onto the corner of an open press door. He cursed loudly in pain, and that was when he put the boot in, blaming her for making him miss and hurt himself!

After she had arrived home and offered some feeble excuses he had waited in a menacing silence, deliberately stimulating fear while she prepared dinner. Mechanically she had gone through the motions, while a cowering sense of the inevitable invaded every fibre of her being.

Everything was wrong. The gravy was too thick. The meat was tough. He didn't like broccoli any more. But it was her new hair-do that seemed to aggravate him the most, until her mobile fell from her apron pocket when he gave her that first push.

That really did it.

Afterwards he went out. He left her on the floor and went without a backward glance.

She lay still for some time, feeling relief in knowing the need to try to protect herself from his blows was over, for the moment. He would not hurry back, she knew he would want to get as far from the scene of his crime as he could, and so she felt safe, for a while at least. Her phone lay beside her, crushed to bits by his heel. With a heavy sigh she got herself up on her feet, slowly and with great effort, for she was sore everywhere. She picked up the bits of the phone and threw them in the kitchen bin. Once again she felt alone and isolated, and cut off from her children. Somewhere in the depths of her being the feelings of outrage and indignation had begun to stir.

They conflicted sharply with her lifelong feelings of guilt, causing an emotional turmoil that she was not yet strong enough to deal with.

So much for her day out.

She tried hard to keep her thoughts on Angela and Thomas. She needed to focus on them to prevent focusing on what had just happened to her. And so she put what little energy she had into taking consolation from the fact that she had spent a few happy hours today with her daughter and grandson. It had been worth it, she persuaded herself lamely, to see them again. Ever since they left she felt like her heart was missing from her body. The ache to see them sometimes became unbearable. And even though she hurt, her heart was alive again within her. She had the satisfaction of knowing they were safe and well.

Thomas was such a surprise. So happy and full of life. So different! And he was taller. Angela said she could not keep him full. He ate everything she put before him.

The things Angela Brennan was saying. She sounded like a mother! Nancy never thought she would hear her daughter say the likes. It was good. It did her sore heart good to hear it. Despite her swollen face, Nancy smiled. And she looked forward to telling Annie Ryan all about it.

It rained all night, and Paddy did not come home.

Nancy didn't care.

Chapter 27

The following morning in Baltinglass Thomas pulled on his wellies to go out to play.

"Take them off!" Angela said when she noticed. "We're going in to see Patrick Cullen and you're not going in them."

Without the usual argument Thomas took the wellies off. Something in his mother's tone told him arguing would be useless. But he didn't mind. He liked going into Patrick's office. And they would see Rose. He could go out to play afterwards.

"And we're going to see about getting you into the school."

Thomas was unprepared for that. He stared at his mother as though she had just told him she had arranged to send him to the moon!

School? God!

His mind tried to comprehend the significance of what she just said, but it was difficult. He had forgotten school. It was part of his other life, where he had been unhappy most of the time. That life where he always seemed to be in the wrong place doing the wrong thing, according to those that looked after him. Where he always ended up annoying *somebody*, no matter how he tried.

Angela did not look at him but the stunned silence told her a multitude.

"You've already missed too much," she said, busy pulling on her jacket. "You wouldn't want Owen to be smarter than you, now would you?"

Out of the corner of her eye she watched his reaction. She saw excitement replace the shocked look. She could almost *see* what he was thinking. Pleased, she told herself she was ahead of him this time.

Owen! Of course! *He* went to the school here. And he *liked* it. He was always talking about his teacher. Thomas said he fancied her. Owen hotly denied it.

"Will I be going to his school?" Thomas asked, half-afraid now the answer would be no.

"If they have a place for you, yes, you will."

"Yes!" Thomas whooped, and he punched the air with his fist. "Will I be in his class," he kept asking, "will I?"

Although Rose had not said how old Owen was Angela figured they were about the same age. "Maybe."

"Yes, yes, yes!" Thomas jumped all over the kitchen, punching the air and almost knocking himself out when he crashed into the door.

"Cut that out before you kill yourself, Tomo Brennan! You'll just have to wait and see if you are in the same class or not."

He did his best not to annoy his mother, but he felt like running all around the front garden and shouting his head off in excitement. Angela was all business. She had a plan to work to and they set off on the walk to town. Thomas forgot the noise he heard last night as he went running down the driveway ahead of her. This morning there was no reason to be around the back of the house, and he did not see the broken clay flower pots, a few old empty ones that had been stacked by the side of the workshop. Nor did they see the large footprints in the muddy ground nearby.

On the narrow country road Mick Furlong slowed his car. Ahead of him Christy Cleary was cycling his bike. As he drew alongside, Mick pressed a button and the passenger window wound down.

Christy glanced at the car to his right and scowled. The luxury of it! Fancy windows and what have you! Furlong was rubbing it in, sitting in the comfort of his cream leather seats. *And* he had a bloody good idea what the other man was going to say, and it annoyed him to have to hear it.

"You'd want to get a move on, Christy. You're taking your time, aren't you?"

Mick was not referring to the pace of the bicycle. Christy knew it and cursed aloud.

"I just want it done – sometime soon would be grand, if you're going to do anything at all!" Mick countered, growling back sarcastically.

The car cruised, keeping pace with Christy, making

him feel like a total eejit as he huffed and puffed against the wind.

"Fuck off!" he roared in through the open window. "Fuckin' get rid of them yourself if yer in that much of a hurry! Only you don't want to be seen to soil your own hands, do ya? The Furlongs have to think of their standing in the town, now don't they?"

Mick would have had something to say to that truth, but another car had come up behind them and he thought it wisest to be off.

"Don't leave it on the long finger. If you don't have the balls for it I can get someone else!" he said with a warning tilt of his head. He wound up the window and accelerated, moving his car off down the road at speed, leaving an enraged Christy cursing rings around him.

From the car behind Seán Mulhearn had recognised Mick Furlong's car as it slowed to keep pace with Christy on his bicycle. He kept his distance and watched the exchange and wondered what it had all been about. He saw an irate Christy shake his fist in the direction of the departing car. It surprised him. He'd been of the opinion that relations between the two men were on a better footing than what he had just observed. He remembered how keen Mick had been on occasion to see the inebriated Christy safely home. And more than once he had sought him out in the pub, bought him drinks. He wondered what could have triggered the level of aggression being displayed by Christy Cleary.

Seán accelerated and passed the cycling man, giving

him a wave of acknowledgement. In his rear-view mirror he saw Christy recede into the distance.

Christy gripped the handlebars of his bike, his knuckles showing white with fury. That blasted Furlong! Who did he think he was anyway? If he didn't want to dirty his own hands then he just had to leave it to Christy, didn't he? Furlong obviously didn't want anyone else beating him to the purchase. He had moved fast, Christy had to give him that.

Furlong might only be interested in results, but Christy wasn't about to put up with being hassled.

"But I don't know a thing about sheep!" Angela was protesting.

Patrick Cullen smiled at her alarm.

She was sitting in his office while Thomas brought Rose up to date on all he had been up to lately. Rose always had time for the boy, no matter how busy she was, and for his part he always managed to entertain her.

"You don't need to know anything about sheep at all – the farmer will look after them himself," Patrick was saying. "He just wants to rent your field."

Angela's brow retained its frown. This living in the country was a very different kettle of fish for sure.

"Daniel used to allow him use it when he needed to, and he pays for the use of it. I thought maybe it might be some help to you . . ."

"Of course it would," she replied, the prospect of making some much-needed cash alleviating her alarm. "God knows we can do with anything that comes along.

271

So, how exactly will it work?"

Patrick assured her it would be absolutely no problem for her. The farmer looked after everything; all she had to do was agree. He would see to everything else for her. She agreed, and made a mental note never to go anywhere near that field while it was full of sheep! They were peculiar things that were likely to suddenly scatter in all directions at once. She had seen a flock once or twice being driven down the road, and for no apparent reason they would unexpectedly run up on the ditch, or change direction, giving the farmer real headaches, especially if there was traffic on the road. It occurred to her then that *they* just might be the same scatty ones that would end up in her field!

But, if all she had to do to make some money was to allow sheep eat her grass, which would have to be cut anyway, and there was an awful lot of it, well, how difficult could that be?

"I'll tell him to go ahead so. There is nothing you need do, he'll look after everything."

Angela nodded and then said hesitantly, "I was wondering if you have any idea yet how long probate will take?"

His face took on a serious look, and he did his usual solicitor thing of asking a question before he answered one. He scratched the top of his head before speaking.

"Is something up?"

"No. It's just that we won't be going back to Dublin. Not to D'Arcy Avenue anyway, and I wondered how long we will be here, before things can be finally settled."

There was a tone of definition in her voice, like she knew something she hadn't known before. Surely she hadn't already agreed to sell, the sale to go through after probate was granted?

"I would say a matter of months. A year is not uncommon. But you sound much more positive, Angela. Why so all of a sudden?"

She told him about the meeting with her mother the day before. About how she knew she had moved on, and going home was obviously not an option. He did not make any response, just nodded. He acknowledged silently a feeling of relief. If he was to fulfil Daniels wishes it would be necessary for Angela to give her inheritance a fair chance. But he had seen families broken up over less. And he felt sure that Angela's mother had got the raw end of the stick.

"In a straightforward case like this things sometimes can move faster. That is as much as I can say. It is down to the Probate Office, and they work at their own pace. Are you still thinking of selling?"

"I don't know. I was just wondering how long we may have to be here, because I need to get work."

Rose and Thomas came in then with the usual tea and biscuits, and Patrick was glad to hear that Thomas was looking forward to school.

"I might be in Owen's class!" Thomas enthused, selecting a chocolate marshmallow that he had put on the plate for himself.

"I'm sure the headmaster will be delighted to have you in his school," Patrick remarked. Thomas nodded in response. He had filled his mouth with the marshmallow biscuit before anyone else had the chance to take it. Angela glared at him for being so greedy. No one else seemed to notice.

"Don't get chocolate all over you," she warned, "or nobody will have you in their school!"

Before another hour had passed Thomas was registered in the boys' school. He and Angela sat in the headmaster's office and discussed everything from Thomas's schooling to date, to how well Daniel had done at school, to what Angela's hopes and plans for the future were. Here she had to freelance a bit, since definite decisions had yet to be made. She only hoped that Thomas would not interject and contradict her.

He surprised her by sitting quietly, not fidgeting, and speaking only when he was spoken to. "Yes, Sir," or "No, Sir," he said, wherever appropriate, so much so that Angela looked at him in surprise. He just clasped his hands between his knees and smiled sweetly back at her!

And that was it. He was in. They would put him in Owen's class for the moment, and see how he got on. From September he must have the school uniform, but for now, since the holidays were so close, he would be allowed wear his own clothes. The headmaster gave Angela an information leaflet on the school, including all facilities, rules, various procedures and school hours. Tomorrow morning was good to start.

Thomas was ecstatic! He could hardly wait to see Owen to tell him the news! He was high as a kite with excitement on the way home.

His antics were as usual annoying his mother who was wondering where she was going to get a job down here. The thought had been knocking around in her mind that if she said it to Patrick Cullen he might know someone who was looking for someone, to do . . . something, anything. It was totally vague, what sort of work she could get, or do. But he did not say a word when she mentioned it. She wasn't even sure he heard her, because Tomo and Rose came in then. She was irritated that it didn't go according to plan, and she wished she could think where would be the best place to start looking.

Her spirits sagged. She needed money. She thought of the electricity bill that had arrived in the post before they left the house that morning. It was addressed to Daniel, and somehow it made her feel very alone. It made getting a job imperative. It was just as well that Tomo didn't need his school uniform till September! But he was going to need copies and pencils at least in the morning. They arrived at the gate. It was open. Thomas remarked that he definitely closed it after them when they left earlier. He noticed things like that.

But then Angela saw why the gate was open. Francie Furlong's jeep was parked up at the door, and he was about to get back into it when he saw them arriving. A wide smile broke out on Angela's face. Instantly her financial problems were forgotten.

Thomas scowled, and kicked the gravel.

"Hi there, Angela. I was just about to leave. Thought

you must be off gallivanting for sure!" Francie gave her his most charming smile.

She beamed at him in return.

Thomas got no greeting.

Thomas did not feel like going into the house and listening to the guff coming out of the ponce! He headed straight for the field where the sheep would be going to graze, and set off around it as if he was inspecting it, trying to make sure everything was going to be all right for them. Down the far end there were a couple of horse troughs filled with water. This field did not have the river running along at the bottom of it. Safer for the sheep, he thought. He found himself wondering did sheep need much water? Would the farmer have to keep the horse troughs filled? Was there anything *he* could do to help? It would be nice if he was allowed help. He could offer – after school, of course.

In the house Angela was making tea, even though Francie insisted he did not want any. She needed to do something. She fervently hoped the nerves didn't show.

Francie sat himself on the edge of the kitchen table, his long legs stretched out in front. He didn't seem to notice that he was actually obstructing her way. She had to be careful to avoid tripping over his feet to get past as she went about her task.

"What about the dance Friday?" he asked lazily as she passed. "Can I pick you up?"

Her heart leapt, even though she froze in surprise. She was holding the half-full milk jug, and had been about to go and top it up.

"I take it that's a yes?" he smiled, his eyes taking in all of her, unabashedly.

"I . . . I thought . . . Clodagh was . . .was . . ."

"Clodagh? No, no, no. Clodagh . . . isn't."

She responded with a little "Oh."

His arm reached out and pulled her towards him, taking her completely by surprise.

Still holding the ceramic jug, she was suddenly standing between his long legs. She was being kissed and she hadn't been kissed in ages, not like this.

This was demanding and the thought went through her head that it was as well that he was holding her so tightly, because her legs almost wouldn't support her. Her free hand went around his neck and she responded eagerly. Somewhere in the corner of her mind it occurred to her that it was ridiculous that she was still holding onto the jug.

"I knew this would happen the minute I laid eyes on you," he breathed. His arms lifted her and in a flash he had moved so that it was she who was sitting on the table. His kisses were rougher, and his hands very quickly and easily found their way up under her skirt. This was just *too* fast for Angela altogether. He misinterpreted her gasp.

"Like it, Angela, don't you? I knew you would, I knew you'd want it."

"Stop!" She struggled against him, suddenly alarmed. "Stop it!"

He paid no heed – no one ever meant it when they said stop to Francie Furlong.

She persisted in struggling hard against him. "No! Francie, no!"

He was becoming annoyed. Briefly he held her away from him a little. "Don't give me that! Your sort doesn't say no!"

She couldn't believe her ears. "What?!"

"You have Thomas! You're no virgin! You put it about no problem!"

Her hand tightened on the jug, and suddenly she brought it against the side of his head with a smack. She was left holding the handle, and Francie was covered in milk, holding his hand to his head.

She was livid! Her face was white with anger.

"You bitch!" he exploded at her, almost floored with surprise and anger. "You're nothing but a slapper!"

But she was even more angry than he, and unafraid. She exploded back at him instantly and with such fury that he was silenced.

"Get out of my house! You bastard, you fucking bastard! Never come *near* me again or I'll fucking kill you! D'ya hear? I swear it! I fucking swear it!"

He backed off quickly, brushing milk from his face and clothes, telling her she would be better off to go back to where she came from, and take her bastard with her!

She looked around wildly for something to hand to fling after him. But her words were her best weapon.

"To think your father wants to buy me out! He'll never get his hands on *my* father's house *or* land! And I will let him know that *you* saw to that!"

The saturated Francie made a quick exit from the house. He had made a right mess of that. Where did it go wrong? She wanted him. Anyone could see that. It should've been a cinch.

He was supposed to make her fall for him, sweep her off her feet, get her onside – at least till she agreed to sell to his father. That was the plan. Mick Furlong was not above using his son's attractiveness to the female gender to further his plans, and Francie had no objections to that, since he was the one who was going to get "it" practically handed to him with hardly any effort at all. But he had just made a right hash of it by totally misjudging their prey.

His father was not going to take this lightly, and an angry Mick Furlong was not something Francie cared to have to face. He jumped into his jeep and sped off down the driveway, scattering gravel in all directions. He drove out onto the road without slowing down, and Thomas, coming from the field, was glad to see him leave.

He went over and closed the gate, and headed up to the house.

"How come *he* left in such a hurry, Ma?"

Angela tried her best to appear normal, but it was impossible. "None of your business."

Thomas was suspicious, and eyed the milk and the broken jug. He wouldn't trust a Furlong. "What did he do?"

"Nothin'!"

"What did he want?"

"I told you! None of your bloody business!" his mother snapped.

As she lay in her bed that night the fury had not abated very much. It went between her and her sleep, and she worried because she had to get Tomo up in time for school the following morning. But the feelings had a familiar ring to them. Francie Furlong thought she was scum. Because she had Tomo he believed she was an easy lay, and he had come to get what he could. Paddy Brennan held much the same opinion of her – she had lived with that insinuation from him for the past nine years. And she was far too familiar with the vulnerable and powerless state such conviction locked her into.

The injustice of it upset and angered her deeply, and kept sleep at bay.

That Francie Furlong should attempt to treat her with the same attitude was the straw that broke the proverbial camel's back. She was surprised that her reaction was so violent, but not sorry. Not remotely sorry. She swore vehemently that no one was going to treat her like that again. It was a pity that the jug was broken, but it couldn't be helped. Suddenly she laughed to herself under the sheets. The stunned look on Francie's face with the milk running down it in little rivers flashed again before her eyes. It was priceless. It gave her a little tremor of satisfaction to have halted his gallop. Did the glamorous Clodagh or anyone else for that matter never say no to the unchained advances of the Furlong playboy? Apparently not. And she'd had that visit from his father offering to buy her out. What her mother had said came back to her. Could both visits be connected? She pulled the covers up to her chin and closed her eyes. She just *had* to get some sleep.

Chapter 28

The snug was cut off from the main body of the pub by a wood and stained-glass partition. It was empty, except for two tough-looking characters who left almost as soon as Paddy came in. He chose the best stool and placed his pint on the bar in front of him. He was still in his working clothes. His trousers were splattered with gravy from his dinner, but it was hardly noticeable now.

It was *her* fault anyway, that he was annoyed. It wasn't good enough that he should work all day and then come home and find that the telly wasn't working! She should have noticed and called the cable company. Or the repairman, or something. He liked to watch the news while he had his dinner, and he told her to turn on the telly. But nothing happened. Nothing but a screen of black and white dots, all jumping all over the bloody place, enough to give a fella the sick!

It wasn't her fault, she said. What a joke! *Everything* was her fault! When he slammed his fist onto the table and accidentally hit the edge of his plate, splattering himself with gravy, she had the audacity to accuse him of being as bad as Thomas! How *dare* she mention that bastard in *his* house! She was becoming too fuckin' smart for her own good! Standing up to him like that!

A few smacks soon shut her up. But it put him right off his dinner. It was a drink he needed. He downed the rest of his pint and ordered another. The snug door opened and someone came in but Paddy took no notice. He sorted out the price of his pint from the change in his pocket, glancing up only when the barman placed the drink in front of him and said, "There you go" and someone else said, "I'll get that."

Redser Reilly sat himself on the stool next to Paddy.

"I like to buy a neighbour a drink," he said quietly, his lightning eyes watching Paddy's face for the slightest sign of hostility. His feet just about reached to the bottom bar on the stool, at a stretch.

He had came upon a totally unsuspecting Paddy, and as always, he expected the element of surprise to give him the advantage. But Paddy was in no mood for being surprised, or disadvantaged, and showed no sign of being either. He cast Reilly a sidelong glance and then fixed his eyes on the pint.

"Shouldn't you be – in hiding or something?" A touch of sarcasm coloured his tone.

Reilly gave a low laugh. "I'm always in hiding . . . or something."

Paddy eyed him up and down. "So, how come you're buying me a drink?" He hadn't touched the pint yet. He didn't know why this chance meeting was even happening, and was unsure how it would go, and the last drinking buddy he would have wanted was Redser Reilly.

Reilly too was unsure how it would go, but as always he'd brought along some insurance.

The snug door opened, and the two characters who had left earlier returned and closed the door behind them. They sat at the back of the snug. There was an unsettling feel to their presence. A silent look of acknowledgement passed between them and Reilly, but Paddy didn't miss it. He looked straight at Redser and from him to the heavies. He was aware his question had not been answered and he felt a bit less cocky now, but Reilly wasn't going to be allowed to know that.

"What do you need them for?" he asked directly.

"Don't mind them," he was told. "They go where I go. Drink your pint."

It was a bad time to attempt to order Paddy Brennan to do anything, and the last few words sounded just like that. The two men were like boxers circling each other, wary and alert, determined not to give way.

"I never drink more than two on my own." Paddy almost believed himself and hoped he had not gone too far.

Redser sat a minute and contemplated Paddy Brennan. He did a little mental adjustment and decided to humour him a little longer. Then he signalled the barman.

"Two more here, please."

Paddy had no more excuse, other than he had no wish

to drink with this scum, and he wasn't stupid enough to say that. He lifted his pint, acknowledged the giver and swallowed a huge amount in one go.

Redser lifted his also but barely wet his lips on the froth.

"I was thinking . . ." Reilly began rather innocuously, "I haven't seen that son of mine around in a while."

The colour drained from Paddy's face. He froze mid-gulp and coughed as the Guinness went down the wrong way. Reilly allowed himself a smug smile: he had the upper hand now.

Paddy would never have thought that Reilly gave a fiddler's curse about Thomas.

"You haven't done anything to him, have you?" asked Redser.

The question sent alarm bells ringing in Paddy's brain. A vivid picture of the last time he set eyes on Reilly's son flashed before his eyes. Reilly must *know* he had beaten Thomas. Was *that* what this was all about? Was he here to get *even*? He became aware that the two behind him had gone awfully quiet. Everyone waited for his answer. He put the pint down, and licked the froth from his lips, slowly and deliberately, while he gained time to compose himself. His hand was beginning to shake.

"Don't be ridiculous! The lad is down the country with his mother!" he declared.

Reilly appeared to take his time to assimilate this information.

Paddy waited for what seemed a very long time for the response.

"Really? I heard talk about an inheritance?" Redser hinted.

"So?" Paddy shrugged.

"Down the country?"

Paddy was worried. Reilly's eyes had narrowed. Didn't he believe him?

"Yeah, down the country – his mother inherited a place in Baltinglass," he said in an effort to make Reilly believe him. He hoped not to have to go into detail about how the inheritance came about. He didn't need to lose face, particularly in front of this gurrier and the two behind him.

One of the men behind shifted noisily. Paddy cast a nervous glance back. Reilly threw the man a look that immobilised him.

"Yeah, I think I heard about that," Reilly said thoughtfully.

Paddy was dismayed. "How did you hear?" he wanted to know. Just wait till he got that bitch for talking!

"Oh, you know, word gets about." Redser gave Paddy a sympathetic look. "You have your own problems, man, don't you?" He took a sip of his pint, ignoring the fact that Paddy appeared to be lost for words. "So the lad is okay, then?" he asked without waiting for a response. "That's good, that's good."

Paddy's anxiety eased. Reilly was just curious. Relief made him reckless. "Yeah, but I'm not so sure they'd welcome visitors."

Reilly's laugh was more of a sneer. "Oh, Angela won't be seeing *me*! Don't you worry! I was just curious. No love lost there, you know – I had to drug that one to get it!" He laughed outright at the shocked expression on Paddy's face. "What do you care? You're not even her father!" Redser slapped the palm of his hand down on the bar. "So long!" He left his pint on the counter, barely touched. "Oh, and I never have conversations with people . . . we didn't have this one, ya hear?"

A jerk of his head and the other two jumped to their feet and followed him out.

He left a shocked Paddy sitting alone in the snug.

Paddy set his glass down heavily on the counter. He felt sick.

Reilly had drugged Angela.

And all those years he had made her life hell.

Nancy was right all along!

The barman glanced over. "You okay?"

With an inclining of his head Paddy ordered the first of many drinks he swallowed in an attempt to blot out what he had just learned. But hard as he tried, the drink would not oblige by obliterating reality for him.

In the house Nancy picked up her knitting and tried to concentrate on that. With no telly working and her mobile smashed, she needed something to take her mind off herself. After meeting Angela and Thomas in Tallaght she'd decided to get back to doing some knitting again. With the lads in America, and her daughter and grandson in Wicklow the house felt like a morgue. Her existence seemed increasingly pointless. She needed to feel she was doing something useful. Knitting was a poor substitute for her family, but at least it gave her something to concentrate on.

Paddy was in the pub, his dinner was in the bin, and Nancy tried hard not to think about when he came home.

Her shoulder was sore where she had been pushed against the door. The previous bruise was still there and still tender. Her ribs were not too bad now – they seemed to be healing okay. She envied Angela the peace she had in Baltinglass. To be away from Paddy Brennan would be heaven. She sighed heavily. Then to cheer herself up she took out the last letter she'd received from the lads in America. She read it over and over. It was short; not exactly much of a letter, typical of the lads, but it helped to transport her from where she was.

In it Finbar hinted that he might come home early. Maybe he could get some holiday work here. Nancy worried about that. She had not told the lads anything about the terrible things that had happened in the family since they left. How could she tell them that she had been unfaithful? That Angela was only their half-sister? What would happen when they came home and found things the way they were now? She absolutely dreaded the thought of it. She clicked away on the needles again, trying to drag her mind back to the task at hand. She was working on a jumper for Thomas, for winter wear. The fact that winter was a long way away didn't matter. Nancy was good with the needles. When her children were young she whiled away many hours at night with the needles. She hand-knitted or crocheted all the woollies her offspring wore. She used to produce beautiful work for others, as well, and more recently Thomas's school woollens. Now she planned on supplying Angela with warm sweaters for both of them to see them through the winter. Winters in the Wicklow Mountains could be very cold, and from her house she often saw them in the distance, covered in snow.

A ring on the doorbell startled her.

Annie Ryan's voice called in through the letterbox. "It's only me!"

Nancy went to open the door and Annie came in to the kitchen and sat herself down, concern written all over her.

"I saw him going out," she said. "Angela was on to me. She's worried. She says she can't get you on your mobile. Is anything up?"

Nancy always had a hard time admitting to what was going on, but she couldn't have Angela worried about her.

"The mobile is broken," she said flatly. "He smashed it when he found it."

Annie Ryan was exasperated. "Nancy! Why didn't you tell me, for God's sake? Why didn't you come over to me? Jesus Almighty! What am I going to do with you?"

"I know, I know," Nancy sighed, "I will. I'll come over tomorrow, I promise. Want a cup of tea?"

She made the tea while Annie admired the knitting.

"I'd love to be able to knit like you do, Nance. What's this you're doing now?"

"It's for Thomas. He is going to need warm woollies in the country."

It was close to midnight when Nancy put the knitting away. Annie had stayed a good while, but she always preferred to be gone before *he* came back. She couldn't trust herself not to make the situation worse by what she might say.

Nancy put the kettle on for a last cup of tea and went upstairs to the loo while the kettle was boiling. That was when she heard the key in the door. Her heart sank. He was back. She had not expected him home for an hour or so yet, if he came home at all. She listened to his footstep. She could often tell by the sound of it what kind of mood he was in. Or just how drunk he was. But she heard nothing. Strange. She flushed the loo and opened the door, her heart pounding fiercely in her chest. A cold fear froze her but anger bubbled away beneath the surface.

He was halfway up the stairs. She said nothing, and he did not greet her either. Not even a growl, which was unusual. She stood by the loo door while he ascended the stairs. She was trying to keep out of his way, which was impossible on the tiny landing. He reached the top stair and turned towards their bedroom. At the very least she expected to be pushed aside, but he went in and shut the door behind him, as though he had not even seen her!

Nancy stood looking at the closed door. She was so surprised by his passive manner that she was almost tempted to go in and ask him if he was all right.

But she turned and went downstairs to get the tea. She had never seen him so quiet with drink taken. Still, she hoped that by the time she was ready to go to bed he would be sound asleep, thanks to the same drink!

Chapter 29

A knock on the door and Angela opened it to see Mick Furlong.

The big farmer rocked himself on his heels and said, "Good evening, Angela, I thought I'd drop by and see how you are getting on. Would now be convenient?"

"No, it wouldn't," she stated, taking him completely by surprise.

Mick paused slightly at the rebuff and smiled weakly.

Thomas had come to the hall to see who was at the door and Mick could see that he was surprised at his mother's discourteous manner.

"Francie tells me he thinks you may be having a tough time settling in. Country living doesn't have all the conveniences of the city, I know, takes getting used to. Some people never adapt –"

"Really?" she cut him short, her tone cold. "Francie seems to think he knows a lot! Maybe he has had his head in manure too long!"

Thomas felt like laughing at his mother's comment. He could see that this time she was well able for Mick Furlong, and he could only stare up at her, his mouth open, while he wondered what had caused such a definite change.

Mick Furlong too wondered at the difference, and felt himself to be at a distinct disadvantage. "I beg your pardon. Did I say something to offend you?" He looked from her to Thomas, trying to understand, in an effort to reassert his grip on the situation.

But Angela decided to keep the upper hand, and only hinted at the problem. "If you did, then offending me seems to run in your family! Good day, Mr Furlong!"

A stunned Mick could only stare at her in amazement. Words failed him. Angela stepped back into the hall, and he realised he hadn't been invited in and his visit was at an end. He stepped back from the door and inclined his head politely, then turned and went down the steps to his car without a backward glance.

Angela closed the door.

Thomas was beside himself with delight.

"Wow, Ma! That was telling him! Good on ya! *Good day*? Posh! Yeah!"

Angela was really quite pleased with herself too. And she had not used "fuck" even once!

Francie Furlong drove his jeep into the yard and jumped out. His father was talking to Andy, the farmhand, and his expression turned to thunder when he laid eyes on his son. He followed Francie into the house and shut the drawing-room door behind him. Francie did not need to ask what was up. He guessed his father had paid a visit to Cleary's.

"What have you gone and done now?" Mick demanded.

Francie figured innocence was the best policy. "Me? Nothing. What are you on about?"

The blatant lie and the attempt at evasion angered Mick even further. He stepped menacingly toward his son. Francie stepped back in submission. He had not seen his father this furious since the time he had been caught in the barn a decade ago with the daughter of a local TD, two evenings before her wedding to someone else!

"Angela Cleary! Or whatever her bloody name is! You were supposed to influence her thinking in *my* favour, not alienate her! I was there earlier and she wouldn't entertain me at all. She dismissed me as being of a family whose members make it their purpose to offend her!"

Francie laughed. Was *that* what she said? The likes of her had some neck taking the moral high ground! "That's a good one!" he answered, "I mean, what's a bicycle for, for God's sake, except to ride it!"

Any other time Mick would have mentally commended his son for his one-track mind, chip off the old block and all that, but when so much was at stake his behaviour was nothing but utter stupidity. Frustration and anger caused Mick to lunge at him unexpectedly and land a lightning skelp of his hand across Francie's ear.

"You blundering asshole! Can you think no other way than with your dick? I want that land, and if your stupid actions have lost it for me, you'll pay for it! So, you get yourself back in her good books and undo whatever it is you've done so far! Do you hear me? Do you?"

Francie took his hand from his stinging ear. This was the second time in two days that the same ear had been walloped. He snapped back in a sullen mood. "I don't think that's possible. She's not going to want to see me, judging by what you say."

Mick's voice had a way of striking fear in his only son. The fact that Francie was a grown man did nothing to diminish that.

"If I don't get that land – you don't get this!" Mick snarled into his face and waved his hand in a circular motion, leaving his son in no doubt as to what he meant. He had hinted before that he could easily bypass his "good for nothing" son in favour of a cousin.

Francie was far from keen on the idea of approaching that slut again. It was not his policy to risk rejection twice, or to waste his time on obvious no-hopers. There were plenty of others around he wouldn't be wasting his time with. But his inheritance was not going to be on the line over a slut like that.

"All right. All right! I'll sort it!" he growled.

"See that you do!" His father's thinly veiled threat followed him from the room.

Francie slammed the door behind him. I'll sort it, he vowed, cupping his hand over his sore ear, I'll sort it out all right and she'll be sorry she ever set foot on Cleary land in the first place!

Chapter 30

The bell went, the doors burst open and twenty-four nine-to-ten-year-old boys stampeded out into the schoolyard, despite their teacher's firm instruction to walk. A football was miraculously produced and the Man. United wannabes got a game of sorts going, while others gathered around Thomas to chat to the new boy.

Owen was chuffed that he was the first to know the newcomer, particularly since he was fitting in so well, and he was charged with showing Thomas the ropes. A lad with sticky-out ears and glasses said he could see the Cleary house from his bedroom window, claiming a tenuous connection.

Everyone wanted their share of the newcomer, and it was Thomas's hour, and he milked it for all it was worth. He gave them the impression that it was no big deal living with a ghost, invented on the spot, and the others were spellbound, and Declan with the sticky-out ears was particularly pleased when Thomas chatted with him and called him Deko.

In the classroom Thomas could see why Owen was in love with his teacher, and he decided if he was very clever then she would ask *him* all the questions and *he* would have all the answers and she would be so pleased with him. That would be so cool!

He fell deeply in love with her himself when some smart aleck in the classroom laughed at his Dublin accent, and she immediately gave the class a short informal lesson in regional dialects.

But in the schoolyard and out of the teacher's hearing, the smart aleck said Thomas's mother couldn't afford a school uniform for him. Straight away Thomas leapt blindly on the bully and with one lucky punch he bloodied his nose! It meant that he was hauled before the headmaster on his first day, but what worried him most was that his mother would absolutely kill him when she heard!

And she heard. As soon as she came to collect him the headmaster strolled over to her as she stood by the gate, and had a quiet word. Thomas judged by the look on his mother's face how deep the trouble he was in was going to be. She nodded her head while the headmaster spoke, and only took her glaring eye off Thomas long enough to make her reply. On the way home she listened to his version of how the day went and what happened to make him lash out the way he did.

"He was being real smart alecky, Ma! And he was slagging me in the classroom! And Miss said –"

"I don't want to know what Miss said!" Angela interrupted him. "And I don't want any more boxing matches in school! D'ya hear me?"

She was dead annoyed.

"But he was jeering at us!"

"I know, I know. I'd have felt like boxing the little git myself, but if you do it again I'll box you, is *that clear*? I have enough bleedin' problems without more from school. Got that?"

Thomas was amazed. She *agreed* with him! She would have felt like boxing the bully herself! He could hardly believe his ears. Instantly he saw her in a new light. His ma was great!

"Got it," he readily agreed, before she changed her mind. The heavy cloud of worry that hung over him evaporated rapidly. His ma agreed with him and he was chuffed! He did not know why exactly, but for some reason he felt safe. Safe from the bully and safe and happy to go back to school tomorrow.

Back in the house, as Angela prepared dinner Thomas got down to doing his homework. It was the part of the school day she always hated. Trying to get him to pay attention long enough to complete the work was always a major hassle to her. Nancy usually had to intervene in order to keep the peace, and Angela would take the opportunity to escape to something else. Now, she was on her own. As she chopped vegetables and kept her eye on the grill, the doorbell rang.

Thomas jumped up from the table.

"Here, you!" she exclaimed. "Get back to that ecker!

I'll get the door!"

But Thomas kept going.

"I'm nearly done with it," he said, as he ran and opened the door.

He came back into the kitchen with Patrick Cullen.

"Something smells delicious," Patrick said, taking in the domestic scene before him. Angela greeted him warmly. "We have enough for three," she offered. She was lying, prepared to do without her own pork chop.

Patrick wouldn't hear of it. He protested that he had a late lunch with a client.

"If I could have a coffee, I'd be much obliged," he insisted. He sat down beside Thomas, who was concentrating on chewing the end of his pencil. "Homework, Thomas? How did your first day go, then?"

Thomas would have told the whole boxing saga with relish, but a darting glance from his mother made him temper his reply. "Great, thank you. I'm in Owen's class." He prattled on as Angela made the coffee and put it in front of Patrick.

"Thank you," he said. "I tried to phone you earlier, but you must have been out."

"Collecting Thomas from school," she replied.

Thomas liked the way she called him by his proper name these days when she was talking to someone.

Silently, Patrick pointed to a misspelled word in Thomas's copybook. At first Thomas frowned at it, and then went "Oh, yeah" and corrected it. A conspiratorial wink passed between them.

"I'm sure your grandfather would have been right proud of you," Patrick was saying. "That's the school he went to as well, you know."

Thomas looked up, pleased as punch. Imagine that, him going to the same school as the famous Daniel Cleary!

That thought triggered a question in Angela's head. "What did my father do?" she asked. "I mean, what did he work at?" It surprised her that she had not asked that before.

"He was a stone-mason. He was passionate about restoration work. He worked on the Heritage Centre in the town, you know. He restored the cottage outside to its original state and then decided to make it his studio. He did some work for a company in Naas too, but mostly he freelanced."

Angela thought of the computer in the front room, and assumed that was where he ran his business.

"Naas? How did he get about then?" Buses were not that frequent in this neck of the woods.

"He drove," Patrick replied. "It's only about twenty minutes at most."

"But there's no car," Thomas quickly pointed out.

Patrick hesitated. The morning Daniel died came into his head as clear as if it was only happening now.

Reluctantly he went over it again, for them.

"That morning your father drove into town. He was changing his car, and he delivered his old one to the man who was buying it. Then he was to come up to my office, and I was going to drive him to a showroom in Tallaght where he was planning to buy his new one. But he collapsed in the street on the way to me."

They were all silenced. The details of Daniel's last day had a very subduing effect.

Patrick perked up first. "But look, I'm keeping you from your dinner. What I came to say is that Rose remarked that Maura is looking for an assistant to help in the bakery. I wondered if you might be interested, Angela? I said I'd drop out and see how Thomas did today and let you know about it."

The offer of a job! That was good news. Perhaps things were taking a turn for the better, for a change.

Part-time for the moment, Patrick said before he left, but that would suit her very well with Thomas being in school. A job would be the answer to a number of things right now.

Chapter 31

Thomas ran in the school gate, calling to Owen and Deko. Angela stood and watched him go, and felt a pang at the sight. Unconsciously, he was forming a little life for himself, based around his new friends, his sudden interest in school, and his love of where they were living. In the past few days the emphasis had changed from "Ma, this" or "Ma, that" to "Deko said this" or "Owen said that", and often it was also what Miss said too. Angela listened to it all, painfully aware of the changes and feeling left out, like an observer standing aside, and watching all the goings-on.

Deko Doyle's dad owned the sheep and lambs that were coming to their field, and Thomas could hardly wait for them to arrive! It was like they were coming on their holliers, he declared. His mother was more inclined to think they were being fattened up before being put on the market, and in case she was right she kept her opinion to herself.

Deko lived further out along the same road, and his mother offered to take Thomas to and from school in their car, since they passed by the gate. Angela had no valid reason to refuse, so she accepted gratefully, and took a lift herself this morning, but it made her feel even further out of her son's life. The irony of it was not lost on her. Not so long ago she *wanted* him out of her life. She knew the problem now was loneliness and isolation, and to sort it out her own life needed filling. She wondered what she could find to fill the aching gap.

Perhaps the job would help. She was on her way to talk to Maura about it. She stood a minute or so watching the energy of the boys as they formed into their lines, ready to file into their classrooms. Thomas would not thank her for seeming to "mammy" him, so she turned and left before he realised she was still there.

She walked down into the main street, taking her time because she was a little early for her appointment, and met Maisie Mac sweeping the footpath outside her shop.

"There you are, Angela – dropping the lad into school, eh?" Maisie stopped her sweeping and leaned on the brush. But as she often did when she knew she was right, she continued without waiting for an answer. "How are you out there now? Managing well, I hope?" She squinted against the morning sun and scrutinised Angela's face.

Angela answered pleasantly, though she did not want to encourage Maisie. "Yes, thank you."

Maisie, as always, had another question. "Going over to the bakery, are you?"

It was irritating how this woman got hold of every scrap of news. Angela took deep breaths to help her dispel the irritation she always felt whenever she came across Maisie Mac. She was convinced that the fuzzy-haired auld busybody deliberately tried to get her going. But just exactly why Maisie Mac had decided not to like her was not going to bother Angela.

She continued on over the bridge and with the wind in the right direction the delicious aroma of freshly baked bread practically led her to the little bakery. Maisie Mac's idiosyncrasies were forgotten as Angela approached Maura's house. It opened onto the street, and the front rooms were converted into a shop for the bakery. The rest of downstairs was where Maura baked the most delicious breads of all kinds. Her living quarters were upstairs. She was behind the counter and was glad to see Angela come in.

She nodded across to her. "Be with you in a moment, Angela."

The woman she was serving turned and on seeing Angela said, "Heard your lad just started up in the school."

Angela nodded and smiled. She was learning how to cope with life in a small town.

The woman took her purchase and nodded to Angela as she left. "You take care, now. There's them that are not pleased to see you, y'know."

Angela nodded in return, wondering what on earth the remark meant.

Maura quickly rearranged the wholegrain bread tray and took off her plastic gloves.

"Don't mind that one," she said. "She always sees the worst of things. Come on inside."

Angela followed saying, "She could be right, you know. I've upset at least one applecart by showing up here."

They went into the back room, Maura keeping an ear alert for customers in the shop.

"Rose was saying you're looking for a part-timer, Maura."

Maura put the kettle on. "That's right, I need someone to do mornings in the shop. My morning girl is off to Australia for a year, and I need someone to fill her hours." She cut a fresh soda bread down the centre and cut and buttered a couple of thick slices.

Angela watched as the butter slowly melted. Everybody was off to somewhere, she thought. The irony of it was the same could be said of her. She was "off" to Baltinglass. She hoped others were more pleased with their destinations than she.

"It's mornings only, Monday to Friday. I have a girl for the afternoons and one who does Saturdays, but if you are interested, the job is yours."

Angela could not help smiling. "Just like that? Don't you want to see references or something?"

Maura laughed and poured two teas. "For what? I don't suppose you had time to look for references before you left Dublin, if you don't mind me saying so, and you were saying at the quiz that you worked in a newsagent's. So you are well used to the till. It will be just like falling off a log!"

Angela smiled ruefully. "You're right there, on both

counts. This bread is gorgeous – do you do all the baking yourself?"

"Yes. I got fitted with new ovens only recently. They are bigger so I can produce more now. I hope to be able to offer full-time jobs soon. That's my plan."

"When do you want me to start?"

The door from the street opened and voices could be heard. Maura lifted her cup to her lips and sipped, then with her other hand outstretched she indicated the door to the shop.

"How about now?" she suggested. "Here, you'll need these." She pulled a fresh pair of plastic gloves from a nearby box, and handed them to Angela. "That coat on the door should fit too."

By the time the morning was over Angela figured she had served about half the population of the town. Maura was thrilled.

"You're drawing customers like a magnet, Angela. I've never been so busy in one few hours before!"

Angela laughed. "For your business I hope it keeps up. But for me, I hope it doesn't!"

Maura was ever logical. "Don't worry. Novelty always wears off. That's when you get to see what level of future business really is out there."

Angela walked back up the main street, her morning's work done. She had enjoyed it. She liked the sense of satisfaction that it evoked. She felt as though she had achieved something, and she smiled unconsciously to herself.

"A penny for them," a voice broke into her thoughts.

Francie Furlong was standing before her on the footpath. He was smiling broadly, as though he expected she should be delighted to see him. Her smile faded. She was amazed at the neck of him! People made their way around them, as Francie stood his ground.

"The dance on Friday," he said in his most persuasive manner, "we still on for that? I'll pick you up at eight thirty, okay?"

Anyone overhearing would have been forgiven for thinking that this was a normal continuation of a conversation. To Angela it was proof of his utter disregard for her feelings. She was supposed to come running simply because he called! Maybe the wallop of the jug had deafened him! Maybe he just did not get it!

"I told you to stay away from me," she warned him, fully expecting him to go away.

"You don't mean it," he said lightly. "You're mad at me, that's all. That's okay, we can start again!"

His assumption that she would still go to the dance with him infuriated her.

"*We* are starting nothing! You don't get it, do you? Now get out of my way!"

In utter surprise he stood rooted to the spot and she sidestepped around him without glancing at him.

She really did mean it! Who did she think she was, snubbing him like that? He watched her go, then realised people were looking, so he turned and went about his business, trying to appear unaffected. But inside he was seething. She was carrying this too far, and for it to happen in public was humiliating in the extreme!

Angela was so mad she practically marched up the street. By the time she realised she was marching in annoyance, she was outside Seán's pub. She pushed open the door and went in, glad to see him behind the bar. She sat herself on a barstool.

"This is a nice surprise," he smiled. "To what do we owe the pleasure?"

She adjusted her position and took a deep breath to calm herself.

"Francie Furlong!" she said through gritted teeth.

Seán's demeanour did not betray either surprise or disappointment. He would have liked to be able to evoke an emotion that strong in her himself. He waited for the explanation, but none came.

"What can I get you?" he offered.

"What?"

"Can I get you a drink? Tea, coffee maybe?"

She let out a deep breath, as if she had been holding it for a while. "Coffee would be nice" she replied, picking up a bar mat, turning it around in her hand and tapping its narrow edge on the counter.

By the time he placed the creamy liquid before her she seemed to have calmed down. He tried a question.

"Want to talk about it?" he asked quietly. He leaned his elbows on the counter and waited while she appeared to make a decision.

She lifted her eyes to meet his for the first time since she came in and was surprised to see the concern in them. "Oh, there's nothing to talk about really." She tried to sound calm and casual.

"You're pretty mad about something, that's plain to see," he prompted.

She sipped the coffee. "You do a lovely cappuccino."

"I'm a very good listener too," he tried again, and watched a little smile spread to her eyes.

"Good cappuccino and a listener as well!" she surprised him by saying. "You'd make someone a wonderful wife!"

They burst out laughing together, and she put the cup down quickly to avoid spilling the coffee.

"No, seriously," she dabbed at her mascara, "that asshole has a problem with the word 'no'."

She had said no to Francie? Seán's hopes lifted. But no to what? A drink, a date? Seán really wanted to know but he couldn't think quickly enough of a way to ask without sounding facetious. It turned out silence was his best ally.

"He thinks I'm a slapper, because I have Thomas."

There. It was out, and she felt the better for having said it. She did not look for Seán's reaction. Her thoughts were focused on how totally wrong Francie was, and how indignant she felt about it. The strength of her feelings surprised her, and slowly but surely another feeling emerged. It negated the need to hear Francie's behaviour condemned. Her gut instinct did that for her.

Seán realised he was watching her self-esteem grow.

"He doesn't know how wrong he is," she stated simply.

Seán would have liked to know what the story was there. "That fellow has a lot to learn," he said quietly.

"Depends too much on his looks and his father's money, if you ask me."

He knew Francie Furlong's style, and he knew therefore that he must have tried it on. He was also hugely pleased because it was clear that the spoiled brat had got nowhere for his efforts. But more so he was angered and would have liked to sink a couple of wallops into the brat's perfect smile.

Angela looked at him and noted that although she did not need approval voiced, it was nice to know it was there.

"I started work this morning," she changed the subject, "got a job in the bakery."

"Well, that's good news. I'm glad for you. How did it go?"

She put down the empty coffee cup.

"Another?" he asked.

"No. No, thanks. It went very well really. Like falling off a log, as Maura said."

It was lunch hour and the pub had become busy as was usual, with people coming in for lunches.

The door opened again, and Angela did not notice Mick Furlong until he stood beside her. He took off his cap and placed it on the counter. He gave her a tentative smile and said, "We seem to have got on the wrong foot, you and me. May I offer my apology for any offence I or my family may have caused?"

Seán was instantly alert. He knew from old that Mick Furlong would never apologise to anyone without an ulterior motive.

Mick's great height towered over Angela, who still sat on the barstool, but for some reason he became aware that his bulk did not have its usual intimidating advantage. She looked him straight in the face, and her steady gaze put her on equal footing with him. Her voice was quiet in its answer but her words roared.

"Okay, accepted. It's a pity your son is not man enough to do the same, though."

Seán had to hide his amusement at the forthright answer and the thunderous look that crossed Mick's face.

Angela stood up and turning away from Mick she said, "Have to go, Seán, or Thomas will be home before me."

The two men watched her leave.

"Getting a bit uppity, that one, isn't she?" Mick remarked, bristling with indignation.

Seán was pulling a pint. "Oh, I don't know," he said, trying to hide his mirth and sound philosophical. "I think she's beginning to find herself. That must surely be good for her."

Mick threw him a quizzical glance. He didn't hold with all this "finding oneself" business. The girl belonged in the city, no two ways about it, and *that's* where she would soon "find" herself, if he could manage it at all.

"Yeah," he replied sarcastically. "It used to be called 'getting too big for your boots'." He waved an impatient hand. "I'll have the usual lunch and I'll have a pint with it."

Something about his attitude got Seán annoyed. So

just for the devilment of it he decided to prolong Mick's discomfort, and put a question to him.

"What was that she meant just there about Francie?"

The bigger man went red in the face, and searched in vain for a fast evasive answer.

"Nothing, nothing at all," he snapped when nothing came easily to mind. "Service in here is getting very slow," he growled. "What's keeping the bloody pint?"

"Nothing, nothing at all," Seán answered smartly, topping up a pint and placing it in front of the irritated farmer. "There you go, I'll bring the lunch over to your table. The beef, isn't it?"

Chapter 32

In D'Arcy Avenue Nancy was at a loss to explain to herself what exactly was preoccupying Paddy. She wouldn't ask. The situation was too precarious, and the atmosphere was fraught with tension. She waited in dread for some indication of what was wrong, and walked on eggshells in the meantime. She was as sure as she could be that he was not sick, and as far as she could tell he was not missing work. He didn't skip going down for his pints, either. The advantage for her was that she was getting some respite from his viciousness, thanks to whatever was on his mind. He had nothing to say to her, so she couldn't read between the lines, or even make a guess. His complaining was greatly reduced, but the loaded silence was in itself ominous and threatening. The strain of waiting for the next eruption was unbearable. She felt relief when he stayed out, and her heart sank when she heard his key again.

She noticed a change in herself too. She felt much less

inclined to tolerate his deplorable behaviour and showed it by daring to voice her objections now and again, despite the fact that doing so was a very real risk to her person. She was still too afraid to be late with the dinner, even by a short while, or even if she suspected he might not be home to eat it. And she dared not be out when he was due home.

But she did buy herself a new mobile phone, a definite act of defiance, and it became the embodiment of her growing anger. Paddy was very frugal these days when it came to giving her sufficient for the housekeeping. There were only two of them now, he pointed out, and he savagely cut the amount she received. But there never seemed to be any shortage for his pints and getting the money together for the new phone wasn't easy. It took nerves of steel on her part, encouraged by her fledgling indignation. She waited for the nights when he came home with much drink taken. It was his habit to drop his clothes on the floor and leave them there and fall into bed. She never went to bed any more till she was sure that he was sound asleep, then she had to pick up the clothes, if only to prevent tripping over them herself. The idea took hold instantly one night when his wallet fell from the pocket of his trousers. Without allowing herself time to be frightened off the idea she whipped a note out and shoved it in her apron pocket. In the toilet she took out the note and was shocked to find she was holding twenty euros! It was too much in one go, but she was not brave enough to chance putting it back. The following day her heart was in her mouth lest he should cop what she had done. Time passed, and she waited with baited breath, but nothing was said, and she rightly came to the conclusion that he assumed he must have spent it in the pub. She collected money in dribs and drabs in the same manner, and when she had enough she bought the same phone as she'd had before, and made her calls or did her texting while he was at work. But something in her needed the satisfaction of him knowing she had another phone, yet she feared him finding out.

It came about quite unintentionally one evening while he was having a cup of tea after his dinner.

She usually turned the phone off when he was home, but that evening she forgot and the tone seemed awfully shrill when it rang. His head jerked up instantly, and Nancy, with the pounding of her heart almost deafening her, jumped up to switch it off. His eyes narrowed as he watched her reach into her bag for the phone.

"How did you get that?" His suspicious growl frightened her.

Her hand clasped the phone to her chest, and she whirled round to face him. It surprised her that he was still seated, not looming towards her. Something in her refused to collapse and lie down, and she straightened her back and lied defiantly.

"The lads sent me a few bob from the States, said to buy something nice for myself!"

She was unable to take her eyes away from his face; such was the fear she felt. If he guessed the truth, she was dead! Yet she remained defiant. Slowly he got to his feet.

"If you lay your hands on me again," she burst out,

"I'll go to the police, I swear it! And if you break this I'll just get another one!"

She was shocked as to where the nerve for that outburst had come from. He came towards her, his icy cold eyes glaring right through her. Her whole body shook, a cold sweat trickled down her back. She had gone *too* far this time. Oh, dear God. Sweet Jesus! Why didn't she keep her mouth shut? He would surely kill her this time! She tried to speak but her voice dried up in her throat. But still she retained the defiant stance.

His arm reached out and he pushed her out of his way. He shoved past her without a word, took his jacket from the hall, and left the house. She stood looking after him, stunned and silenced by his indifferent reaction to her outburst. That was when she knew that *he* was the cause of whatever was bothering him, and she felt no trace of pity or compassion. It served him right. Whatever it was, clearly he had brought it on himself.

She checked the phone. One missed call, it said. She decided to phone Angela back in a while, but now she was going straight over to Annie Ryan. She was elated and absolutely bursting to tell her what had just happened with Paddy!

Chapter 33

Orla gave Thomas a lift home after school. She drove her car up to the front door and Angela heard it and came out. Thomas ran into the house.

"I told Declan's mam I'd take Thomas home," Orla said. "I was intending to come over later, but I have an awful lot of paperwork to do. So here I am, for a short visit."

"I'm glad to see you, anyway," Angela replied. "Come on in, I'll make some coffee."

She led the way into the kitchen, and gave Thomas the usual instruction.

"I know, I know," Thomas said mimicking his mother, "homework before play."

He plonked his bag on the table and took out his books.

"Is he always this good about it?" Orla asked after observing him for a minute or two.

Angela looked over at her son, busy chewing the end of his pencil.

"I think it's the lead he likes," she laughed, "but yes, he is since he started here." She crossed her fingers lest the miracle should cease. "At home was another story!" She rolled her eyes to give Orla a silent indication of the past horrors of homework.

She poured two coffees, and a glass of milk for Thomas.

They took their coffees, out to the sunshine while Thomas worked away at the table. Chatting away as they sat with their backs to the workshop Orla noticed something.

"What happened to the window?" she asked, looking up at the house.

Angela followed her gaze. A pane of glass in the bathroom window was broken.

"I don't know," Angela replied, suddenly troubled. "Was it broken before?"

"No, it wasn't. It's the bathroom. I couldn't not have seen it."

They looked at each other, a measure of concern in their eyes. Without a word they went inside and up to the bathroom. Glass lay splattered on the floor and a large stone was found at the far side of the room.

Angela's face paled.

"Who would *do* that?" Orla whispered.

"It wasn't like that before we went out this morning – I would've noticed."

Silence ensued for a moment while the implications sunk in. Each could almost hear the other think. Who would deliberately do such a thing?

"It's such a childish thing to do," said Orla, "but there was never any vandalism like this around."

Was it Christy, thought Angela. Would he be that bad?

Then Orla asked the question: "Could it have been Christy Cleary?" Everyone knew how much his nose was out of joint over Angela inheriting.

"I don't know," Angela replied, so thoughtfully that Orla was curious.

"Who else do you think?"

The answer was slow in coming but Angela just had to say it: "Do you think Francie Furlong would do this?"

"*What*?" Orla's reaction was utter disbelief and even amusement. "Why in God's name would you think *that*?"

"Francie came over here a while ago and thought he had nothing else to do but have it off with me," Angela confided, watching Orla's mouth drop. "Thomas was out and Francie wasn't about to take no for an answer so I hit him over the head with the milk jug! It was halffull."

Orla was speechless! Finally she burst out laughing and Angela couldn't help joining in, especially when she thought of the milk pouring down the front of Francie's shirt and trousers, and dribbling off his chin!

"My God, Angela! You're priceless, you really are!"

"Yeah, he was furious all right. That's why I thought it might have been him."

Orla became more serious. "I can see now why you would think that," she said thoughtfully. "Francie Furlong is a spoiled brat and thinks he is the cat's whiskers. I wouldn't imagine he comes up against much opposition. You should tell the police – it sounds like he assaulted you."

"Oh, I couldn't! I'd *die* if they asked for details! And you know the gassest part of it is I met him in the town yesterday, and he just assumed he was taking me to the dance on Friday! I mean, how cocky is that?"

"Unbelievable! But typical enough. Actually, I was going to ask if you were coming to the dance," Orla remarked, carefully making her way over some glass. "It's over in Stratford. I'll pick you up if you like. Thomas could stay in our house, of course."

Angela's mind was on the glass. It was going to have to be fixed, and the bits and shards cleaned up off the floor. But who had done this? Why would they do it? Even worse, would they be back?

"I'll phone Patrick Cullen," Angela said worriedly. "He'll know where to get someone to fix this."

They headed back downstairs.

"Let me get back to you on the dance?" she said.

Orla had an idea. "Maybe you could ask Seán Mulhearn to take you. That would be a right smack in the face for Francie! I think Seán most likely would."

"I'm not asking him any such thing! If I go to that dance, it will be on my own."

Thomas was finishing his "ecker" and putting his copies back into the bag.

"Can I go out now, Ma?" He was already heading for the door.

Orla decided it was time she was off too, such was the

amount of work she had to get through.

Angela waved her goodbye from the door and Thomas ran down and closed the gate after her car. Then he headed off for his daily "inspection" of the fields, while he decided what activity he would get up to before dinner.

Angela cleaned up the broken glass and phoned Patrick. After discussing the incident with her he gave her the phone number of a local glazier. She made the call and he agreed to be out with her within the hour.

Thomas was not out very long when he came running and screaming back towards the house. In the house Angela could hear him long before she laid eyes on him.

"Ma! Ma! Come quick, come quick, Ma!"

Her heart almost stopped. *What now!* She uttered a sudden impromptu prayer: "Jesus! Don't let it be more trouble!"

Forgetting the potatoes she had on the cooker she ran out the door, just as a wildly excited Thomas raced up the driveway.

"What?" she called anxiously, running towards him. "What is it?"

Thomas was almost dancing in excitement. He babbled incoherently, trying to get it all out at once.

Angela's alarm grew. "*What*! Jesus, Tomo! What the fuck *is* it?"

"The sheep!" Thomas could hardly contain himself. "It's the sheep! They're in the field! Lots of them!"

Angela stopped dead. Sheep! She'd nearly had the heart put crossways in her over fucking sheep!

"Come and look, Ma. There's loads of them. And little ones as well!" He caught her arm and began to pull her towards the gate.

She didn't want to get close.

The gate from the garden to the field was a wide one, made of tubular steel, and Thomas quickly climbed up on it.

"Get up here, Ma," he urged her. "You can see them all the way down to the back of the field from here."

There was no way that Angela was going to climb onto that gate. If those stupid animals decided to run her way she could break her neck in her hurry to get down again. At the sudden sight of them, the sheep nearest the gate immediately turned tail and ran away, but not very far. Then they turned again and stood looking towards the gate. Thomas was thrilled to bits.

"They're going to charge!" said Angela.

"No, they're not! Sheep wouldn't charge!" Thomas laughed.

"Since when did you become such a bloody expert, then? I'm not taking any chances with that lot! They have lambs with them, so I wouldn't trust them one iota! And don't you be going near them either. That farmer doesn't want the likes of you running around in there, d'you hear?"

Thomas wanted to know everything about the new arrivals. "When did they get here, Ma? How long are they staying?"

Angela had no idea. She hadn't even noticed them when she got home from work. The sheep couldn't be seen from the driveway, and unless she went across and looked down the field from the gate she wouldn't have seen them.

"Declan's da must have put them in while we were out. I'm sure he'll be over to see me about them so you can ask him then."

They didn't have to wait long. As they made their way back to the house a car pulled up outside the driveway gate, and Thomas got the job of going to open it. It was something he never seemed to tire of doing.

"Hi'ya, Mr Doyle, we were just looking at the sheep. I think me ma is afraid of them!"

Declan's father came up to Angela and introduced himself. He wore a waxy gilet over a wool jumper in spite of the warm weather, and he looked exactly like Angela's idea of how a farmer should look.

"You don't have to bother yourself in the slightest about the sheep, Angela," he assured her. "You won't even know they are there."

"Oh, but I will," she replied much to his surprise, "because Thomas here will give me an account of every move they make."

He laughed with relief as he understood her meaning. He handed her a cheque to cover the rental, and told her how much it meant to have the use of the field.

"Your father and I were good friends, you know, as well as neighbours. How are you getting on with your other neighbour, Mick Furlong?"

She wasn't quite sure at first exactly how to answer that. She wondered should she tell him that Mick offered to buy her out, and decided why not?

"One of the first things he said to me was that he would buy me out, so I suppose he isn't too pushed about being overly friendly."

Declan's father didn't appear to be very surprised to hear that.

"There's not a farmer around who wouldn't make a fair offer on this place, given the chance, so don't you let Furlong bother you, girl. Don't think he is the only option you would have. But it would do justice to your father's memory to have you keep this place on, and I wish you all the best with it. We could do with some young blood around the area – there's plenty of us would like to see you make a go of it."

He shook her hand warmly, and said he must be going. But before he did he appointed Thomas chief sheep-watcher, and stressed how important it was to make sure that the gate was never left open!

While Thomas sat on the gate watching sheep, Angela and Mr Doyle moved away. It occurred to her that he might have seen someone about the place earlier. He looked very concerned when she asked. He had seen no one at all and was relieved to know that Patrick Cullen had been told.

"You be careful, girl, there's plenty pleased for you, as I said, but clearly there are those who are not. Keep your doors locked. It was never like that around here. But you never know."

Angela mulled over Mr Doyle's advice as she turned back

towards the house and suddenly she remembered the potatoes! She broke into a run and pushed open the door of the kitchen, only to be greeted by a pall of black smoke coming from the burned-out potato pot! The smell was choking her but there were no flames, and she grabbed a towel and lifted the pot from the cooker and placed it outside the back door. The pot was totally ruined, and the potatoes were seared to the bottom, never to be removed!

"Well, fuck that!" she cursed. "Fuck whoever broke the window and fuck them bloody sheep, anyway, I knew they'd cause something!"

She heard voices and, going around the side of the house, she saw Thomas and Seán coming around to the back door. She swore to herself again, because they could not help but notice the burned dinner – the smell was everywhere.

"What's the smell, Ma? Something is burning."

"Yeah, go on," she muttered to herself, "make a song and dance about it!"

"It's under control," she replied aloud, and ignored the question. "Hi, Seán, what brings you out?"

Seán saw the pot. "Well, I was going to invite myself to dinner, but I won't now," he joked, picking up the pot carefully by the tip of the handle.

"Yeah, yeah, very funny, put that down. No need to make a meal of it!" she warned him, and they all laughed at the unintentional pun.

They went into the house and Angela made tea.

"I was wondering if you have any plans for Friday?"

Seán asked. "I have to go to Blessington in the afternoon and I wondered if yourself and Thomas would like to come for the spin?"

"Yes!" Thomas decided straight away.

"Just a minute, you," his mother checked him. "You have school and homework before you go anywhere."

Thomas's face dropped but Seán was quick to say that it could wait till later in the afternoon.

"If you would give me a buzz when you are ready, I could pick you up then," he suggested. "Would that be a good idea?"

Angela thought of the arrangement she had made with Orla. They would probably be back in time. She agreed.

Thomas clenched his fist in the air and went "Yes!"

His mother was busying herself peeling more potatoes, but Seán had another idea. He got up, took the knife from her hand and said, "Why don't we go into town and get something to eat there?"

This time Thomas stayed quiet. Something told him this was grown-up stuff, and not his decision. His mother was about to say something, but Seán was already prepared for a refusal and joked with her that it would be safer all round if someone else did the cooking, and preferably somewhere else too!

"The cheek of you, Seán Mulhearn!" Angela declared. "But I can't. Thomas, go and wash your hands, and take off those wellies."

Thomas didn't see the point of all that, and looked at Seán for support, but Seán just directed his eyes towards upstairs, and coupled it with a helpless gesture.

Thomas went reluctantly.

"I'm waiting for the glazier," Angela explained and told Seán about the broken window.

He didn't like the sound of that. He wondered if Christy would do such a childish thing. He was a known begrudger, and he had plenty of reason to begrudge Angela this house, but would he do *this*?

Angela didn't say anything about her suspicions of Francie. It would be too embarrassing to explain that one, and anyway she probably had him all wrong. They dropped the subject when they heard Thomas coming back down the stairs in a hurry. His eyes were wide with the surprise of seeing the broken window in the bathroom.

"Who did that?" he demanded.

"Calm down," said Angela. "The man will be here soon to fix it. We don't know what happened to it."

Just then they heard the glazier arrive and went outside to meet him.

In no time the window was fixed. When the glazier heard that they didn't know how it came to be broken he whistled softly. The question in his eyes was clear: Christy?

After having a cup of tea and some chunks of Maura's fresh soda bread, he left. It would be all over the town by morning.

Seán's advice was to report the broken window to the Gardaí. Angela wondered what they could do. It was so easy for anyone to go around the house and land without being seen. And it could have *been* anyone, but she didn't think so. They dropped the subject rather than worry Thomas about it.

Seán stayed for what Angela called a make-do dinner and produced a bottle of wine from the boot of his car.

The grown ups took *so long* to eat, Thomas thought, especially when they were busy drinking wine as well though it seemed to him Seán wasn't drinking much at all. He drifted away from the table, more curious to see what was on the telly. Angela was enjoying her make-do meal immensely, the conversation was interesting, and she relaxed and chatted away as if she had nothing else to do in the whole world. Seán was aware of nothing else in the whole world and wanted the meal to go on and on.

"What of Thomas's father?" he asked unexpectedly, changing the subject.

The spell was broken. Angela had difficulty finding an answer that she would be willing to give. She became visibly uneasy and Seán actually felt her withdraw from him. He saw in her face that there was a lot of emotional turmoil going on, and the fact that she felt unable to talk freely about it told him clearly that there was some other dimension to be contended with. He quickly came to the conclusion that it had not been a regular boyfriend/girlfriend situation. He could have cut his tongue out, and deeply regretted having asked at all.

"Thomas has school in the morning, and I have work," Angela said suddenly.

"Angela, I'm terribly sorry, I really was very out of line there. I – I . . . it's really none of my business . . ."

She raised a hand and cut him off. "It's okay. I didn't realise myself that I had such a problem with it, really. I thought I –" She broke off, searching for a way to voice her feelings.

"Look, I shouldn't have been so crass in the first place."

"No . . . you weren't . . . it's just that I haven't given much thought to that lately," she sighed. "I suppose I was busy just getting on with things. I imagine I'll have to deal with it . . . sometime."

She let out a deep breath, as if to expel the unpleasant reminder, and he was glad to see she still had a smile for him.

He rose to leave.

Thomas was engrossed in watching the telly so for once he didn't go with their guest to close the gate after him.

"Are we still okay, then? Friday still on?" Seán enquired tentatively on the doorstep, searching her face for an indication that he had not done *too* much damage by his tactlessness. He did not dare to touch or kiss her as he would have liked, lest he distance her any further.

"Yeah, Friday is grand."

Relieved, Seán drove home and took a shower before going down to the bar to begin the evening shift. He was in a very contemplative mood and he wondered about a lot of questions concerning Angela and Thomas. It struck him as odd that she never had any friends or relations visit her from Dublin.

Where were her parents, for example? What about sisters, or brothers? She never mentioned them. It seemed to him that if someone inherited the likes of Daniel's place, there would be friends and relations all over the place, coming to view the inherited property. He knew that she and her mother had met in Tallaght, but it seemed odd that her mother didn't come here.

It seemed even odder that a chatty fellow like Thomas should settle in so easily to life in the country, without ever mentioning any friends that he must have left back in Dublin.

They had problems, both of them. It occurred to Seán that a fellow would be better off finding himself someone else to be interested in.

But Seán was not that fellow.

Chapter 34

Angela had been on the verge of cancelling the trip to Blessington. She didn't delve too deeply into exactly why, but somewhere in the back of her mind was the thought that Seán might read too much into it. For his sake she didn't want him to get the wrong impression. And she worried that he just might. She knew that she was going to have to put him straight about things, sooner rather than later, and resolved to do it as soon as she got the opportunity.

"Can we phone Seán now?" Thomas wanted to know, "I'm nearly finished."

"In a few minutes," she answered and went upstairs to get ready. Getting ready in the country was not the ritual it was at home. She managed to achieve satisfaction in the way she looked in what seemed like half the time.

Thomas put his books and copies back into his schoolbag and called out, "Finished!"

"Go and check that the back door is locked," she called down to him, "and close the little window in the back porch!"

Just before Seán arrived Thomas ran down to the front gate and opened it for him, and he took a look at the sheep grazing while he was down there. He liked to reassure himself that they were perfectly happy in the field, now that they were well settled in. He regarded them as his personal pets, and watched over them like a mother hen. He was particularly fond of the black-faced ones, and already he could recognise some of the ewes and their lambs.

On the way out of the town Angela was curious as to why Seán was heading to Blessington.

He had no hesitation in saying, "Business – we have another premises just before you get into the main street. I visit it on a regular basis. Certainly keeps me busy, spreading myself between the two."

In a rather pleased tone Thomas chipped in. "See, Ma? I *told* you Seán owned the pub! You didn't believe me!"

"Okay, okay. So you were right! Does that make you happy?"

"You own *two* pubs, Seán?" Thomas was really impressed. "Wow!"

Seán was amused. He cast a glance at Angela, who was shaking her head in disbelief at her son's frankness.

"It's not manners to ask things like that!" she rebuked him.

"I didn't ask, did I, Seán? You said, didn't you?"

A slight nod kept him happy.

That young fella was getting far too smart altogether, Angela told herself yet again.

"Did you ever go out on a lake?" Seán asked out of the blue, changing the subject to rid them of the slight narkiness he sensed in the air.

That silenced them both for a moment or two. But again Thomas was quickest. "I saw a lake once, in the park where me nan used to bring us."

Angela turned on him. "Don't be stupid! That was only a *pond*. The duck pond in St Steven's Green!"

Thomas looked injured – he didn't want to sound stupid, especially in front of Seán. But Seán took no notice of the exchange and said they could go and see the Blessington lakes when he had done his work. Thomas perked up and Angela was glad her remark was ignored.

They arrived at the pub and while Seán attended to business Angela and Thomas sat at a table outside in the sunshine, and minerals and tea were taken out to them. Then they continued on to the lakes. Angela, who had only ever seen the River Liffey, or the sea at Dollymount, was quite taken with this expanse of water in the middle of the countryside. Thomas was speechless, for once. Then his eye caught all the activity going on around him and he could hardly take it all in. Out on the water were all sorts of craft – boats with sails, brightly coloured canoes, and windsurfers with tall elegant sails which mesmerised him. On land, there was an archery class in progress and they could hear the guns at a clay-pigeon shoot.

"Come on," Seán said, "we'll see if the waterbus is going out."

They cruised the lakes on the waterbus, watching people being instructed in the various craft on the water. Later they watched the archery class and strolled about taking in all the sights.

But what really took Thomas's fancy were the stables, the horses, and the pony trekking!

"Can I have a go, Ma? Can I? Please? Can I?"

He was practically begging, and Angela was worrying about the cost. She had no idea of how much it would be and she wasn't sure if she had enough money in her purse. So she said there wouldn't be enough time, Seán might need to get back.

"I think we have plenty of time for you to have a go, if that's okay with your mother?" said Seán. "And it's my treat." He looked for Angela's nod and got it. "You told me you already know how to ride horses, so let's see if they have a good one for you."

The excitement was almost too much for the lad. He was absolutely bursting to get going. The smell of horse was instantly familiar. He hadn't realised how much he missed those wonderful animals till his nostrils tingled with their peculiar odour.

Things went very differently to what Thomas expected. In the first place he told the stable girl that he didn't need a saddle, just a rein would do. But that was not allowed. And neither did he get to ride where he pleased. He had to stay in line, and they didn't get to gallop as he would have liked.

"There were beginners on the ride, and we had to go slow for them," he told his mother and Seán afterwards, with a note of disdain in his voice, but he was so thrilled at being on a horse again it didn't really matter. He had *such* a cool day. Just wait till he told Owen and Deko about it!

They had dinner in the Lakeside restaurant before heading home. Thomas talked horse all the way, and his mother just knew she was in for it again about horses. By the time they were approaching the last stretch to their house she was already utterly fed up with horse talk. But she said nothing. There was no point. Thomas was on a high and she knew he would simply talk himself out.

They were approaching a curve in the road just before Daniel's house and saw that the two cars in front of them had stopped. Seán pulled up behind them, wondering aloud what could be the hold-up – there certainly weren't any roadworks in progress – at least there weren't when they had passed this way earlier. Because they were unable to see beyond the curve they simply waited for the traffic to move.

All the time Thomas talked.

"I hope this hold-up isn't an accident," Angela said, no longer listening to him.

Telling them to stay where they were for safety, Seán decided to step out and have a look. He walked forward towards the curve, as did the driver of the car in front of them. The two men approached the bend in the road and looked ahead to where they saw the cause of the problem.

Sheep!

Sheep were all over the narrow road! From one ditch across to the other they filled the width of it. No one seemed to be in charge of them, and their combined bleating signified the great confusion they were in. They were so tightly crammed together in the centre of the flock that they had to hold their heads aloft above the backs of other sheep. Lambs were in among the mêlée and in serious danger of being crushed or injured. Looking way ahead to the far side of the flock Seán could see that the approaching traffic was also stopped, some of the drivers out of their cars, and he quickly realised the sheep were from Angela's field. In fact, he now saw that some of the flock were blissfully happy munching on Angela's lawn. The field gate must be wide open.

Doyle's sheep! Loose and all over the road. And obviously panicking. Christ Almighty! The drivers were quick to see the danger to the animals, and to other unsuspecting drivers as well. They were trying to prevent the sheep from straying any further by blocking their escape either up or down the road, but the problem was to get the ones nearest the gate to turn around and go back in. But they were too tightly jammed against each other to be able to go either way. They were simply following their instinct and following the ones directly in front.

Seán ran back to the car. Angela had just stepped out to see what was going on.

"What is it? What's up?"

"You won't believe it – the sheep are out all over the road!"

She stated at him in disbelief while Thomas jumped out of the car. His sheep! How could they have got out? He had made very sure they were safe in their field before they left for Blessington. He *always* made sure the gates were closed.

"Stop it, Seán Mulhearn, that's not a bit funny!" said Angela.

"I'm deadly serious! Most of the flock is on the road in a panic back there!"

His tone alarmed her, and she realised he wasn't joking.

"Both of the gates are wide open! I can't understand it. Thomas checked them before he got into the car!" No sooner had he the words uttered than the obvious hit him. The gates were deliberately opened! It *had* to be that. But there was no time to wonder about it now. The sheep must be got back in before some of them were injured in the crush! Or worse.

"Angela," he said decisively, "go up there and help those men to keep them from scattering any further! Thomas, you come with me!"

Leaving a shocked and immobilised Angela staring incredulously after him he ran towards the near ditch and jumped across at a point where the hedgerow was less dense. He held out a hand and helped Thomas after him, because there was no way they could have got by on the road through the tightly packed sheep. They ran through the field to Angela's garden and around to the gate that led to the road. Some of the sheep near the gate ran safely back into the garden, while the ones just outside the gate made frantic efforts to run forward and away from them. But there was nowhere to run to, only more sheep in front of them, and they panicked further at the fuss being made behind them. Seán made a quick decision as to how they should handle it.

"Listen to me, Thomas, we have to get these nearest ones back into the garden so there is space for us to turn the others around. Are you with me?"

Thomas had no hesitation. "Yes!"

"Good lad. Now, I am going to grab them one by one, and pull them back. When I do, I want you to shoo them out of the way, so they don't try to jam it all up again. Okay?"

"Okay."

On the roadway Angela screamed frantically as a panicked ewe got past the other drivers and came frighteningly close to her. One of the drivers whirled in alarm, and then let out an irritated shout at her when he saw she was being worse than useless.

"Don't make a bollix of it, woman! Stop the fuckin' animal before they *all* follow!"

She stared at him stupidly. It was a *sheep*, for Christ's sake! Did he actually expect her to get *near* it?

"Move!" he roared.

She jumped, suddenly not knowing which frightened her more, the sheep or the man.

"Get back there!" she heard herself order the ewe, as if she expected it to understand her. "Shoo, shoo!" Encouraged by the sheep's hesitation she shouted again, "Shoo! Go on, get back!" and she waved her arms wildly, while taking a very brave couple of steps towards it. Her actions worked, and as the sheep rejoined the outer edges of the flock she came level with the front car.

"Keep at it!" the second driver told her, while he and the other man did their utmost to cover the width of the road. "Keep them together!"

Angela took up a position level with the men, and between them they managed to prevent the main body of sheep from fragmenting and escaping further down their end of the road.

At the far side of the flock other drivers were doing their best to keep that side together. A few determined sheep managed to get loose, but they had to be let go, rather than lose the whole flock all over the place.

Working as fast as they could Seán and Thomas did their utmost to unblock the sheep jam at the gate. It was frustratingly futile. The sheep kept running the wrong way, despite their best efforts. Thomas "whooshed" at them when Seán grabbed them by their thick wool and pulled them one by one into the garden, but the animals' instinct was to rejoin the others. Thomas was becoming frustrated and so he whooshed louder and waved his arms at them, but it was useless.

"Grab them by the wool before I let go and shove them away from you towards the garden," yelled Seán. "They might get the message then."

Thomas grabbed big handfuls of warm living wool, and pushed the sheep away. When he let them go the frightened animals were only too glad to be free of the manhandling, and ran at last in the required direction.

Slowly but surely the escaped animals became less crammed, and Seán was able to get outside the gate and turn the others back towards the garden. One followed the other, and eventually a steady flow of sheep began to head into the garden and away from the road.

They still had to be got from the garden into the field, but at least in the garden they were safe. The ones still loose they had to leave to the skills of Mr Doyle with his sheepdog, and he had to be told right away that some of his sheep were loose on the roadway. It was getting late and the light was beginning to fade.

Angela was in a state. How could this have happened? What would he say? He paid good money for the use of a secure field, and his animals were running amok on the dangerous narrow roads. Could she not even keep a simple gate closed?

One of the drivers called into Mr Doyle's house and alerted him to the situation. Mr Doyle did not utter a word when he arrived. He got straight to work and paid no heed to anyone till his flock was safe.

Thomas watched enthralled as Mr Doyle and his dog herded the sheep through the gate and back into their field again. With a series of whistles Doyle gave orders to his dog and they both worked steadily till all the animals were returned to the field. It took quite some time for the last of the escapees to be safely rounded up, but finally all the flock was back in, and none of them seemed to be any the worse for their experience. By that time it was dusk.

Angela dreaded facing Mannix Doyle. But there was no way out of it. She approached him as he dug into his waxed gilet pocket, pulled out his pipe and some tobacco, and began the ritual habit of lighting the pipe. He gripped it between clenched teeth while he rolled the tobacco to reduce its volume in order to pack it into the bowl of the pipe.

Angela, thinking this was her opportunity, began her apology.

"Mr Doyle, I'm terribly sorry – I *know* the gate was closed –"

He cut her short, speaking surprisingly clearly, even while his teeth gripped the treasured pipe. "I paid good money for a secure field." He was a straight talker, and expected the same in return. He did not hold with excuses. He took the pipe in his hand and pointed it towards the sheep. "That flock is my livelihood. If I have to move them again it's no good for either them or us. But they are my first concern."

Angela wanted to die. She felt *so* incapable. So much of a *townie*!

"Your father and I have had this arrangement for years without mishap." He was pulling no punches.

She felt worse, but decided the best thing to do was be straight with him too.

"I don't know what to say to you, Mr Doyle. I do realise how serious it is, but I can only assure you that both gates were properly closed before we left this afternoon."

He gave her a strange look. "You were out?"

"Yes," she answered, "but the gates were definitely shut."

Seán came up to them and heard the conversation.

"I can vouch for that. I watched Thomas double-check the gates before he got into the car."

It was Mr Doyle's turn to be baffled. He drew on the pipe, and his brows were drawn together in a worried frown.

"Is there something else?" Angela tentatively asked the question, prompted by the sudden reflective manner of Mr Doyle.

"It's just that I thought you were in. I thought your Uncle Christy was visiting you. I passed by earlier and I saw him cycling up the road.

The shock that reverberated through his listeners was all too apparent. They looked silently from one to the other, while the enormity of the situation sank in.

Angela said, her voice a whisper. "First the broken window? And now *this*?"

Seán was worried. If they were right, Christy was surely going off the deep end.

"Broken window?" Mr Doyle asked.

"Too much to be a coincidence," said Seán.

"And now this . . ." The farmer was very concerned for the safety of his flock.

All this while Thomas was sitting on the gate anxiously surveying the sheep.

"Might I suggest a padlock on the field gate? A good strong one?" said Seán.

There was no immediate response from Doyle who was obviously weighing up whether to leave his flock there or move them.

Angela surprised herself by wanting him to leave them but being worried as to their safety.

"Will you come in, Mr Doyle and have tea? It's almost dark, we can talk inside."

But her neighbour had come to a decision.

"No thanks, I won't come in, but thank you for the offer. What I will do, though, is take Seán's suggestion. I have a strong padlock and chain up in the shed. I will put it on the gate for tonight anyway, and then we'll see."

Angela nodded. At least that would keep the sheep safe for now. If anyone tried to break a padlock in the silence of the country night, the whole place would hear it.

"Mr Doyle, I *am* sorry for this . . ."

He looked straight at her. "I know, but if you have a problem with Christy, or anyone, I don't want it impacting on *my* sheep."

"I understand."

He settled the pipe between his teeth again. "You watch out for yourself, girl," he advised. "That uncle of yours is not the most balanced person, y'know." He whistled for his dog which was lying on the grass at the bottom of the gate where Thomas sat.

When he was gone Seán went on about Christy.

"Surely to God the police can warn him off?"

"If it was him."

"What does that mean? Who else could it be?"

"Don't know," she answered lamely, thinking of Francie.

But she decided to ask Patrick Cullen if the police could have a word with her uncle. If it was him then it might get him off her case.

Chapter 35

Later that night Mick Furlong paid a visit to Christy's cottage.

"You asshole!" he hissed at the older man as soon as the door closed behind him. "You don't endanger livestock, for Christ's sake!"

Christy recoiled under this attack. But he was quick to defend himself. It was pointless – Mick Furlong was much too enraged to tolerate any excuses.

"You were seen! The whole damned place knows it was you! You'll get no fucking sympathy putting *sheep* at risk!"

Mick was having a seizure! Christy was totally taken aback. He never saw Mick Furlong lose his cool before.

"People will be firmly behind her after this," Mick growled thumping his fist on the grubby table, all previous fears of contamination overridden by anger. "You don't put a man's livelihood at risk, you fucking eejit! It was *her* you are supposed to get rid of, you blasted imbecile, not the bloody livestock! You fucking *moron*!"

Christy wiped Mick's spittle from his face and felt the turbulence of a volcano of fury bubble up inside. He clenched his fists so tight that his longish black fingernails dug into his palms. He did not feel it. He felt the urge instead to smash the bulging face that stuck itself in front of him, pulsating veins and all. He wanted to box the mouth that roared obscenities and likened him to a fool!

Instead he said, "What are you fuckin' yelpin' about? What bloody sheep?"

"Don't come the innocent with me! You let Doyle's sheep out all over the road! You were seen up there just before they got out!"

It was Christy's turn to be stunned, but he recovered quickly. "So I can't cycle where I want now but I am accused of something, is that it, eh?"

He leaned towards the farmer, his voice so low that Mick automatically felt himself draw in his horns.

"If you can't prove your accusations then you had better clear off out of here while you still can, you hear me? You want to hide behind me so that you can hold your head up in the town! Do your own bloody dirty work, you two-faced bleedin' hypocrite!"

He lashed out with a closed fist and caught his antagonist square on the chin. His fist felt like he had smashed it into the wall. Even so he positioned himself, ready to fend off Mick Furlong's retaliation.

The speed with which he had moved had taken Mick by surprise, and he staggered backwards, despite his larger size. He instantly knew, even in the heat of his extreme anger that he did not have the agility or the viciousness to take on Christy Cleary. He steadied himself against the door and straightened himself up, brushing his hair smooth again, with a hand he hoped could not be seen to be shaking.

"You just keep your end of the bargain, Cleary, or else you can fucking wither away in this hovel! And make sure you don't make stupid moves! Do you think people are fucking eejits?"

Behind him his hand searched for the doorknob, and just managed to find it as Christy made another lunge at him. He whipped the door open and quickly stepped outside.

Christy stopped at the door, while Mick hurried out the gate and got into his car.

"Go on, run, you bleedin' coward!" Christy bellowed after him, still shaking a clenched fist.

He went back into the cottage and vented his temper on anything in his way. That Mick Furlong should call to his house and call him an eejit, a moron, an imbecile, was to push Christy Cleary *too* far! He kicked a chair out of his way. With his arm he swept the few dirty dishes he had used for his tea onto the floor, and kicked at the pieces till they were in smithereens. In his blind frenzy he swore to show them they could not push Christopher Cleary around! They would regret treating him like dirt! By God they would! As sure as there was breath left in his body! He went into the bedroom and from under his mattress he took a half-empty bottle of whiskey. He had been saving it for whatever he considered to be a good reason. This was as good as any.

Driving back down the winding road Mick was unaware of the dangerous state of mind he had left Christy in.

He had plenty of reason to want the girl gone, but if accusations were flung he had no wish to be implicated. And with Christy the way he was, that was highly likely. He would deny everything of course. He would say that Christy had flipped entirely, as a result of being left out of the will. Many would believe it. But if Christy was telling the truth then who opened that gate?

It should be a simple matter to get rid of a slip of a girl, a raw novice to country living. But time was passing and she showed no indication of leaving. The boy had started school. A bad sign. Even Francie had failed him miserably. He made a right botch of what should have been a simple matter for him. Despite Mick's threats his son was hitting a brick wall in his efforts to inveigle his way back into the girl's good graces.

He did not give a damn about Mr Doyle's sheep or his livelihood. That speech was protection for himself. If it made Christy feel stupid, so much the better. He might be less reluctant to spill the beans if he thought it was going to result in making him look like a total moron. Still, Mick feared he might have just struck his plans a fatal blow by exploding at Christy the way he did, because if all else failed he would end up having to make *her* an offer she could not possibly turn down. A last resort.

But somebody was being stupid. The cover of night was obviously the time to open gates.

Chapter 36

It was Saturday and The Square in Tallaght was crowded with weekend shoppers. The shops were having mid-season sales, and Angela and Thomas were afraid they wouldn't find Nancy in the crowds. Angela knew she would have already arrived: it was a while since they had met and Nancy was looking forward so much to the hour or so she could spend with them that she was unlikely to miss even a minute of it.

"Yoo hoo! Angela! Thomas! Over here!"

There was wild hugging and instant visual assessment of each other before they settled on where they would have lunch. As always Thomas wanted McDonald's, but his mother and Nan went 'Oh, no! Not again!' in unison, and Thomas knew he had lost this time.

They settled themselves in a nice little café on the first level, and were lucky to get a table before the lunch mêlée began. Thomas was bursting to tell Nancy the news about the sheep, forgetting that she had not heard about their arrival in the field.

"There's loads of them, Nan! They even have lambs, and some have black faces and all, and they were all over the road yesterday, and Deko's da had to get his dog to get them back in – oh, and I got a go on a horse as well, you should have seen me! I was the best! And do you know what? Seán brought us to the lakes, and we were on a waterbus!"

"My God! Hey hey hey! Take it easy a minute, I can't take all this in, in one blast!" Nancy laughed, delighted to see he was as happy as ever with his new life. She looked at Angela for some kind of confirmation of all Thomas was babbling about. "Don't tell me you've gone into *sheep farming*!" She could hardly believe she was even *saying* this.

"God forbid, Ma!" Angela grumbled. "The bloody things run everywhere! They are so stupid!"

"They are not!" Thomas denied it hotly, and was offended as if it was *he* who was responsible for their intelligence, or lack of it.

Angela relayed to Nancy how they came to have sheep in the field. "Money, Ma, that's what brought it on. Mr Doyle rents the field. Apparently he has been renting it for years from Daniel – not all year – just for a while around now when he has need of it. So I wasn't going to say no when I heard he pays."

Nancy felt an envious desire to see things for herself. This life they talked about seemed to be getting better and more settled each time they met, and she was not part of it. They were moving in another world, far removed from hers, and deep in her heart she feared they would eventually be separated by the gap.

"Why don't you come down and stay, Ma?" It was as if her daughter had read her thoughts. "We'd love that, wouldn't we, Thomas?"

Nancy noticed how Angela had got into the habit of calling him by his proper name.

"Come on, Ma! I'm always asking, and we have plenty of room. Do you never get curious to see the house where *he* lived or anything?"

Nancy smiled a little wistful smile. "Of course I get curious. I know you're always asking, love, I appreciate it, really I do, but I couldn't go. Not just yet, anyway."

Angela studied her mother. Then she took out her purse and gave Thomas money to go to the counter and get some chocolate biscuits. He hated being sent for biscuits or Coke when they wanted him out of earshot but he reluctantly went off.

"Why not, Ma?" Angela lowered her voice. "You said there was none of *that* anymore?"

"I know. There's not, that's the funny bit."

"How do you mean 'funny bit'?"

Nancy's brows were twisting in an effort to find words to explain. "He's gone all quiet. I don't know what brought it on, but one night he came home from the pub, and he was just . . . different. I can't say it any better than that. But he couldn't be bothered raising a hand now. Mind you, I'm grateful for whatever it is, since it keeps him away from me! You should hear me!" She smiled, obviously quite pleased with herself. "I even answer him back! The things I say to him! And nothing. Just nothing. It seems like he's not even listening. I think he has something else bothering him."

Angela was as perplexed as her mother. "Any idea at all what it could be?"

Nancy shrugged. "Naw. But as long as he leaves me alone, I don't care. But I feel to go away for a while, even a couple of days, might be pushing it a bit too far. I'd love to come down, love, but not just yet, you know?"

Angela did. She well understood the fear her mother felt. Memories of what it was like that last day had not faded much from her mind. But she was happy that at least her mother was not still being beaten. She could relax about that. Whatever was bothering Paddy Brennan was his problem. Not something to trouble themselves about.

Thomas came back from the counter. He was allowed listen to the conversation again, but he knew he had missed the best bits.

"The job is working out well," his mother was saying. "It's still part-time though!" She gave a rueful laugh. "I can imagine what *he* would have to say to that!"

Thomas knew that "*he*" meant his granda.

"Don't you mind that – it's bringing in some money, isn't it?" Nancy said supportively. "Yeah," Angela replied wistfully, "but it's not actually *being* something, is it?"

"How do you mean?"

Angela took her time answering. She had not really articulated what was in her mind before – the question had just come out of nowhere. Now as she thought about it she was easily able to see what was going on in her head.

"Y'know," she said pensively, "practically everybody I have met since I got here is *something*. Like, I mean, a teacher, or a secretary, or having their own business. And me? I have only a part-time job. Yeah, a part-time job, and a field full of someone else's sheep!" The last sentences were said in a very derisory tone.

Nancy was dismayed to hear such talk. She looked across the table at her beautiful daughter and cursed Paddy Brennan for continually beating her self-esteem into the ground over the years.

"I never heard such a load of tripe in my life!" she declared so indignantly that people at the next table actually halted their conversation to see what would happen next.

Angela too, waited in surprise. Nancy lowered her voice, but the urgency of it was sufficient to convey her meaning.

"Look, love, I look at you and I see a fine young woman who has been dealt a raw deal in her life. And I see how she has taken control of that life, and is doing what is necessary for herself and her son, and making a grand job of it too! And that is very admirable. As for someone *else's* sheep? Remember, it's *your* field they are in!"

Angela was quietly nodding her head. "I know, Ma. I appreciate that, I really do, but maybe if I had finished school or something . . ."

Nancy could see where this train of thought was leading, and it was no good for Angela. She tried her best to turn it around. "People having more education doesn't

355

mean they have more intelligence, or more character, or integrity, you know. It only means circumstances weren't right for you at the time. Your life so far has made you bring out qualities in yourself you can be proud of. Other people might yet have to develop these skills, you know, even educated people. You should be proud of yourself. I know *I* am proud of you."

Thomas was getting tired of this heavy stuff. He moved away from the table and began to inspect the cakes under glass at the counter. Some of the bigger ones were birthday cakes, decorated with coloured icing depicting things like a football match, or a pink Barbie doll, and he wondered what he would like on his cake, if he ever had such a cake. But his nan called him back as she delved into her shopping bag.

"Thomas, I knew there was something!" She pulled out a package.

His eyes lit up. Something big was in a large brown paper bag.

"You've grown so much, I hope this fits."

Thomas looked in at the woollen garment and couldn't help feeling a little disappointed. It was only a jumper. But his nan had knit it for him, and so he would wear it, when the weather was cold enough.

As always, they parted in the same manner, with Thomas asking when Nancy was going to come down and see them. And as always, she answered in the usual way.

"Soon, love, I promise, soon."

She could not have known how true her words would prove to be.

Chapter 37

When she finished her morning's work Angela called in to see Patrick Cullen. Rose was just going off on a late lunch, but Patrick was in his office.

"We haven't seen you lately, Angela," Rose commented. "How have you and Thomas been keeping?" She was rummaging in the bottom of her black leather handbag for her car keys as she spoke.

"We've been very well, thanks, Rose. I'm with Maura at the bakery, as you know. And I'm kept busy enough, I suppose."

Rose found the elusive bunch of keys. "I'm always threatening to get myself a smaller bag. Stuff gets lost in this monstrous thing, and then I think I have really lost it."

Angela smiled. She could never imagine Rose losing anything, not even in the "monstrous thing" she used as a handbag. She was far too organised for that.

Rose turned towards the door. "Orla says you missed a great night on Friday, you know. I hope it wasn't

357

because you were stuck for a sitter for Thomas."

It wasn't a question. Angela knew Rose would not hear of her being stuck, and she assured her it wasn't.

"I heard Francie Furlong was disappointed you weren't there," Rose teased. "Well, I must be gone."

The door of Patrick's office opened.

"I thought I heard a familiar voice, Angela. Nice to see you, come on in."

Of the two seats opposite the desk she chose the big leather chair, and Patrick rambled around to his own chair and sat down also. He clasped his hands in front of him on the desk and looked at her thoughtfully for a moment.

"So, how have you been?" he enquired kindly.

She never felt uneasy with him. He always was genuinely interested in how she was.

"I'm fine thanks, Patrick. How are you?"

"My doc says I'm A1," he replied lightly. "My body doesn't believe him of course, but there you are. Tell me, this story I hear about loose sheep – what happened?" He leaned forward on his desk, all attentiveness.

"That's what I wanted to ask you about," she began. "You see, Mr Doyle said he saw Christy cycling along our way that evening, and he assumed it was him who let them out."

Patrick was shaking his head disapprovingly as she spoke. "And was it?"

"I don't know." Angela was reluctant to say any more. "We were out, Thomas and me, with Seán Mulhearn."

Patrick's eyebrows went up. There was a little smile about his eyes.

"It's not like that!" she answered the unasked question, feeling herself get a little hot under the collar. "When we got back the sheep were all over the place."

"And the gates?"

"Wide open, both of them."

"And they were definitely closed when you left? Can you be positive about that?"

"Thomas minds those animals as if they were his very own pets. He gave himself the job of checking their safety. He never leaves without making sure the gate to the field is shut. He would drive you mad, because there's no reason to open it in the first place. He has to go right over to it when you can see from where you stand that it is properly shut. It was the same on Friday. We were in the car waiting while he 'just made sure' as he put it. You can ask Seán, if you like, and Thomas also closed the garden gate after the car was out."

Patrick was amused. In his mind's eye he could see Thomas at the gates. He remembered how the boy always ran down and closed the garden gate each time he paid a visit.

"So, they were opened while you were out. And Christy was seen in the area," he mused. If Christy wanted to cause trouble it would have made a lot more sense to open the gates at night. But while that might be so, patience was not Christy's strong point, and Patrick, knowing Christopher Cleary of old, knew he would be very likely to do it as soon as the opportunity presented itself.

"Can we get the police to make him stop?" Angela

asked anxiously. "I mean, he was there, and there was the broken window too. Can't they arrest him, or something?"

Patrick was extremely concerned about the situation. Without doubt Christy was very angry when he had attacked him in the office, but it was difficult to judge just how far he would be likely to take his troublemaking, assuming it *was* he who had released the sheep, and broke the window. But Patrick did not work on assumptions. Neither did the Gardaí.

"What we seem to have, at the moment, is circumstantial evidence. That is what the police will say, even if they suspected that it was Christy who did it."

Angela sighed hopelessly. She was afraid he was going to say something like that.

"But people get arrested on suspicion of things. You see it all the time on the telly."

Though Patrick could well understand her fears, he was wary of aggravating Christy.

"I'll tell you what I can do in the short term. I can ask them to have a word with him. They could say he was seen there at the same time, and that they will be watching his movements. They might do that, off the record." Even as he spoke he worried that such a thing would make Christy flip. "But I'm not at all sure it's a good idea – it might aggravate the situation," he finished.

Angela's shoulders sagged dejectedly. "And long term? Is there something you can do long term?"

He grimaced, and moved his hands in a seesaw manner. "Short of an injunction to keep him away from the house, or from you and Thomas, not really, and he has to be found guilty of something in order to get that."

"That puts us back to square one," Angela sighed.

"The best thing at the moment, I think, is vigilance. Be extra cautious."

It wasn't a lot of help. She was sure something tangible was needed, and would probably be more effective, like the heavy padlock Mr Doyle had installed on the sheep's gate. Angela would have preferred if they just locked the bloody lunatic up. At least, she hoped there was only *one* lunatic out there.

Chapter 38

A period of peace and quiet followed the sheep incident. Angela began to relax on the Christy issue. Although she had not heard, she figured the Gardaí must have "had a word".

Other matters were coming to the forefront, like what was she going to do about Thomas while she was at work in the mornings? The school holidays were looming, and she could ill afford to pay for a minder. Neither could she leave him alone every morning while she was in the bakery. At nine years of age there was not a great deal of minding to be done, but neither was he old enough to be left alone. She hadn't mentioned it to him. His reaction, she knew, would be one of disgust if he thought she was looking for a "babysitter" for him. Because no matter how she put it, that would be the way he would see it.

She remembered wistfully how it was when she was in D'Arcy Avenue. Who would mind Thomas was never an issue. She went to work, or out at night, always without even thinking that she was leaving someone else to look after her child. The load she allowed her mother to take off her shoulders was massive. The enormity of it swamped her now, now that there was no one convenient to do it for her again. No one to do it without expecting to be paid.

She allowed her mind to roam over all the people she knew who had schoolgoing children. Rose had Owen, and she worked full time. But then Rose had Orla, and Orla was on holidays the same time as Owen because she taught in his school. And as well as that, his father worked at home.

There were others whom she sometimes met at the school gates, or served in the bakery. Some of them had farms and the school holidays were an opportunity for the children to contribute with much-needed extra help. There were the Doyles up the road – she knew Deko was expected to help his dad.

So, it was a real problem. If she didn't find a way around it she was going to have to stop working. If she stopped working they would have no income. If they had no income . . . God, she didn't want to dwell on that. Apart from lack of funds, she couldn't bear to think of all day with time on her hands.

The job in the bakery was not rocket science, and she had recently begun to feel that she would like something a bit more challenging, but the interaction with other people was something she was enjoying. And she knew she would miss it as much as the money.

She didn't want to ask Patrick Cullen, *yet again*, how much longer he thought probate might take. The last time she mentioned the matter he'd said the Probate Office had been on to him, seeking various bits of information on Daniel's affairs. It was his impression then that things were progressing quite well, judging from previous experiences, and that there should be no unnecessary delays.

So, there was nothing for her to do but wait. It seemed like a case of "Live horse, and you'll get grass". That was what her mother was always saying.

The kitchen door was slightly ajar, and Angela heard Thomas in the back porch.

"Don't come in here with hay from that loft all over your clothes!" she called out in warning to him. He didn't reply, and she heard the kitchen door squeak, as it usually did when it was pushed wide.

"Did you hear me?" she turned to say, but the words froze on her lips. The doorway was darkened with the unfamiliar and deranged presence of Christy Cleary! Instantly she was terrified. She recognised the shape in the grubby cap and the belted overcoat immediately. She had often seen it in the town, but not close enough before to know the twisted features and the manic expression in the eyes. Fear immobilised her. Her mouth was wide with a silent scream, her arms went up for protection.

He stood but a few feet from her. He reeked of the smell of unwashed body and clothes and stale alcohol. His hands gripped the door frame, which he seemed to be about to use as a means of launching himself at her.

He sprang like an animal springs for the kill, his outstretched hands making straight for her throat. His weight staggered her, forcing her backwards. Her legs almost gave way. In his fury he had not allowed for the sudden tottering, and he found he had relaxed his grip to steady himself. Anger at not having secured a tightening grip with his first attempt fuelled his viciousness.

Angela knew not what moves she made, only that she fought in sheer panic. Anger that he should even attempt this, fury that she had suffered enough at the hands of others, rage that anyone seemed to be able to inflict what they liked on her, welled up from her depths, and shot through her mind in an instant! Savagely she fought back. His grip, at first clumsy, became vicelike and she knew she could not fight him much longer. There was no one to come to help her. She was on her own!

Angela's world went dark. Air hissed through her teeth in an effort to get to her lungs. She did not hear the succession of dull thuds that served to distract her attacker. Sound had been obliterated from her world, other than the pounding of blood in her head. She sensed rather than heard other movement in the room. Thomas! Oh, God, no! Why didn't he stay outside where he was safe!

The grip relaxed. Something else was happening. Suddenly the hands released her, flung her aside, and blessed air raced down her windpipe, sucked down by a desperately struggling pair of lungs. She steadied herself against the table, and saw in horror that Thomas was the new target. With her hands gripping the table for support she suddenly thrust her foot out in front of the frenzied Christy in a desperate effort to obstruct his advance on Thomas, for what she hoped would be long enough for him to get away.

His progress instantly halted, Christopher Cleary lurched forward, and as he plunged to the floor his head and the corner of the heavy pine table came into contact so hard that the force turned him around and he landed face up.

Shock caused Angela to shake from head to toe. She was deathly pale but for the deepening red marks on her throat and jaw.

Christopher Cleary stared up at her. He didn't move. Just stared.

Thomas edged warily towards the prostrate form.

"He's dead," he said flatly.

"He's not!"

"He is!" Thomas insisted.

"Fuck it!" Angela swore. He couldn't be. "How the fuck would *you* know?"

"I've seen dead birds in the field. And a dead dog too. They had the same kind of stillness as that."

She couldn't move away without having to step over the body, he had landed so close to her feet.

"Gimme your hand, Ma."

She took his hand, closed her eyes and jumped across the body. The two of them stood back, holding onto each other tightly for support and comfort.

"Jesus, Tomo, what are we going to do? Oh God! Oh fuck it, fuck it!"

And suddenly memories swamped her and she was in another time and place. She was barely aware of Thomas's presence as he led her out of the kitchen and into the drawing room. She was unaware of the fact that she had begun to babble.

Thomas was seriously worried about her. She was talking to herself and making no sense.

But the babbling made perfect sense to Angela. Only it referred to another time and place when another attacker had forced himself upon her. One terrible memory after another rushed back. Redser Reilly's thugs had threatened to hurt her if she refused to swallow the drink he offered. He was just being sociable, they said. They had half-walked, half-carried her upstairs, and stood and laughed while they cheered him on. No one came to her aid then. No one dared. Now Thomas had saved her. How ironic – the result of Redser's efforts that night had saved her life!

She pushed away the glass of brandy that Thomas was offering her, her mind whirling.

"I knew it all along, I knew it wasn't my fault!" she was telling herself as she tried to dispel the shaking in her body.

"Drink this, Ma!"

She kept pushing the glass away. "I know now," she whispered, "I know now."

"This will help, Ma. Just have a little sip!"

She took the glass and drank, and then at last became aware of the frightened face of her young son looking anxiously at her.

"Are you all right, Ma?"

She was all right. She was going to be all right now. She would be fine. While her body shook both inwardly and visibly, she knew in her gut that she would be okay. *They* would be okay. She nodded determinedly.

"Did he hurt you badly?"

She would have answered him but for the fact that a noise startled them both. In their fright they could not decide where it had come from, or exactly what sort of noise it was.

Their heads swivelled towards the door together, then in alarm they looked at each other, wide-eyed. A terrible silence prevailed while they waited for something awful to happen, their hearts almost stopped in suspense.

Angela got to her feet and felt Thomas's restraining hand on her arm.

"Don't go, Ma," he whispered, even as he moved with her.

As stealthily as a cat stalking a bird they moved into the hall and towards the kitchen. Thomas had left the door open, and from the doorway they stooped low and looked across the room under the table.

Christopher Cleary was gone!

"Oh Christ!" Angela moaned.

"He can't be gone!" Thomas couldn't believe his eyes.

"I thought you said he was dead!" Angela hissed.

"Well, I thought he was! But where *is* he?"

She feared he might still be in the house. She was too afraid to turn around. It occurred to her that she should phone someone. They needed help. What if Christy was lurking around? What if he had collapsed and died outside in the yard?

"Ma, he's the oul fella we always see on his bike," Thomas was whispering.

"Thomas," she said, trembling, "that oul fella is not just any oul fella. He's Daniel's older brother, and he's pissed off that we got this place, instead of him."

The boy's mouth fell open. He stared at her in disbelief.

"Swear to God!" she insisted, her throat sore and her voice rasping. "Patrick told me. Now, come with me, I'm going to phone him."

She immediately felt a little better. Patrick Cullen would know what to do.

The phone in Patrick Cullen's office rang. Rose was at the large filing cabinet there, her arms full of files.

"I'll get it," Patrick offered, and Rose continued with the filing, her mind on the proper alphabetical order.

"Angela. How are you?" an unsuspecting Patrick asked by way of greeting.

Rose smiled to herself. Patrick was like a father talking to his favourite daughter when Angela was around. Since he had no family of his own, he looked on his word to Daniel as the nearest thing to being a father he would ever get.

"*What!* When? Are you hurt? You don't sound okay."

Patrick stood up suddenly in shock, the phone to his ear, as he tried to grasp what had happened. Rose spun round, alarm in her heart, her eyes fixed on her boss, willing herself to know what was wrong.

Patrick's face had gone a deathly white. "Is Thomas all right? Thank God! Where is Christy now?"

"What *is* it?!" Rose demanded, worried sick now, with only half the information.

"Is he still in the house?" Patrick was asking. "Well, don't move. I'm on my way right now. Two minutes, I'll be there in two minutes! Hold tight, Angela, hold tight!"

He dropped the receiver on the table, and headed for the door.

"*What?*" Rose almost shouted after him in her anxiousness.

"Christy attacked Angela in the house! Get the Gardaí out there now! And phone an ambulance – she said that bastard is hurt. She's not okay herself either. He tried to strangle her!"

Rose dropped the pile of carefully organised files on the floor and grabbed the phone.

She found her usually panic-proof hands were shaking as she dialled the number of the local police station.

Patrick ran back and grabbed his jacket. His car keys were in the pocket.

"Get the doc as well, just in case," he advised, as he left, "he may be needed."

He arrived at Daniel's house first, and for the first time ever he did not have to open the gate. It was already open, a sure sign that all was not well. Without seeing anything else amiss he drove on up to the front door.

Thomas opened it to his knock. The lad was white as a sheet, and very clearly afraid.

"Thomas, my good man, are you hurt?"

The boy shook his head. "Ma is. And we thought the man was dead but he's gone!" Thomas's voice was a whisper. He was very relieved that an adult was there. He led Patrick to the kitchen where Angela was sitting at the table. Patrick was shocked at the sight of her. She was in a dishevelled state. Her eyes were like big black sockets in her head. The finger-sized round bruising on her face and neck was particularly ugly, clearly showing the force used. The sight of Patrick's kindly and concerned face released the tears and her helpless sobbing was heartrending. He could do nothing but put his arms around her, listening to the rasping in her throat, and wait for the tears to subside.

Thomas sat nearby, looking very worried. Patrick reached out a hand and placed it on Thomas's shoulder, so that he would feel cared for also.

"I don't know where he is now," Angela whispered in fear of Christy's return, her swollen throat making speech difficult. "He just burst in and went for me!" The tears threatened to disrupt her again, and she clasped a hand over her mouth, but the pain made her flinch.

Helplessly, Thomas could only sit and watch.

"Take it easy, we'll find him, we'll find him," Patrick assured them.

The singular wail of a siren told them the Gardaí had arrived, and Patrick advised her just to tell it as it happened, then went to let them in. Angela and Thomas heard voices in the hall for a minute or two, then Patrick and a garda came into the kitchen.

Thomas moved beside his mother. The garda interpreted the move and was at pains to reassure the boy that he had nothing to worry about.

Between them mother and son gave an account of what happened.

The garda wanted to know if the door was open when Christy came in. He took one look at the hideous bruising on Angela's face and neck, and whistled silently to himself. She was one lucky young woman.

"How did you manage to fight him off?" the puzzled garda asked. He was thinking she was only a slip of a girl compared to the brawn and strength of her uncle. And he'd had first-hand experience of the strength of Christy Cleary. Trying to get him into a police car when he was in fighting form took at least two hefty gardaí.

In answer, Angela put an arm around Thomas's shoulders and pressed him to her. "Thomas saved me," she said gratefully. "He fought him off with the coal shovel!"

Thomas was surprised at the unaccustomed affection, and for a second or two he had no response. When he looked up at the garda there was a new light in his eyes, his expression a mixture of smiles and nerves.

"Yeah," he laughed nervously, "I whopped him as hard as I could, and then he went for me and I dropped the shovel and ran like mad!"

Immediately the order went out to search for

Christopher Cleary. They first searched the house and to Angela's immense relief they quickly established that he was not inside.

The doctor and ambulance arrived and attended to Angela's injuries. She was given an injection to help her over the shock, and ease the acute soreness that would result from her bruising, but she flatly refused to go to hospital. The doctor's advice was that she should go at least for overnight observation – apart from the swelling, shock could do things to a body, but she insisted she would be better off at home with Thomas. Christy to be found and taken away was all she needed. And for him to be locked up too, she thought, but didn't say it. After all, if he was going to be taken to hospital, and it seemed he might, she could not rest being in the same building as him. The doctor could well understand the logic of that, and reluctantly agreed to her staying in the house, but only if she went straight to bed, and had someone stay with her. Thomas too was thoroughly checked out, and the doc concluded that copious amounts of patting on the back for his bravery was the only necessary remedy the boy needed.

It did not take long to locate the badly concussed Christy. Staggering and disoriented he had left the house, confused as to aim or purpose and with no rational grasp of place or direction. He made only a few metres before falling, but managed to get upright and stagger aimlessly on before collapsing again. Being unable to rise, he lay there where they found him, at the far end of the garden.

The repulsive swelling on the side of his temple bore

out Angela's version of what had happened. The ambulance crew took over after the doctor had seen to him, and in less than five minutes he was on his way to the hospital. His pallor was alarming, his pulse extremely erratic, but he held on tenaciously to his miserable life.

When the ambulance drove away, Angela felt she was able to breathe more freely. It was a feeling that was more psychological than physical. Her throat was very sore.

"Y'know, Patrick, I feel better just knowing they've got him."

"Yeah," Thomas said, his head going up and down in agreement.

His mother cast him a concerned glance. "Are you sure you're okay, Thomas?"

She looked hard at him, searching his face for indications of residual shock. Not that she could put a name on it, but she feared him cracking up on her later, nightmares maybe.

"Ma, stop worrying, I'm all right," he insisted. Then with a sudden rush he declared, as his natural vivacity returned in leaps and bounds, "We really socked it to him, didn't we?"

She couldn't resist a smile, even though it hurt. He was a tonic.

Patrick watched the exchange between them with an easing of his worries. They had gone through so much in the last couple of months, and from his observations they each had the character to rise above it all.

He thought of Christopher Cleary on his way to the

hospital. The police would want to talk to him, assuming he was fit to talk. Patrick thought it unlikely that charges would be brought against him. With his years of experience in legal matters Patrick Cullen thought it more likely that a psychiatric evaluation would prove Christy to be mentally unfit to stand trial to the charge of attempted murder, or anything else. But that was ahead. For now he delighted in Angela's relief that, for the moment at least, her tormentor was unable to cause her any more trouble. There was a knock on the back door and a very anxious Orla stuck her head into the kitchen.

"Mum phoned me, Angela. She's sick with worry. Oh, my God! Your face! What happened to you?" She sat down suddenly, appalled at the sight of the bruising.

Patrick did the explaining, while Thomas put on the kettle at his mother's request.

"If you like, give your ma a buzz, Orla," Angela suggested. "Let her know we're okay."

"Right."

Patrick intervened then. "Actually, thanks, Orla, but I think I'll phone her myself."

Orla was glad not to be the one to break such awful news.

Patrick took control of the situation and insisted that Angela follow the doctor's orders and take herself up to her bed. She raised no argument. The injection she'd been given was taking effect and bed seemed like an excellent idea. Orla accompanied her and Patrick stayed in the kitchen to phone Rose.

With his mother settled in her bed Thomas poured two mugs of hot tea and joined her and Orla in the bedroom. He was glad to be able to tell of his part in all this himself. Orla was bubbling over with praise for him.

Angela had a proud smile on her face. "He's something else, isn't he?"

"He surely is. What about your own mother? Have you phoned her yet?"

Angela sat propped up against a number of pillows and cupped her mug of tea in her hands, turning it around slowly as she replied.

"No, I haven't. I don't think I'm going to either," she told a surprised Orla. "She has enough problems of her own. I can't burden her with this, at least not at the moment. I probably will tell her at a later time, maybe when I'm sure that lunatic won't be able to cause us any more trouble. She'd only worry."

That was understandable to Orla. She admired Angela's stoicism, and she wondered if she would be able to bear up as well herself in similar circumstances.

"Is there *anyone* you want to get in touch with, then?" she asked. "What about Seán? I'm sure *he* would like to know."

"Can I tell Seán *my* bit myself, Ma?" Thomas butted in.

Angela answered, "You can tell anyone you like *your* bit, Thomas. I might be dead this minute if it wasn't for you."

It was a new experience for him to have his mother so pleased with him. He swelled with pleasure, so much so that Orla began to tease him.

"Make sure you don't burst there, Thomas, before you get to tell your bit!" Seeing that he didn't know how to take it, she relented and confessed to teasing him.

He decided he didn't mind. She was pretty. He liked her.

Patrick knocked on the door, and assured them that he had put Rose's mind at ease. Rose told him that the news had hit the town. Somebody passing had seen the garda cars and the ambulance at the house.

That bothered Patrick. He felt they did not need people arriving, even with offers of help. They'd had enough excitement for one day. So, when Seán arrived, Patrick was glad, and went down to have a quiet word with him first.

"Seán, see to it that she gets rest. The doc doesn't want her pestered, even though people mean well. He insists she have complete rest – you know, the shock and all."

He gave the younger man a thank-you nod and felt better about leaving Angela then. He was keen to get to the hospital to find out the condition of Christopher Cleary.

After Patrick had left, Seán approached the stairs and called aloud as he reached the return. "Hallo! Anyone home? Can I come up?"

"It's Seán!" Thomas exclaimed and jumped to his feet.

"Tell him to come on up," said Angela.

Thomas's excitement at Seán's presence caused Orla

to raise her eyebrows as she threw a querying look at Angela.

Angela simply nodded back with a smile. She tidied the bedcovers a little nervously, and handed the empty mug to Orla.

"I'll be downstairs." Orla quietly got to her feet.

"Don't you dare!" Angela retorted as best she could. "You stay right there!"

A bemused Orla put both mugs on the dressing table and turned as Seán came into the room. He put his head around the door first, then slowly tiptoed in and across to the bedside. Orla watched quietly as the horrific appearance of Angela's bruising twisted the contours of his face. His mouth set in a hard line, but his eyes were full of concern. Thomas was babbling away about the attack but he was not being heard.

"Thanks for coming." Angela tried a smile.

Seán took hold of one of the hands that held the bedcovers. His anger at Christy Cleary was too strong for him to be able to hide it completely but he was mindful of upsetting Angela any further, and he did his best to control it.

"How are you?" he asked softly. "You going to be okay?" His eyes tried to fix themselves on hers and avoid being drawn to the spectacle of the deepening bruises. Easier said than done.

She looked down at his hand holding hers and nodded a little. "I'll be fine," she said with difficulty. Her whole throat was now objecting to the vicious attack and the swelling was becoming very noticeable. The doctor told her that would happen, and she was not to be worried by it. It would settle down again in a little while, he assured her.

"That must have taken some guts," Seán commented, "fighting him off like that."

She shook her head, while she deliberately fixed her eyes on her son, thereby identifying *him* as the gutsy one. Thomas was bursting to tell his part in the whole thing, and Angela nodded at him to tell "his bit" as he called it, while she lay back on her pillows. Orla just sat listening, and silently admired the resilience of both of them, while Thomas went through the motions of showing exactly how he had used the coal shovel to fight Christopher Cleary off. At first he said he gave Christy two blows, then it became three to four, and soon anyone listening to Thomas's version would swear he was beaten to a pulp! Orla and Seán exchanged a quick smile at how carried away with his story the lad was becoming, but one thing was a dead cert, he certainly had saved his mother's life. And Angela thrusting out her foot the way she did might well have saved Thomas in return.

Seán turned to Angela. "I hope he got him good while he was at it! He deserves it for this!"

But she had fallen asleep somewhere during Thomas's re-enactment.

"Perhaps we should leave her," Orla suggested. "Let her have her rest, she must be exhausted, poor thing."

Down in the kitchen again Seán was worried about how she might be during the night.

But Orla had already thought of that.

"We were just talking about that before you arrived. Patrick was saying the doctor wanted someone to stay the night. I said I would. I wouldn't think it a good idea to leave them on their own either. Not tonight."

Seán was relieved. "That's very good of you. I'm sure she will appreciate that."

Orla waved away his thanks. "It's no problem at all. Thomas will be able to show me where stuff is, won't you, Thomas?"

"Yep."

Orla thought he looked a little pale. "Did you have dinner, Thomas?"

"No."

"You must be hungry. I'll get something ready. What would you like, eh?"

Thomas decided he wasn't really that hungry. "Don't know."

He had gone rather quiet and Orla concluded he must be at last feeling some effects from the whole debacle.

"I'll tell you what," she said, "I'll get you some milk and a sandwich, and if you'd like to go to bed that would be okay."

He gave her a quizzical glance.

"What I mean is, I won't tell a soul if you'd like to go a bit earlier than usual."

"Nor me," Seán put in supportively. "After all, heroes need their rest as well!"

Thomas brightened a little. He wouldn't want them thinking he was a real baby if he went to bed early. But now that he felt it would be all right he was suddenly very tired. His mother was fast asleep in her bed, and he wished he were in his bed too. Orla produced the milk and some sandwiches, but he couldn't eat them.

Seán took his cue and decided it was time to leave them to themselves, telling Orla quietly to call him anytime, if need be.

Thomas headed for the stairs after Seán left, even though it was still a bit bright outside.

"Goodnight, Orla," he said, his voice betraying his exhaustion.

"Goodnight, Thomas, God bless. Would it be okay if I look in on you later, when I look in on your mother?"

He just nodded and kept going, dragging his feet up the stairs. His bedroom seemed miles away.

When she was sure he was in his bed, Orla went upstairs and looked into his room. His little shape was lost, curled up in the big double bed, and he was already fast asleep.

She checked on Angela too, and found her sleeping soundly, and then set about finding where she could sleep herself.

She crossed the landing to the other rooms and opened a door. She figured she was standing in Daniel Cleary's bedroom.

It felt a little weird. The room was very tidy. The bed was freshly made and Orla was surprised to see a number of very well executed paintings propped against the tallboy. Clearly it was a man's room, and out of respect for the dead she decided to try the last room to sleep in.

It was quite small and there was no bed in it. Though

Orla didn't know it, in times past Mary Cleary had used it as her dressing room. Now it was stacked with boxes and files, old suitcases, framed pictures and other household items and obviously was used as a boxroom.

The last door on the landing was the bathroom, so Orla decided it would have to be Daniel's room after all, or the couch downstairs in the front room. She decided Daniel wouldn't mind.

She went downstairs, put on the kettle, and helped herself to the sandwiches she had made for Thomas. While she waited for the water to boil she phoned her mother, and learned that Patrick had already filled Rose in on what happened and how Angela and Thomas were.

"I'm staying over here tonight, Mam. I'll be back in the morning. I'm sure they're going to be fine. Although you wouldn't believe the state of Angela's bruising. She came within a hair's breath of being choked! Honest to God, Mam, that Christy Cleary should be done for attempted murder!"

"If he survives!" Rose replied.

"If he survives? How do you mean?"

"He hasn't really regained consciousness properly yet, Patrick was saying. He was up to the hospital to see how he is. Apparently he is babbling now and again, rather incoherently they say, but it looks like Michael Furlong might be mixed in there somehow! If Christy's ramblings have any truth in them!"

Orla was aghast. "Are you serious? Francie's dad?"

"Yes, it could be trouble for him if Christy sticks to

his story when he recovers, and is declared fit and of sound mind."

Orla doubted that would happen. "Really, Mam, when was Christy Cleary *ever* of sound mind?"

A knock on the back door startled her.

"Someone is at the door, Mam – hold on while I get it, will you?"

Deko's mother was calling to enquire as to how Angela and Thomas were.

"It's Mrs Doyle, Mam. I'll hang up now, and I'll talk to you later, okay?"

Mrs Doyle came in and sat down. She was a surprisingly small woman and yet she worked like a Trojan about the farm. She was well used to sitting in this kitchen. She felt quite at home. When Mary Cleary was mistress of the house they were good friends. She looked around her and was pleased to see that Angela had not changed anything. To Mrs Doyle that meant appreciation. To Angela it meant lack of money.

"Angela and Thomas are both in bed asleep," Orla explained. "God love them, they're wrecked, both of them. I'm staying tonight. But have a cup of tea with me. I've a fresh one made."

"What did the doctor say?" Mrs Doyle wanted to know. "That poor slip of a girl and that bloody brute Cleary! Good Lord! She is unfortunate, the trouble he is causing her! I can understand him being put out about the place, but to go this far? It's not even as if he would make something of it, if he got it. No. It's better that she has it, jackeen or no. This house has needed youth in it for quite a while now!"

She muttered away to herself while she sugared her tea. Orla smiled understandingly. Mrs Doyle was country stock through and through, and the land was all that mattered to such as she. But she was not one to condone such an attack.

"I'd be prepared to bet next year's lambs that that young lad upstairs will turn out to be a fine countryman!"

"Like his grandfather," Orla put in her pennyworth.

"Better than Daniel," Mrs Doyle was adamant. "I can see the makings of it in him already. He comes over to our place to Declan and as sure as God, you'd think he was born on the land to listen to him. He has names on all the sheep, did you know that? Says he can tell them one from the other. I ask you. Declan wouldn't be that interested."

She finished her tea, having talked most of the way through it, and decided she really must be going. She had an early start, as always, she said. She would see Angela and Thomas sometime tomorrow.

After Mrs Doyle left Orla sat in the kitchen, wondering what to do now. Sitting alone in someone else's house was the quickest way to feeling you had nothing to do. The telly did not interest her, her mind was much too active for that, what with all that happened that day, so she took out her mobile and phoned her mother again.

"Are you okay there on your own?" Rose wanted to know.

"Of course I am. I have the doctor's number. He left it, just in case, so stop worrying."

"How are they now?"

"The two of them are conked out, absolutely. I think young Thomas was only delighted to get to his bed. He was like a sheet, poor thing. I'm going to go on up myself now. Might as well get the early night while I have the chance."

"Okay, Orla, but make sure you ring me if you need me, you hear?"

"Okay. Night, Mam."

She couldn't resist a smile when she hung up. All the people she was to phone "if need be". Heaven forbid! The night wouldn't be long enough for all those calls!

She settled into Daniel's double bed, and before she slept she said a little prayer that he would be okay with that. She did not consider herself to be a superstitious person, but surely there was no harm in being cautious.

Thomas woke her, and for a minute she had no idea where she was. Then it all flooded back with a bang and she sat bolt upright in the bed.

"Thomas. Good God. What's up? Is your mother okay?"

"It's morning," he informed her. "We'll be late for school."

"*What?*" She looked out. He was right, it was broad daylight and a fine day it was too.

"Is your mother okay? Did you sleep all right?" She yawned and rubbed her eyes.

"Yeah, she's okay. I brought her up some tea and toast."

Orla looked at him in amazement. Another child would be looking for a *week* off school. She had them in her class who were given time off by their parents for the piddliest little reasons.

When she was dressed she went in to Angela's room. Angela was sitting up having her tea and toast.

"My God!" Orla remarked. "The two of you are something else! I'd be splattered if that happened to me. Did you know Thomas says he wants to go to school?"

Angela nodded. "If he feels up to it, why not? He seems fine to me."

Orla admitted he certainly did seem okay.

"And you?" she asked. "How are you?"

"Relieved, to say the least," was the reply. "Glad to be alive and glad that fecker is finally put away somewhere safe. If I have to bring charges against him I will, if it will put him where he can do no more harm."

"You must have been awake very early to figure all that out!"

"I was. I woke up and my mind wouldn't be still. It went over and over so many things. The attack yesterday brought up so much stuff. Even some things that happened before Thomas was born." She fell silent, then went on as if she had made a decision, "I'll tell you about it sometime."

"You don't have to, if it upsets you." Orla thought to save her some angst.

"No, I don't mind talking about it, but not just yet."

This was a huge advancement for her. Things were settling, becoming less traumatic, more understandable, more . . . something. Definitely more . . . something she could cope with. Something she could find a box for, put a label on, and thereby keep it in its place. Control it . . . instead of the other way round.

"How's your throat this morning?" Orla was looking at the state of her hair in the oval mirror of the dressing table.

Angela swallowed some of the soggy toast. Thomas had put plenty of butter on it while it was still hot so that it would be soft. He had cut the edges off it so it would be easy to eat. He remembered that his nan did that when he had a sore throat.

"Not as bad as I thought. I thought last night I was losing my voice. How do I look? Truth now," she warned Orla, "no codding me!"

Orla took stock of the evidence imprinted on Angela's skin. The bruising was more noticeable than last night, it had turned darker and it was likely to become more so for a while, but Orla thought the swelling had gone down some and said so.

"I think so too," Angela agreed. "It doesn't feel so puffed now. Before I fell asleep it felt like a bloody balloon!"

Thomas was downstairs having his breakfast. It was the last few days before the holidays, and he didn't want to be absent. Miss had said they would put the finishing touches to their art projects today, and Thomas was as keen a student as any. His project was almost complete.

Using paints and other items he had gathered, such as wool from the sheep where they brushed against the hedgerow, and twigs and leaves from the trees, flowers that grew wild in the hedges, and small stones from the shallow edges of the river, he was making a collage representing their land. He was very proud of the soft fluffy barn owl feathers he collected in the loft. No one else had barn owl feathers for their project, and Thomas promised to give Owen some, if he had any over.

"So, what are you going to do with yourself today, Angela? Take it easy, I suppose, while the rest of us work?" Orla asked. "Would you like more toast?"

Angela put her cup on the bedside table. "No thanks, Orla. I'm going to get up. The doc says no work today, he will be out to see me later, but I feel like getting up."

"You sure?"

"Yeah. Look at that day. Gorgeous. I have a feeling of freedom about me. Queer, isn't it? Must be something to do with Christy Cleary being off the streets, I think!"

Orla was still at the mirror, examining her face for blemishes. "You wouldn't want to overdo it – you've had a fair auld shock, you know."

Angela laughed. "You sound like my mother!"

"This is a great mirror, Angela, you can see really clearly in it!"

"And if you don't get your face away from it, you'll be late for school!" Angela replied. It was Orla's turn to laugh. "Now *you* sound like *my* mother. But you're right; I'd better get a move on. I'll take Thomas in with me, and I'll see you later, okay?"

Angela was pleased that the doctor called early to see her. It meant she didn't have to sit around the house for ages waiting for him. Announcing how pleased he was with her, he made a speedy exit, saying with a wink that he had some *sick* people waiting for him to call on them. He encouraged her to return to work as soon as she liked, and she was glad to hear it.

"Not much point in making a speedy recovery and then sitting around letting idleness whittle it away, is there?" he smiled. "Back to work it is, the sooner the better."

After he left she went to the back porch door and stood looking out. It was not the usual looking out, like when she wanted to call Thomas. This time she was actually *looking*.

What did Thomas see when *he* looked out? To listen to him talk anyone would think there were magical things out there!

She walked over to the workshop, remembering when Christy had wrecked it before. She thought again of his rage and viciousness the day before. It was hard to believe that dark day was only yesterday, but she did not allow herself to stand and brood over things.

She moved along by the hedge towards the river. The water was fairly shallow, the level low because of the recent good weather, and she found a small mound of grass near the edge and sat down. There was no sound other than those Mother Nature made. Rippling water gurgled over stones on the riverbed and a soft breeze rustled the leaves on the trees.

High overhead the crows and magpies vied for favoured branches in the trees, and without looking up she found she could visualise their antics. The sun warmed her bare arms and legs, and she realised it was a long, long time since she sat for any length in its healing rays. Warmth and quietness flowed through her, melting away the turmoil of confusion that for so long had occupied her mind and heart.

So, this was the magic Thomas referred to.

She got to her feet at last and walked along by the bank, then turned her back to the river and headed up through the field. She walked slowly, with no feeling of need to hurry. There was a slight weakness in her legs – the shock would do that, she thought – so she took her time. She plucked a long blade of grass and placed it between her teeth, feeling its sharp edges against her lips, and the straight ridge down its centre. She stopped her rambling a moment and looked around. This field was quite large, and the emptiness of it struck her. The field in which the sheep were grazing was smaller, and yet it was being put to profitable use. The other fields were bordered on all sides by hedges, save for the smallest one, at the bottom of the yard, which met the riverbank for only fifty metres or so. But this one had the river flowing past the full length of its fourth side. She found herself wondering if it would be safe for Thomas to ride here. She had a mental picture of him cantering about the field.

She was shocked at herself that such a thought should come into her mind, unprompted by him as it was. He saved her life yesterday, and she was feeling like she would give him anything he wanted . . . if she could.

In D'Arcy Avenue there were horses but no safe land. Here there was plenty of safe land, but no horse, and no means of affording one. She knew she was not going to trigger him off by saying anything, but it did strike her as odd that he had not mentioned it himself. Not yet anyway.

She looked back towards the river, and across through the hedge to the house and garden, and to the field beyond where Mr Doyle's sheep grazed contentedly, and realised for the first time the extent of what Daniel had bequeathed to her.

She approached the gate where Mick Furlong had let himself into her garden and marched on the house to prove beyond question that the lad in the tree was lying. She crossed her garden, just grass, and approached the gate of the opposite field with some nervousness. The sheep took no notice of her at all. She half expected them to remember that it was she who roared and shouted and shooed at them only a number of days ago, but the juicy grass was much more interesting to them than she was. Slowly she climbed onto the gate and sat the way she had seen Thomas do. She eased her legs over the top bar and, having sat still for a little while, slid to the ground on the other side. Stillness or no sudden movements seemed to be the key to not scattering the sheep.

Standing still a moment to reassure herself that none of them were getting aggro she took a deep breath and stepped forward. Some heads raised, looked at her steadily, and went down to business again. Feeling a little more daring she took a few steps into the field, making sure that she was within escaping distance, just in case. No panic. She dared herself take some full-sized steps forward.

The sheep immediately ceased their munching and for a second they remained motionless, looking questioningly at her.

She had pushed her luck *too* far for their liking. As if they were responding in unison to some unseen signal, they turned tail and ran away from her in a semi-circle, like ripples on a pond surface, blown by the wind. Then they stopped running and turned to look again. When she backed off and climbed the fence again, they returned to their grazing. She left them to graze in peace and walked back up the gravel path, feeling quite elated. She felt she had conquered her fear of those silly woolly things and she was so very pleased with herself.

Approaching the house in the bright sunshine, she was struck by how different it looked to when she first arrived. The front of it was quite impressive after all, she thought, and the large steps up to the front door gave it quite a grand appearance. Going around by the side again to the back door, she resolved to have the additional carving done on Daniel's headstone as soon as she could gather the money.

The phone in the house was ringing as she came in.

"Hello?"

"Angela! My God! I've been trying to get you for ages!"

She was immediately alarmed. Thomas? He must

have had a reaction. She'd been so afraid of that. Her heart almost stopped. "Why? What's happened?" She was terrified of the answer.

Seán was thrown by her surprise. His words suddenly sounded like he was overreacting.

"I called out this morning to see how you were. There was no sign of you. I've even tried the hospital!"

Relief swept over her and a little laugh escaped her lips. "Oh, Seán, I'm so sorry. I thought something was up with Thomas. He went to school today and I thought . . . oh, I'm so relieved!"

"Oh God, I'm sorry! I didn't intend to give you a fright – but I was anxious about you. Were you out?"

She told him how she walked around the fields, and sat by the river, and listened to the peace and quietness, and felt the tranquillity and braved it with the sheep. Everything.

"But I didn't think I was gone *that* long!"

"Well, everyone is looking for you, worried about how you are. Rose, Patrick, Maura, to name a few. We were thinking of organising a search party!"

"You're joking!" she gasped.

She heard the laugh in his voice as he answered. "We were, you know."

As she hung up Mrs Doyle appeared at the back door, wearing her apron and her oven mitts and carrying an ovenproof dish full of a delicious-smelling lasagne. Angela was amazed because the Doyles' house was the distance of about three fields away, but then she saw the little Opel Corsa parked at the side of the house.

"Thought you might not feel like cooking, Angela. How are you today?"

Mrs Doyle did her best not to show her shock at the sight of the bruising, but her lips tightened in an effort to silence the exclamation that surged up. She placed the casserole dish on the cooker top.

"I feel much better than I thought I would, Mrs Doyle, thanks. You shouldn't have gone to all that trouble. It smells gorgeous, though. I can't thank you enough."

Mrs Doyle flapped away the thanks with a mitt-covered hand. "It's nothing. Nothing at all. I'm glad you're up and about. And Thomas? How was he during the night?"

"Not a bother!" Angela was saying while she filled the kettle. "Couldn't keep him home! He was up so early *he* called Orla!"

Mrs Doyle removed her mitts, sat herself down, and then placed the mitts on top of each other on the table beside her. She smoothed her apron as she reminisced.

"But sure isn't that youth for you? Bounces back like a rubber ball!" She sighed wistfully at the memory of how it was. "Didn't appreciate it when we had it, did we? Thought we would never grow up, eh?"

There was a huge age gap between her and her much younger neighbour, but out of respect and gratitude Angela answered appropriately with "I know what you mean!"

She didn't really know what it was to wish to be older. She only remembered wanting to grow younger. Younger than fifteen! She only ever wanted to be back at a time when she was her daddy's darling. Growing up suddenly became impossible for her, and adulthood frightened the life out of her. She did not have the benefit of her teenage years in which to adapt. She was instantly catapulted into a bewildering situation in which she was prevented from adjusting by the condemnation and animosity that poured ceaselessly from her once adoring dad.

But enough of that. Mrs Doyle was chatting away and Angela was glad of it.

Then her neighbour remarked, "I was in the town earlier this morning."

She waited for a response, but Angela was not sure what was expected of her.

"And?" she prompted, playing it on the safe side, while she cut some tea-brack.

"There is plenty of talk going on about the attack," said her neighbour.

Angela took the milk from the fridge. "What are they saying?" She knew well that Mrs Doyle was only waiting to be asked. Otherwise she might feel that she was gossiping.

"Well, it's more what Christy is saying, apparently," said Mrs Doyle.

Angela frowned. Was he saying *she* attacked *him*? Putting the blame on her? In her own house? "What do you mean?"

"It seems that he keeps saying that Mick Furlong put him up to it."

"*What*?" She wasn't prepared for that.

"He isn't coherent all of the time, but they say he managed that much."

"I don't believe it. Why would Mick Furlong *do* that?" Angela's recently acquired sense of security was being eroded. She remembered what Mick had said the first time he had darkened her door: "Don't be stuck with this place, now. I'm sure we could come to some arrangement if you want to head back to Dublin." Very quick off the mark, getting his plug in first. Was she using her loony, begrudging uncle to do his dirty work for him? Another thought flashed across her mind. My God! Francie! Had he roped his son in to driving her out, too?

Mrs Doyle saw the appalled look that registered on her face. "What is it, Angela? Something struck a chord, did it?" She took the liberty of getting up to pour the tea. She'd be there all day if she waited on Angela to pour. She liked a chat but she was a busy woman too, and it looked like the girl had just been rendered motionless.

Angela sat as her neighbour did "mother".

"If that's what they are saying, Mrs Doyle, my only hope is that this is the end of it."

"Please God, indeed. Mick Furlong will probably say the man is nuts, and there's them that would believe it. But another thing, what are you going to do with Thomas next week?"

Angela's mind was slow at adjusting to the change of subject, and at first she didn't catch on to what she meant.

"The school holidays, girl! Don't tell me Christy Cleary fuddled your brains! I was thinking you could leave him up with us if you like, while you work. We always get off to an early start in the mornings, even during the holidays, and Declan would certainly love it – keep him from being bored."

Angela could certainly identify with *that*. Trying to keep Thomas occupied and away from the Reillys and the rest of the gurriers all summer long was something that used to cause continuing conflict. It was a constant source of aggro and a battle she hardly ever won. Summers in D'Arcy Avenue were always the most troublesome time of the year. What was *wrong* with her this morning? Why was she going back over all *that* stuff now? Why on earth did all these things insist on coming into her head? Had Christy Cleary *really* fuddled her brain? Or maybe it was all the fresh air, *clearing* her head?

She fervently hoped so. She took a deep breath and said, "I really don't know what to say, Mrs Doyle. Are you very sure it would be okay?"

Mrs Doyle milked her tea again, even though her mug was already half empty.

"Are you ready for another?" Angela got up for the teapot.

"No, no, I'm grand here, pour your own. That's settled then. Good. He can just run across before you go to work. We'll be expecting him so." Mrs Doyle emptied her mug and picked up her mitts, telling Angela to be sure to go easy on herself, for a little while anyway.

"How can I thank you?" said Angela. "I was really stuck on that one, about the holliers. There must be something I can do in return?"

Mrs Doyle gave one of her prophetic smiles, and made her way to her car. "When there is, and no doubt there will be, I'll let you know. Sure, isn't that the way it works, eh?"

She threw her mitts onto the car seat and hopped in behind the wheel. Angela was gobsmacked by the speed with which the petite little woman drove out onto the road, and hoped her neighbour's prophecy wasn't brought about by her own driving. She also hoped she didn't drive like that when she had the lads in the car.

When Thomas was dropped back home after school he brought with him further talk of yesterday's happenings. The Gardaí were at the hospital, waiting to be told they could question Christopher Cleary. Stories abounded among the lads in school about how exactly he attacked her. Some said it was with a hatchet; another story was that he had tied her up and was going for Thomas. Angela was sure of one thing, Thomas wallowed in the attention.

But the day was not over yet. She was in her bedroom when she saw Mick Furlong's car coming up the driveway. What the heck did *he* want? If the stories were true he had some nerve calling to her door. If he wanted to see for himself if his tactics were working, she thought, well, let him see.

He got the surprise of his life when she greeted him at the door and invited him in. This was looking positive, he thought. He followed her down to the kitchen where Thomas sat at the table doing his homework. He looked up from his books and Mick ignored the scowl that spread across the boy's face.

"Hello there, Thomas, knuckling down, I see?"

Thomas made no reply. What did his ma have to ask him in for? It felt threatening, him being in their house. His mother offered tea, and a chair. Mick refused the tea but sat down. No point in arsing about with tea, wasting time.

"Well, I heard of your trouble," he began, noticing the bruising on Angela. It was worse than he had expected. Christy had nearly succeeded by the looks of it.

"And how brave this young lad was too," he continued. "I'm glad you're all right."

A peculiar pause followed his words.

Angela just nodded. Now that he was here she didn't know what to say to him. Was he responsible for the attack? Maybe it was stupid of her to ask him in.

Mick was gaining confidence. He rested both hands on the handle of his walking stick. Did he ever go anywhere without it, Thomas was wondering? He bent over his book again.

"Been difficult for you since you arrived," Mick remarked, wondering how he was going to get around to what he wanted to say.

Thomas's head shot up. "Everybody is saying *you* got him to do it!"

"Thomas!" Angela checked him sharply.

"'Cos you want *our* land!"

Angela felt like silencing him with a wallop – she didn't want this to develop into an argument.

Mick also regretted the child's outburst, but it gave

him an opening and he decided honesty could be the best policy here. "Everybody knows I want to buy this land, son," he smiled his best paternal smile, "but I am not the one who was disinherited. I do not have the gripe about it that your uncle does. Yes, I made an offer to your mother, and yes, my offer still stands. Do you think I asked someone to *murder* you for it? My God, son, I would never do anything of the sort!"

That was true. He had not *asked* Christy to do any such thing. He could hardly be held responsible for what that madman made of his words. They looked put out by his straight talking, and feeling he had the upper hand he went on, "I would pay a fair price, as I first promised, enough for you to have whatever you want. We could agree a deal and close it when probate comes through. Then you could start making plans for something you would really like. Something you would be better able for. People around here would well understand if you sell up. This is all too much for a slip of a girl from the city."

It wasn't said in a belittling manner and he sounded so persuasive. They were taking it in, he thought. Hearing his logic. Coming over here today was a good move. There was a perceptible change in the mother's manner. He was about to ask if he could change his mind and have that tea after all.

It was the last sentence that did it. His utter belief in what he had said. Angela felt severe indignation rise at the suggestion that she didn't measure up. She heard Paddy Brennan talking: *"Useless! Totally fuckin' useless! It's a pity you hadn't the brains to pass your exams!"*

401

Francie also ran her down. A slapper. That's what she amounted to in his mind. That's all she was good for! "Putting it about" was what he had said. And Christy thought he could inflict what he liked on her and get away with it.

Daniel didn't think this way of her. Patrick Cullen didn't. Mr Doyle didn't, even after his sheep got out. But most important of all, Angela didn't. Not any more! She drew in a deep breath. Thomas felt his heart stop. He didn't want to hear what she was going to say.

"Mr Furlong," she began, "I should be clear on a couple of facts. Firstly, I know you offered to buy me out. But I also know that there are a number of farmers around who would also be glad of the chance to buy this property."

Ah! So she was going to haggle, was she? Well, no harm. When it came to bargaining there was no better man than Mick Furlong. He settled himself on his seat. Might as well get comfortable.

"The other fact is that whether I have one willing buyer or ten I have absolutely no intention of selling. None whatsoever. Do you get that?"

His jaw dropped momentarily. Thomas's jaw dropped half a mile.

Furlong found his voice. "Don't be too hasty. You'll never manage –"

She cut him short. "What I will or won't manage remains to be seen, Mr Furlong. Any further attempts, by anyone, to get me out will be dealt with by the law. This is my rightful inheritance, whether you like it or not, and

I am staying. Now, I ask you again, do I make myself clear?"

Her heart was pounding. She was sure he could hear it in the pause that followed. The silence that was emanating from her son roared astonishment. She could just *feel* he was all agog.

Wow, he was thinking, look at his ma! She was socking it to Mick Furlong. She was bossing *him*. Young as he was, Thomas could see the farmer was not dealing very well with the situation.

His mother dared not flick a glance at his face. She knew it would knock her off her stride. She kept her steady gaze fixed on their visitor, waiting for his response.

He stood up. "Very clear. But if you change your –"

"Good. I'm glad we have that sorted out. We both know now where we stand. So, if you don't mind, we have had enough for one day, I think."

Rage and disbelief fought inside Mick Furlong for supremacy. Where in Christ's name had *that* come from? Was this the result of pushing *too* hard? She had bounced the wrong way. Was she more like her father than he had given her credit for? How on earth had he managed to judge her so badly? In a fog of incredulity he was aware that he was being dismissed. Wordlessly he went to the front door.

She followed him cautiously, feeling that at any second he wouldn't be able to contain his rage, and would lash out, such was his demeanour. The thought came to her that she should ask Patrick Cullen if he could send a letter confirming what had just transpired. If he would do that it would leave Mick Furlong in no doubt that she meant every word she said, and the fact that she made it an official refusal might deter any further attacks on her and Thomas.

She opened the door and without a glance at her he marched out to his car. She closed the door without waiting to see him drive down to the gate.

Thomas ran from the kitchen door and flung his arms around her.

"Do you really mean it, Ma? Do you *really* mean it?"

She hugged him back.

"I really mean it."

Chapter 39

The pub was buzzing with talk. The lunchtime chatter had reached a higher pitch than usual. There was only one topic of conversation. The attack was on everyone's lips. The fact that none of them had actually seen Angela yet gave rise to stories of *terrible, horrific* wounds, which got worse each time the story was relayed. Those few in favour of Christy tended to make less of the situation. One very unkindly soul muttered under their breath that she had it coming, and then sweated in case anyone had actually heard.

The other school of thought was that Christy had been going off the deep end for a long time. A large number of people were not surprised to hear that Mick Furlong would love to get his hands on the land. That was common knowledge to some. But whether or not he actually put Christy up to it was the question.

An ominous silence fell as people nudged each other as soon as the door swung open and Mick Furlong's large frame filled the doorway. He approached the bar with an air of calculated indifference, and placed his big hands on the counter. Slowly he looked to his left, then to his right, and suddenly the hubbub of voices filled the pub again.

Seán came and stood in front of Mick.

"What can I get you, Mick?" he asked, as normally as he did every other day at lunchtime.

As normally as always Mick replied, "I'll have the usual, Seán. And I'll have a pint with it."

Seán studied the man's expression surreptitiously while he drew the pint. He judged he was preoccupied with something other than the speculation running around as to his guilt or innocence – there was an air of anger about him.

After the initial hiatus, an air of relief ran around the pub. Mick Furlong was ordering the usual, and carrying on as normal, and surely that was proof enough that he was not involved in any wrongdoing? How could he behave the same if he planned to have his neighbour attacked? Still, there *was* the fact that the police were in the hospital, waiting for the doctors to allow them to question Christy, and also the fact that Christy, with every waking moment denigrated "that fucker Furlong".

Seán placed the pint before Mick.

"Nasty happening at your neighbour's place yesterday," he commented, watching the older man's eyes carefully.

Mick looked back at him with a hard glare. "So I heard."

Seán tried a more offhand approach. "Been up to see

Christy yet? I believe he got a bad crack on the head."

Mick put the pint to his mouth and took a fair gulp before answering. "What would *I* be doing up there?" His eyes narrowed in an attempt to make Seán go away.

But Seán wasn't done yet. He feigned surprise. "Oh, I thought you two were pals lately. I mean, you've been very helpful to him, haven't you, seeing he gets home, getting his bike fixed, buying him the odd drink. I saw you up at his cottage the other week –" He stopped short.

It looked like his customer was going to explode.

"Nonsense!" Mick became flustered at the mention of being at the cottage. "Haven't been there in years!"

Seán knew he was lying, and Mick knew he knew it.

"But I saw –" Seán was persisting with his antagonism, disguising it as surprise.

"Nothing!" Mick dropped his voice to a low growl, suddenly aware the whole place was earwigging. "You saw nothing!"

Seán was quiet for a few moments during which the customers became aware that it was evident they were listening. The babble of voices started up again, as people pretended they were otherwise occupied.

"Did you know," Seán dropped his voice too, "that Christy keeps saying you put him up to it?"

Mick had leaned forward to hear Seán's words, but he straightened suddenly, apparently ready to pop a blood vessel.

Seán raised a hand in apparent self-defence. Secretly he was enjoying this. Watching Mick Furlong squirm was nearly worth risking losing his custom, but he didn't want to push it *that* far, unless of course he was guilty.

"Take it easy," he said. "I'm only saying what I heard! You know Christy. Runs off at the mouth from time to time."

"Happens to more than Christy!" Mick glared at the barman. "You have customers waiting while you stand there spreading idle gossip."

"So I have," Seán observed pleasantly, and he wisely moved down the counter to the taps and began pulling some pints. He was well aware that the customers would gladly have waited longer if they were being treated to some juicy gossip. As he lowered the handle of the tap over the glass his thoughts were not entirely on what he was doing. He would have liked to ask other questions but didn't get the chance. Like who was that fellow he saw chatting to Mick in his car the other day? The one who wore the black knitted hat pulled down over his ears in spite of the warm sunshine? When Seán acknowledged them Mick started the car and drove off. Something about it stuck in his mind. He hadn't recognised the guy, and he thought he knew everybody in the town. Nor had he thought much of it at the time but now speculation was rife and he was concerned about Angela and Thomas.

People deferred to Mick Furlong. He was a man of substance and standing in the community. Never questioned, never doubted. So much so that Mick himself took it as a given. Seán had never seen him flustered. He had seen him angry, or bluffing, or throwing his considerable weight around. But never actually flustered as he certainly was now.

He was on edge about something, and Seán wondered if there was at least a grain or two of truth in what the demented Christy was saying. He served his other customers, and couldn't help noticing how they made a point of greeting Mick directly. Seán knew they wanted to judge for themselves whether or not Big Mick Furlong had a guilty look to his demeanour. If the mighty take a tumble, the gossip is all the sweeter.

It didn't go unnoticed that Mick finished his lunch in record time and left the pub. He got into his swanky Mercedes and took out his temper on the gearbox. He fumed. He threatened all sorts of damnation on that fucking imbecile Cleary. If there was any point to it at all he would sue the fucking pants off that moron. So, he got a bad crack on the head, did he? Pity it didn't knock sense into him. But then, you can't get sense into a head that doesn't have a brain in it, can you?

When he screeched to a halt and yanked on the handbrake he found he was in his own yard. He sat in the car. His countenance would have frightened thunder, while he sought to separate speculation from fact.

The first fact was there was nothing concrete to connect him with what Christy did. If he was being nice to him, what was wrong with that? If he *did* call to the cottage, so what? If that *amadán* suffered a bash on the head and woke up voicing hallucinations, what right-thinking judge could take them as evidence? *If*, that was *if*, Christy could be considered stable enough to *give* evidence.

Judging from what he heard, Cleary was highly unlikely to be declared fit. Indeed, he thought with a curling sneer, even in the whole of his health Cleary would hardly be considered normal. No psychologist worth his salt would be willing to risk his reputation by declaring Christopher Cleary normal.

The more he thought about it, the less Mick figured he had to worry about. Leave Christy to it, let him keep blabbering away and he would talk himself into the asylum.

But if Mick had sought to get away from the insinuations of the townspeople, he walked right into it again at home.

Francie, coming in from the field, drove the tractor into the yard and saw his father's car parked there. He turned off the engine and jumped down as his father got out of his car. Francie glared coldly across the distance between them. Mick turned and went into the house. Obviously Francie was still "in a humour" after the last words they'd had. But, unknown to Mick, Francie had been to the town early that morning, and heard the talk.

The sitting-room door slammed. Mick spun round. His son stood glowering at him.

"You got Cleary to do your dirty work! He nearly killed her, *do you realise that?*"

Whatever Francie thought of Angela Cleary, it didn't make her dispensable just because she was in his father's way. That was too heavy for Francie.

Mick made a supreme effort to remain calm. "Christy has his own issues there," he began. "If he decided to –"

"What did you promise him to get rid of her?" Francie practically spat. "*Well*? Did you tell him *strangulation* would be easy? Did you?"

"Enough!" Mick roared, pushing Francie against the door. "I've had all of this I'm going to take!"

Francie made no attempt to retaliate. But the enmity was so palpable that Mick took an involuntary step backwards.

"You put that lunatic up to it – for a bit of land!"

Mick was ready for him. "And what about *you*? You were put out big time at her rejection!"

Francie's eyes shifted uneasily away from his father's glare. He wasn't proud of what he had done. He wanted to be gone. And he became afraid. Afraid of the fact that his father was prepared to go to any lengths to get what he wanted, and he himself could well be implicated by association. He wasn't prepared for that either.

He gripped the door handle and wrenched the door open.

"I'm not going to be involved in your antics and –"

"You wouldn't have the balls for it! You're not man enough to take what you want," Mick cut in derisively, "you never were. It only suits you if it is handed to you on a plate. You always were a wimp!"

Stung by the remarks Francie furiously hurled back, "I'll go to the police!"

Mick was taken aback but not for long. "You ever do anything of the sort and you can sing for *this*!" His gesture indicated Francie's inheritance.

"Shove it!" was the reply.

Francie went out, slamming the door again, leaving his father looking at the closed door, his jaw gaping.

Had Mick heard correctly? His own flesh and blood, standing up to him over *her*? Threatening to go to the Gardaí? He'd see him in hell first.

Chapter 40

Paddy Brennan sat staring into his pint. He didn't really feel like drinking, but he could hardly sit at the bar without something in front of him. Anything was better than sitting at home, watching Nancy's face, knowing what he had done. He found it very difficult to sit there. Every minute he was in her company he was reminded. He'd never be able to tell her. He was sick enough with himself as it was.

Apart from anything else, Nancy was different these days. It was not something he could put his finger on. He was unable to pinpoint what changed her. Or when it happened. When did she begin to seem taller? Why was it that her presence seemed to fill the room? What was it that made her seem stronger, formidable almost?

It wasn't that there was much talk between them. If he were honest, he would have to admit that he spoke to her as little as possible. He could hardly blame her if she spoke very little in return.

The fact was that Paddy spoke very little to anyone these days. He had things on his mind and, even when they were in his subconscious, they tended to keep him quiet. Put plainly, he was deeply troubled. But he was afraid to examine too closely what troubled him. That might make it too real. So, sitting in the pub and staring into a pint he was not pushed about was preferable to sitting at home and risking things surfacing in his head. Anyway, after a couple of pints, be they good or bad, he usually began to forget his troubles.

"What's it like?" someone at his elbow asked, pulling himself onto the barstool.

"Not bad," Paddy responded, without looking up.

The man settled down to making small talk, hoping to get enough response to keep the exchange going, for a while at least.

Paddy sighed inwardly. This was always the price for sitting at a bar. Someone always took the opportunity of inflicting themselves upon you, whether you liked it or not.

The man ordered another pint, and one for Paddy. Then Paddy did the same, and the chat picked up, became livelier, and in a short while they were telling lewd jokes, loud enough to be heard by anyone who wanted to listen.

But people took no notice. They had their own conversations going, and the more they drank, the more *they* wanted to be heard as well.

Paddy's new friend made a trip to the gents, and Paddy took to looking around to see if he could find someone to fill the short gap, till yer man got back. He felt very much like chatting now, now that the Guinness had done its work. He turned slightly on his stool, and cast his bleary eye over the crowd in the bar.

He surveyed all the usual suspects, the ones who only came in for a couple, the ones who were there every night, and the ones, like him, who were there because they preferred not to be anywhere else.

One face across the crowd caught his eye and the sight of it paralysed him. Its owner looked back directly at Paddy and the shifty look in the eye sent a cold feeling of fear down his back. The thug held his gaze and sniggered when Paddy was forced to be the one to look away.

Paddy had not laid eyes on him since his talk with Redser Reilly, and something about the look in the thug's eye gave him the distinct feeling that something was about to go very wrong. His mood changed. His new friend came back from the gents to find a very different personality.

"One for the ditch, eh?" the man joked in his friendly manner.

"Ditch yourself!" said a very surly Paddy, and he got up and left the pub.

Outside he walked a little way and checked that he was not being followed. He heard the thump of the bar door as it swung shut behind someone, and his heart missed a beat, but the emerging customer simply hitched up his trousers and headed in the opposite direction. Paddy told himself he was being ridiculous. One thug on his own would never have the nerve to approach anyone. He felt somewhat better, and laughed at his own fears. Not for long though. One thug on his own? *One* thug? Thugs were notorious for being in pairs, at the very least. Weren't they? The uneasy feeling returned with a bang. He knew that thug in there was one of the two who were never far from Reilly's side. They were a regular trio, never seen apart. So why was it that this fellow happened to be on his own? The worry of it tormented Paddy's addled mind. A bad feeling of foreboding dug itself into the pit of his stomach, and refused to be dislodged.

He got home, and reached his bed, and the drink was kind enough to grant him oblivion, at least till morning.

Nancy did not expect him to rise before noon, since he was on the night shift, and Paddy himself would not normally have expected to waken much before twelve. But when sleep left him shortly after ten, the blessed relief he had enjoyed whilst asleep left with it, and the torment returned.

In the starkness of broad daylight he could not lie there and pretend all was well. He had to be doing something, so he got up and dressed, and when he went downstairs he skipped breakfast. Without as much as a "Morning" he went straight out into the garden, took his spade from the shed and set about turning over the soil in the flowerbeds. He plunged the spade into the soft earth with a vengeance.

Nancy watched from the kitchen window, while he put his back into the work, stabbing at the ground as though he was severing a head from its body. She was eternally perplexed by his behaviour these days. But what mattered was that he left her alone, made no attempt to raise a hand. She was done with accepting that kind of behaviour.

Perhaps he knew it.

Chapter 41

Angela was glad to be back at work, and Maura was very glad of it too.

"I don't know how I managed without you," she said. "I hadn't realised how much you took off my hands – trying to do it all myself again was murder!"

Angela was very pleased to hear it. Her spirits lifted immeasurably. "But I thought you had help?" She got into her shop coat. The delicious smell of the bread baking in the ovens was welcome back in her nostrils.

Maura turned her eyes to heaven. "Oh, I had help all right, but there's more to helping than looking good behind the counter, and I won't say *who*. I'm glad you're okay, though. Are you sure you are up to it? Take a break whenever, right?"

As if to emphasise her concern Maura vanished into the back and promptly reappeared with two cups of coffee, and fresh rolls that she had smothered with her own home-made strawberry jam.

"Oh, that's yummy, Maura! You'll get no good out of me if you keep feeding me like this! These rolls are gorgeous!"

She reassured her boss that she was only too glad to be back. She needed the money for a start, although she didn't voice that.

Customers varied greatly in their reaction. Some gaped at her face and neck and tutted loudly, declaring that Christy Cleary was in the best place, and they should keep him there. He had been moved to a psychiatric hospital for evaluation, just as Patrick Cullen had anticipated. Others tried to have a good look at her bruising without being so obvious about it. These were the ones that made Angela wish they would just come straight out with it, and be done.

Thankfully the bruising began to fade day by day, and the attention went onto whatever was the next most interesting topic. Christy was safely out of circulation for the moment and thereby forgotten, until such time as a decision on his condition was made, or he reappeared in his cottage to await charges, whichever was the outcome.

It was about two weeks after the attack that Angela got a phone call from Patrick.

"I just wanted to tell you the latest on Christy."

"Yeah?"

"It looks like he'll be on psychiatric medication for the future. There's not much likelihood of a charge against him. That's pretty much what I expected. I had a word with the doctors. They will observe him for a while and see how he is. In all probability he will be back in his cottage soon."

There was a silence on Angela's end.

"Is that a problem for you, Angela?"

"No . . . not really. As long as the doctors say he will be okay, I suppose."

"Placid as a lamb, they say. I just thought you should know."

She felt Christy would never be right, medication or not. Her arrival must have been the final push. Still, she decided to do her best to put him out of her head.

When at last Christy did arrive home it was Maisie Mac who told her the news.

"I heard Christy is home."

Angela wasn't too surprised. She had been expecting it any time.

"When?"

"Few days ago, I believe. He's keeping a very low profile, it seems. Haven't seen him about the town at all."

His medication must be working, Angela thought. If Christy was to be seen, Maisie Mac was the one who would know. Placid as a lamb, Patrick had said. She hoped to God that was right.

Thomas had been going up to Doyles' since the start of the holidays and life looked like it had finally settled down. He fired Declan with enthusiasm according to Mrs Doyle and miraculously they managed to stay out of devilment, most of the time. When he came in at lunchtime he was always full of stories about what he got up to with Deko. Angela listened with great interest, often thinking that no one would believe he was not even six months living in the country. He sounded so much like a countryman, born and bred!

The summer holidays were heaven for him. When he wasn't with Deko he was with Owen, or all three were together in the afternoons when he was back from the Doyles'. They made a "hideout" in the loft, where they held secret meetings, and the sign on the ladder said *No Adults Allowed!*

Angela could hardly believe her life had changed so much. Six months ago in D'Arcy Avenue she'd thought her life not worth living. Now look at you, she told herself with a wry smile, owner of a country mansion – well, not exactly, but near enough for her, and a terrific son to boot.

It was with a good level of surprised acknowledgement that she reflected on how her life had changed. Without question the major part of it was her relationship with Thomas. She found she looked forward to him coming back from the Doyles' each day after she got in from work. She enjoyed the way they chatted over meals, telling each other things that had happened in their mornings. They laughed together over things, and it had even happened that she gave him the occasional quick hug when she was particularly pleased about something. She came to know his personality, his character, and thanked God that she could see no trace of his father in him. If he took after anyone it had to be her father Daniel, judging by the things she was hearing in conversations with people who knew him.

Thomas's company was always cheery, he never objected to helping out about the house. He amazed her, it was as if he actually appreciated it, and things didn't get wrecked like they did before. She liked how he chatted away with news. Mrs Doyle said this or Mrs Doyle said that. Amused, she thought it was like the way he was always quoting his teacher before the holidays.

He didn't quote his nan. If he mentioned Nancy it was to ask a question. When were they going to see her again? When would she visit? Would she stay a while?

If they were sure that Paddy was actually at work they would chance a phone call. Nancy sometimes would text them to let them know. Thomas's delight was to dial her number himself and chat a little with her. The call always ended with him asking the same question: "When are you coming to visit, Nan?"

Recently Nancy had said she just might manage a trip down soon. It was only a *little* might, but better than no hope at all. Angela took more interest in the house, partially because of her mother's half promise as she wanted her to be impressed, and partially out of a growing sense of pride.

She never thought about Paddy.

What he would make of her now didn't matter one little jot. She felt wonderfully free of that old need that had sapped her energy, and hindered her so much. She knew the beatings had stopped, and that was really all that concerned her about D'Arcy Avenue. She never asked about Paddy. Nancy never mentioned him any more.

This morning before she set off for work she had promised Thomas that after lunch they would take a walk up to the cemetery to inspect the new carving on the headstone at Daniel's grave. She was pleased it was finally done. As Maisie Mac would have said with a degree of satisfaction which was unusual for her, she "had done right by Daniel".

When she finished in the bakery she walked up the main street and met Maisie Mac emerging from her shop with her sweeping brush.

"Are you ever done with the brush, Maisie?" she greeted her.

Cheek, Maisie thought, smiling her sugary little smile. "Sure how would I ever see anything from inside?" she asked.

Angela smiled at the very honesty of it.

"Well, I'd better get on," she replied, determined not to delay. "Things to do after lunch, y'know?"

"Off for the day are ye, eh? It's well for some."

"Off to get Thomas's lunch, and me own. I'm a bit late getting out today. See you."

Angela walked up the road and hesitated outside Seán's place, thinking she would drop in just for a minute to say hello. Then she decided not, telling herself it would only delay her more, and she knew how much Thomas was looking forward to going to the graveyard. So she set off on the road towards her house, walking quickly, because there was always the possibility that she might not get a lift. Today was one such day. Walking briskly she reached home without so much as a tractor passing. She closed the gate, and let herself into the house.

Thomas would be down from the Doyles' any second with his stories of the morning's comings and goings. She turned on the radio, something which had become a habit, and she lost no time starting the lunch. She was thinking he was late when the phone rang.

"Angela?" It was Patrick. The tone of that one word told her there was something up.

"Is Thomas okay?" she asked at once.

"What makes you ask?" Patrick was immediately concerned.

"It's in your voice."

"It's not Thomas, it's Christy".

Not him again. But she didn't need to ask because the solicitor continued.

"He's in the hospital. They found him unconscious on his floor."

"Oh!"

"Apparently someone passing saw his bike out the front, and he never leaves it there, and the side gate was open. Unusual it seems. They say the gas was left on."

The back door opened and Thomas came in.

"Will he be okay?" Angela asked.

"I'm sure they will do their best, just thought I'd let you know."

According to Thomas, Mr Doyle was telling Mrs Doyle that the drugs might have made Christy drowsy and he might not have known the gas was not turned off properly.

In the age-old cemetery on the western slope of Baltinglass Hill, outside Baltinglass town, a small group of women gathered by an open grave. Standing back a bit to allow room for relatives by the graveside, they waited for the hearse to arrive. From their elevated vantage point they watched as it approached on the sharply curving road, which climbed steeply from the main street to the gates of the graveyard and beyond.

The hearse and the mourning car turned into the cemetery and slowly made its way up the narrow path as far as the old tower. It stopped, and the coffin was hoisted carefully onto the shoulders of six men, none of whom were related to the deceased, but all of whom considered it a tragic end to a very tragic life.

The women waiting by the graveside watched as the oak casket was carried up the narrow path between the headstones. They stood gathered together, as they did at every funeral in the parish, summoning their most sorrowful expressions, with their rosary beads wrapped around their fingers.

"Would you just look at the little face on Thomas," Maisie Mac said. "That poor lad has been through so much in his young life."

"His mother has been through as much," someone countered. "I don't know that I would like to be in her shoes, inheritance or no inheritance."

"Well, she has it all now," Maisie declared none too quietly. "She will probably get the cottage as well, unless of course, *another* relation is going to come out of the woodwork!"

"Shut up, Maisie, that's very unkind," Betty O'Gorman declared.

Taken aback by the manner of the usually quiet Betty, the group fell silent.

Following the coffin to the open grave beside Daniel and Mary Cleary's, Angela felt herself to be a spectacle for the town. She was glad of the comforting presence of Patrick Cullen, Rose, Orla, Mr and Mrs Doyle and Seán. Thomas held her hand and, apart from when they needed to bless themselves, they held onto each other the whole time.

The priest, standing solemnly beside them, raised his hand, and made the sign of the cross upon himself. The people did likewise.

"In the name of the Father, and of the Son, and of the Holy Spirit," the priest began. "My dear friends, let us pray for the repose of the soul of our dear brother, Christopher . . ."

Chapter 42

A plush car with a soft-top and a Dublin registration plate was unusual in the town. Its driver got out and looked around, then crossed the road and went into Seán Mulhearn's pub.

The man in the suit who sat down at the bar immediately aroused Seán's interest. To Seán's mind he was a peculiar mix of rich and rough. He was very well dressed, and he wore two large gold rings, one on each hand. They were somewhat ostentatious and not in keeping with the subtle dark-grey business suit. His silk tie was held with an equally big gold tie-pin, and Seán thought ruefully that his valet, if he had one, should have known tie-pins were very naff these days and dressed him more subtly.

The visitor was short but well built, and the thing that Seán thought odd was that he sported an extremely tight haircut for a businessman. Almost a blade one!

He looked around, his lightning-quick glance

reminding Seán of someone who was wary. He did not
sit with an air of calm and unhurried ease, as a
businessman used to spending much time in various
hostelries would.

Seán's interest deepened. He sauntered down behind
the bar, wiping the bar top and replacing beer mats.

"What can I get you?" he asked easily, smiling.

The man avoided his gaze. There was no smile in
return, just a fixing of the man's cuff.

"Coffee thanks." The two words were enough to
identify the customer as a Dubliner.

Since it was lunchtime Seán felt quite at ease asking,
"Would you like something to eat? We do a very tasty
menu." He picked up a menu and placed it in front of his
customer.

The man didn't even look at it.

"Coffee's fine." The words were spoken quite
deliberately, the menu was ignored.

Seán took no heed of the rudeness and put the menu
back in its place. But the feeling he got about this
character was one he did not particularly like.

But that was bar work for you: you get all sorts and
you treat them all the same. He smiled, produced the
coffee and went on with his work.

The man's mobile phone rang.

"Yeah," he said and listened for a moment. "Right."
He got off his bar stool and went out of the pub.

Seán looked from the closing door to the unpaid-for
coffee.

"Well, did you ever?" he asked no one in particular,

standing with a pint in his hand.

"By God! He was in a big hurry, all right!" a customer answered. "What a neck! Here, are you going to hang onto me pint till it goes flat or what?"

"Would you believe that?" Seán put the pint down. He was annoyed, but not surprised.

Mick Furlong never came in for his lunch that day, and that was another strange thing.

The last two portions of Mrs Doyle's delicious lasagne were already defrosted and in the oven being heated up for the lunch. Angela was dicing some cold boiled potatoes, left over from yesterday, to make a potato salad to go with the lasagne. Nothing was wasted in her kitchen. She remembered with shame the countless times she saw her beleaguered mother scrape almost untouched dinners into the bin.

That didn't happen here. Thomas never left anything on his plate these days. No wonder Nancy always remarked how well he was growing. But then, he had a lot of catching up to do to begin with. In D'Arcy Avenue he was always the smallest in his group.

With the salad ready and the lasagne making a mouth-watering aroma, Angela thought it was about time Thomas got back from the Doyles'. She heard a car door close – that would be Mrs Doyle with Thomas. She always parked her Opel at the side of the house.

Instead of Thomas coming in through the back porch, there was a knock at the front door.

"What's he playing at?" Angela muttered, but went

into the front hall and opened the door.

Shock reverberated through her. The colour drained from her face. She felt she had been dealt a body blow.

Redser Reilly was standing on her doorstep.

"Well, if it isn't little Angela!"

The sneer and the sickening lechery in the eyes were still the same. She attempted to slam the door on him, feeling as if she was moving in slow motion. But then he was standing in the hall, and it was he who pushed the door shut.

"Don't want the neighbours gawking in, do we?" he breathed into her face.

She backed off instinctively, but he kept coming towards her. She turned suddenly and ran into the kitchen, thinking to escape through the back door. She knew both it and the kitchen door were open, for Thomas to arrive home.

Reilly was ahead of her like lightning. The speed of his reactions was unbelievable. In the kitchen she stopped dead to prevent herself from bumping into him, because he had got ahead of her. He gave a little laugh. Blocking her, he tormented her by not even bothering to close the door of her escape route. He advanced on her, forcing her to back into the centre of the room again.

"How – how did you find me? Who told you where I was?"

Her voice was a whisper, strangled in her dry throat. She was afraid to hear the answer. Her eyes darted each way about the room, trying to see a way round him. He blocked all possibilities merely by standing in front of her. The power of his body was very evident – she could almost feel the strength he had at his disposal. It frightened her into making futile efforts to escape. But, every time, even before she moved she knew it was useless.

"Now why do I get the impression you're not pleased to see me?" He moved to block her again. "After I came all this way?"

The chilling grin looked like it had been plastered onto his face. His beady eyes never left hers. He saw the imminent movement before she moved at all. Thus alerted, he thwarted her every attempt.

"You're not wanted here!" she blurted as she slowly backed away, but there was only the sink behind her. Her mind raced. Her eyes searched for something to fling at him, preferably something that would disable him. Bleach, oven cleaner, anything.

He saw the intention.

"Take off your tights!" he ordered her.

She froze, staring at him in abject horror.

"You heard me."

The vicious undercurrent froze the blood in her veins.

"No . . . no. No. Never!" She almost broke down pitifully. History was repeating itself. Oh, God not again! But she forced herself not to let her knees buckle under her, and she repeated, "Never! You scum, never! You'll have to kill me first!"

He drew his hand from his pocket and she saw a flash of steel, heard the click as the blade shot into position. She did not see the rapid movement that brought his hand up, but she certainly felt the cold point of the blade on her cheek.

"That can be arranged, little Angela, no bother at all." His eyes were like slits, the pupils dilated. The hand that held the knife moved slowly from side to side in front of her face. There was no hurry about him, no tremors, no nervousness, just a cold determined knowledge that he was good at what he was doing. And he was enjoying it immensely, savouring every minute.

She looked like she had been turned to stone. Any second she expected to feel the steel puncture her flesh, slowly, deliberately. The warm blood would run over her chilled skin, and he would watch it flow, smiling that same icy smile.

"Maybe we don't have to go *that* far . . ." His facial contortions betrayed his pleasure. "We could make some nice patterns on that pretty face instead, couldn't we? Nice deep cuts that would never really heal properly. *Lots* of them. Then you'd *wish* you were dead. That what you want, is it, little Angela?"

Her mouth was dry as a bone. Her lips moved and formed a silent "No".

"Then the tights it is, so."

She fumbled with her skirt, pathetic whimpers escaping her. Thomas came into her mind. Dear God, she prayed, don't let him come in. Please don't let him come in.

Redser watched every embarrassed move she made, a smirk on his face. The tights were removed and with his free hand he grabbed them, spun her around and had both her hands tied behind her back before she knew it. Then roughly he pushed her onto a chair and tied the remaining length of the tights to the rungs at the back of the chair. It had been no effort to him. He tossed her about like she was a mere feather. Suddenly his hand was clamped tightly over her mouth and she realised she was screaming. He leaned against the table and placed one foot on the seat of the chair, against her thigh. The blade was waved in her face.

"Make another sound like that and this will slip! Badly."

He waited for her acquiescence, then thrust the blade frighteningly close till she nodded frantically.

Her thoughts raced. She had expected the intention was to rape her, but once she was securely tied to the chair he relaxed but continued to watch her like a hawk. She refused to meet his eyes. She didn't want to look upon his countenance – to do so was tantamount to accepting what was happening, and utter fear caused her to deny this.

Why was he here? What did he want? Were there some of his thugs outside?

He double-checked the knots. "That will stop your stupid ideas," he laughed into her face, "while we wait for the lad."

She swallowed hard. Thomas! He was after Thomas? The nightmare got worse. Thomas was due in any minute. Christ Almighty! He was going to walk right into it.

Reilly saw her expression change. You could tell

everything by watching a person's eyes. That was the first thing he had learned. It always served him well.

"Where is he, by the way?" He made it sound so like an offhanded casual question.

She remained silent. Stubborn.

"Talk!"

The knife brushed against her face, instantly causing a hissing intake of breath. Wide with terror her eyes followed the blade as it swayed hypnotically before her.

"He's not here," she gasped. "He's gone off for the day. He won't be back for ages!"

He studied her carefully. He did not believe her.

"Why do you want him? Leave him out of it!" she entreated him. "He's only a child!"

Reilly just smirked and said dispassionately, "But we can't leave him out of it, little Angela. I need you both!"

Then it came to her. Reilly was on the run! He needed to lie low. Hide. And she was perfect for it. This house was perfect for it. But he needed them both under his control in order to stop either of them from talking. So he would wait like a predator till all his prey was in the net!

He almost could see her mind racing. She was trying to work it out. His look became more menacing. He leaned forward, pointing the knife at her lips.

"Trying to work it out, eh? Smart, are you?" He made it sound like something distasteful. "I don't like smart women. They think, and that's never a good idea. So you just keep your trap shut, and we'll wait for my son to show up."

She felt sick to hear him refer to Thomas in that way. Anger rose inside her suddenly.

"You'll never get away with this!" she shouted. "The Gardaí will find you and –"

She broke off with a gasp as the back of his hand lashed across her face.

"I told you – enough!" The knife was within a hair's breath of her face again. "Another word out of you and I'll cut you!"

He was angry. He could not allow himself the luxury of becoming angry. It clouded his thinking. Caused him to make mistakes. In his business mistakes could cost him his life. His anger was directed at Angela, she had made him angry.

She was instantly silenced, and kept her head turned away from him while he growled his warning.

Thomas came across the fields, and saw the smashing-looking car parked at the house. He wondered who was visiting them. No one he knew in Baltinglass had a soft-top car like that. Then he noticed the Dublin registration plate. His mother hadn't mentioned anything about them having a visitor. He got to the back door, sat down and pulled off his wellies. The weather had been dry for a while now and the boots were not muddy, but his mother would not allow them in the house under any circumstances.

He was just about to call out that he was home when he became aware of the raised voices. One of them was his mother's, the other was strange. For one awful minute Thomas thought that Paddy might have found them. But no. Paddy would never have a car like that. Feeling quite apprehensive he went to the slightly opened kitchen door and took a peek before going in.

The sight before him petrified him. Reilly!

He saw the knife. His mother tied up. Redser threatening her.

He couldn't move. He couldn't save her this time. He couldn't stand up to Reilly. Not Reilly! In absolute panic he turned and ran. He ran blindly through the fields, stumbling and crying, his breath coming in sharp gasps as he plunged headlong through the hedges.

When he reached Doyle's yard he called out, "Mrs Doyle! Mrs Doyle!"

He burst into the house, and a very alarmed Mrs Doyle came towards him, wiping her hands on her apron. She knew something terrible was wrong when she saw the state the state of him. Then she saw he had run all the way in his stockinged feet.

"Jesus, Thomas! What is it, child?" His obvious distress put the heart crossways in her. Thomas found it difficult to get the words out. His heart was hammering and he was out of breath. Tears ran down his cheeks.

"It's – it's – Reilly! He's in the house! He has me ma! Oh, Mrs Doyle, he'll kill her, he has a knife!"

It all gushed out in one go, and Mrs Doyle did her best to get him to calm down and tell her exactly what was up. She tried to keep a cool head, and wished that Mr Doyle hadn't already left to go to Tullow, taking Declan with him.

"Who's Reilly, Thomas?"

"He's . . . he's . . ." Thomas couldn't bring himself to say "he's me da," because he was so ashamed, "he's . . . from Dublin! He has a knife . . . he was pointing it at me ma!"

Mrs Doyle began to get the picture. She knew there were unsavoury elements in their past. She tried to calm the panic-stricken child, and think what to do.

"I'll tell you what, Thomas, I'll phone the house. If that gurrier knows there's someone close by he'll be afraid to do anything."

She tried to sound confident, but she could see the boy wasn't going for it. But she had to do something. She picked up the phone and dialled Angela's number. After what seemed like forever the receiver was lifted. There was a long silent pause before Angela said hello. Her voice was different, strained.

"Angela! Are you okay?"

"No!" came the shaky reply. "No. Thomas isn't here."

Mrs Doyle was sure that Angela had tried to alert her, and she was convinced the lad was right and there was a very dangerous situation in the house.

"He's safe with me – I'll get help –" was all she had time to say.

There came a rushed "Goodbye" before the line went dead.

She looked down at Thomas's tearstained face, and tried to give him hope.

"Your mam is okay. I'm going to ring the police now.

They'll know what to do. They're probably looking for that man, even now. They'll be glad to know where they can get him." She did her best to sound reassuring, and it worked a little. Thomas just nodded and sat very subdued, his face white and drawn.

Mrs Doyle made her call. Thomas barely listened. He could still see the knife, his mother's fearful face, and he felt awful that he had run away and left her with Reilly.

Mrs Doyle was talking to him.

"Thomas, do you know the man's full name?"

"Redser Reilly," he said dully.

"The garda says can you describe him? Do you know where he lives?"

Thomas was such a mine of information that Mrs Doyle handed him the receiver and let him talk to the garda himself. The garda asked him all sorts of questions. Was anyone else in the house with his mother? Did he see any other strange men about? Did he see any other weapon besides the knife? Did he know the registration number of the car? The questions were endless. Then he passed the phone back to Mrs Doyle and while they were talking to her another garda was on a different line and found out the low-down the Dublin force had on Reilly. They were looking for him all right and the car was stolen, they said, and they stressed how violent Reilly was. They gave instructions to stay away from the house, and not to alert Redser that they were on to him.

The phone call over, Mrs Doyle tried her best to comfort Thomas. "They're on to him now, love. They'll get your mother out safely, you'll see."

He looked up at her with wide fearful eyes. "I shouldn't have run. I left her there with Reilly. He could kill her."

The poor little thing! He had so much trouble in his young life. And now he felt guilty because he could not save his mother from a vicious thug. At only nine years old! She sat down beside him and put her arm around his shoulders.

"Now, Thomas, you listen to me," she began decisively. "*Are* you listening?"

He nodded.

"Because you did the *wise* thing and came over here to raise the alarm, the police are on to it, they will get her out, and that's all thanks to you."

He didn't look so convinced. She tried another way.

"Well, let me put it like this. What do you think would have happened if you had gone into the house?"

He couldn't answer that. But he knew. He knew for sure, now that he thought about it, that he was too afraid of Reilly to have been able to do anything. Mrs Doyle was right. They would both be prisoners, and no one would be able to help because no one would know.

He sighed heavily. He still wished his mother wasn't on her own. He wished *he* wasn't on his own. Mrs Doyle was very kindly but he needed someone else.

"Mrs Doyle?"

"What is it, Thomas?"

"Can I ring me nan?"

Chapter 43

After Reilly put the receiver back in its cradle he rambled round the kitchen, then sat himself down at the table. He appeared to be thinking; yet his face was a veritable wall of blankness. He kept turning the knife over and over in his hand. The blade was still extended and he frequently ran his finger the length of its sharp edge. He admired the cold steel, the ability of the weapon to inflict the most awful injuries. Or, in the deftest of hands, such as his own, the ability to score the flesh with delicate intricate wounds, thereby causing the maximum of terror.

Angela watched this withdrawal from her. She knew it was merely temporary. Any second she expected him to switch back on to her with renewed viciousness, because of the waiting. The waiting was worst.

Waiting for Thomas to walk into his trap.

But that wouldn't happen, Thomas was safe, thank God. But she knew instinctively that that did not bode well for her. Reilly would not take kindly to having his plans go astray. And she was a sitting duck. She wondered what Mrs Doyle meant when she said she would get help. It worried Angela. They did not know what Redser was capable of. It was not only she who might get hurt.

The phone rang, shattering the oppressive silence.

Angela jumped. Redser lifted his head unhurriedly. He was very much in control, and he took his time going to lift the receiver.

"If it's Thomas, tell him to get himself back here double quick, y'hear?"

She nodded. It was no problem for her to say that because she knew Mrs Doyle would never let him walk into this mess.

"If it's anyone else, get rid of them! Don't let anyone think they can call over, or it will be the worse for you!"

He held the receiver to her ear, but far away enough so that he could hear too.

"Hello?"

She was unprepared for Seán's voice.

"Seán!"

Instantly Reilly covered the mouthpiece with the palm of his knife hand.

"Say you are on your way out," he mouthed at her.

She did as she was told; trying to sound normal, but the blade was so close she dared not breathe lest she came in contact with it.

Seán hesitated for what seemed like ages. "You okay?"

"Yeah, fine. See you later."

Reilly hung up. He gritted his teeth.

"What's with the 'see you later' act?" he snarled.

"I had to end the call somehow," she protested, "otherwise he might have gone on."

Reilly scrutinised her, searching for trickery. Not finding any way to fault her, he reasserted his control by deciding there would be no more calls answered. If she were supposed to be going out, then the phone would have to be allowed to ring out.

Her eyes followed him, frightened as she was of his unpredictability.

"Something smells good," he remarked, suddenly seeming normal and becoming aware of the smell of food. She sat watching him in disbelief, noting how frighteningly Jekyll-and-Hyde-like he was. The lasagne was well heated by now, and he went and took a look in the oven. He straightened up with a twisted smile on his face.

"Two portions! And you said Thomas was gone for the day – wouldn't be back for ages, you said! Lying bitch! And you with his lunch ready in the oven. Just as well I didn't believe you."

He removed the tray, placed the lasagne on a plate and sat himself down.

"Want some?" he jeered.

She remained silent. The food she had so anticipated enjoying was sickening to her now. He had no such compunction about it. "If that lad can't be on time for grub, we can't waste it – now, can we?"

The words chilled her. He spoke as if he lived there. If he was on the run, did he think he was going to stay?

Seán was very uneasy. His call to Angela had been strange. She sounded very tense. She didn't usually cut a call short. He went about his work and tried all sorts of ways to convince himself that he was being paranoid. But in the end he could not stick the uneasy feeling any longer and decided to take a run out there and . . . and what? Check up on her? She might not appreciate him doing that when she obviously decided not to mention anything to him in the first place. He was in a right quandary over what to do.

Finally he decided to risk incurring her wrath. Lunches were almost finished and, leaving the others to finish up, he took the car and headed for Daniel's house. Angela still called it that.

But a surprise was in store for him before he reached it. A squad car stopped him at a roadblock when he was still about half a mile off and told him he could go no further. There were a number of police cars parked ahead of him on the roadway.

Seán's unease turned to alarm.

"What's up, Joe?" he asked, recognising the garda from the local station.

"A bit of trouble up ahead," he was told. "You'll have to go back, take the other road."

"Would it involve Angela and Thomas?"

The garda's ears pricked up. "What would you know about it, if it was?"

Seán told him about the peculiar phone call. Another car pulled up behind Seán and the garda went to inform the driver that the road was closed. He ambled back to Seán.

"Just between ourselves," he confided, "there's a hostage situation at the house. Dublin fellow. Wanted for murder, it seems. They're just waiting for back-up to arrive."

"Who? Who's at the house?" Seán asked in alarm.

"Just the mother – the lad is over at Doyles'."

Angela! His heart pounding, Seán stared ahead in the direction of the house, searching his brain for some way he could help. Murder! But thank God Thomas was out of it at least! He thought of the fellow in the pub earlier. Him? He had known there was something about him.

"Anything I can do?" he asked, knowing it was useless even to offer.

The Gardaí had procedures to follow in these siege situations, he was told. Procedures that did not include civilians. He tried again.

"Any chance of getting up to the gate at least? I could leave the car here?"

The garda was very apologetic but there was no way he would allow Seán to go any further.

"Sorry, but this could go on a while, you know. We don't know how well armed he is. Can't risk anyone getting injured."

Armed? For Christ's sake! Angela was *in* there. What if *she* got injured?

"Look," Seán reasoned, "surely you can let me get through to Doyles'? Thomas might be better off if he had someone he can relate to, and we get on great." He detected a slight hesitation, a human heart under the navy blue serge, and he moved on it before it vanished in a puff of officialdom.

"Aw, come on, the lad has no one else, his mother is being held hostage and –"

"Okay, okay, okay," the garda relented, "but make sure you go straight to Doyles', y'hear?"

Seán's car pulled into Doyle's yard. Mrs Doyle was very glad to see him.

"I'm so glad you came, Seán! The lad is in there and I can hardly get a word out of him. Me heart goes out to him."

"They nearly didn't let me through. They have a road block in place and they are just waiting for back-up."

"It's terrible," Mrs Doyle lamented. "The problems that are inflicted on that poor girl!"

Thomas had assumed that the car outside was Mr Doyle returning from Tullow.

Then Seán walked into the kitchen and, on seeing Thomas's stockinged feet, said: "Cowboys *never* lose their boots!"

Thomas jumped from his chair and threw himself at him, almost slipping in his stocking feet on the tiled floor. Seán caught him and steadied him up.

Thomas suddenly was all talk, gushing about how he had seen Redser with the knife to his mother's face, and how she was tied to the chair, and how he was so afraid that he turned and ran.

"You did the right thing, man, you raised the alarm. Somebody had to do that, and the Gardaí are on the ball. Don't you worry, Thomas, they know how to deal with these situations." He hoped he sounded very positive, but he knew "these situations" could go very wrong sometimes. "But tell me, who is this Redser fellow? Why would he do this to your mother?"

Thomas's talk suddenly faltered, and Mrs Doyle immediately said, "Oh, dear, excuse me! I left the tap running!" and went out.

Seán buttered a slice of bread and looked enquiringly at the lad.

Thomas cupped his hands over his mouth and whispered, "He's me da! Don't tell anyone, will you?"

Seán disguised his shock. "Of course not!" he said stoutly. "We'll keep it between ourselves."

His mind was whirling around this latest piece of the jigsaw puzzle of Angela and Thomas. No wonder she didn't want to talk to him about Thomas's father. Did the lad know his father was wanted for murder? Was Angela aware of it? Thomas said he had a knife. Surely Reilly would be unlikely to use it on the mother of his own son?

While his mind was still trying to get itself around the situation Mrs Doyle returned, after taking a very long time to turn off a tap, and poured two delicious bowls of home-made soup, and told them to "wire into the brown bread".

Seán began to eat his own, and put some buttered bread next to Thomas's bowl. The boy started to eat but obviously had no appetite.

Mrs Doyle very much wished that her husband were home.

Chapter 44

Reilly belched loudly after the lunch and laughed.

"Not bad at the cooking, are you?" he remarked.

She made no answer. The muscles in her arms had begun to ache from the angle at which her wrists were tied.

"That stupid young fella missed a good lunch."

"He's anything but stupid!" she retorted.

Redser was amused. "Oh, chip off the old block, is he?"

She was sorry she had said anything.

His belly full, Redser seemed in better humour.

"Why are you here?" she dared ask. "What do you want? You can't stay here."

He glared across at her with such a weird look in his eye that she was instantly sorry she had spoken. His sneer frightened her. Had she hit the nail on the head?

"Oh, I'm not staying here," he was quick to assure her. "I'm leaving just as soon as I get my money."

"Money? What money?"

What could he possibly be on about? Did he think there was money here for him because he was Thomas's father?

Feeling his plan was well and truly secure Reilly enlightened her. "You are going to sell to Mick Furlong. I am here to ensure that, then I get my money and I am out of here. Simple as that." He flicked the blade of the knife back and forth in quick succession as if to emphasise how simple it was.

"*Mick Furlong*?" Her heart thudded at the way this was going. What had Mick Furlong to do with anything? "How do you know Mick Furlong?"

Redser just smirked at her and tapped the side of his nose with his finger. He had his ways.

She tried another angle. "I don't own this yet. I can't sell it!"

"But you can agree *now* to sell it when it becomes yours. That's what you are going to do. Today." His voice was silky with menace. "Then I get my money and I go. Today. Simple." He reached into his breast pocket and slammed a very officious-looking document onto the table. "You will sign *that* as soon as Thomas gets here. If you don't, one phone call and my mates take him. You might not get him back in one piece."

The implications of his statement cut to her heart. Her head swam as if it had been deprived of oxygen. How could he even think of this? She knew without being told that he – they – had it all worked out.

"Mick Furlong put you up to this?" She was incredulous.

She couldn't believe Furlong was involved in this, that he would go that far.

"He only wants what he wants. How I work is of no interest to him. He gets your agreement, I get my money, and I'm off. And you won't try to backtrack later – Thomas could vanish at any time . . ."

Angela had always thought Reilly had access to all the money he wanted. Again he saw her unspoken question but did not enlighten her. He didn't need to.

Of course! They would have frozen any assets he had acquired through criminal activities. She heard it often enough on the news. He couldn't run without money to sustain him, at least enough for a while. And Reilly was not used to slumming it.

Angela's thoughts ran riot. Talk of Reilly's spies had long abounded. But she knew now the rumours had to be true. Did he have her followed from the start? Was he having her watched all the while, waiting for the chance to turn her misfortune to his advantage? Simply because he was Thomas's dad? Then another more awful thought occurred to her.

"The broken windows . . . the open gate . . . did Mick Furlong get you to do all that?" "No, no, no . . . think of those as little greeting cards from me."

It was all more than she could grasp immediately.

Reilly was getting edgy. He got up and tossed the blade in his hand, his face darkened, his manner changed.

"What's keeping that git?" he growled. "Why don't you seem worried about him?"

It was well past the time when Thomas should have been home, and Reilly had become aware of it. He was growing very uneasy. He paced the room and cast frequent glances at his watch. He tossed the knife from hand to hand, and made impatient noises with his mouth. Angela's anxiety grew with every minute. Reilly eyed the kitchen door and decided to have a look outside for any sign of Thomas, the windows in the room being too high to see through. He went into the back porch, nearly tripping over some boots lying there, and looked through the window. No trace of the boy. He stuck his head outside the door to look around.

Then he saw it. The flash of navy as a garda dived for cover. Reilly had too much experience with the law not to know exactly what he sensed. He jerked his head back inside and slammed the porch door shut, turning the key in the lock.

"Cops! Fucking cops! Everywhere!"

He rushed back into the kitchen. But there was no key for that lock. He rushed at Angela and grabbed her hair, jerking her head backwards. She felt the blade against her throat.

"How did you do it? Was it the phone call? How? You fucking bitch!?" he raged at her. Such was her fright that she could not answer coherently. In fury he shoved her head forward. Thinking this was her end a cry escaped her, but he was already moving back to the porch to see what was going on outside.

He couldn't afford to step out into the porch again and so his view was limited. He went back into the kitchen and paced up and down, up and down, his brain working overtime.

"In the house. Reilly! This is the Gardaí! You are surrounded! Send Angela out and we'll talk!"

The loudhailer startled both of them. Angela's reaction was fear of retaliation from Reilly. Reilly's reaction was to embed the blade of his knife in the table in front of her, and push his face towards hers.

"I don't get out of this – *you* don't get out alive!"

"Thomas!" she cried. "Think of Thomas!"

He spat, "Fuck Thomas! Fuck you! I'm not here to think of either of you!"

He was back at the porch door, but only for a split second, no point in making a target of himself. He whirled away from it again, and pulled the blade out of the table.

He kept turning to her and pointing it ever closer, while his behaviour became more agitated. The loudhailer was heard again, increasing the tension in the room. The phone rang. Redser spun towards it, but refused to pick up.

It continued to ring.

"Pick up the phone, Reilly, we want to talk!"

Reilly strode across the room and yanked the receiver from its cradle. Then slowly he put it to his ear. When he spoke his voice chilled Angela. His initial panic was over. He had regained his wits, and was coldly in control of himself again.

"Fuck you!" he snarled into the mouthpiece. "Fuck the lot of you!"

He wrapped the cord of the phone around his hand and wrenched it out of its socket. Angela felt despair. With the connection to the outside world broken she began to lose hope. Reilly now paced slowly back and forth, like a caged animal. His menacing manner became more threatening, more volatile. Her eyes followed him to and fro, waiting in agonising tension for him to snap.

Chapter 45

Apart from the rustling of Paddy's newspaper, and the news on the radio, there was silence in the kitchen at D'Arcy Avenue. Paddy was sitting by the side of the fireplace, in his armchair, perusing the paper after his lunch. Nancy was listening to the news while she finished her cup of tea.

The lack of communication between them was the norm these days, and Nancy did not regret it.

When the phone rang she answered it and Paddy listened to the conversation, pretending to be absorbed in his paper.

But today he got the shock of his life.

It was obvious that a very distressed Thomas was on the other end of the line. Paddy's shock automatically blocked out most of what his wife said, but one thing was clear: Reilly was down there.

He could not concentrate on the words on the page. He had dreaded something like this ever since the time

Reilly approached him in the pub and asked about Thomas. He found himself to be immobilised, unable to show concern. He was unable to feel anything other than bald, raw guilt. An overwhelming sense of the inevitable washed over him and he wished himself to be anywhere else on the entire planet!

But it would make no difference. He could not escape what he had done.

His wife was clearly in shock at the news she was given, and from the responses he heard he garnered that the Gardaí had been informed and were at the house. Obviously Thomas was not in his own house, but his mother was, and Reilly was holding her at knifepoint.

And he had brought it all upon her. The feeling of self-loathing which began after his conversation with Reilly intensified a hundredfold.

What Nancy's reaction was he was hardly aware of. Guilt prevented him from looking at her, but he rightly knew that her face would have lost its colour, that she was in a state of shock.

When she put down the receiver she turned towards him in utter disbelief. Then, looking at his face, the truth dawned on her.

"You," she breathed. "*You*! This is your doing. I know it. It's written all over you!"

She came towards him, propelled by sheer wrath, and for the first time in his life Paddy Brennan knew what it felt like to be afraid of her. He was transfixed to the chair by eyes that pierced accusingly through him, and saw the black sin of guilt on his soul. Disgust, abhorrence, hate, flowed in a torrent from a silent Nancy, so much so that he cowered in his chair, recoiled at the fury that directed itself at him.

He opened his mouth to utter something, anything, in his own defence, but there were no words in existence which could exonerate him, either in his own eyes, or hers.

She loomed ever closer. She placed her clenched hands on the table to support her trembling body.

"You miserable coward!" she flung at him. "You betrayed them! Told that bastard where to find them. He has her at knifepoint, you spineless shite!"

Nancy's voice rose to a shrieking pitch. But she was not about to lose it now. Not now that they were in such danger. Her breath came in gasps, such was the fear she felt for her daughter's predicament.

He could not meet her eyes. The paper was in his lap and part of it slid to the floor.

She swiped the rest of it aside in her fury, and he made no move to avoid what he thought was going to be a ferocious blow.

She withdrew her hand. "I wouldn't want to touch you!" she said with such derision that he felt like scum. "Not even in anger would I want to come in contact with you. You are beneath contempt. You are nothing but a pitiful wimp, a gutless creep! I'll tell you this much – I'm *glad* you're not her father. You don't deserve her."

Somewhere in the depths of her subconscious she thought it strange that her words evoked no reaction from him, but she was beyond caring, beyond being afraid.

"Daniel Cleary has been more of a father to her than

you. *He* would have had her with him no matter what. Her *and* Thomas. I'll be sorry till the day I die that they never knew him. And I'll tell you something else. I'm going down there, today, and you can burn in *hell* for all I care! And even that would be too good for you."

She whirled away from the table and rushed upstairs. He heard her moving about, and he knew she was throwing some things in a bag. He did not move from the chair. The blackness he had feared for weeks now had finally descended upon him, and he already knew it, like a nightmare he dreamt so often that when it became reality he was already familiar with it.

The bus moved agonisingly slowly. Nancy sat with her holdall at her feet. In her mind she was already there, doing what she could to protect her daughter. And still the bus was only moving through the city traffic. She stared unseeingly out the window, and had some understanding of what it must have been like for Angela and Thomas when they took the same journey out of their familiar life and into an unknown town, in an unknown place, and into a very uncertain future.

She turned over and over what Thomas had said to her on the phone, and wondered just how accurate it was. Thousands of "what ifs?" ranged round and round in her head till she was almost demented with worry.

What was happening now? Right now. Was it over? Did the police get Angela out? She tried to remember the stand-offs she heard about on the telly. How many ended happily?

She knew how vicious Reilly could be. And to think that Paddy Brennan had told him their whereabouts! Oh, God. Why couldn't the bloody bus move faster! She didn't know what she was going to do when she got there. She had no idea where to go. Or how far it was. Angela always said it was miles. And no means of transport.

Nancy tried to think more logically. She tried to remember the town and how it was when she used to go down to Baltinglass all those years ago, to visit her friend.

It was on the bus, just like she was now, that she had met Daniel. The instant electricity between them came as a huge shock to her. She remembered it as though it was yesterday. He had taken the seat beside her, the only one left, and for the duration of the trip she forgot what she was going to Wicklow for. She forgot Paddy, her husband of less than a year. She forgot she was married. So did Daniel. But she was not aware that he was experiencing the same wave of emotion that carried them through that journey. She only knew she was lost.

Difficult though it was, they both behaved with proper decorum, and did not really expect to meet again. The second chance meeting, also on the bus, put the seal on things, and as Nancy often told herself afterwards, the rest was history . . . and inevitable.

But she had never been in Daniel's house. And she had no idea how she was going to get there, if the bus *ever moved*.

Her mobile phone was in her handbag. The urge to

dial Angela's number was strong, but she was afraid that somehow it might add to the problem. It occurred to her also that if all was okay Angela would phone her, once she heard that Thomas had told her what was going on.

That thought worried her desperately, because she realised that if there was no call, then neither was the crisis over. And if the police were at the house then there was a real hostage situation. Oh dear God. Could the bloody bus not go any faster?

The need to do something got the better of her and she took out her phone and dialled. But the constant engaged tone at the end of the disconnected line worried her more.

Chapter 46

The hostage situation had already dragged into its second hour. Gardaí surrounded the house, but apart from the glimpse of a uniform Reilly got at the beginning, there was nothing else to see. The loudhailer jerked into action from time to time, trying to coax him to give up. It was useless, they said. He was surrounded, there was no way out, they said. They tried to persuade him to send Angela out. It would go better for him if he did, they said.

Reilly believed none of it. He knew full well why they were after him. With that and his long record, there was no way they would be about to grant concessions.

He was also well aware that to show his face could be the height of folly. He needed to think. And he needed his hostage. She would be his guarantee of getting out of here alive. Time was unimportant to him. The cops did not know how well armed he was, and since they hadn't stormed the house so far, he guessed they were unlikely to, yet.

Outside an edginess had crept into the situation. Stalemate was the worst thing that could occur, and when siege situations dragged out like this, mistakes were easily made.

But the officer in charge wanted Reilly too badly to risk fouling up. He was a plainclothes man, down from Dublin, and he had no intention of going back empty-handed, so he settled in to wait.

Word was passed from man to man: we wait.

At the Doyles' house a car pulled into the driveway. Declan and his father, arriving back from Tullow, came into the kitchen.

"What's going on up the road?" Mr Doyle wanted to know. "I nearly couldn't get back into my own house with that roadblock up there!" He looked at the grave faces of those in the room, and at once became alarmed. His first thought, because of the loose-sheep incident and the presence of Thomas and Seán, was for his animals, and he asked, "It's not to do with the sheep, is it?"

"The sheep are fine, absolutely fine," his wife assured him. "It's Angela that's in trouble."

"What's up with her?"

Looking at Thomas and considering him when she answered, Mrs Doyle told the story so far. Leaving out her own thoughts on the matter and what she thought should be done with that gurrier from Dublin, she gave her husband a clear picture of the situation. Seán and Thomas added their explanation of their encounters with Reilly that day. Thomas told again of how he had seen Reilly in the kitchen and his mother tied to the chair.

Declan took it all in with a huge sense of disappointment at having missed most of the dramatics, big time. He had gone to Tullow with his dad for something interesting to do, and as it turned out he missed the best bit.

"And is he still holed up in there with Angela?" was Mr Doyle's question, the grim look on his face telling them clearly what he thought of the situation.

"Afraid so," Seán answered. "Hope to God it's over before nightfall. Otherwise that scum just might get away in the dark."

Mrs Doyle was appalled at the very thought of Reilly getting away after all the trauma he was causing. "The likes of him should be shown no mercy, since he shows none himself, and probably is incapable of it!" she declared.

Seán looked at Thomas. They were coming down very heavily on Reilly, not that he didn't deserve it, but Thomas was listening, and Seán could see it worried him more.

"I'm going to change my clothes," Mr Doyle said and left the room.

Declan was eager for Thomas to tell him *everything* that happened, and couldn't understand his friend's reluctance to go over it all again.

Mrs Doyle put on the kettle. She knew her husband would like a cup of tea after changing into his working clothes. She busied herself at the cooker, glad that Thomas now had Declan to occupy him; to help him pass the time and maybe distract him a little. In her own mind she prayed to God that this situation would be over with soon. Her thoughts were with Angela and how she was bearing up. Was she hurt? Was she even alive? Dear God Almighty, it didn't bear thinking about, all the things that could go wrong! She wet the tea and cut some tea-brack to go with it.

Declan helped himself to a big slice.

"That's for your father!" his mother told him sharply. "He'll be in any second now."

But Mr Doyle didn't come back into the kitchen.

"What's keeping him?" Mrs Doyle asked. "He's taking his time changing."

Declan wanted some tea-brack for Thomas and himself.

"Dad's not there," he told her. "I just went to the toilet. He's definitely not there."

Chapter 47

After what seemed like an endless journey the Bus Éireann coach pulled into the terminus in Baltinglass town. Nancy gripped her holdall and was among the first to alight. The place had hardly changed in the last twenty-five years, she noted. There was a peculiar sense of familiarity, in spite of the two and a half decades that had elapsed since.

But now what? Where to?

She was standing looking about for someone to ask for directions, when she thought she heard her name called.

Can't be me they want, she thought, assuming there was another Nancy around, but a small woman with a sweeping brush outside a shop seemed dead bent on attracting her attention. With the evening sun in her eyes Nancy found it difficult to make out the person. The woman stood looking at her in utter disbelief as she approached, as if she were an absolute apparition. Then she broke into a wide smile.

"Nancy Brennan! My God, I don't believe my eyes. How are you? What brings you back to Baltinglass, for God's sake?"

Nancy drew closer and the woman before her took on a familiar look. Different, but familiar. It was her turn to be gobsmacked.

"Maisie MacArdle! God bless us! I thought you were married, living in Kilkenny."

The two women regarded each other with surprise and disbelief.

"Ah, no," Maisie said sadly, the sight of Nancy Brennan bringing her jilted status flooding back into focus. "He found someone with more land than I had."

"The bastard!" Nancy exclaimed. "I always thought you were too good for him anyway."

Maisie gave a genuinely jolly laugh. "You always were sharp, Nancy Brennan. But for God's sake, come in and have a cup of tea and you can tell me all about yourself. What are you doing here, anyway?"

Nancy caught her breath, suddenly feeling ashamed for letting Angela slip her mind even for a moment.

"I can't come in, Maisie, I came down to see my daughter. I have to find my way out to her place as quickly as possible."

Maisie's astute mind began to put two and two together. *Could* it be? No. It surely must be a coincidence. But she asked with bated breath. "Your daughter, Nancy? *Who's* your daughter?"

"My daughter, Angela. And my grandson Thomas."

Nancy was aware of the astonishment on Maisie's face. "You know them?"

"*Daniel's* daughter? Good Lord, Nancy! I'd never have taken you for a scarlet woman!"

"Me neither!"

The two women laughed together, at the very improbability of it, and at the old-fashioned term used, but Nancy's merriment was short-lived.

"How can I get to her place, Maisie – she's in trouble."

The laughter quickly faded from Maisie's face too. "I know, Nancy. We shouldn't be laughing. I'm just so surprised it's *you* who was Daniel's woman! The news is all over town about what's happening out there. I'm so sorry for your trouble. How can I help?"

She had just asked the question when over Nancy's shoulder she caught sight of Betty O'Gorman coming towards them. Clearly, Betty was late with the news, again.

Maisie greeted the newcomer before she had time to open her mouth, with, "Betty. Are you doing anything in particular at the moment?"

It was a peculiar way to greet her and Betty could only reply, "No."

"Good," said the ever-practical Maisie. "I wonder could you drive Nancy here out to the Cleary house? She's Angela's mother."

Betty's mouth hung open for a split second before she thought to shut it. She stared at the personification of Daniel's mistress who was looking expectantly at her.

"Of course. Hello, Nancy," she agreed, while her mind gave vent to annoyance at the fact that though she thought she had the best news ever, Maisie Mac had usurped her yet again.

"Are you sure I'm not putting you out, Betty?" Nancy asked politely.

"Not a bit of it. Glad to help, I'll bring the car down, won't be a minute."

While they waited for Betty to arrive back with her car Nancy asked, "How come you're in a shop, Maisie? What happened to the farm?"

Maisie nodded her head in reflection. "Ah the farm, yeah. The good old days they were. Y'know, when you used to come down to see my sister-in-law I used to envy you, coming from Dublin and all that. Then, after she died Joe couldn't bear the place without her. And I thought it was my chance to do something else, especially after my fella took off. So we sold up and bought this place."

"And Joe?"

"He died about sixteen years ago, Lord rest him. It's not the same now. Too bloody lonely, y'know?"

Nancy nodded. It was strange the way things hardly ever turned out the way you planned. Strange how life messed about with your intentions, and left you with a completely different situation to cope with. She picked up her holdall. Betty had arrived with her car.

"We'll get together when all this is sorted, Nancy. I hope things go okay out there."

Nancy got into the car. "Thanks, Maisie," she said

out the window. "I look forward to seeing you soon. We'll do that."

Betty was glad to be able to help, but she had heard of the roadblock.

"I don't know how far I can take you, Nancy," she remarked as they headed off. "The Gardaí have the road blocked, but we'll get you as far as we can. We'll be there in a couple of minutes."

Nancy fell into silence, watching the countryside slide past the window, and thinking: Daniel's country. Now Angela and Thomas's country. Life was strange.

"How do you and Maisie know each other?" Betty was wondering.

Nancy had no wish for small talk right now, but it occurred to her that Betty might be trying to help by distracting her.

"Maisie's sister-in-law and I were good friends. We worked together in Dublin, and I used visit her and Joe after they married. Maisie always lived with them."

"That's right," Betty mused. "Joe's wife was a Dublin girl. Oh here we are, this is as far as we can go, I think."

She slowed the car down as a garda stepped out and stopped their progress. The road was blocked with a police car parked crossways on it. Nancy got out and spoke to the garda, and at first there was no way he was going to allow her to pass, until she told him she was Angela's mother, and she had been called down by her grandson.

That put a very different light on the matter and he told her he would drive her in the police car as far as the gate of the house, but she could not go further. After speaking via his radio to the other gardaí up ahead he told Nancy they would allow her to wait in one of the garda cars there, if she would agree to stay in the car, no matter what.

Nancy would have agreed to anything then.

Thanking Betty for her help she transferred herself to the police car, and was driven to the gate of Daniel's house. The amount of gardaí and plainclothes men around drove home the gravity of the situation. Nancy watched as they moved about, being careful to keep down low. Everyone and everything was kept well hidden, and the only view she had was of the narrow roadway and the garda cars and the ditches and hedging. The gardaí kept in touch by radio, and now and again the car radio crackled to life. Not understanding the jargon, the things Nancy heard only served to worry her more. Despite the amount of communication going on, there was no action evident, causing her anxiety and worry to rocket astronomically.

Angela was losing hope of ever getting out of this situation. She couldn't understand why, with the Gardaí all around outside, there wasn't some attempt to get her out. Waiting for Reilly to give in was like waiting for mountains to crumble. It would never happen. But what worried her now was that he seemed to be going into some sort of *thing*. He had stopped talking, and when he looked at her she felt he did not see *her*, but someone who was causing his problems. He was doing a lot of thinking, walking back and forth, and he kept tossing the knife over and over in his hand, almost mechanically, while he paced. Suddenly he turned to her and, startling her because it had become so quiet in the kitchen, demanded to know: "What was Thomas wearing on his feet when he went out?"

His eyes had a different glint in them, and she couldn't think for the moment.

"I – I – don't know…"

"Liar!" he shouted. "He was wearing wellies, wasn't he?"

He was, she realised, but how could Reilly know that?

"I knew it! The little bastard! The fucking Judas, *he* turned me in!"

Alarm and fear for her son gripped Angela afresh, a new depth of anxiety swamped her.

"No – no! He couldn't have, he's not even here!"

Reilly turned and pushed his face close to hers. The manic eyes held the worst threat she had seen thus far.

"But he *was* here, the fucker!" he snarled. "His boots are in the porch!"

In the Doyles' house Seán was finding it extremely difficult just to sit and wait, and wished he could know something of how things were going at Angela's house. Mrs Doyle was still going on about where her husband could be when Seán excused himself and went outside.

The Doyles' land was on a rise, giving good views over the surrounding countryside, and Seán hoped he might see something positive happening in the distance.

What he saw almost made his heart stop. Striding across the fields towards Angela's, carrying his double-barrel shotgun, was a very determined-looking Mr Doyle. What was the man thinking of? Surely to God he wasn't thinking of intervening? He could blow the whole operation, taking a chance like that. But he was already too far away to hear even if Seán called him.

Seán went back into the house just as Thomas and Declan came running down the stairs.

"Dad is on his way to Angela's!" Declan shouted. "We saw him from the window. He has the shotgun with him!"

Thomas's eyes were wide with alarm. He looked to Seán to be told "It'll be okay," but he could see by Seán's face that it might *not* be okay. He immediately headed towards the door but Seán grabbed him.

"No, Thomas! It's too dangerous. Your mother would never forgive me if I let you go down there."

"Then come with me," Thomas begged. "I can't just stay here, Seán, I just *can't*."

Mrs Doyle had sat down heavily, her face distorted with worry. "Mannix Doyle," she whispered through white lips, "if you get yourself killed I'll never forgive you."

Thomas broke free of Seán and dashed through the back door. Leaving Mrs Doyle to recover as best she could, Seán ordered Declan not to follow and set off after Thomas. Wearing a borrowed pair of Declan's trainers Thomas ran as fast as he could after the disappearing figure of Mr Doyle and by the time Seán managed to catch hold of him he was practically halfway home.

Inside Reilly paced the floor, switching the blade from hand to hand as he went. When the loudhailer began again he cursed aloud – the damn thing was interrupting his thinking.

"Reilly? Talk to us, Reilly, you can't stay – what the fuck is going . . ."

The loudhailer broke off mid-sentence and Reilly's attention was immediately turned to the porch window. He could see no more than before but something was obviously going wrong from the cops' point of view.

Outside a very determined Mannix Doyle had emerged from the hedge, taking the police completely by surprise. Using the few seconds gained to his advantage, he automatically drew two magnum cartridges from his gilet pocket and loaded them into the barrels of his gun as he strode purposefully towards the back porch door. Obscured from Reilly's view by the door itself he levelled his gun at the lock and pulled the trigger. The blast was deafening. In one smooth movement he covered the remaining ground and kicked in the door in one go.

A number of things happened in unison at the sound of the blast.

Angela screamed and instinctively pushed her chair backward away from the blast, using her feet against the floor. This distanced her from Reilly who, shaken at the unexpected discharge, missed his grip on the knife and it dropped to the floor, hitting it at an awkward angle. It bounced away from him, landing under one of the chairs. He leapt towards it and bent down to reach for it, but before his fingers could close over the handle he froze at the sight of a shotgun pointed straight at his head.

Looking up from his crouched position, his mind tried to gauge how real a threat it was. This lunatic of a farmer had just shot a door, but had he the bottle to fire at a person at almost point-blank range?

Reilly read eyes and learned all he needed to know, and the steady determination he saw in Mannix Doyle's face answered his question. His nerve was shaken, causing him to hesitate.

"Give me an excuse, scum, just give me an excuse!" Mannix growled.

His finger closed over the trigger. Reilly saw the experienced deliberate movement, and for the first time ever he knew fear.

Afraid to go for the knife, he was equally afraid that a movement, even of retreat, might push this reckless hero into firing. There was a sudden rush of footsteps as gardaí rushed into the kitchen.

"We'll take over now," one of them said to Mannix, his manner clearly indicating that he considered he had interfered gravely in police business.

Mr Doyle stepped back, released the pressure on the trigger and lowered the barrel of his shotgun out of harm's way, while a couple of gardaí overpowered the crouched Reilly, who just for pig iron, threw himself backwards, taking two burly policemen onto the floor with him.

There was a scramble to get them all back on their feet, and a sneer on Reilly's face told them he enjoyed causing the cops to have to roll on the floor. He wasn't going easily. Mr Doyle held his position till he saw the handcuffs clamped on Reilly's wrists. Then he removed the remaining cartridge from his gun and took a scissors from a drawer and cut Angela free.

At the sound of the shotgun blast Nancy had screamed and jumped out of the police car. A startled garda grabbed hold of her as she attempted to run through the gate, but she struggled, kicked him on the shin, and broke free. He lost his balance and she had a head-start when he set off after her.

Crossing the field Thomas also tried to wrench free of Seán's hold, and almost succeeded, for Seán was equally taken aback by the blast. He knew what damage a shotgun could do outdoors, but if it had gone off inside the house . . .

He held his grip on the frantic lad and tried to get him to stop struggling and listen.

"Look, Thomas, we'll go down to the house, but let's be careful – we don't want to run headlong into Reilly, now do we?"

That had the desired effect and they hurried together across the field.

In her house with a white-faced Declan, Mrs Doyle buried her face in her hands and cried silently with worry, as the sound of the blast reverberated across the fields.

Mr Doyle was a little embarrassed as a grateful Angela threw her stiff arms around him, tears of relief streaming down her face.

A garda car sped up the driveway to the side of the house, and a scowling handcuffed Reilly was led out of the house and marched past the stolen car.

Before he was bundled into the cop car he was stopped in his tracks by the sight of Nancy Brennan running towards them. The look she gave him was enough to kill. The contempt she felt towards him was tangible. He had threatened her offspring and in his gut he realised there were some aspects of human nature he knew nothing about. Some boundaries he could not cross and expect to live.

Nancy burst into the kitchen.

Angela turned at the welcome intrusion, and quickly released a very relieved Mr Doyle when she saw her mother standing there with her arms outstretched, tears in her eyes.

Another sound of feet running over the fallen back door caused them both to turn. Thomas stopped dead in his tracks.

"Nan!" he squealed. "Ma!" and he hurled himself at the two women.

Seán and Mr Doyle took refuge in each other's company, with great handshaking and a fair bit of backslapping.

"That was some hell of a chance you took there," Seán remarked, smiling broadly. "Thank God it worked! You're a brave man!"

Mr Doyle nodded. Only he knew the misgivings he felt prior to pulling that trigger.

"I knew I was taking a huge risk, but too much has happened to this unfortunate girl here. I had to do *something*. I couldn't bear that bastard getting away with this. I figured that if that gurrier was armed with a gun then I would drop mine, and at least Angela would have company – me. I knew the Gardaí would be right in once the door was down."

It was a long speech for a man such as Mannix Doyle. He seemed ill at ease with people's gratitude. He was glad to be able to transfer Seán's attention to the noisy, tearful, happy reunion, taking place at just arm's length away where Thomas was happily being squeezed between his mother and his nan.

Chapter 48

It was still fairly early, and Angela and her mother sat having breakfast at the kitchen table. For once Thomas was still in bed. The events of the last few days had finally exhausted him. Apparently, happiness and exhaustion combined made for a powerful sleeping potion. The porch door had temporarily been replaced. Apart from the door, all traces of Reilly's visit were gone, except in people's minds, where memories could not be erased, only buried.

Nancy sat wrapped in Daniel's dressing-gown, her holdall was under his bed, empty. Its contents were distributed between his wardrobe and his chest of drawers.

"Last night was good, wasn't it?" said Angela.

"It was nice to have those people over like that," Nancy agreed. "They're lovely people, every one of them."

It was Nancy's idea to have the get-together. It had

been a terrific success. She was glad to have the opportunity to meet all the people she had only heard about. Glad to thank them personally for how they had received her daughter and the help they had been.

Daniel's house was filled with laughter, the laughter of adults and children. Everyone made a contribution. Mrs Doyle had come up with another of her now famous lasagnes, Rose supplied the salads, Maisie Mac brought ham, and Seán supplied the drinks and the lemonades. Angela provided the roast potatoes and vegetables. Patrick Cullen was in his element. He delivered a very amusing brief speech before the meal began, which got everybody in great form.

Dinner was served on the large mahogany table in the dinning room, which had got the once-over for the occasion. A dinner service from the long sideboard saw the light of day for the meal, and the potatoes and vegetables were placed on the table in large matching tureens.

"Posh, isn't it?" a delighted Thomas remarked.

A fire had been lit in the huge marble hearth, making the house very welcoming.

Afterwards, Nancy, Rose, Mrs Doyle, and Maisie Mac settled themselves on the long sofa, a glass of Seán's best wine in hand. Maisie was in her element. She wore lipstick and her treasured cameo brooch for the occasion, and never once said anything that sounded remotely like a snide remark.

Mannix Doyle, Rose's husband Brian, Patrick Cullen and Seán got talking about manly issues over by the fireplace, while outside in the hall Thomas was busy demonstrating the skills of sliding down the long banisters to Deko and Owen.

Angela and Orla remained at the table, sipping wine and getting as tipsy as the others.

"Would you look at them sitting there!" Orla remarked watching the women chatting away, "You'd think your mother knew all of them all her life!" She sipped her wine and went on, "Imagine your mother and Maisie Mac knowing each other all that long ago."

"Yeah. Funny how things go, isn't it? Imagine a few months ago Thomas and me lived in a totally different world."

"Yeah! Can you imagine going back to it?"

"Good Lord! Banish the thought. Would *you* if you had a Judas for a da?" She lowered her voice, "I don't think me ma is going back either."

Surprised at this news, Orla thought about it for a minute. "Well, good for her!" she declared, and laughingly they slapped the palms of their hands together in the air.

Now, at the breakfast table, mother and daughter sat, each with their own thoughts of the previous evening.

"What about the lads?" Angela asked, breaking the easy silence.

Nancy shook her head. "Don't know, love. Oh, they're keeping great, thank God. Fergus loves it, but Finbar is talking about coming home soon. He'll be in for a bit of a land, I'm afraid." She decided not to think about that right now. Nor her own future, either. Time enough for that in a few days or so. When they'd had a chance to settle. In a more positive tone she asked, "And what now for you, Angela?"

Angela lazily buttered herself a slice of toast. "What I'd really like is to go back to school."

This surprised Nancy.

"Yeah," Angela was saying, "I could actually afford to do that now. I was thinking I wouldn't really want to keep the cottage. Not after what Christy did. But I could sell it, and use the money to tide us over while I go to school, couldn't I? I'd like to be like the lads, y'know? *Be* something. Have options. Be the somebody I would've been if my life hadn't gone so off the rails."

"And you're back on the rails now, eh?" Nancy smiled, happily anticipating a positive response.

Angela grinned. "Yeah, I suppose you could say that."

THE END

Published by poolbeg.com

POOLBEG *Crimson*

ellen mccarthy
Guarding Maggie

All her life, people have looked after Maggie
Breslin. She is happy enough with her quiet
life in the heart of rural Donegal. But when
a face from her past surfaces, disaster follows,
and Maggie is left alone to pick up the pieces.

Who would want to harm Maggie and her family,
here in the place she has known since she was a
child? Whom can she trust? As tragedy follows
tragedy, she doesn't know where to turn.

For the first time, Maggie must take control of her
own destiny and find out who her tormentor is –
before it's too late.

ISBN 978-1-84223-322-1

Fiction with an edge